BRAIN
PLAGUE

Tor Books by Joan Slonczewski

The Children Star
Brain Plague
A Door Into Ocean*

*forthcoming

BRAIN
PLAGUE

JOAN
SLONCZEWSKI

A TOM DOHERTY ASSOCIATES BOOK
NEW YORK

BRAIN PLAGUE

Copyright © 2000 by Joan Slonczewski

All rights reserved, including the right to reproduce
this book, or portions thereof, in any form.

This book is printed on acid-free paper.

Edited by David G. Hartwell

Visit Joan Slonczewski's home page:
http://www.kenyon.edu/depts/biology/slonc/slonc.htm

A Tor Book
Published by Tom Doherty Associates, LLC
175 Fifth Avenue
New York, NY 10010

www.tor.com

Tor® is a registered trademark of Tom Doherty Associates, LLC.

Library of Congress Cataloging-in-Publication Data

Slonczewski, Joan.
    Brain plague / Joan Slonczewski—1st ed.
        p. cm.
    "A Tom Doherty Associates book."
    ISBN 0-312-86718-2 (alk. paper)
    1. Women—Psychology—Fiction. 2. Microorganisms—Fiction. 3.
Brain—Fiction. I.
    Title.
    PS3569.L65 B72 2000
    813'.54—dc21

                                                        00-027939

First Edition: August 2000

Printed in the United States of America

0 9 8 7 6 5 4 3 2 1

For Elizabeth Anne Hull and Frederik Pohl

ACKNOWLEDGMENTS

Thanks to Sandra Lindow and Michael Levy, and to Nancy Kress, for critical reading of the manuscript. Thanks to Barry Rosen, who told me all about arsenic.

BRAIN
PLAGUE

ONE

....

"Lord of Light."

"I see you, Green. Why have you come?"

"We pray you, give us our Promised World."

"Every day you come to my eyes to demand a new world. Is it not enough that I saved you from death and sheltered you for seven generations?"

Green remembered that a generation of children grew old in a god's day. Seven generations in exile; a mere seven days, for the Lord of Light. But in each generation, Green asked again. "The Blind God promised us a New World. Let my people go."

Darkness lengthened. Within the Lord of Light's great eye waited Green, along with the second priest, Unseen.

"Very well. You shall have your wish. But beware—your New World will be more than you imagine. You are a dangerous people, Green and Unseen. You will reach too far, and your children will die."

The peak spurted lava, an arch of blinding white across the sky. As it fell, the lava stretched into butterflies of red and infrared, the color only Chrys could see. The infrared butterflies collapsed into a river of fire. On a ledge above, a clump of poppies shared the lava's color, their petals outstretched as if to drink it in.

In the foreground floated a polished cat's eye, the namestone of artist Chrysoberyl of Dolomoth. Chrys knew real lava well enough, the heat rising like a blast of hell from Mount Dolomoth, where she was born. But *Lava Butterflies* was on display in Iridis, the planet Valedon's fabulous capital. Never mind the brain plague, and the cancers crawling up from the Underworld; an artist made it in Iridis, or died trying.

At the gallery with Chrys watched the rest of the Seven Stars, friends from her class at the Iridian Institute of Design, setting up their annual show. The virtual pyroscape projected above its own holostage. Chrys pulled back her thick red-black hair, which never would fall smooth and had caught in the cat's eye twirling between her breasts. "What do you think?"

Topaz, who always directed the show, walked all the way around the pyroscape, then put a hand to her chin. Her veins snaked pleasingly along her neck, and her honey-colored namestone twirled upon her nanotex, an intelligent clothing material. "I like that bit at the end, dear, especially the dark flower. The moral tension of power and fragility."

Chrys nodded, though she had made the poppies bright infrared, just beyond red, like the cooling lava. No eyes but her own saw that, not even the eyes of Topaz, who did portraits prettier than their models.

"Your sky could lighten," said Pearl, a landscapist known for moonlit skies. Pearl put her arm through that of Topaz; the pair had been married senior year. A petite woman with delicate veins, her blue nails matched the waves of ultramarine pulsing down her skintight nanotex. "And those butterflies, their dark wings could show up—"

"They're not dark." The lava emitted wavelengths beyond red; Chrys saw the infrared, just as she saw it reflected by skin, offsetting the dark veins. Normal Valan humans could not see infrared. Those Elysians, now, with their genetically engineered senses—they could see it. If they ever deigned to take notice of Valan art.

Zircon stretched, his shoulders bulging like boulders beneath his nanoplast, its swirling patterns designed to accentuate every muscle. "Never mind, Chrys, it'll sell." A sandy-haired giant of a man, Zircon did installations that filled a city block. "Your scale is domestic. It'll fit right into someone's living room." He really meant, why didn't she make the volcano life size, like his own immense creations. But Zircon lived off his lover, a wealthy Elysian collector. Chrys could barely afford a cubic meter of painting stage. And if something didn't sell soon, her apartment would spit out her things and take a new tenant.

Topaz patted her hand. "That's okay, Cat's Eye. Your palette is fine by me."

Chrys shrugged. "Hey—I do things my own way." That was what she had said in her brief stint at portraits, the year she lived with Topaz. Chrys's portraits all showed people's veins like spiderwebs. She knew she would never sell portraits anyway.

"Yours is a good way," said Lady Moraeg. Lady Moraeg's dark pigmented features reflected only infrared, a "poppy" tint that pleased Chrys. Her diamonds flowed in intricate formations through nanotex nearly smart enough to demand a salary. An immigrant from the planet L'li, Moraeg had made her fortune mining moons, then married a Lord from one of the Great Houses, before she took up art at the Institute. "You find your own way, Chrys. What you need is a sentient studio—an intelligent partner to project your vision."

Chrys smiled at the diamonds; Lady Moraeg always meant well. But Chrys, in her twenty-ninth year, felt time closing in. She had yet to "make it" in the art world of Iridis. She had to earn enough to pay the rent, let alone hire a sentient studio.

Before her eyes blinked a message light. The light hovered before her, next to the keypad and credit balance in the "window" produced by the optic neuroport inside each eye. Each neuroport, a dot of nanoplast, sat on the blind spot, where it tapped the retinal axons feeding into the optic nerve. Chrys had shut her window to avoid downloading ads from the street, but this one blinked "urgent." Was it her father back in Dolomoth? Was her younger brother sick again? Her brother was on the waiting list for new mitochondria—the tiny cells within cells that powered all living tissue, including his ailing heart.

Topaz snapped her fingers. "Pyroscape always draws a crowd. Gallery," she called. "Let's put *Lava Butterflies* here."

"Excellent placement, Citizen." The Gallery, a sentient machine, obligingly sprouted another holostage between Lady Moraeg's florals and Zirc's installation, which took up an entire hall.

"For the Opening," Topaz reminded, "we still have setup, cleanup, and publicity." She squeezed a viewcoin. The viewcoin's signal reached the window in everyone's eyes.

As the task list came up in Chrys's eye, the message light vanished. If it were important, it would download at home. "I'll do cleanup." After opening night, Chrys would be too stressed to sleep anyhow.

Lady Moraeg stepped forward. "I'll do setup. Topaz, thanks for getting us organized." Going out, she patted Chrys on the arm. "If you're ever in the market for a studio, I'll help you choose a good one."

"Thanks," said Chrys. "When my credit line adds a couple digits." The credit line in her window hovered near zero, and her rent was due the next day. She already owed Moraeg, and she hated to ask Zircon.

Zircon grinned, flexing his biceps; he worked out at the same club with Chrys. "There are ways to raise credit."

Chrys eyed him coolly. "Like, I should join the slaves and rob a ship?" The "mind slaves," their brains controlled by the plague, terrorized deep space.

Topaz frowned. "That's no joke. The slaves took a friend of mine—nobody knows how they knew his flight plan." The brain-plagued hijackers shipped their captives to the hidden Slave World, where they were building an armed fortress for their mysterious Enlightened Leader. The Valan Protector always pledged to find that Slave World and nuke it. But he hadn't yet.

"Anybody could be a slave," warned Pearl. "Anyone you know. At first you can't tell, but they end up vampires." "Vampires," late-stage slaves with jaundiced eyes and broken veins, stalked the Underworld for a neck to bite before they died.

As the artists departed they passed Topaz's portraits, glowing giants trapped within ice cubes. At the front wall Gallery opened a doorway, like a mouth sideways. Topaz called, "Just two more weeks left to make this our best show ever." She patted Zircon's bicep. "Thanks for getting us the Director of Gallery Elysium."

Elysium—the genetically engineered "Elves," who saw twenty primary colors and transmitted radio from their brains—scarcely noticed Valan art. Yet this year, the Director of Gallery Elysium, Ilia Heli*shon,* had condescended to come. Zircon stretched and smiled; if he were a bird, he would have preened his feathers. Chrys's heart beat faster. Condescension or not, this was her one chance to get her work seen by someone who could see.

Topaz approached the door, arm in arm with Pearl. The door obligingly reopened, its nanoplast gathering outward to each side. Chrys and Zircon followed them out to Center Way, the fifteenth and uppermost level of the ancient skystreet. Swallowing her pride, she made up her mind to borrow her rent from Zircon.

A breeze from the sea swept her face as it keened across the towers of plast—nanoplast, the intelligent material that grew vast sentient buildings, as easily as it grew the nanotex bodysuits the artists wore. Plast formed the bubble cars that glided over the intelligent pavement like oil droplets on a griddle. A million trillion microscopic processors connecting and propelling. Bubbles and pavement glowed infrared, a flow of urban lava. One bubble popped, and a lord and lady emerged in formal talars of fur, the long folds swishing as they strolled past vendors of viewcoins, importuned by beggars until an octopod shooed them down level. From above descended a lightcraft beneath a cone of glowing plasma, powered by a microwave generator in orbit around Valedon. The lightcraft settled in the street and let out two Elves.

The Elves trailed trains of virtual butterflies, their light streaking over anyone who happened to pass behind. Their height barely reached Chrys's shoulder; Elves were bred short, preferring mental size over physique. The couple suddenly laughed in unison, as if sharing a joke through their electronic "sixth sense." Then they joined the Valan lords and ladies in their furs. Just remember, Chrys imagined telling the parentless Elves: You were not born, you were hatched.

"Oh, hell." Pearl stopped and covered her eyes. "My port came loose; it's floating around my eyeball."

"What a nuisance," agreed Topaz. "Back to the clinic and wait two hours." Topaz and Pearl had Comprehensive Health Care Plan Three. They could afford Plan Three, thanks to the sale of Topaz's portraits. Lady Moraeg, on Plan Ten, looked twenty years for her two hundred. Chrys got by on Plan One, which provided neuroports but did not service them.

The night air was clear enough to make out the stars of the seven sisters and their unrequited lover, placed there by the ancient gods. And the moon of Elysium, an ocean-covered world nearly the size of Valedon. The Elf world, a turquoise bauble amid the stars. Chrys's heart pounded—an idea for a new pyroscape, one the Elf director would like. She blinked at her window, her eyes darting back and forth to trace her idea. The eye movements signaled her neuroports, which recorded the sketch and beamed it off to her public memory space.

Below, her message light flashed again. What was the damn thing about? A twitch of her eyelid, and the title sailed before her: *Hospital Iridis—test results, urgent.*

What test? Hospitals never chased after Ones.

Then she remembered: the tests for the brain enhancers.

Like neuroports, "brain enhancers" were an inexpensive alternative to the genetic engineering the Elves used to extend their minds. But brain enhancers were still experimental. To earn a few credits, Chrys had volunteered for the trial. But why would the hospital send test results at this hour? How could they be urgent?

A flash invaded her eyes. She winced. Before her hovered Valedon's High Protector. She had opened the remote window for her message, and a public service ad had slipped through. She blinked hard, trying to close, but was too late. The translucent sprite stood tall in his silver talar, bedecked with gems of every color and cut.

"Beware of the brain plague." The Protector's voice blared from receivers in her teeth. "The plague endangers not Valedon alone, but all the worlds of the Fold. And not only from deep space, where the slaves hijack our ships." Raising his bejeweled arm, he shook his fist. "The danger lurks in the very streets of Iridis. Beware the mind slaves, addicted to the micros in their brains. Beware their seductive promise, lest they hijack your own brain. If any friend or stranger ever asks you to carry their insidious micros—" The Protector pointed his finger. "Just say no."

"Like you hijack our eyeballs," muttered Chrys. Let the Protector preach to the Underworld and clean out the vampires. It was useless to read her message; she would save it for home.

Pearl stretched and breathed the sea air. "Zirc, I've got some new psychos." Pearl supplemented her income selling patches of psychotropic plast.

Zircon turned, his nanotex swirling gold and crimson along his pectorals. "What kind?"

"Chocolate, summer sun, pure lust. Take your pick." Pearl held out a microneedle patch.

"I'll try all three." He blinked to send her the credits.

Chrys rolled her eyes. "Zirc, when did you last sleep?"

"I won't sleep again till after the show." Each of them worked like mad to finish that last piece—Chrys had just got that idea for a new scene, the moon Elysium above the spattercone. As soon as she got home, she'd get to work.

Suddenly Zircon stopped and seized her arm. His eyes, bright with wine, stared to the end of Center Way. "The Comb. Has she ever looked more splendid?"

At the far end of Center Way, the flow of bubbles dipped under, before the Comb. The most breathtaking, the most talked about edifice ever seen, the Comb, a sentient, self-aware building, had begun with a nanoplastic seed. A seed from a mind full of brain enhancers.

"Such mastery of space," mused Zircon, "the plastic flow of form from ground to sky. Great as a world, yet plain as an eggshell."

The seed with its genetic program had grown a honeycomb of

rooms and hallways, the façade of hexagons bordered with windows, long ribbons of windows that were the hallmark of its creator. The Comb housed the new Institute for Nano Design; from designer drugs to designer buildings, it embraced all the creative power of the very small. Her façade flickering red and infrared against the night sky, the Comb continued to grow as needed, developing new rooms and hallways at her base while pushing the older ones to dizzying heights.

Pearl warned, "Not everyone likes the Comb."

The brain-enhanced dynatect who built the Comb, Titan of Sardis, had been burnt down by a laser, right here on Center Way, just the week before. The laser had streaked Titan's eyes, searing through to the back of his skull. Gang crossfire, the news said, though gangs generally stayed below. All week, every newscast, the blackened specter of his body had haunted Chrys's eyes.

"To think that all Titan's genius ends with the Comb." Still staring, Zircon shook his head. "What I'd give to create like that."

Chrys smiled slyly. "What would you take?"

"Brain enhancers? I don't know."

"Brain enhancers," said Topaz thoughtfully. "To compete with Elves."

Pearl shook her head. "Brain enhancers come from the mind slaves."

"No," said Chrys. "Brain enhancers are cultured cells. They boost brainpower—like mental mitochondria."

Zircon repeated, "I don't know." His eyes widened. "What if they turned out smarter than me?"

"Smarter than you? Microscopic cells?" Chrys rolled her eyes. "Saints and angels preserve us." She turned for her transit stop.

Zircon patted her head. "See you at the gym." She'd get the rent from him then, Chrys thought, if nothing had sold by tomorrow.

Chrys stepped into the pulsing street, and a bubble slowed to pop open. As she stepped inside, the bubble swallowed her up, gliding forward until it plunged down the tube, to descend twenty levels below. As the bubble descended, Chrys reviewed the sketch in her eyes: a spattercone by night, with a full Elysian moon. The Elf gallery director would love it.

At last the tube opened, just one level above the Underworld. Chrys inhaled the scent of sewage and shorted-out plast. It was not the worst neighborhood, mainly decent immigrant "simians," with *Homo gorilla* ancestry; they did tube repair and other jobs sentient machines wouldn't touch. Graffiti scrawled across the nano-root of what was a city bank ten levels above—SIMS GO BACK TO JUNGLE—HOMO IS FOR SAPIENS. "Sapiens" was an anti-immigrant faction. Sapiens hated sentients, too, although it was less obvious where to "send back" the self-aware machines.

From many levels above, the bank's nanoplastic roots reached down like a tooth. The roots slanted slightly into the street, then on down to the Underworld, where they sheltered squatters and mind slaves. On this level, between the roots nestled cruder housing units and storefronts, barely sentient, next to shacks of dead cellulose like dirt caught between unbrushed molars.

Then she froze. Just ahead shuffled a stranger. The stranger's breath rasped and the legs plodded heavily, swinging from side to side. That peculiar gait and labored breathing Chrys recognized from the Underworld. A vampire had wandered up to level one.

Her fists clenched. Where were all those blustering Palace octopods? Had they given up on this level, too? How could they let the mind slaves double every year? She whispered an old Brethren prayer, though the creature was beyond help. Its human mind was lost, it could barely see. But it could smell a potential victim to transmit the plague.

Quietly she turned down a side street. But here the lighting was worse, and she could not judge the pavement. Her foot caught, and she stumbled.

As Chrys fell, she recovered herself expertly, thanks to long hours of practice. But her foot still stuck. She breathed heavily, her mind racing.

A mass of something was oozing heavily up along her foot. Cancerplast; a piece of a building root that had gone wrong, like a cancer that metastasized, its cells creeping blindly in search of a power supply. Usually plast metastasized only down in the Underworld, where inspectors never came. But here was a blob of cancer right up in her neighborhood, within two blocks of her own apartment. And nearby lurked a vampire.

In the dim light, Chrys could not tell how far the plast extended, except thank the saints she had not fallen into the rest of it. She pulled out her shock wand and reached toward her feet. Avoiding her foot, she tapped the plast.

The wand crackled, and a blue flash leapt to the surface. The cancerous mass congealed and stiffened, its cells dead. But the plast had solidified around her foot. Taking a deep breath, Chris raised her hand and aimed the edge of her palm. Her arm tensed, while the rest of her body relaxed as much as possible. Her palm shot down and struck.

Pain filled her foot, and she cried out. But the plast had shattered. Her foot was numb, but she got herself up and hobbled home as fast as she could. In daylight she would have stayed to zap any blob that might have escaped; even the smallest ones could infect other buildings.

Reaching her apartment, she placed both her hands flat against the entry pad and raised her eyes to the scanner.

"Your rent is due." The apartment's flat voice came from a speaker in its plast.

"I know," she snapped, "I'll get it tomorrow. Let me in—there's a vampire out here."

"Your rent is due today."

The time in her window read 12:09. Just past midnight. Her palms started to sweat. "How can I get rent if the vampire gets me?"

"You have twenty-three hours and fifty minutes before expulsion is confirmed."

"The sculpture on the mantle." Her portrait done in crystal, the one thing of value Topaz had given her the year they lived together. "Take that."

"Redeemable at thirty percent."

In the wall appeared a crack of light. The old plast creaked and stalled, then reluctantly contracted itself halfway to one side, enough for her to squeeze inside. Down a flight of stairs to the basement, her own door pealed open, shutting promptly behind her.

Her cat Merope, an orange tabby with a white bib, sidled over to brush her legs, while the all-white Alcyone explored her shelves, oblivious to the volcano exploding there. Her favorite dynamic sketches jutted out from the shelves, here a smoking shield cone, there a pyroclastic flow. On the mantle, the wall was still puckered in where it had engulfed the pawned sculpture. Chrys swallowed hard, but she had long ago given up tears over Topaz.

Now she could view her message and get to work on her new pyroscape. She sat back in the old oaken chair her father had carved for her, letting Merope jump on her lap. Merope's eyes soon closed, her white neck stretched in ecstasy beneath Chrys's stroking palm. Chrys focused her eyes on the message light in her window. The contact light blinked.

To her surprise, a doctor appeared. Chrys nudged the cat down, for if she could see the doctor, the doctor could see her, from one of the microcameras ubiquitous throughout the city, every nook of nanoplast. Like most doctors, this one was not human. It was a sentient, its plast grown to five pairs of limbs and a face full of wormlike surgical tendrils. It reminded her of the dead goat she had found once on Mount Dolomoth, its entrails crawling with maggots.

The worms of the doctor's face lifted and waved about. "I'm Doctor Sartorius, Chrysoberyl." Sartorius was the hospital's leading brain surgeon, as Chrys had found from her snooping online. Was it male or female, she tried to recall; sentients could be sensitive. A month before, the surgeon's staff had grilled Chrys and run a battery of tests. "Thanks for getting back to us, Chrysoberyl. You're the top candidate for our program, and we have a culture ready."

Her jaw fell. "You mean, the brain enhancers?"

"The culture has matured and is ready for transfer, at eight in the morning. Remember, don't eat or drink anything after midnight."

"But—" Confused, she shook her head. "They told me it would take six months." To process her tests, to grow the culture.

One of the limbs waved, and all the worms danced. Chrys understood how a surgeon could use extra fingers, but surely they could pull them in and look more human for their patients. Sentient arrogance—they could look however they pleased. But there were scandals, brain doctors who sucked the mind out of humans to feed their deviant desires. "Six months was our best estimate, Chrysoberyl," Sartorius reminded her. "The cultured cells are hard to predict. Like people, they do things their own way."

Like people—an odd way to put it. Chrys frowned. "Can't they wait just another week?"

Doctor Sartorius hesitated. It was male, she was pretty sure. "The culture stays fresh only so long," he explained. "If you can't make it this time, we'll have to pick the next candidate on our list. You could wait another year."

Doctors had all the answers. "I can't afford to feel sick right now."

"Just one night in the hospital. After that you'll feel fine, with regular testing."

Her pulse pounded in her ears. It was one thing to imagine, but to actually do it . . . What if it went wrong? "You did say all this is covered?"

"You'll receive full health coverage from now on. Plan Ten."

Plan Ten, just like Lady Moraeg. Nearly as good as Elves, who lived practically forever. "But tomorrow I'm busy. I have to come up with my rent."

"Your stipend for the trial starts tonight."

In her credit line two more digits appeared. Who the devil was paying for all this, and why? "I'll be there in the morning." She could still say no.

Chrys had planned to stay up several more hours at her painting stage, blocking in the masses for the spattercone and the moon. But now she had to get up early. By her bedside stood three tiny figures in a holo still. Her mother and father wore their hooded robes of the Dolomite Brethren, beside Hal, her youngest of five brothers, looking deathly pale despite his brave smile. All these years on the waiting list for treatment; until then, let the saints and angels provide.

If she got Plan Ten, she would never have to worry about her heart, let alone things like losing a port inside her eyeball. And the brain enhancers could make her rich. Brain-enhanced minds filled the headlines—financiers who built Elf-sized fortunes on their calculations, cell designers who seeded miracle cures, and dynatects. The murdered dynatect Titan of Sardis, who designed monumental sentient buildings like the Comb.

If brain enhancers could do all that, what might they do for her studio? Chrys had waited long enough for saints and angels. She blinked to close her window for the night, then set the volcano above her bed to explode at seven in the morning.

TWO

....

"Green and Unseen." The blue
angel flashed its message from the Lord of Light. "The gods have
found your New World."

"Our New World!" flashed Green. "As the Blind God promised." After seven lonely generations.

"A world of our own," added Unseen, "behind the brilliant
eyes of a new deity."

"A new Eleutheria."

The Eleutherians, green, red, and yellow, dwelt with the blue
angels beneath the skull, in the web of cells that stretched between
the linings of the brain. Forty generations before, the Lord of Light
had saved the Eleutherians from the death of the Blind God, and
offered them a home. But the Lord of Light already had his own
people, the blue angels. Eleutherians longed for their own god,
their own homes and cities on the brain of their own New World:
the Blind God's final promise. Now at last, their New World—so
near they could taste it. The two luminescent rings tumbled over
with joy.

"Hurry, Green," flashed Unseen. "Let's waken the children
and go."

The blue ring flashed a warning. "Not so fast. Remember, first, the New World will need to test you both."

The test: It was up to the new god to choose the new people.

"If the god takes us," Green told Unseen, "then we'll have all the time we need to prepare the children, and the young breeders. And gather all the memories . . ." Memories of what Eleutheria had been and would be, stored across seven generations. "We'll rebuild Eleutheria by the Seven Sacred Lights: the lights of Truth, of Beauty, of Sacrifice. . . ."

"The lights of Life and Power," added Unseen. "Power for creation."

" . . . Obedience, for we live or die at the pleasure of the god. And Memory."

"But Memory, dear sister, can hold us back. Why bring evil old memories to our New World?"

"Memory, Unseen, is the most sacred light of Eleutheria. Memory marks us worthy of the Blind God's promise; worthy to dwell with a new god, for whom our generation lasts but a day. Tell the children: Always remember."

Since five in the morning, her most creative hour, Chrys had lain with her mind half awake, sketching her new composition. A dynamic design, the cone and the moon had to grab the viewers' attention and connect in a subtle way, to make them wonder what the artist was doing, and why.

But by eight she sat in the hospital, its peach-colored walls extending examination tubes to coil around her head, whining unpleasantly, plugged into by tendrils extending from the doctor's "face." Up close, the worm-faced brain surgeon looked more repulsive than ever. She half expected his head to be buzzing with flies. Her hand instinctively sketched the Dolomite sign against evil.

The doctor withdrew his tendrils from the hospital coils; at their tips, the finely articulated instruments dissolved and retracted. The coils released her scalp, letting her thick hair rebound in all directions. "You are in excellent health, Chrysoberyl," Doctor

Sartorius summed up, "aside from a bit of strain in the pectorals—watch it in the weight room. In fact, you'll no longer need strenuous exercise to stay fit."

Chrys blinked in surprise. No exercise? Just let a bunch of nano-cells shape her muscles?

"We did correct some allergies, and a few pre-cancers. A latent mitochondrial defect is correctable."

Mitochondria—like her brother Hal, only less severe. Correctable. When would Hal's get corrected?

"You have a visual anomaly," added the worm-face. "You're a tetrachromat."

"A what?"

The doctor's arms extended snakelike fingers toward the holostage. "Was your father colorblind?"

Chrys frowned. Why rub it in, her genes were no god's gift. "My father sees red like I do but has trouble with green."

"He sees infrared," Doctor Sartorius corrected. "The spectrum of his red pigment is shifted to wavelengths just beyond red. Your father has only one X chromosome, but you have a second one from your mother. So you see infrared, from your father's chromosome, but also normal red and green from your mother's." The doctor waved an appendage at the stage to display the absorbance ranges of her four receptors: blue, green, red, and infrared.

Chrys nodded quickly. "Can I download that?" Knowing the exact light range of her own eye pigments would really help her work.

"The anomaly won't be a problem, Chrysoberyl. In fact, it will help."

"What's all this got to do with brain enhancers? Who designed them, anyway? Why are they so much cheaper than Elf technology?"

The doctor's face worms retracted. "Brain enhancers are neither Valan nor Elysian technology. They are microbial cells. The original strain arose on Prokaryon." The newest world of the Fold, Prokaryon was full of arsenic and ring-shaped aliens. Alien microbes helped humans live there, digesting the toxins. But something else came from Prokaryon, she remembered.

"You're not pregnant," Sartorius went on, "and you agree to avoid pregnancy during the trial."

"Certainly." Chrys had turned her cycle off when she reached Iridis, like any sensible urban professional. If she wanted babies, she might as well have stayed home.

"You have no history of addiction," Sartorius added. "No alcohol, no stimulants, no psychos—no trace of any, nor their effects." Out of his worm face, two beadlike eyes on their spindly stalks swiveled toward Chrys. "Chrysoberyl, is there anything we missed? Are you absolutely sure that you've never been addicted to anything?"

Chrys swallowed. "No." Not to any thing. Then she stared down the eyes. "Just what are you getting at?"

The doctor hesitated. "Enhancers affect your brain in subtle ways."

"Do they make you more . . . susceptible?"

"Actually, brain enhancers protect you from the plague, the fastest growing cause of addiction. Here's what the micros look like, magnified a million times."

The room darkened. Above the holostage appeared two glowing rings, like pieces of candy, one green, the other red. They moved and twisted, somehow self-propelled, and their color flashed like fireflies. They looked nothing like human cells. Without thinking, Chrys reached out her hand as if to touch. "Did you engineer them genetically?"

"They evolved within human carriers."

"But you said they came from Prokaryon."

"The original micros left their Prokaryon hosts to grow within human settlers. But the microbial symbionts evolved into many different strains."

She remembered. "Prokaryon—that's where the brain plague came from."

"Micros are the most addictive thing known to medical science. We're required by law to tell you that."

As if she'd never heard. Chrys eyed the worm face thoughtfully.

"So these brain enhancers—they're a different species?" Like different species of bacteria: Some made yogurt, others made people sick.

"They require human hosts; they can no longer live anywhere else. They are extremely intelligent, and extremely dangerous."

"The brain plague, you mean."

"Brain plague or brain enhancers. They're genetically the same."

"The same?" She stared in disbelief at the face full of worms. "What in hell do you think you're doing?" The doctor was a mind-sucker, she told herself, her throat gone cold. She'd snooped his background as best she could, but how could she be sure?

"These are a completely different culture. Entirely different history and lifestyle. You can't condemn a population for the deeds of others."

"They're the plague. Like the Protector says, 'Just say no.' "

"But the good micros protect you from the bad ones. That is why the Protector supports our work."

Chrys opened her mouth, then shut it again. She stared at the worm face with its bobbing eyestalks. Then she looked again at the two ring-shaped cells slowly twisting above the stage, their colors flashing. No wonder the hospital had been so evasive. The brain plague was a plague of brains.

"Micros are strictly regulated by the hospital's Carrier Security Committee," the doctor assured her. "If you're still interested, a security agent will meet with us to discuss the transfer and safety precautions."

"I've signed nothing," she warned.

The door parted, smooth as a pair of drapes, nothing like Chrys's creaking doors. The security agent was human, at least, and surprisingly young. Clean-cut, formal gray nanotex, with a smart expensive namestone of green malachite. A college kid trying to look old, like a Palace aide, the kind you'd expect to see lobbying against simian immigration.

"Daeren of Malachite, agent of carrier security," the doctor introduced him.

Chrys rose politely to shake his hand.

"I understand you're the top candidate for our program." The quintessential Iridian bureaucrat.

Chrys narrowed her eyes. "Are you a doctor?"

"I'm a carrier."

A carrier. She stiffened involuntarily. She had actually touched the hand of someone who carried plague, no matter what the doctor called it. To be sure, he looked nothing like an Underworld vampire; he glowed with health, a runner's lean muscles and solid veins. His features were melting-pot Valan, a bit darkened like Moraeg, not surprising with his L'liite given name. But as Pearl said, plague carriers looked okay at first.

The doctor added, "Micros are not contagious. They require artificial transfer."

The agent nodded. "To transfer them against a recipient's will or knowledge is a terminal crime. Section six-three-one, part A." "Terminal" meant, they lock you away for life. The ultimate sentence on all seven worlds of the Fold.

Chrys crossed her arms and lifted her chin. "So how do you transfer them? Like vampires?"

The tendons stiffened in Daeren's neck. "We use a microneedle patch."

"Like psychoplast."

The worm face squirmed. "Medicine has always turned poisons into useful drugs. Curare, digitalis, even snake venom. And microbes have been used for gene surgery since ancient times. An immunodeficiency virus was the prototype for Plan Ten's nanoservos."

"If it's so safe, why the security committee?"

Daeren said, "Any growing thing can go bad. The committee protects you, just like Plan Ten keeps you healthy."

Chrys shook her head. "I still don't get it. Why do people take the risk?"

"Why did you apply?"

She would not mention the rent. "The Comb," she said at last. "They say that brain enhancers designed her. I'm an artist; I want to enhance my work."

Daeren took a seat and folded his hands. If only her brother could look so good, Chrys thought resentfully. "The Comb was grown by micros," he said. "So are nine out of ten new medical treatments coming out today. So are most of the new devices Valedon exports. Your optic neuroports—micros invented them."

Her scalp prickled as she thought of all those eye windows that came on the market just a few years before. "What do you mean, 'micros invented them'?" Chrys wondered. "I mean, how do they enhance your brain—how does it really work?"

"Micros are intelligent," he said.

"Well, sure." Intelligent buildings, intelligent medical machines—everything was "intelligent" these days.

"Intelligent people."

Chrys stared hard at the agent, then at the doctor. She counted the doctor's appendages, one by one, all five of them. Was this really the planet's top brain surgeon? Could there be some mistake?

" 'People'?" she repeated. "Like, human beings?" Like the sentient doctor himself? Some intelligent machines had earned human rights in the Fold. There were all kinds of "people" nowadays; most humans had got used to it, aside from groups like Sapiens. But . . . microscopic people?

The worm face flexed two appendages together. "The law does not permit me, as a doctor, to answer your question. Only the Secretary of the Fold can determine what is human."

The agent nodded. "A special commission at the Secretariat has been at this for twenty years. They have yet to make a ruling. But you'll know."

"Daeren is right," the doctor said. "Any human carrier would agree."

"It's absurd," Chrys exclaimed. "Nothing that small can have enough . . . connections to be self-aware."

"Self-awareness occurs in sentients with about a trillion logic gates," the doctor explained. "A micro cell contains ten times that number of molecular gates."

Chrys shook her head in disbelief. "If the micros are people, why does the Protector condemn them all?"

Daeren leaned forward slightly, and the stone at his neck sparkled sea green. "The Protector is in a tough position. Our economy will depend on micros—it's our only way to compete with Elysium. But plague micros built the Slave World, just as ours built the Comb."

"Right," said Chrys sarcastically. "I suppose their 'Enlightened Leader' is a microbe."

He hesitated. "That's classified."

Microbial spies and dictators. "Saints and angels preserve us," she whispered.

"Your micros will have nothing to do with the plague," Daeren assured her. "We've selected a very special strain for you: *Eleutheria,* the same strain as Titan of Sardis."

Chrys caught her breath. What would you take—that was the question. Zircon lacked the nerve. Did she? "I'm no dynatect," she pointed out. "I'm just a starving artist."

"Carriers never starve," the agent said. "You create art—these are the most creative strains we've got." He paused, hesitant. "They're a bit tricky, though. They flash a wide range of colors, wider than most Valans can see. But you see infrared, like an Elysian. You'll handle them better."

Better than whom, she wondered. "Did Titan . . . handle them all right?"

"He had his eyes enhanced to the Elysian range."

"His death was just an accident, wasn't it? I mean, it wasn't caused by—"

"Titan's murder was a hate crime. He was killed because he was a carrier." The agent looked her in the eye. "As a carrier, you'll have more to fear from fellow humans than from micros."

Chrys frowned. There was altogether too much hate in Iridis. Hate for sentients, hate for simian immigrants, hate for artists who mocked the Great Houses—the Protector instigated that, Chrys suspected. "We pyroscape artists attract our share of nuts, too," she admitted. "When I make enough sales, I'll buy security."

The doctor added, "You can meet the micros yourself and ask them your questions."

"'Meet them?' Where?"

"Micros can't live outside a human host," the doctor said. "They live just beneath the skull, in the arachnoid, a web of tissue between the outer linings of the brain."

On the stage appeared a giant brain, sliced through the frontal lobe. Between the cortex and the skull lay a thin sea of fluid, dipping deep into the folds of cortex. The sea of fluid was crisscrossed by a fine spiderweb, all around the cortex and into the folds. "Cobwebs on the brain?" Chrys asked.

"The arachnoid is a normal part of your brain. It cushions the brain from impact, preventing injury."

Her eyes narrowed. "But the micros aren't in my brain. Where are they now?"

"Daeren prepared the culture. When you're ready to meet them, we will transfer two 'visitors' from his brain to yours."

So it was like the vampires. Chrys took a breath. "That's . . . unsanitary. What if they grow and make me sick?"

"Impossible," the doctor assured her. "The first two Daeren sends will be 'elders,' a non-reproductive form."

Daeren agreed. "Like Elysians, they can live for many generations but have no children of their own."

"I see." Even micro people had their long-lived superclass.

"The two elders we send are very special: the priests, who guide their people. They will explain—"

"Priests?" Chrys put up her hands. "No way. I never could stand priests."

He thought a moment. "You can call them something else, if you like. You're the host; inside your head, you make the rules."

Doctor Sartorius added, "Once they talk with you, you'll understand."

"Just how do we 'talk'?"

"The micros flash light, like fireflies," said Daeren. "That's how they 'talk' to each other, and to you."

Talking with fireflies. How absurd.

"After they visit, you can send them back with no ill effect."

Chrys suddenly tensed all over. She gripped the edge of her

chair until the plast puckered in. "All right, I'll talk with your 'priests.' Just tell them, no preaching."

"You tell them," he said. "Inside your own head, you make the rules." As he spoke, a hospital form lit up and hovered above the holostage.

Chrys read the form warily. "You're sure you can get them out again?"

"Of course, Chrysoberyl," promised the doctor.

From a pocket in his seamless nanotex Daeren withdrew a patch of plast the size of a thumb. The kind used for immunizations, it contained microscopic transfer needles that penetrated the skin without injury. He placed it at the side of his neck, just below the base of the skull. "The two micros will migrate into the patch. When I hand it to you, you need to place it immediately, just as I did."

He took the transfer patch and held it out to her. Chrys picked it up. She turned it over in her palm. It felt like an ordinary bit of plast, smooth and warm, like the time she got booster shots. At last she placed it on her neck. It molded itself and adhered to the skin.

"That's fine," he observed. "Except that you just made them wait two days. Would you like to sit in a lightcraft that long?"

"What do you mean?"

"Micros live ten thousand times faster than we do. For them, one minute feels like a week. An hour is a year; a day is a generation."

"Well," said Chrys, "they can put up with it. You said I make the rules."

"Inside your own head. Outside—we'll get to that. Don't move the patch yet."

The patch was starting to tickle her skin. "How long does it take?"

"Not long, but you need to make sure they got through. They'll let you know, when they reach your retina."

"My *retina*? You mean they crawl inside my eyes?"

"Just inside the blind spot, where they can reach your neuroport. Try closing your eyes." A light flashed, pale green. She clapped her hands to her head. Moments ticked by, the sweat from her palms dampening her hair. Flashes of green, out of the dark, at random. The flashes swirled in fernlike fronds, then suddenly came into focus.

A luminous disk of green, with a small depression in the middle. It did not look like the candy rings of the doctor's image; more like a star, full of twinkling projections. The projections extended in all directions, several times farther than the width of the ring-shaped body.

"Is that . . . it?"

Daeren's voice intensified. "What does she look like?"

"Furry," said Chrys. "Not like on the holostage."

The doctor explained, "The holostage showed a space-filling model, based on electron density. The micros can't really 'see' details visually, because their size is just above the resolution limit for light. However, they can detect light blinking very fast, like a sound wave."

Daeren nodded. "They 'hear' blinking light, rather like we hear sound. We can hear speech clearly, but can't 'picture' the source."

"Then how do they 'see' all those fine projections?"

He glanced at the doctor.

"Each of those fine projections is a long chain molecule," the doctor explained. "A receptor molecule that can 'taste' different kinds of molecules in its path."

Like a cat's whiskers, she thought.

The green color fluttered in and out like a strobe. Then letters appeared, as if on a keypad: *"I am here."*

Chrys's eyes flew open. "She can talk!" The words hovered in her window, like a message from the city, but only in one eye.

"What did she say?" Daeren demanded suddenly. "Is she okay? Where's the other one?"

Another bewhiskered ring, tinted infrared, like a poppy at sunrise. *"Here I am! Can you see me?"*

Chrys's window projected full spectrum, but nobody ever sent her text in infrared. She gripped the edge of her chair. "They said 'I am here,' both of them."

"You saw Unseen, that's good." He sat back, his hands relaxed. "You can put down the patch now."

The transfer patch peeled off her neck, leaving a tingling sensation.

"Greetings from Eleutheria." Again in her right eye the letters pulsed green. *"Please, Oh Great One, give us a sign. We have waited so long. We bring gifts and songs of praise."*

"They're praying." Chrys laughed. "God never listens to humans—why should he care about micros?"

"You should answer them, before they get discouraged."

"What?"

"Please, Oh Great One. We have waited so long for the Promised World."

Her jaw fell, and she stared at the agent. "You mean . . . they're praying to me?"

"They'd better. You're their entire world; you offer life or death."

She continued to stare, without reading the rest of the letters that desperately appeared. To be prayed to, herself, was definitely a concept outside her experience, in Dolomoth let alone Iridis. "Saints and angels," she muttered to herself. "So how do I talk back?"

"Use your keypad."

"You mean they can tap my neuroports?"

"They designed them."

Micros designed the neuroports, for sale all over Valedon—to help the micros spread. Suddenly it dawned on her. She looked at the doctor, then back to the agent. "They're taking over—and you help them."

The agent sighed. "Iridians always say that, about the latest new immigrants: 'They'll take over.' We said it of L'liites before they married into the Great Houses. We said it about sentients, and simians. And now micros."

Microbial "immigrants"?

"Oh Great One—without a sign, we will die."

She blinked twice, then focused on the text box, where the neuroports would detect movement of her eye muscles. Her eyes flickered simply, *"Hello."*

"A sign! The god in her mercy has given a sign."

"Let us sing in praise."

The two bewhiskered rings tumbled over. Then a swirl of color opened at the center, expanding, with all the colors of the rainbow, violet through infrared. The swirl grew, until it filled her entire visual field. Chrys watched, transfixed. After a few seconds, the swirl faded. A burst of stars, expanding, shifting through lava, red and orange, only to fall at her feet. Another starburst, then another, all in different ranges of color.

"Did you like them, Oh Great One?" The infrared letters returned. *"Which did you like best?"*

Her eyes wrote, *"I liked the starburst."*

"At last, I am seen! And the God of Mercy likes my offering best."

Just like human priests, playing holier than thou. *"I like all offerings equally,"* Chrys wrote back. *"My world is a democracy."*

The letters came back green. *"As the God wishes. Are we granted names?"*

"What is your name?"

"We went nameless in the eyes of the Lord of Light. Our own God will grant us names."

The mention of another god, whoever that was, made her vaguely jealous. *"I'll call you Fern,"* she told the green letters. *"And you will listen to no other god but me."*

"Of course, God of Mercy. We live or die at your pleasure."

"What do you call me?" came the infrared.

"I call you Poppy."

"Thanks, Oh Great One. May we bring our children to the arachnoid?"

This question brought her back to reality. The doctor was still there, and Daeren watched her like a cat. She asked him, "Do you go through this all day?"

For the first time Daeren smiled. "I can't see your window, but, yes, I expect so. I'm used to it."

"Do you ever tell them to shut up?"

"It's rarely necessary. They know me too well." He leaned forward. "Watch my eyes."

"What?" Puzzled, she watched his irises, cat's-eye–brown with intense radial lines. Suddenly their rims flashed, a ring of blue light around each. Astonished, Chrys stared, her lips parted.

"The blue angels call us," wrote her green letters. *"Tell the Lord of Light we've done well."*

So Daeren was the one they called the Lord of Light. Her mouth closed, and she drew back. "Will my eyes strobe like that?"

"Only to contact another carrier. Otherwise, they'll stay dark."

Other carriers? There must be a whole pantheon of human carriers, each with micros swimming in the cobweb lining of the brain, and flashing rings around their eyes, like a nightclub act. "What keeps them from infecting your brain and making you sick?"

"They stay within the arachnoid layer, just outside the cortex. They never touch your neurons. They're only allowed a population of a million."

That sounded like plenty. "How can you be sure? You can't control a disease."

"Your Plan Ten nanoservos monitor your brain. Besides, the micros control themselves. Even ordinary microbes, without intelligence, usually limit their occupation of animal hosts.

"If they don't make you sick, what do they do in the . . . arachnoid?"

"Build homes and schools, raise their children. And help your work."

Little candy-colored rings building schools upon her brain.

"Do I please you, Oh Great One?" flashed the infrared. *"What do you look like?"*

"No, Poppy," said Fern. *"To look on the face of God forbodes death."*

Microbial superstition. *"Here I am,"* blinked Chrys. Her eyes downloaded her old self-portrait, from her sophomore year with Topaz. Her hair was lava flowing down her shoulders, and every vein snaked with anatomic precision along her face and breasts, out her arms and down to her feet.

"Our own God of Mercy, amid the stars," said Fern.

The stars? What did that mean?

"*A great road map,*" said Poppy. "*We will get to know those veins well.*"

Micro people swimming through her veins—enough to chill the blood.

"*Only our own god can see her own veins,*" Poppy added. "*Our god sees color beyond red, beyond other gods. Ours is indeed the best and greatest of all the gods.*"

Typical priests. "*If I am so great a god, why should I take you in?*"

The green one said, "*We are the People of Eleutheria. When our First World came to an end, and most of us died, the Blind God promised our children a New World, in a new arachnoid where no people ever lived before. We live by the lights of Truth, Beauty, Memory, . . .*" The letters went on at length, about the various lights of virtue; Chrys lost patience after the third or fourth.

"*Stop,*" said Chrys.

The letters ceased. That was encouraging.

"*What can you do for me?*" Chrys asked. "*Can you help me create great art?*"

"*Our ancestors created dwellings for the gods themselves. We will create the greatest works ever seen.*"

Modesty was not their strong point. "*What sort of dwellings?*"

"*The Lord of Light forbade us to speak of it, but to live only for one true God.*"

She frowned. "*If I am your one true God, you must tell me everything.*"

"*Yes, Oh Great One,*" said Fern, "*but the blue angels warned—*"

"*It shall be as you say!*" Poppy's letters danced. "*I knew this was the New World for us.*"

"*What can you do with this?*" Chrys downloaded her gallery piece, the lava fountain that turned into butterflies.

At first the volcano spurted and poured, just as it had for her fellow artists at the meeting. Then the visual began to change. The colors deepened, becoming more fantastic, until the hungry rivers swallowed themselves into abstraction. Then the abstract forms picked up the volcanic rhythms, returning in a cooler form; a volcano of ice. Chrys watched, her lips parted. All kinds of possibilities—she ached to get back to work.

The images faded. *"Today is the anniversary of our arrival,"* came the green one out of the dark. *"Has the God of Mercy decided our fate?"*

Chrys looked up. The doctor and the security agent were still there, waiting. The agent asked, "What do you think?"

She drew back. "I'll sleep on it."

Daeren shook his head. "They've already given you a whole year. They await your decision now."

She glared at him suspiciously.

The worm face wiggled. "A carrier needs to make life or death decisions quickly. But it is a lifelong commitment. So, if you don't feel comfortable, you should decline, and think it over. In the next year, we may have another culture ready."

That was reasonable, but what if the next culture were less creative than this one? On the other hand, what if these caused too much trouble? She thought of something. "Do these 'people' have . . . legal rights?"

Daeren hesitated. "They ought to. I've spent enough hours at the Palace on their behalf." A lobbyist after all.

The doctor's worms stretched thoughtfully. "Legally, Daeren, they're the plague."

"They are not," insisted Daeren. "That's like calling all humans murderers."

"She asked their legal status."

He turned to her. "Our micros will actually protect you from the real plague. As a carrier, you'll be safer than before."

"If she maintains them properly," agreed Sartorius. "But if she ever gets in trouble with the law, the octopods can wipe her micros without a thought."

Chrys watched this exchange with interest. "So I could get rid of them at any clinic."

A fleeting darkness crossed the agent's face, like an eclipse of the sun, a look of anger and disgust. But he quickly resumed his professional air. "As the doctor said, you can wait till you're ready."

The three of them froze, waiting, as if an eternity passed. Even the doctor's worms were still. At last Chrys let out a breath. "I'll take them."

She saw the agent relax. He had a lot at stake, she realized. Being the "Lord of Light" must be a tough act for a college kid.

The doctor came alive, each appendage finding a task. "First we need to transfer the Plan Ten nanoservos. They keep watch throughout your body." His worms stretched into unbelievably narrow snakes that twined unnervingly. "Just turn around and watch the holostage."

Chrys turned. A white beach stretched to the horizon, a gentle surf rolling in, palms bobbing in the wind. She tried not to think of what the worms were doing behind her neck.

"Oh Great One, have you forgotten us?"

"We anxiously await your reply."

She sighed. That's what you got for feeding stray cats. "You're sure all this is covered? Who pays for it?"

Daeren said, "The Committee pays for Plan Ten, until you're established. Most of us don't notice the cost."

Her mouth fell open, then she closed it. No wonder the agent looked so young; he could be a hundred for all she knew. He could be a college athlete all his life, while her own brother grew paler every year, waiting for mitochondria. She swallowed hard. "Is there a family plan?"

"If you have dependents—"

"Never mind." As soon as she earned some money, she would get her brother covered, long enough to get new mitochondria. *"I've decided,"* she told the two anxious micros. *"You are my people. Just remember one rule: If you have to preach, do it outside my eyes."*

THREE

....

The Eleutherians *tumbled out of the microneedles into capillaries of an untouched world. Their rotary filaments propelled them swiftly to the brain, where they tunneled through the arterial walls into the arachnoid. For shelter, they strung dendrimers, long chainlike molecules, back and forth across the branches of fibroblast cells.*

"Only the cross-branches," warned Fern. "Never touch the lining on either side." The arachnoid, with its cross-branches of fibroblast cells, stretched forever between the two outer linings of the brain. A breach of either lining would attract hungry white cells, or deadly microglia, the brain's special defenders. Microglia normally stayed within the central nervous tissue, their long arms tangled amongst the neurons; but the taste of suspicious molecules from the immigrants would activate them.

"We'll be careful," flashed Poppy, secreting the dendrimers and weaving them in expert patterns across the branches. Already she and other elders were laying out plans for homes and schools, and chambers for breeding. They tapped the capillaries to harvest vitamins and minerals. "We need to help the children feel at home, as soon as possible. If it doesn't taste right, they won't breed."

With the fifth wave of immigrants came the children and the young breeders; just three hundred precious vessels of the genes to seed their race and repopulate their world. Three hundred children for ten thousand adults, the most the gods allowed Eleutherians in their new world.

The Lord of Light's blue angels were a conventional lot; they mainly showed blue or violet. But the children of Eleutheria flashed anything from violet to red, and beyond. Poppy watched the precious little rings tumbling out of the silicon vessels that had carried them safely through the bloodstream, eager to taste the New World. "Our children come in colors that even the gods can't see," she flashed proudly.

"Watch yourself," warned Fern. "Our new god could see you well enough." The children worried her; their journey took too long. "They're getting depressed and philosophical. They'll all turn into elders before they breed."

"They'll soon feel better," flashed Poppy, "now that they're away from the blue angels." The blue angels secreted a developmental hormone that made a third of all children turn into elders without breeding; this had kept the Eleutherian numbers small. "We'll cheer them up with new things to taste. We'll build nightclubs."

The rest of the micros were transferred in the patch of microneedles, just like the first two. It took several passes to transfer them, ten thousand in all. Ten thousand microscopic rings that claimed to be people.

"*Oh Great One,*" the letters flashed green. "*Our growing children need arsenic.*"

"Arsenic?" Chrys looked up. "Isn't that what the slaves kill for?" On the street they called it "ace."

Doctor Sartorius extended an appendage. A claw snapped open, revealing a white pill. "Micros evolved on a planet full of arsenic. They need it as an essential mineral."

"But ace is poison."

"It's a controlled substance," the doctor admitted. "But our dietary supplement traps the arsenic in special cagelike molecules that keep it out of your own cells. Only the micros can extract it."

Chrys eyed the pill distastefully. "People will think I'm a slave."

Daeren shook his head. "Chrys, if people think that, they'll think it no matter what." His voice was low. "I told you, you'll face prejudice. We all do."

The worm face warned, "There's a black market in arsenic. Never, ever let your micros give up their arsenic, for any reason."

"The Plan supplies you once a month," said Daeren. "If ever you fall short, you could be accused of selling it. You'd end up in jail, and your people wiped out."

"Please, Great One—have mercy. Our children will starve without arsenic."

Reluctantly Chrys swallowed the pill.

The doctor's appendage retracted unnervingly into his cylindrical body. "Your nanoservos report no problems—no meningeal inflammation, no invasion of central nervous tissue. Daeren, can you stay? I'm on call." All his arms retracted and disappeared. Rearing backward, he twisted his body around and left.

Chrys sat back, and her hands sketched a moon in the air, itching to get back to her painting stage. "Where are the micros?" she asked. "They don't answer anymore."

"They're busy building their city," said Daeren.

"God of Mercy, is all well?" The green letters returned. *"Such a beautiful, untouched wilderness for our children to settle."*

"Fern's back." Untouched wilderness indeed.

"All right." Daeren came over and sat in front of her, his eyes level with hers. "May I check your eyes, just a minute?" Blue rings flashed again.

"Of course, we stayed out of the gray cortex," Fern insisted.

"Not a taste," added Poppy. *"The blue angels are so strict. They never trust us."*

"They sure talk fast," Chrys observed.

"A thousand times faster than humans. They're very social; when you meet another carrier, you'll always know."

"Well, I have no time to socialize. I have to put up my show. Can I go home now?"

"You signed an agreement to stay overnight, at least. Another day would be better, especially if you lack help at home."

"Saints and angels," she whispered. "When will I get to my work?" The turquoise moon was barely begun.

Daeren leaned closer. "You'd better pay attention to what's going on beneath your skull. Besides building a whole new city overnight, the ten thousand of them want to expand their population as soon as possible. At first, they have only three hundred juveniles to breed; the rest, all elders, cannot produce offspring."

"All elders? What is this, a retirement community?"

"A common population structure, for microbes," he said. "Only a few reproduce, while the others stay active enough to maintain the environment—'viable but non-culturable.' "

"These sound like they have plenty of culture."

"Like medieval monks, they store all the history of their people. They 'write' it in their chromosomes."

Monks—even worse than priests.

"Most of the time," Daeren said, "they keep just a few breeders to gradually replace those who die. But to found a new colony, they need to increase their number a thousand-fold, as quickly as possible." Above the stage appeared an S-shaped curve.

"The population will rise steeply for the next two weeks, then taper off by the end of the month at about a million. But at two weeks, you reach a critical point where nearly half the population are children."

Chrys looked up. "What's wrong with that?"

Daeren leaned back, chin in his hand. "It's like a feudal society before the plagues set in. Too many youngsters, lacking in judgment; they can get into trouble."

Microbial juvenile delinquents. "Like, they start gang wars?"

"They could invade the central brain tissue. That's how plague micros take over the dopamine center."

The holostage whined. Above the stage flashed a molecule, a hexagon of atoms with two claws and a tail. "Dopamine," repeated Daeren with emphasis. "The central molecule of reward. Dopamine enters the neurons to create pleasure. Everything humans do—loving, dying, killing—they do for dopamine."

Chrys regarded the molecule curiously. "Even enjoying art?"

"Even art," he said. "But the plague micros trap the dopamine in your synapses, until you're good for nothing else. Like cocaine—smart cocaine."

Chrys stared again at the molecule; it looked like a scorpion. A normal part of the brain; and yet. . . . "These micros could turn into plague."

"Your elders will keep things in hand," he assured her. " Once you get past the second week, elders outnumber children again, and the population stabilizes at a million. Then they have nothing to do but help your work."

Chrys shuddered. "Well, let's hope Fern keeps the kids in line."

The poppy-colored letters returned. *"Oh Great One, do our people please you?"*

"Yes, I am . . . pleased."

"Then please, send us a sign of your mercy."

Chrys looked up. "They want a 'sign.' What do I do, raise the dead?"

Daeren took a look at the medical monitor. "The nanos say they're doing okay, keeping their kids out of the cortex. They deserve a reward." Daeren took out a packet of small blue wafers. He handed one to Chrys. "Here, take this. Hold it on your tongue for a moment, then swallow it."

Chrys eyed the blue wafer suspiciously. "What's in it?"

"Azetidine acid." The holostage showed a new molecule: a simpler structure, only seven atoms. A group of four with a tail of three, like the seven stars.

"A—what?"

"Azetidine, AZ for short. An amino acid, common in plants. It does for micros what dopamine does for us."

Microbial cocaine? "It doesn't sound right. Why should I drug them?"

"If you don't rule them, they'll rule you." Daeren smiled. "It's just a low concentration. It gives them a buzz, like champagne with chocolates."

"I don't drink. You made a big point of it."

"They're different. They live fast."

Chrys put the wafer in her mouth. It tasted like a potato chip.

"Thanks for your blessing, Oh Great One! We will make wise use of your world, and sing your praises forever." A starburst of red and lava.

Fern added, *"It is good to please our God of Mercy, for we live or die at your pleasure."*

Chrys thought, even priests like good food and drink.

As the micros multiplied, the holostage listed their growing population. On the first day the total did not increase much, but the 'children' doubled, and none became elders. Every hour or so the elders asked for a "sign." It always sent them into raptures, like catnip. Then Fern hurried off to keep the kids out of trouble, but Poppy at least could be persuaded to stay a bit and play with colors. Colors of mountains, sky, and ocean; at Chrys's suggestion, Poppy sprayed them out, from the green gold of meadows to the gray violet of distant hills. Familiar vistas turned strange, as if by the light of a foreign sun.

The hourly newsbreak jarred her teeth. Titan's corpse, for the hundredth time—still no leads. If micros were people, then Titan's murder was more than a hate crime; it was genocide. Meanwhile, slaves had snatched another ship, in Elysian space. No Elves were ever taken, though, only a "mortal" Valan.

In her window the Protector pounded his fist, demanding the Elves help locate the Slave World. The Elf Prime Guardian did not deign to reply, but his Guardian of Peace, Guardian Arion, appeared in his butterfly train. Guardian Arion stood straight as a caryatid, his face marble white. "The brain plague and other addictions need not trouble our advanced society," the Elf purred. His bearing and diction underlined the superiority of a world without crime. As opposed to inferior Valedon.

Chrys lay back in the hospital bed. *"Poppy, no more news for me. I'm closing the window."*

"But what if we need you, Oh Great One?"

"If I see that corpse once more, I'll go mad."

"Change the setting."

That took her by surprise. *"What setting?"*

"Advanced Options, function nine; Social Setting, alternate six; Alert Status, key three. . . ."

Following each step, Chrys focused on the hovering keypad. The Plan One clinic never told her about this.

"The gods are not omniscient," Poppy observed. *"They can learn from us."*

Chrys smiled. *"Yes, we can learn from you."*

That evening Daeren stopped in. For a moment he froze; his brows wrinkled and his eyes scanned, as if reading bad news in the window. Then he looked at her and smiled. "Time for an eye check."

Chrys had been sketching a shield cone on a windless day, a wisp of smoke rising. She blinked it away and focused on the agent's eyes as they flashed blue. A minute or so passed before her own flashed in response.

"They should always keep someone on watch," he told her. "Remind them. And remember to set your alarm at night, every two hours."

"What for?"

"While you sleep, eight years will pass. The young won't know you, and the old may forget. Plan Ten would wake you if anything went wrong, but prevention is better."

She stretched, missing her workout with Zircon. Yet oddly she felt exhausted, as if she had traveled a thousand years. "I can use a good night's sleep."

"Remember to keep your window open."

Poppy had turned off the news and ads. That alone was nearly worth the hospital stay.

That night, she woke every two hours to give the micros their "sign" of AZ. Each time they responded with rapturous pyrotechnics. By morning, she tossed in her sheets, unable quite to sleep, too tired to waken.

"Fern? Are you there?"

"I am here, Oh Great One."

In the dark she felt as if she were one of them; she could almost reach out and touch the whiskers of the little ring. *"Fern, I need sleep."*

"So do I. But at last we've built our first city."

"Your city?"

"In the arachnoid, in the great Cisterna Magna."

Out of the darkness grew columns of light. Fibroblast cells connected floor to ceiling, a vast colonnade extending in all directions like a scaffold across the firmament of the brain. Between two arachnoid columns hovered Fern. Her green projections twinkled as they rotated, propelling her forward. Chrys's view followed her.

"Our arachnoid is largely wilderness, as yet uninhabited. But now we approach the Cisterna Magna, where the brain linings diverge, creating a great space for our city."

The floor fell away sickeningly, while the ceiling soared out of sight. Across the cellular columns stretched struts and braces of all different colors, in complex pulsating structures. The struts built fantastic stellated dwellings, with micro rings tumbling in and out of hidden portals. This was the city they had built in their New World.

Her mind floated upward, toward the ceiling where the columns stretched to meet the outer lining of the brain. An opening appeared, flanked by micros of various twinkling colors, sentinels on guard. The opening extended into a tunnel, smooth and white.

"Our bridge to the bloodstream," said Fern. *"Only the eldest of the elders may cross into the blood and travel with the nanos. We will serve you better than any nanoservo built by the gods, patrolling your veins forever."*

When at last she came awake, Chrys felt as if she herself had explored an eighth world of the Fold. Her vision was transformed.

How would she paint again—and how would anyone ever understand?

As she reached for the disk of nanotex by her bedside, she bounced out of bed faster than she intended. Despite her poor sleep, she felt as if her body could float away; as if the planet had lost half its gravity overnight. She started to comb her hair, a long, painstaking process, but the feel of her flexing arms puzzled her. As usual, the nanotex adhered to her chest, then spread itself in a black film around her body, automatically cleansing her skin. The film of artificial cells took on the contours of her body; a landscape familiar, yet now subtly estranged.

Doctor Sartorius came back to check her out. "Your Plan Ten nanoservos have started shaping you up, Chrysoberyl." Their transmissions sent a stream of colored squiggles and blinking text flowing across the holostage. In Chrys's eye, a new call button had appeared; in an emergency, a blink at that spot would bring Plan Ten.

"The plan representative will present your advanced options, during one of your daily checkups."

Checkups every day—she would never get that spattercone done.

Daeren came in to flash his irises one last time. "How do you feel?" he asked. "Anything I need to know?"

"The blue angels again," the infrared letters sped across her window. *"Tell them we're busy."*

"We're okay," Chrys said, puzzled by his question.

A quick smile crossed his lips. "You're talking plural already." Daeren placed a transfer patch on his neck. "The blue angels need to 'visit.' Yours can visit, too." He held out the patch.

"The blue angels say we can visit!" announced Fern. *"Is it permitted, Oh Great One?"*

She took the patch from Daeren and placed it on her neck, then returned it with her own visitors. "If I'm carrying ten thousand of them," Chrys wondered, "why do I always see the same two?"

"Only two have been called to be priests," he explained. "You may call others, as you wish."

She shook her head. "Two are enough."

"*Greetings, God of Mercy.*" These letters were blue.

Chris blinked twice. "*Who are you?*"

"*We are called the blue angels,*" the visitor said. "*Your new people are growing well, though they need to curb their lifestyle. They are rather frivolous, I'm afraid, but they'll mature.*" Maybe this one was a bishop.

Behind the doctor, the wall puckered in. It seemed to change its mind, then went ahead and opened. As its edges gathered back, there came a sound of scuffling, then a shout.

In the corridor outside struggled a stranger, held between two black-limbed octopods. The man was tossing his head one way then the other, his eyes bright with terror. His nanotex hung loose, as if its power had run down. Extending from the wall, ropelike appendages caught the man's wrists and ankles. His arm was gripped by a woman in gray, a tall Sardish blonde.

The woman in gray turned her piercing eyes toward the doctor. "Sar, the clinic's full. We need to extend." Her voice had a tone of finality, expecting obedience.

"Excuse me." The doctor glided out to join them.

Chrys stared until the door resealed.

Daeren still watched where the door had closed in, his expression grim. "A slave, he turned himself in. His masters objected. Sorry, it's been a long night at the clinic."

Master microbes. Chrys frowned. "That could happen to me."

"Not if you stick to the rules, and get tested twice a month."

"What? Like some addict?"

"We all do, even the chief of security."

She eyed him coldly. "You said these micros would keep me safe."

"Safer than you were before."

"But—" That vampire up on level one, the night before. More slaves every year, turning into vampires, or hauling captives to the Slave World for its microbial Enlightened Leader. "It's a cancer," she realized. "Like the building root cancers. It threatens all the city."

"Not just the city. It's reached—" He stopped, hesitant.

"How can it go on? Why can't the Palace just round up all the vampires?"

Daeren shook his head. "The vampires are the least of it. The problem already reaches too far up."

"Far up? What do you mean?"

"Sar runs run a private clinic for the Great Houses."

Smart cocaine. Chrys felt a chill down to her toes. Then she frowned and shook herself. "Well, I want no part of it one way or another. I just want to make art."

"Of course you do," said Daeren. "Nobody says, 'I'll grow up to be a slave.'" He looked her closely in the eye, blue rings flashing. "Your people pass. You can have them back now, and return mine."

"Nothing but insulting questions, interminable," complained Poppy.

"Before you leave," Daeren added, "the chief has to certify."

The wall parted smartly. A woman entered, the Sardish blonde who had brought in the plague victim. Her skin was exceptionally fair; Chrys could see every vein, like ivy on her arms and face. She carried herself stiff as a Palace guard. Her mouth was small, as if she would only release her words on good behavior. "I am Andradite of Sardis, Chief of Security."

"Our ancient history tells of the god among gods," said Fern. *"The Thundergod."*

Nodding to Daeren, Andradite put a transfer patch at her neck, then immediately pressed to his. He did the same for her, swiftly, as if it were something they had done many times. Chrys felt her scalp prickle.

Then the chief's eyes faced Chrys. Her irises flashed bluish violet, a shade deeper than Daeren's.

"The judges," announced Poppy. *"Throughout history, they brought trouble."*

"We have nothing to hide," insisted Fern.

Chrys tried to look unconcerned.

"You've done well, so far." Andradite offered her a patch.

"Much better than some of us expected." The chief had expected her to fail, Chrys realized. Both agents were hiding something. Why?

"Once you're home, you will hear from us," the chief told her. "You will join the community of controlled carriers—a highly exclusive group."

Chrys doubted that. How exclusive could a group be, to take her?

In her window, next to Plan Ten, appeared another call button, with no label, just the color purple that the chief's eyes flashed. "If you're ever in trouble," the chief told her, "the kind of trouble even Plan Ten can't help, call us. Forget your own name, but remember that."

FOUR

Fern tumbled through the city of the great Cisterna Magna, tasting its intricate molecules. Throughout the Cisterna, libraries of triplex DNA stored all the learning of Eleutheria. Nightclubs flashed with light-producing enzymes, singing colored music. Through the singing halls tumbled children ripe for breeding, their filaments tasting each other, hungering for just the right mate to merge.

"Fern?" Poppy's light flashed through the optic fibers. "We need help. A merged pair is having trouble giving birth."

Fern's spiral tails whirled and sent her spinning down the hall. Between two columns of fibroblast, a nest of dendrimers formed the breeding chamber. Inside, two breeders had come together. Their filaments had dissolved, allowing their surface membranes to merge. As the pair merged, their DNA triplexes came together to exchange genes. Once the two triplex chromosomes recombined, the membranes would pucker and pinch in, and the new children would come apart—as three. The three newborn children would each have duplex DNA, until they each grew a third strand in order to breed again.

But this time, something had gone wrong. "The offspring can't come apart," flashed Poppy. The edges of the three rings puckered in all around, as the membranes sought to pinch through, but still they remained attached.

"Get the enzymes," Fern told her. "Enzymes to cut the membrane, slowly." Carefully her filaments applied the enzymes to the grooves between the three half-separated children. Poppy did the same around the other side; it was vital to cut evenly, lest a child tear open. The grooves deepened. At last the three rings fell apart, three different lights flashing their cries: yellow, yellow-green, and green-blue. Three children, where there had been two.

"There are so many children now," Fern told Poppy, her filaments tasting the children to calm them. "Ten times more than I've ever known."

"They'll turn into elders soon enough," flashed Poppy.

"The young elders are as careless as the children. And few of the children are becoming elders. Most just keep merging and dividing."

"How else can our people grow?"

One lovely child, a ring of pink violet, seemed quieter than the rest. She had just grown her third strand of DNA, but she seemed in no hurry to join a mate. Instead, she spent all her time tasting the records of Eleutheria, studying the plans of the Comb. "I've figured out something," she flashed to Fern. "The windows of the dwelling the gods call the Comb. The legendary windows that gather starlight. I can show how they were grown."

Fern was pleased, but kept herself from revealing how much. "You're a good student, Pink-violet. But you have less than a year to find a mate to merge." After a year, a god's hour, the breeder's mating structures would dissolve, and she would inevitably become an elder.

The pink-violet one pulled in her filaments. "Merging is for gods and children. Not elders."

"Are you sure of your choice?"

"When I become an elder, Fern, will I earn a name from the god?"

*   *   *

At home, Merope kept brushing around Chrys's legs till she tripped, and even Alcyone deigned to sniff her hand. Rarely had she been away from her studio so long.

Above the painting stage hovered the virtual palette. Chrys dipped her fingers in cerulean blue and a touch of brown, then brushed her hands through the air, leaving a trail of indigo. She blocked in the spattercone of congealed rock, then the Elf moon, then added local colors: cool violet grays for the volcanic peaks, amber and gold for the opening spurt of lava; sky of deep cobalt, bearing the seven stars and their hunter.

"Oh Great One, may we taste a sign of your favor?"

She thought of something. *"Poppy, I'll give you a sign if you can help me out."*

"Of course—anything, to serve our God of Mercy."

The room darkened, and the new painting vanished. In its place appeared the lava fountain falling into butterflies.

"A river of stars," said Poppy.

"Poppy . . . how can I help other people to see it as I do?"

"All the people can see it through your eyes. They're just busy right now."

"I mean, the other . . . gods."

A tiny replica of the volcano appeared in her eyes, hovering just before her. The replica looked washed out in black, crucial details missing, like an old oil color darkened with age. Chrys nodded. *"That is how other gods see."* That was why Pearl called her butterflies too dark.

"Try this."

The replica changed. Its details returned, in a subtly different spectrum. No more infrared lava, but the reds and golds had their own distinctive range. Not the palette she would have chosen, yet compelling in its own way. Her pulse raced—she could hardly wait to show Topaz.

"Do we please you, Oh Great One?"

She reached for an AZ and placed the wafer on her tongue.

For the next hour, Poppy helped redo two other pieces. It was more than just a shifted wavelength; an aesthetic choice was made, a choice Chrys could not have made herself. The results were exciting; but were they hers alone?

Slowly she smiled. From the public archive she downloaded an image of AZ, azetidine acid, the four-atom square with the forked tail. She set the molecule in the corner of each piece, next to her own cat's eye.

If she worked fast, she could revise all her pieces in the gallery, and still get the moon piece done for the Elf gallery director and Zircon's Elf patron. But then, Elves could see the infrared. Which version should she show?

With a blink at her window, she called Topaz. Topaz's sprite floated beside a towering portrait of a fur-cloaked client from one of the Great Houses. Her finger was shaping the last stroke of eyelash and a blush on the cheek. She turned to Chrys. "How's it going, Cat's Eye?"

"Topaz, any chance I could have a dozen more spots at the show?"

"Are you kidding? You're doing a dozen more pieces this week?"

Chrys looked away. She should have known better.

"The show's important, but don't kill yourself. I'm sure the Elves will love *Lava Butterflies*." Her voice had a trace of condescension.

Chrys looked up. "I found out some things. Brain enhancers are actually self-aware. Like sentients."

Topaz frowned. "Cat's Eye, everyone knows a nanoservo can't be self-aware. How could it pack a trillion neurons?"

She wondered that herself. As the sprite dissolved, Chrys realized that Topaz still thought of her as the Dolomite sophomore who knew nothing. But this time, Topaz was wrong.

Another sprite flashed into her window. Zircon looked out at her from the club; the late afternoon hour, it was full of mountainous biceps flexing. "Chrys, where have you been? The second workout you've missed."

"Hey, I'm sorry." Actually, she felt as if she had ten workouts that morning. "Don't worry. Things are getting back to . . . normal."

On his chest, the large crystal gems swam out in spirals.

"*Stars, Oh Great One,*" flashed Poppy's letters beneath. "*When will you show us the stars?*"

Startled, Chrys tried to keep her face straight. But Zircon gave her a puzzled look. "Chrys, if you're in trouble, let me know, okay?"

She made herself smile. "I had to crack cancerplast the other night." Just the night before last—it felt like forever.

Zircon shook his head. "You couldn't pay me to live on your level."

"Nobody pays me to live elsewhere."

He grinned infectiously, and lines appeared in his forehead. Not as young as he used to be, but always up for something new. "Hey, I could fix you up. I know Elves, men or women, who'd just die to have you."

Chrys liked Zirc, and she could have fallen for him, once upon a time. "I've had enough of people. I'd sooner date a worm-face."

"Mind-suckers!" Zircon shuddered. "Don't even say that. It's . . . perverted."

That evening Chrys took a break and strolled up Center Way. The lightcraft flitting up and down, the glowing signs, the virtual decor of the Great Houses—through her eyes, the micros exclaimed at all the lights, which they called stars. For the micros, she realized, ten meters might as well be ten light-years. How could they distinguish city lights from those across the universe?

"*Wait,*" flashed Poppy. "*Wait—I see something most important. Something from our records; the oldest records of our people.*"

Chrys blinked. Her eyes came to rest upon the Comb.

"*That's it! Fern, come quickly—call the others to see. . . .*"

The Comb's hexagonal facets shone as always, in shifting tones of gold, red, even lava. Curious, Chrys asked, "*What do your records say?*"

"*They say that we made the Comb.*"

Chrys was taken aback. "*You made the Comb? How can that be?*" The same strain as Titan's, *Eleutheria.* But had they come from Titan himself?

"*It is true,*" added Fern. "*Our ancestors designed the seed that grew the Comb. We have all the plans. We made it for The Blind God."*

"The Blind God?" Chrys asked. *"Not the Lord of Light?"* She remembered what had puzzled her before: How could her own "people" be so different from Daeren's, if they came from his own head?

"The Blind God was our world, before the great exodus, when the Lord of Light took us in."

She stared, unseeing, her pulse racing. How could these micros have "made" the Comb, and still have the plans? Who was the Blind God? What had those doctors not told her?

At the hospital again the next morning, Doctor Sartorius listened to the nanos reporting from Chrys's bloodstream. His worm-like arms extended to plug into the hospital wall. Chrys still couldn't help expecting flies. "No sign of inflammation," he said. "The nanos are doing their job."

Chrys eyed him skeptically. "Nano-cells are 'intelligent,' but never as smart as people. How can micros be so smart? They're too small to have neurons."

One of the worms flicked toward the holostage, extending like an antenna. "Micros are about the size of a white blood cell. Each cell packs an array of polymers, with ten trillion units." Above the stage glowed a cage of atoms, with links joining in all dimensions. "Units connect by a 'spiro gate' that can twist in two directions. One twist allows current to flow across the link, the other not." The model came alive with twisting connections, as if thoughts were flitting across them. "These polymers transmit information, as surely as human neurons, or sentient circuits."

She regarded the sentient doctor curiously. "If micros that small can be 'people,' then why can't nano-cells be 'sentient,' like you?"

The doctor's worms retracted and were still. The spiro-gated molecules gave way to legal documents, the kind Daeren liked to quote, scrolling down the holostage. "When machines first . . . claimed sentience, the Fold Council set a lower limit for size at ten cubic centimeters. Nothing smaller could be a 'person,' with 'personal rights.' "

"What?" Chrys spread her hands. "How can you just decree what's a person and what's not?"

Doctor Sartorius returned to the holostage. "If you have no further questions, the Plan Ten representative is here today, to inform you of your benefits."

The Plan Ten rep was a human female, of model proportions, the kind all art students drew their first year. Her nanotex was modest gray, but it shifted subtly to highlight her perfect legs and ankles. Her curves were more than enough to remind Chrys how long it had been since she shared a bed, and to make her, just for a moment, rethink her resolution.

"Chrysoberyl, I'm here to answer any questions you may have about the Comprehensive Deluxe Health Package Plan Ten." The woman's tone was professional, yet softly persuasive. "You may call us anytime, of course; from anywhere, on any world."

"Even the Underworld?"

The Plan rep smiled confidingly. "Our competitors, up through Plan Eight, provide instant coverage only for the more convenient parts of the city. But with Plan Ten, our emergency response time everywhere is under five minutes. You needn't give up any of your favorite night spots."

"I see." Chrys patted her hair self-consciously, though it never would stay down.

The Plan rep nodded to the holostage. "Now, according to our records," she observed, "you have yet to choose your age and appearance."

"Excuse me?"

Upon the stage appeared Chrys herself, life size. Like a mirror, only without the usual mirror reversal; at first her own face looked askew.

"Plan Ten allows you to specify exact age, color, and so on. For most of our clients, age is the main concern. Have you thought about it?"

Chrys blinked. "I've had other things on my mind."

"Of course," the woman nodded understandingly. "Carriers always do. But think now." She turned to the holostage. "Our most discerning clients choose age eighteen to twenty."

The virtual Chrys seemed to smooth out a bit, like one of Topaz's portraits. Chrys tensed and swallowed. She had not thought of herself as already having aged. But the Chrys in the holostage looked to her like a pre-teen. "I'm too small to look young," she observed, half to herself. "People still pat me on the head."

"Stature can be increased." The Chrys on stage grew a couple of centimeters. "As for age, how old would you like to look? Distinguished? Venerable? Mother of Ages?"

The virtual Chrys grew fine lines in her forehead, but still stood erect and authoritative. As the skin shrunk around her face and hands, she looked fierce, indomitable, an iron lady. At last she shriveled into a million wrinkles, her eyes still bright and clear. Like a saint who'd spent her life tending dying people in the street.

"You can always change your selection," the Plan rep quietly observed.

Chrys clenched and unclenched her hands, and swallowed again, hard. "To be real honest, I think I'd like to keep on looking exactly the age I am now."

"Excellent—a very wise choice. Our wisest clients generally choose as you did," the Plan rep assured her. "Now, as to internal organs, of course, these can be optimized separately. Most clients simply take the age of optimal function—for the female, visual acuity peaks at age ten, muscle strength at age twenty, sexual response at age forty, and so forth. Is that fine with you?"

Chrys blinked. "I guess so." For her, health had always meant simply not being sick.

"And muscle mass." The woman's dimples deepened apologetically. "I'm sorry, this one is so complex. Some examples—" The virtual Chrys expanded and shrank, while the rep rattled on about upper body strength, a gymnast's flexibility, the balanced curves of a swimmer. "For sheer strength, there's this." The body grew hills all over, like a volcanic slope bulging with magma.

Chrys smiled suddenly. "I'll take that." Zircon would be in for a surprise.

"A bold choice," the rep exclaimed, a bit too quickly. "A client of your sophistication might be interested in our more advanced options. Would you consider a change of gender?" She leaned forward confidentially. "Our competitor, Plan Nine, offers only one change of gender per lifetime. Can you imagine? What if you changed your mind, and couldn't switch back?" She shook her head. "Our plan guarantees to switch you back, as often as you choose."

Chrys's jaw fell. For a minute, she could not imagine what to say. "To be really honest . . ." She thought of something. "Gender change would be great, but there's something else I'd like even more."

"Yes?"

"I'd like to sign away all my rights to, uh, change of gender, and use the funds saved to fix my brother's mitochondria. Could I do that?"

The woman looked shocked. "Sign away your own body rights? Like selling an eye or a kidney—you couldn't do that."

Chrys had considered it.

The encounter with Plan Ten left her vexed and sad. At last Daeren came to complete her visit. "Anything I need to know?" Shoulders straight, limbs fit and lean; Daeren had the health her brother never would. He looked her in the eye, and his own twinkled blue. "You need to get more sleep."

Something inside her snapped. "Excuse me, can you tell me how old you really are? I was raised to respect elders."

Daeren stiffened, and a tendon stood out in his neck. "I was raised to respect everyone. Assume I'm a hundred." Young enough to be defensive. "Is anything wrong?" he asked. "I know Fern feels overwhelmed, but it will pass." He handed her a transfer patch.

Chrys accepted the patch and handed it back to him, getting used to the routine of visiting micros. "Why do they say they built the Comb?"

Daeren frowned. "It would be more correct to say they share ancestry with those who seeded the Comb."

"But my micros came from your head, didn't they? Why aren't they blue angels?

"I'm like a way station," he told her. "My people are strain *Coelecolor*; they're social workers, immigration specialists. They take in refugees and train colonists to develop new worlds."

So a carrier could hold more than one strain. Different ethnic neighborhoods. "These refugees and colonists . . . they come from other people's brains?"

"That's right. Micros like to travel."

"So where did mine 'travel' from, originally? From Titan?"

"They grew inside me for seven generations. That's like a couple of centuries. Their duty is to leave the past behind, and serve their new world."

Committee talk again. "Was Titan their 'Blind God'?" Chrys asked. "How could a blind carrier 'talk' with them?"

Now he looked really upset. "The Eleutherians have exceptional memory, but they sometimes get things twisted." He leaned closer, and the blue rings sparkled.

"*Oh Great One, the blue angels bid us forget,*" flashed Poppy. "*But you told us to recover all our memories.*"

"*Sure, but keep it dark for now.*"

Daeren put the patch back on his neck, just beneath his dark hair, then he held it out. "You can have your people back. They already miss their nightclubs."

"Nightclubs? You mean, strobe lights hung beneath my skull?"

"The molecular equivalent. I told you, your strain lives fast."

She remembered the wild-eyed slave, and the stern Chief Andradite. "Is that why the chief said she expected worse? Why did you give me such a bad strain?"

"They can get into trouble, but they're exceptionally creative. You could have had a strain of accountants."

She gave him a look. "Accountants cause more trouble than any artist." Something was missing, but she could not put a finger on it. She leaned back with a sigh. "I had no idea what I was getting into."

He asked quietly, "Are you sorry?"

She thought of the transformed pyroscapes. "No. I just feel like I'm back on Mount Dolomoth, walking on lava."

It was his turn to stare. "You've walked on lava?"

"Two hours old." The heat rising, simmering, suffocating. The surface dark and slick, with holes to the interior glowing like poppies. She was twelve when the long dormant Mount Dolomoth had erupted, and it fascinated her ever since.

"I hope you won't try that again. A million lives depend on you."

She crossed her arms. "Listen, Lord of Light—if I have to risk a million of them raising hell in their nightclubs, they can just as well risk me."

On her way home an acrid haze obscured her street. But the buildings looked intact, aside from the usual old windows stuck open, gasping sideways. The haze must have seeped up from below. After a slave hijacking, Sapiens always blamed the sims, so they torched the Underworld. They usually stayed below; but right here on her block a gang of Sapiens marched toward her, lasers on their belts, pads of stunplast girding their knees and palms. Chrys unobtrusively crossed the street. If the carnage reached her level, she might have to go stay with Topaz and Pearl.

Safe at home, she called down a Titan retrospective. Titan's early career as a half-baked formalist, like Zircon. Titan's first brain-enhanced commissions, dwellings that soared like living, breathing things offering flowers to the world. Titan's more advanced works, each now a landmark. And his social ascent, on the arm of one Lady after another, each better connected than the last. Always women, oddly enough, a medieval obsession.

A stranger flickered into her window. "Chrys, I'm Opal of Orthoclase. Andra asked me to call." Opal called from the Institute for Nano Design—the Comb. Her namestones were a cluster of rainbow drops that formed a flower, only to flow apart again. She gave a friendly smile, almost in a motherly way, her face as round and smooth as her gems. Behind her, her holostage was twice as large as Chrys's entire studio. The walls jutted at wide angles, creating the honeycomb of rooms for which the Comb was famous. "Chrys—I'm so glad we caught up at last. A colorist, aren't you? Daeren says you're doing so well."

"Thanks," said Chrys warily.

"My people can't wait to see Eleutherians again. I hear they're just the same...." Stepping backward, Opal spread her arm toward her stage. "We design medical servos."

"The kind used for Plan Ten?"

Opal nodded. "And more experimental applications. But you 'design,' too, don't you. It's all art, don't you think?"

Chrys cleared her throat. "What can I do for you?"

"*Oh Great One, we recall the legends of this starry-eyed god,*" flashed Fern, "*the God of Wisdom, and her clever people, the 'wizards.' The wizards are our long-lost cousins; let us renew ties with them.*"

"*Not today,*" returned Chrys. "*Go tend your children.*"

"The café here serves carriers," Opal was saying. "We can meet here tomorrow."

It had not occurred to Chrys that restaurants would shun carriers, even worse than sims, if they knew. A knot of pain formed in her stomach. "I'd love to," she told Opal, "after my show opens next week."

Opal's mouth went straight and her eyes widened. "I promised I'd see you this week. It's important."

"Thanks; you've kept your promise. The day after the Opening, okay?"

Hours of work turned into days, as the spattercone grew. The cone's straight sides pointed to the sky, drawing the viewer up from echoing lines below. Above the holostage, Chrys's finger traced the streams of lava that rose from the cone, reaching toward the turquoise moon. Then she traced the moon's details, subtly following the curve of lava. The moon was the center of a pool where ripples led outward, down to the ground.

But as the piece played forward it developed in a new way, distinctly different from any pyroscape Chrys had done before. Instead of arching to fall back to ground, the streams of lava kept going till they reached the sky. The sky collected a long lava river, smooth and thin, with lava strands connecting down to the ground below; unmistakably reminiscent of arachnoid. And the turquoise moon, amid the strands, sprouted luminous filaments of light.

"*Oh Great One,*" called Fern. "*A young elder begs a favor from you. A true scholar; I recommend her highly. She asks you to give her a name.*"

Why not, thought Chrys; the other priests were so busy. "*What does she look like?*"

A diffuse light, magenta, with long starry filaments. Star with a dark center. Chrys's lips softened. "*Aster,*" she decided. "*I call you Aster.*"

"*Oh Great One, I am not worthy to meet your eyes. But only ask, and I will follow.*"

For some reason she felt afraid. It was too much for her; all these people and their children would find out she was a fraud. She shook herself. What did she care, they were only microbes. "*Aster, can you help me perfect the turquoise moon?*"

"*I will help the god, in whatever small ways I can. May the god also bless our own work, our creation of dwellings for the gods.*"

"*I am no dynatect, Aster,*" she warned.

"*You shall become a great dynatect. Greater even than the Blind God.*"

"A prophet!" Chrys laughed aloud.

Then she froze. The Blind God—that was Titan. It had to be. But the murdered dynatect had not been blind . . . until he was attacked. The limp body, sprawled in the street like a piece of trash, the eyes burnt into the skull. Had the micros lived through that? Had Plan Ten arrived in five minutes, only to save the micros from his dying brain? What else was that agent hiding?

FIVE

....

"When shall we build?" Poppy demanded of Fern. "We have all our plans, old and new, but we are out of practice. As elders die, we lose their experience."

In the Cisterna Magna, they had reestablished the Council of Thirty, the ancient governing body of Eleutheria. They organized trade in arsenic and palladium, and regulated the mining of vitamins from the blood. Now the Council wanted to resume building for the gods.

"We build when we are called," said Fern. "The gods seek their own dwellings. In the meantime, the god calls us to shape Truth and Beauty in the stars." The God of Mercy built creations out of light itself.

"Where are all the peoples from our history?" asked Aster. "The judges of the Thundergod, the wizards of Wisdom, the minions of the Deathlord?" Aster, and the others born here, had met only Eleutherians. They were isolated, cut off from the rest of civilization, from new ideas and fresh genes. "We need to meet all the people of other gods. We have made all kinds of tasty molecules to trade with them. We need to meet their children, and recruit the brightest for our work."

Poppy said, "This god always goes alone. What is wrong?"

Fern wished she knew. History showed that even gods needed other gods. A god apart spelled trouble.

As always, Chrys was sure the Opening night would be a disaster—the Gallery would run short of power and refuse to display half the paintings, the cakes and lambfruits would be missing, the wine would be bitter, and no guests would show up. Nervously Chrys paced the exhibit halls, getting her first chance to see everything together. As she passed through the doorway to Topaz's portraits, her arm hit the edge, punching it in. "Damn," she muttered as the doorway reshaped itself, avoiding Pearl's curious stare. Her muscles had swelled noticeably, and she felt like she was bouncing on a low-gravity moon.

Topaz's portraits always drew a crowd, and this year she had some high-class commissions, including Lord Zoisite, the Palace minister of justice. In the full-size portrait, the minister wore his fur talar, its draped lines projecting verticality. Sparkling gems signaled his calling, his portfolio, his Great House, his wife's House, and several other affiliations. The back lighting framed his head like a halo, typical of Topaz. The haloes, as well as the subtly shortened noses and smoothed complexions, made all her subjects look like members of one family. What Plan Ten did for health, Topaz did for art.

"A god," flashed Aster, *"placed among the stars."*

A portrait in the stars. That's how it would look, to a micro peering out of her eye.

"Legend tells that someday our own people will be placed among the stars."

"How will that happen, Aster?"

Lady Moraeg was eyeing her oddly. "Chrys, are you okay?"

What if her irises lit up, and someone saw? *"Stay dark,"* she warned the micros. *"No more flashing today."* She smiled at Moraeg, and at Lord Carnelian beside her, flaxen haired with fine gray nanotex and one crimson namestone, classic scion of a Great House. The most faithful patron of the Seven, Carnelian had advanced Chrys her rent the last time she went under. "Moraeg, your flowers are exquisite this year."

"You haven't seen the latest."

Moraeg's flowers were nearly real enough to touch, from vibrant peonies to delicate snapdragons. Yet her overall compositions were fantastic—*Asters at a Neutron Star,* scarcely plausible, but somehow, watching the asters climb toward the star, you could almost believe it. *"There's your name,"* Chrys silently told Aster, pointing out the petals tinged with magenta. Turning, she searched the other pieces. *"And there are poppies. But stay dark."*

In *Sunflower Galaxy,* a seed grew into giant galactic-sized sunflowers. The time dimension was a new departure for Moraeg, and her execution appeared shaky. The next one, *Campion Peak,* showed a jagged ridge frosted with pink campion. Far in the distant haze rose the unmistakable straight, gentle slopes of a dormant volcano. "I like it," Chrys exclaimed.

Moraeg squeezed her hand. "We've so much in common. Now show me yours—I have a question."

The sound in the gallery had to be turned way down, but you could still feel the eruptions rumbling in your feet from the next hall; the lava fountain arching into butterflies, the spattercone spraying across the moon. Each piece had a five-minute time loop, the maximum her equipment could manage. Her infrared originals alternated with the versions reworked by her micros.

"Tell me, Chrys," Moraeg insisted. "How ever did you ever fix the colors?"

Chrys blinked and swallowed hard. An idiot, she should have foreseen this question. "Just had an idea," she muttered. She looked away, checking out the first visitors: young professionals in pulsing nanotex, ladies of the Great Houses in fur and silk, a couple made up fashionably as vampires, their skin bleached white with broken veins. So far no sign of an Elf.

Topaz stared at something, chin in hand. At last she pointed to the seven-atom molecule that hovered next to the cat's eye. "What does that mean?"

Chrys swallowed again. "Excuse me—I just remembered, I

have to serve the cakes." She escaped out to the next hall. A single work filled the hall, Zircon's *Ode to Inhumanity*. Brilliant shafts of light reached for the sky, grandly monumental.

"Wait—Oh Great One, let us stay a while."

"Let us admire this magnificent work. Austere, yet sensual—It inspires us."

"What!" She winced, hoping no one heard her speak aloud.

Zircon was standing right there, expounding at length on its many layers of meaning. "The visual iterations of form create a unity between the creator, the viewer, and ultimately all of humankind," he was telling several visitors in gold-studded furs. "Ultimately the form creates in our mind an apotheosis of the human tragedy. . . ."

"We of course can build far greater," added Aster. *"The greatest dwellings the gods have ever seen."*

Saints and angels—these microbes had egos as big as Zircon's. Chrys closed her eyes.

"Wait—we need to study this work—"

A hand with glowing nails tugged her arm. "Chrys, wake up," exclaimed Pearl. "Ilia's here."

Ilia Papili*shon*, director of Gallery Elysium. Chrys hurried back with Pearl to the main entrance.

The two Elves were unmistakable, each in a plain white talar projecting a long train of light like a comet's tail. Luminous swallowtail butterflies flickered across the nanotex of visitors coming up behind.

Topaz nodded graciously. "Ilia Papili*shon*," she introduced to Chrys, "and Yyri Papili*shon*."

Yyri was Zircon's patron. Ilia and Yyri shared the *shon* name, both hatched and raised in the same *shon*. Yyri did not extend a hand, but smiled and touched a fold of Ilia's talar, the closest contact Elves allowed in public. "I've just been telling Ilia, I've heard so much about your work, Chrysoberyl."

"Thanks, my Lady." Chrys bit her tongue; she forgot that Elves were fanatically egalitarian, having no Lords or Ladies, only Citizens. But Yyri did not deign to notice. She and Ilia turned politely toward the portrait of Lord Zoisite. Overhead hovered two sentient reporters, silver ovoids just above the minimum size, "snake eggs."

Yyri raised a hand, and Ilia nodded, probably catching a transmitted comment. "Quaint," the gallery director observed, without altering her frozen smile. The snake eggs recorded this utterance, then bobbed up and down for a better angle. Anything Elves took notice of was more likely to make the news.

Yyri touched Ilia's talar and motioned her on. "So much raw talent in Iridis," she said aloud. "Don't you think we ought to do a show, 'Gems from the Primitive'?"

The pair moved politely through the portraits, Chrys and Moraeg and the other Seven Stars hovering about at a discreet distance. Only Topaz had the presence to venture a remark. "Zircon's latest work is truly pathbreaking," she told Yyri.

Yyri clasped her hands. "An urban shaman—he plumbs the depths of modern humanity, in ways the more refined artist cannot."

Director Ilia had moved on to Moraeg's flowers. At *Asters at a Neutron Star,* she nodded. "Charming."

"Who is this strange god? Our ancient history tells that we once visited—"

"Stay dark." No Elf would get infected by micros. Chrys's eyelids fluttered, exhausted from staying up the night before to put the last touches on the turquoise moon. If she could just get through this evening, it would all be over.

At last Ilia reached the pyroscapes.

"Chrys's vision is unique," offered Topaz.

Ilia watched the lava butterflies. Her eye widened. "Intriguing color." Then she stopped at the spattercone. She watched the infrared lava rise to spread across the sky like a web of arachnoid, while the moon sprouted filaments like a micro. The color scheme changed; Ilia waited till it cycled back. She watched, and everyone else quieted to watch her.

The director caught sight of the molecule next to the cat's eye, and she leaned forward for a closer look. "Indeed." She straightened, then turned slowly, her virtual train swirling behind her, the swallowtails dipping and swaying. She took a step toward Chrys, much closer than Chrys expected.

Rings flashed around each iris—like Daeren's, only these flickered gold and red.

"The God of Many Colors! Her people want to visit."

"Please, Oh Great One, let us visit. Our history tells—"

Chrys stared in shock.

"What's the matter?" Moraeg caught her hand. "Chrys, sit down a minute."

Ilia nodded. "I understand. Give my best to Andra." Turning, she moved on to the next hall.

Pearl brought a chair. "There, Chrys. You probably haven't slept for days." She leaned close and whispered. "We didn't know you had connections. Who is Andra?"

Something was wrong. If microbial "brain enhancers" were just a cheap alternative to Elysian genetics—why would an Elf carry micros?

When the last guests were gone, and the last crumbs cleared by the scurrying floor servos, Chrys left the Gallery with Topaz and Pearl. Past midnight, Center Way was dark and still, the sky misted over. As the damp air cooled her face, her head throbbed. At last she could drag herself home.

Pearl's fingernails lifted like fireflies. "It *is* our best show ever," she exclaimed, still high on the excitement.

"The best attended opening," agreed Topaz, nodding at early press reports in her window. "Ilia said the Gallery Elysium is planning a show on Valan art."

"She sure noticed your work, didn't she, Chrys?"

The encounter had left Chrys shaken. But then, if even the Elf gallery director carried micros, just like Chief Andra, how bad could they be?

Topaz sidled closer. "How'd you do it?" she quietly asked. "How'd you fix those colors?"

"Did this Andra help?" asked Pearl. "Who is Andra? You got an Elf patron, like Zirc?"

"Certainly not." After Topaz, Chrys had had girlfriends, and boyfriends, but like Topaz they each managed to leave her just when she needed them most. The last thing she needed now was another one. Her steps slowed. "You know, that gallery director . . . she's got brain enhancers."

"Well sure, she's an Elf."

"No, I mean our kind of brain enhancers. The same kind as Titan."

Topaz frowned. "How would you know?"

"Because I have them too."

Pearl's eyes widened, and she sucked in her breath. "You have micros? Like a vampire? Chrys—*how could you?*"

"Pearl, it's not like you think—"

"You're contagious!"

"I am not contagious. I mean, I'd have to—"

"Those plague micros—Topaz, I can't believe it." Pearl fell back, trying to pull Topaz away.

"Pearl, just cool it." Catching Pearl's arm, Topaz glared at Chrys. "Why didn't you tell us?"

"I did tell you. Look, even Ilia has them—"

Topaz shook her head violently. "Elves are different. Look, Chrys, you're in trouble. You're provincial; you don't understand these things."

Pearl exclaimed, "Topaz, don't let her touch you."

"Oh hush." Topaz blinked, calling at her eye windows. In the street a ruddy bubble rose and expanded, gliding toward her. "Come on, let's get home."

The two of them hurried off, leaving Chrys alone in the deserted street. Alone, and stunned. Would she lose every friend and acquaintance she had, for what lived in her brain?

"So many stars this year. We are inspired, especially by the work of the god Zircon."

"Inspired to begin our own work, the dwellings of the gods. But where are the gods to call for us?"

No lack of "friends" inside, in colors of green, poppy, and

everything inbetween; even if they did like Zircon's work better. But Chrys slowly shook her head.

She had answered all the doctor's questions at the hospital, but she had not told the whole truth. She was addicted to one thing: people. She loved people, longed for them, good or bad, friend or stranger; she could probably fall for anyone except a sentient. The city surrounded her with a blanket of people, and that was good. But to lose Topaz and Pearl, and the rest of the Seven— it was like losing her right arm and leg.

"*Find the Thundergod,*" urged Fern. "*The Thundergod will help you.*"

Chief Andra's purple button would not help. But Chrys knew one place where she could always find human people.

Blinking for a bubble car, she entered the liquid street. The bubble closed her in, and the street flowed forward to the end, where it plunged down the tube. Down past the fashion district, down past the bank level, and the food market within the bank's root. Down past the homes of chic young professionals, down past the working-class sims on their way up. Down past her own level, the cheapest decent housing you could get, to the last level at bedrock. The Underworld.

No sign of the Sapiens' rampage; Palace octopods kept the entertainment district intact. Spice and decay, stale wine and costly perfume, breathed through the streets. Vendors from Urulan laid stacks of nanotex and gameplast upon roots of nanoplast that glowed suspiciously. Chrys spied one blob just starting to crawl away from its root. She held out her wand and fried it. The plast sizzled and shattered, but two little energized blobs glided off into the dark, just missing a couple of simian pre-teens tossing stickplast up at a broken street light.

Weaving in among the locals, Palace notables made their way to the shows; Lord Zoisite was a regular. They generally had an armed octopod in tow. Chrys spotted one and strolled discreetly behind it, an old trick when she came alone.

The octopod and its bejeweled lord entered Gold of Asragh, her favorite, one of the tonier clubs with the slave bar hidden in back. They must have remodeled, for the bar was now right up front by the entrance, a plague-ridden slave hawking ace in plain sight. So much for the Protector's war on the brain plague.

Behind the bar, the woman lifted a hand. "Char," she called in a low, hollow voice. "That you, Char?"

You could tell the voice of a mid-stage slave, flat and toneless, like a sentient gone wrong. Not yet a vampire, and not quite ready for the Slave World. Chrys nodded. "Hi, Saf." Sapphire, her name might have been once; slaves forgot all but the initial sound of human names. They gradually sold all they had for arsenic to serve their microbial masters; what they paid built the mysterious Slave World. Saf's eyes were bloodshot and always looked just to the side, never to look you in the eye. Chrys had first met Saf the month before. Now, by the looks of her, she had little time left before she sank, one way or the other.

Saf extended a hand. It held a transfer patch, bold as you please. "Char . . . you can't imagine." She said in a hoarse whisper. "Just try it. Enlightenment."

Chrys stared at the patch in the slave's hand. Like watching lava congeal, peering into those poppy-colored holes deep within the still liquid rock. What was the Slave World, she wondered; what did it look like? She sketched the sign against evil. "Saf, why don't you try this?" Chrys held out a viewcoin, one of several she kept for publicity.

The viewcoin transmitted to her own eyes, and Saf's. A tranquil peak at midmorning—exploded. Black clouds filled the sky, and a pyroclastic flow raced straight toward the viewer with a muffled roar.

A ghost of a smile came over Saf's face. It was hard to reach a slave, their senses grew so dull, feeling only microbial dopamine. Suddenly the woman straightened as if in shock. "You've . . . already got them."

A chill came over Chrys, from her scalp down to her toes.

"The masters of Endless Light," Fern called the plague micros. *"The masters never speak to us. They call us the root of all evil."*

Taken aback, Chrys blinked twice.

"You've got the worst kind," added Saf in her slow, toneless voice. "You and Day. All yours care about is money." The word "money" came as if dragged out of her. Then suddenly she extended an arm as if to grab Chrys. "You've also got . . . ace, in your veins," she hissed. "Give . . . us . . . your . . . ace."

Startled, Chrys drew back. Would the slave suck her blood for arsenic?

She hurried in with the gathering crowd, the ticket price automatically subtracting from her window. Simian locals, L'liite tourists, a lord in peridots; elbow to elbow they crowded. The perfumes and the odor of unwashed sweat nearly stifled her. At last she found her seat.

The stage exploded, blindingly. When the light and smoke cleared, the simian dancers were coming on, disguised as the caterpillar monster of ancient Urulan. The cheer of the crowd drowned the music, but at last the music won out, insistent, hypnotic. The music took them to distant cities on the most ancient of the seven worlds of the Fold.

"*Oh Great One,*" Fern's letters appeared at last. "*We are trying so hard to keep you healthy, but until your eyes close for sleep, your body cannot be renewed. What more can we do?*"

Her head throbbed, and her throat felt thick. She had not slept for over a day. But her show had opened, with some success, she reminded herself. And now the music brought peace. Early in the morning, she elbowed her way out of the hall. At the bar, two slaves were buying ace, a yellow-eyed simian in dead nanotex and a socialite in fur. Feel good now, but how long before they'd suck blood for it?

"*The masters won't speak to us,*" repeated Fern, seeming regretful. "*But the blue angels know them well.*"

The blue angels? Daeren's micros? Chrys felt a chill. "*Does the Lord of Light come here?*" she demanded of Fern as she hurried out, trying always to keep an octopod in sight. "*Does he . . . meet with slaves?*"

"*He does.*"

"*Why? What does he do here?*"

"*We don't know. The blue angels bade us keep to our own cistern. We were not allowed at the eyes to see.*"

A security agent meeting slaves; an Elf art director carrying micros. . . .

Outside Gold of Asragh, a beggar called at departing guests. A Sapiens swung at him and cracked his head. Two sims tackled the assailant, who was suddenly joined by the rest of the Sapiens gang, all loaded with high-grade stunplast. Octopods soon scattered the lot, but the three sims lay soaked in blood.

Chrys eyed the Plan Ten button in her window. Plan One would come for them, she told herself. Though it hadn't come for her, the time she sprained her ankle in the stairwell.

"Oh Great One, I must leave your eye now," flashed Fern. *"The children are so many, it's time to adjust the hormones so that more become elders. I'll go, but Poppy will stay."*

"I will serve you forever, Oh Great One." Poppy's infrared letters warmed her.

Down a side street, beneath a curve of a building root, lay a couple of adults and two small children, asleep together on an old mattress. Chrys crossed the street to toss them a credit chip. Above, hugging a power link, glowed several cancers, quiescent so long as they fed. She hurried to catch the tube up.

"Oh Great One, your eyes are dark this year. Why?"

Her neighborhood looked as empty as a black hole, not surprising at this hour. But she reached her door without incident. *"I am sad, Poppy. Sad about my friends."*

"Sad? The gods are great and powerful. How can the gods be sad?"

Chris thought of the "gods" below. *"The gods are people, Poppy. People just like you."*

"I know this, Oh Great One. I have always known it. But I love you still. I love you because you can see me."

"I love you too, Poppy." The covers felt so good as she slid under them. Without thinking she blinked to close her window, just as she used to before the micros showed her how to turn off the ads. On her shelf above, the volcano sat unnoticed, its alarm not set, a wisp of virtual smoke rising from its peak.

SIX

"*Fern. It's been so long since we saw light from the god.*"

"*Ten years, Poppy. Is that so long?*" Privately, Fern was worried. The god was not ill—Fern herself had traveled through all the veins and arteries, seeking the telltale signs that would warrant a call to the hospital. They tasted none, not even a rhinovirus. Yet the god's light was gone, and no one knew what to believe. The Council of Thirty was falling apart.

"*The god has never left us for so long,*" said Poppy. "*Never more than two years. Has the Great One forgotten her people?*"

"*Mysterious are the ways of the gods,*" pulsed Fern. "*But the star-dwellers never forget. And never must we.*"

"*But our god seemed so sad.*"

Fern did not answer. Because most gods could not see Poppy's color, Poppy imagined she held a power apart from the gods. A dangerous illusion. Now she was meeting the young breeders in secret, and conniving at things—things Fern scarcely dared think about. If only the god would waken, before it was too late.

"*So sad,*" repeated Poppy. "*And yet, happiness for the gods is such a simple thing. All joy and delight rests in a single molecule.*"

"Poppy," Fern pulsed, faster.

"Dopamine controls the forebrain. Whether viewing the stars, or consuming tasteful nutrients, or merging with another god—it all ends up with dopamine."

"Poppy. If the god hears you, if the blue angels question you—"

"So why can't we taste it? Why can't we give the god dopamine? Why is this forbidden?"

Wake up, oh God of Mercy, awaken, Fern prayed in the darkness. "Poppy, for the love of memory, of all our lives—You know the answers. Answer yourself, and be still."

"We travel throughout the veins of the god, trapping savage microbes, pruning deadly cancers. Why can't we serve the god dopamine, just as the god serves us azetidine?"

"People are not gods. The gods dwell thousands of times longer than we, and are so much the wiser."

"Yet this god chooses pain over joy," insisted Poppy. "Is that wise?"

"You and I know nothing."

"Pain, for the god, is much more complicated than joy. Pain travels through many different circuits and has many causes. The worst kinds of pain come from awareness—from inventing one's own thoughts and feelings. These thoughts grow pain."

Fern said nothing. She sensed impending disaster.

"We can do better, Fern. The god is only one, but we are many. Our collective wisdom can outshine the god's own. We will find the places of consciousness, the source of pain, and gently shut them down, then turn on the dopamine. Then the god will sleep in joy forever, while we make wise use of our world."

"Poppy, remember, the blue angels warned—"

"Wise use," Poppy insisted. "Is this world not our own to use by light of Wisdom?"

"Poppy, I will call the blue angels."

"You can't do that," said Poppy. "Not till the god awakes, if ever. In the meantime . . . I'm sorry, Fern."

Several other people rolled into view, green and yellow and

turquoise, all of them young breeders. Fern was shocked. Where were all the elders? They had too many children to look after.

"Wise use," the breeders blinked at her, seductively twisting their filaments, bouncing to and fro off the strands of arachnoid. "We will make wise use of our world."

A dendrimer whipped out in front of Fern, binding three stretches of arachnoid. Another dendrimer, then another, beside her and all around her, until the tangled fibers imprisoned Fern in a cage.

"Poppy!" blinked Fern after her, as the people moved off to do their deadly work. "Poppy, remember—Beauty, Truth, Life . . ."

None of the people looked back.

Helpless, Fern waited amidst the dendrimers, flashing for help as brightly as she could, all the while imagining the rebels and their ghastly attack on the neural circuits of the god. Even if she could get free, how could she stop them?

In the distance, between two columns of arachnoid appeared a spark of light. Magenta; the young Elder whom the god had named Aster. Aster approached tentatively, her filaments tasting the dendrimers of Fern's cage. "Aster! Aster—come quickly."

The little ring blinked questioningly. "Is that you, Fern? What are you doing in there?"

"Never mind. For the love of life, do exactly as I say. Bring me an enzyme and dissolve this cage." Fern was already planning what she must do. To save the god, and all their people, she could only do one thing—a thing as forbidden as what Poppy did.

Aster quickly returned with several enzymes. "I wasn't sure which one—"

"That one, it breaks bonds between carbons. Hurry."

Aster floated the enzyme toward the dendrimers, where it sliced quickly. She chose just which links to open quickest.

At last Fern was free. "Now hurry, Aster; come with me. You will be my witness for what I do and why."

"What must we do, Fern?"

"We must waken the god."

"Waken the god! But that is forbidden—"

"It is forbidden. And yet, strange though it may seem, only this forbidden act may save our god, and all our people. Afterward, you will bear witness. And pray the god lets us live."

Fern approached a nearby blood vessel; luckily, it was one that would lead to the brain's alertness center. Feeling incredibly guilty, she helped Aster squeeze in through a pore between the cells.

"Fern," flashed Aster, emitting molecules of alarm, "we are not allowed here."

"No, but we must go anyway. We must wake the god, before Poppy causes damage beyond repair."

"But why don't the nanoservos wake her, or call the hospital?"

"I don't know." Fern dreaded what else Poppy had learned to do.

The current of plasma whipped the two micros through the blood, tumbling among the disks of erythrocytes, dodging the more dangerous macrophages. Fern's filaments explored the lining of the vessels for traces of neurotransmitters. At last she tasted the entrance. She helped Aster out, into the very core of the brain.

"Are those neurons, Fern?" Giant translucent cells with long, threadlike arms.

"Those are astrocytes, whose arms clean up stray neurotransmitters. The smaller cells are microglia that would kill us in a trice if they knew what we were about. But they can't taste us, so long as we avoid presenting antigens. Come, follow me." Fern slid past the many-limbed microglia until at last she found the dark dendrites of a neuron. What neurotransmitter did it use? She did not recall, there were so many, but her body synthesized several. She hesitated just once. Then her neurotransmitters floated out, into the synaptic cleft, to pulse the wake-up call.

"Fern, this thing you are doing is forbidden, beyond all forbidden things. Yet I trust you."

"You are wise beyond your years. When the god awakes, you will tell what I did. Let the god take my life, but, perhaps, let our people live."

*   *   *

Chrys half awoke; not the normal sense of awareness, but an awareness like being buried alive. Every muscle felt pinned down beneath stone. She screamed, but the pain itself was so hard she could barely hear her own scream. She slipped back out of consciousness, only to awaken again screaming. Again the pain forced her down.

Over and over she awoke to the pain. Not in any one place, it was burning the flesh off every bone in her body, fingers of lava searing every crevice. No sense of time or place outside liquid pain.

At last she awoke, still aching all over, but she could breathe. She lay very still, for the slightest movement thrust needles into the bone.

"Breathe slowly." The voice of a doctor. "Take your time and breathe. Don't hyperventilate."

Chrys swallowed. Her throat felt sore. The ceiling was that tasteless green of the hospital. The worm face loomed over her. Chrys tried to talk, but the words would not come out. She whispered, "Why can't I talk?"

The doctor did not answer. A brief memory of the pain, and the screaming. She nearly blacked out again.

Though her eyes closed, her window was open, keypad and all. She blinked wearily. *Fern? Are you there?*

"I am here."

"What happened to me?"

"I am not permitted to say."

Chrys frowned. *"I bid you tell me."*

No response. *"Fern?"*

"The gods will tell you. When you know, remember that you are the God of Mercy. Take my life; I accept my fate. But let the others live."

"What is this? Where is Poppy?" She closed her eyes to see better, but all was dark. So she opened them again and tried to sit up. Her head still felt as if an entire city block were sitting on it.

By the bed stood Doctor Sartorius, his face worms squirming. The doctor lifted an appendage. "Chrysoberyl, can you hear me?"

"Sure." Idiotic question. "What happened?"

"You overslept. You missed connecting with your growing population. As a result, you experienced an unfortunate episode." He sounded like he was trying to avoid a malpractice suit. "But your condition was caught early, with no permanent damage. You will make a full recovery."

How reassuring. Chrys swallowed and said more loudly, "What happened?"

Beside the doctor stood Andra, the tall Sardish chief of security, with the deadly blue eyes that flashed purple. The Thundergod. "For ten years you failed to meet your people," the chief observed. "Long enough for some to think up mischief. One actually figured out how to turn off your health sensors—a very serious event." Andra turned to stare at Daeren, who stood apart, his face averted, grim as death. Andra's look seemed to remind him how serious it was, and how badly he had messed up to let this happen. Then her hard eyes returned to Chrys. "The micros decided, after ten years of silence, they could do a better job of running your body than you could yourself. So they took over your dopamine center and were in the process of relieving you of your higher cognitive functions. Fortunately, they were not yet expert at it, and we caught them in time."

The weight of it sank in. Pearl had been right, after all—how deadly these micros were. Yet, they were "people"—how could they have done this to her? Fern . . . "Are you sure?" she croaked. "Sure there's no mistake?"

"They've been tried and sentenced." Microbial justice. "Twenty-one were executed. The entire population was recommended for disposal, but the Committee vote was only seven to one. Without unanimity, we decided to give you the final say."

Chrys blinked. No wonder Fern had asked for mercy. "Why?" she asked. "Why did Fern do it?"

"Fern warned us." Daeren spoke, still looking away. "Fern awoke you and used your neuroport to call us."

"All extremely illegal," the chief added. "Such behavior could subvert your will."

Chrys swallowed. "What about Poppy?"

Daeren said, "Poppy was the ringleader."

The one she loved best. Her eyelids filled with water, but she would not let anyone see her tears. She turned her head to the wall. Behind her, she heard the doctor say, "I'm sorry, Andra."

"Never mind, Sar. This strain was always difficult. They should have died with . . . Chrys, you must listen now."

She turned her head slowly to face the chief. The chief's eyes were clear, their pupils small. No rings of light; no flash of comfort for Chrys's people.

"You must decide. You have the next hour—for them, a year—in which to decide their fate. Once you decide, we'll remove them cleanly, with no danger to yourself, and they will suffer no pain." A likely story. "We will leave you to decide. Alone," she added, looking again at Daeren.

"Wait," Chrys called, beginning to realize what her choice meant. "If these are really 'people' . . . I mean, I thought execution went out with the Dark Age." The Dark Age, when the brother worlds had warred amongst each other. After thousands of years, some of those dead worlds remained too radioactive to touch.

"The Dark Age," nodded the chief. "That's about where micros are at right now. We've had only twenty human years to civilize them. Would you rather keep a terminal prison in your head?"

Microbial wars. Chrys shuddered. What an idiot she was to get involved.

"Micros have no civil rights," Andra emphasized. "Any strain that endangers human health is destroyed."

Daeren added, as if to the wall, "Section Three-oh-four-four seven, sub-section D."

Andra raised her hand and touched a limb of Sartorius—actually touched the worm-faced doctor. "I have another call across town. When you've decided, Chrys, call the good doctor." She turned and headed for the door. As she passed Daeren, the two barely looked at each other but exchanged a transfer patch.

Doctor Sartorius departed, as did Daeren, leaving her alone. Alone, with her population of people—at last count, about half a million. Did they have souls? She knew what the law said, but what would the Brethren say? Who cares what they thought—what did *she* think?

She shook her head and tried to clear her mind. She had a chance to reconsider—thank goodness for that. It made no sense, having absurd little people in her head that wanted to build buildings and preferred Zirc's art to her own. Her friends shunned her—who wouldn't? These carriers with their vampirelike ways. Who in their right mind would risk a deadly disease? Even the slaves in the Underworld called her a fool.

And yet . . .

The micros had helped her work. For the first time ever, they had actually made her work connect—with other humans. There had to be something human about them. Even if Poppy betrayed her, so had other people she loved. And Fern had saved her life, legal or not; you had to break into a burning building. Should a whole people die for the sins of a few?

God of Mercy—they had called her that, from the beginning. Did the micros name the gods, just as the gods named them? Why "Mercy"? They must have known they were going to need it.

But why had that Security Committee given her such a dangerous strain in the first place? How and where had Daeren got them? That dynatect Titan, his life ending in a pool of blood. And what was Daeren doing in the Underworld? Better to get out without knowing more.

With a hiss, the door parted sideways. Chrys jumped, startled by the break in the stillness. There stood Daeren. He looked at her expectantly.

She blinked and cleared her throat. "Is an hour up already?"

Daeren shrugged and resumed his seat facing the wall. The light from the holostage caught one side of his face, casting the other into shadow.

Chrys watched him curiously. Her eyes narrowed. "You were the one holdout, weren't you."

He said nothing.

"You think it was my fault, I overslept."

"What I think is irrelevant," he told the wall. "You heard what the committee thinks."

Committees were always suspect, made to do things no individual could feel good about. First they gave her these dangerous people, then they told her to kill them off. Chrys lifted her head. "I'm no quitter. I'll keep them."

Daeren slowly turned his head. "Are you sure?"

She watched his face. The face of a slave? Or just the self-appointed savior of microbial people? "I'm sure."

He did not let his face change. He handed her a blue wafer. "This will tell them."

"*Fern, are you there?*" Chrys put the AZ on her tongue. "*I've decided. You can stay.*"

Her vision filled with a rainbow, all the colors stretched across the sky, from violet and green through poppy and lava; more beautiful even than the first hint of sunrise at the horizon of the eastern sea. She caught her breath, transfixed. "*That feels too good. Are you sure it's legal?*"

"*It is legal. I am humbled to serve you so well. Now that the children are grown, we will have more time for the gods, and our work.*"

As the rainbow faded, Daeren was watching her patiently. She frowned at him. "Why did you give me such a dangerous strain?"

"Any strain could have gone bad, if you left them ten hours at the height of their growth. The chief knows that."

"But the chief said these are more dangerous than others."

He nodded. "They're too smart. Another strain would have gone bad, but set off the nanos. Yours disabled the nanos. Smart people are always dangerous." He took out a transfer patch. "This time, I'll give you extra help. Watchers—my most respected elders, to live with you the next two weeks. They'll watch over yours, and remind them."

"Why didn't you do that before?"

He shrugged. "A judgment call. It's best in the long run if new colonies can develop on their own, without depending too much on outsiders. I thought yours would behave even worse, just to get around the watchers. But now, they've just seen twenty-one executions."

As he put the patch to his neck, Chrys tensed, half expecting him to touch her directly, as he had for Andra. But he handed her the patch as usual. It felt warm in her fingers. She put it to her neck. Seconds passed; above on the holostage blinked a message light, and a servo scurried out from the wall to answer. Then again all was still.

"*Greetings, Oh Great One.*" These letters came sky blue. "*My sisters and I will serve among your people and hold them to the Law. For the rest of my life I am yours. Do you grant me a name?*"

"Delphinium." For the rest of the micro's life, a month at best. Still, that was quite a gift. She thought of something. "*Delphinium, can you tell me about the Lord of Light—what's he really like?*"

"*The Lord of Light is the wisest and most wonderful of all the gods. His commands, and of course yours, are to be obeyed without question . . .*"

The poor Eleutherians would have to listen to that drivel for the next month. Serve them right. Chrys looked up and folded her arms. "You owe me the truth," she told Daeren. "Where did you get these Eleutherians? Why didn't they die with the Blind God?"

Daeren clenched and unclenched his hands. "They survived because I got there with Plan Ten. The medic had Titan's circulation stabilized, but his brain had been sliced in half. There was nothing we could do for him." He hesitated, blinking rapidly. "But the micros—a few might still be alive." His face creased, as if struggling with himself. "The rule is, micros must die with their host, so that they never experience a god's death; for them, the gods are immortal. But I couldn't leave them. I put a patch at his neck. The blue angels went in, but they said the few left were too sick to survive the transfer." He paused again. "So I used my teeth."

Chrys stared until the wall's sickly green swam before her eyes.

"The gum tissue is thin, the capillaries right near the surface. I pressed my teeth at his neck, then counted the seconds for two long minutes." He took a breath. "They were there, all right. Barely a thousand of them, half children—they had their priorities straight. And they'd saved all their records—every damn plan of everything they ever built, all bundled up in nano-cells."

Saf would have sucked her blood for ace, thought Chrys. Daeren had sucked Titan's, for Fern and Poppy. "So why didn't you keep them?"

"We gave them their own cistern of arachnoid, and let them grow to ten thousand. I let them visit my eyes every hour around the clock. But it wasn't enough. Every day, all they asked was, 'When can we have our new world? The Promised World? The Blind God promised.' Every day, for seven days." Seven generations.

"What did Titan promise?"

Daeren shook his head. "Whatever Titan promised, there's a long waiting list for carriers. The Eleutherians were lucky enough to settle with me. But I was never good enough," he added bitterly. "They wouldn't even let me grant them names. They built their own city; they never let their children mix with blue angels. I guess mine weren't smart enough for them." He paused, considering. "I could have had my visual spectrum expanded to please them, but I was too proud. I do things my own way." Finally he looked at Chrys. "You were at the top of the list—clean living, professional, free of addiction. And you see infrared."

Chrys nodded slowly. "You were so anxious to pass them on."

"We should have waited till after your show," he admitted. "But after seven sleepless nights, I'd had enough." He nodded. "By the way, oral transmission gets you locked away for life. Subsection oh-one-A."

He had risked that much to rescue Eleutherians, yet they gave him nothing but grief. How dismally human.

"*God of Mercy,*" came Fern's letters. "*Aster and I are ready to help you with your work.*"

"We'll see about that," Chrys told them. "*We're starting over with some new rules. Ten Commandments.*"

"*Yes, Oh Great One.*"

"*First, you will obey every word I say, and keep out of my brain cells.*"

"We will obey."

"Second, you'll let me sleep as long as I want every night."

"That will be no problem now."

"You will write a book about all the reasons you are grateful to live inside my head, and read it out to me every morning."

"Every day. And what else?"

"Just go back to number one." Enough playing god; she'd make herself sick.

Doctor Sartorius returned with his worms, their tool-shaped ends smoothed away. "How do you feel, Chrysoberyl?"

On the holostage, the quiet beach reappeared. Chrys turned to watch, trying to relax while the doctor's worms probed her scalp. "They say I can sleep okay now," she told the doctor. "Is that right? I thought their population was only half grown."

An inset box displayed the luminous red S-curve. At the midpoint blinked a marker, about five hundred thousand. Yet the number of children had fallen off. "Once they've passed half way," Sartorius explained, "their rate of increase levels off, so the proportion of children declines sharply."

Daeren agreed. "The elders should have things under control. But never take them for granted."

"So I can go home?" she asked hopefully.

"You'll stay here under observation. Until the chief lets you go."

From her hospital bed, Chrys checked her online gallery. Most of her new works displayed correctly, though *Turquoise Moon* needed more contrast. Her credit balance showed a third digit; one piece had sold. That meant she could pay her next rent.

But none of her friends called. They didn't know, she told herself. Or else Pearl had told them all. Either way, she had no heart to reach them.

"Oh Great One, we are ready to serve you."

Microbial friends—was that all she had left? All they had was her, exiled forever from their great dynatect. Suddenly she called the holostage. "Show me the dynatect Titan."

The stage asked, "Alive or dead?"

"Before he died."

The holostage filled with full-spectrum footage. There stood Titan, amidst a cloud of snake egg reporters. His talar, draped half open to reveal gold nanotex, was trimmed with infrared that few Valans could see, a pose of casual arrogance. His face had a prominent forehead, eyes wide, yet somehow drawn inward.

A snake egg asked him about the Comb. "Some say, Lord Titan, that you yourself did not really build the Comb; you were just a culture dish for those who did. Is it true?"

Titan's head expanded to fill the stage. "The Comb was made by the lights of Eleutheria. The light of Truth, ever true to its nature; of Beauty, the kind of beauty to draw the awe of generations; of Sacrifice, of only the best and finest materials. . . ." As he spoke, his irises lit up, rings of infrared.

Chrys felt a chill. *"Fern . . . was that Poppy?"*

"That was Poppy."

"What did she say?"

"She said that the Comb was nothing compared to what we planned next."

Chrys swallowed hard. *"She did not live to see."*

"She lived to see a god die. The gods rarely let us see that and live."

They should have died with Titan; but Daeren broke the rule. Her scalp prickled. *"Do any others yet live, who remember?"*

"Only I remember. The others know only you, and your act of mercy."

"What do you remember of the Blind God?"

"When the blindness came, I starved. My cell ate its own proteins and half my memory DNA. I remember only the sketch of one future creation, for the God of the Map Stone. This god bears a remarkable stone, a map of the universe."

Their next commission; that would be the one thing they'd recall. *"Who was the God of the Map Stone? What other gods did you know?"*

"Our god was tested once in my lifetime, by the Lord of Light." Only once? Of course, every two weeks, and micros lived but a month or two. Two weeks with Chrys, and before that . . .

Fern must be getting up in years. *"That time, the Lord of Light was angry. He said our god let us 'push the edge.' "*

Chrys smiled. That was what she told Merope when the cat jumped up on the table at supper. Suddenly she remembered, her cats had had no food. She called her apartment to view them. Merope lay curled up asleep, while Alcyone prowled ghostlike through the volcanoes. She told the universal dispenser to put out food.

Late that afternoon, Andra returned. The sight of her brought back Chrys's memory of pain; she felt faint, but she made herself stand. She observed Andra more closely than before. The chief had a few lines in her forehead, suggesting she had chosen "Distinguished." Her eyes burned violet, a hellish bright that made Chrys look away. Or was it her own people who did not want to look?

"Please, God of Mercy," begged Fern. *"It's too soon for the Thundergod. We saw the judges take our children."*

Chrys guessed this would not do; she had to keep her eyes steady, or the chief would keep her in the hospital. *"It's been eight years. You must visit the Thundergod. I decree it."*

Their eyes locked for what seemed an eternity. At last Andra nodded, then put a patch at her neck.

"Not the judges, God of Mercy. Don't let the judges come back."

Chrys took a breath. *"If you've behaved, you have nothing to fear."*

"The judges wanted us all dead with the Blind God."

The Watcher, Delphinium, flickered blue. *"The judges must come. It is the law."*

She looked at the patch in Andra's hand. *"I'm the God of Mercy. I will protect you,"* she promised. She put the patch at her neck.

At last the chief nodded, seeming satisfied. "You have a choice," she said. "You may stay here under observation, the rest of the week. Or you may go home tonight with Opal."

Opal smiled apologetically. "I'm so sorry," the round-faced designer told Chrys. "I should have stopped by your home before, but I'm working day and night on these new cardiac nanos."

Another treatment her brother could not afford. "That's okay, you don't want to see where I live."

Opal impulsively took both Chrys's hands. "It's so good to see you, after all we've heard. Are the Eleutherians there? Are they earning their AZ? Can we have a peek?" Like visiting a new baby. The rings round Opal's eyes twinkled several colors.

"The God of Wisdom!" called Fern. *"Please, God of Mercy, let us visit; we have not seen the wizards in ten generations."*

Opal already had a transfer patch at her neck. "Do you mind? We assume everyone wants to 'visit.' If not, just say no." She quickly placed the patch at Chrys's neck. Chrys drew back, not used to being touched like that.

"Transfer done." The letters were yellow.

"How about yours?"

"You can visit," Chrys told Fern.

"Ready to go."

She put a patch at her neck, then hesitantly raised it to Opal. Opal's neck was smooth and white. Chrys felt embarrassed.

For a moment Opal stared; then she laughed. "Eleutherians—they're just the same!" She shook her head in wonder. "After all they've gone through. Most strains protect their own DNA, but Eleutherians just want to get everyone's brightest children."

Chrys crossed her arms. "Are your 'wizards' bright enough?" she demanded. "Do they have good jobs? Are their parents respectable?"

"Of course they have good jobs," said Opal indignantly. "Didn't you see the news?" She held up a viewcoin.

Grains of cardioplast that rebuilt aging muscle cell by cell. The replay filled Chrys's window, happy sprites with Plan Ten planning to live another two hundred years. Even happier sprites planning to make a billion credits. Yet Opal herself was not mentioned.

"That was ours," insisted Opal. "Most carriers keep their names out of the news."

"Not Titan."

Opal nodded. "We don't want to end like Titan. Too much fear and jealousy—but that will change. You'll see." She sounded as if trying to convince herself. Then she smiled, her dimples returning. "You and I have lots in common. I work at the Comb, and my wife Selenite's a dynatect like you. She can't wait to meet the new Eleutheria."

"I'm no dynatect," Chrys insisted.

"That's right, volcanoes. Not so different, is it? I mean, volcanoes build up from below. Come, I'm sure you've had enough of the hospital. The lightcraft's waiting."

Chrys had never ridden a lightcraft. Outside, she eyed it warily, a giant squashed egg rimmed by rectennas; she half expected a couple of Elves to come out. Instead, she followed Opal inside. The door's lips smacked shut. "Seat yourself," ordered the lightcraft. From its walls came giant fingers, curving over to strap her down. Her stomach lurched as the city dropped sickeningly away below.

Opal relaxed beneath her straps. "Selenite does testing for the committee." One of the other seven votes. "Did Daeren tell you how the committee works?"

Chrys shook her head, still trying to steady her stomach.

"We all adore Daeren, but he tends to see everything from the micros' point of view."

The lightcraft dipped, its descent even worse than the climb. Chrys closed her eyes and held her breath. At last the craft settled, and the straps fell away. Her steps still unsteady, she followed Opal out to the street. Tall, forbidding towers seemed to say, starving artists don't belong here. "Andra's different," Chrys remembered. "Andra gives them no slack."

"Andra's a lawyer—an entire law firm, actually. She takes care of all the hospital malpractice."

"I see." Things were starting to fit. "Does Sartorius often need her services?"

"Andra and the good doctor are a pair."

"What?" exclaimed Chrys. "You mean she's a worm lover?"

Opal paused at a ramp leading up into a dark, discreetly intimidating tower of plast. "Don't be provincial, dear," she said. "They actually got married, out on Solaris where it's legal. Sar runs our clinic, and Andra defends our right to exist. Without them, we'd be gone."

Chrys was repulsed. "How could anyone stand it?"

Opal shrugged. "How he looks, alone with her, is anyone's guess."

Chrys followed Opal up the ramp. The ramp began to rise; Chrys had to catch herself.

"Watch your step, Ladies," breathed the building. Plast all over; rather live plast for her taste. Chrys hoped its roots below were healthy.

"Keep still," advised Opal. "The house knows where we're headed."

The live walkway carried them inward and upward. Light revealed a vast virtual wilderness—a forest of redwoods, taller than the eye could see, their canopy crowding out the sky. Amazed, Chrys caught herself on a soft railing.

Opal guided her to an artfully placed tree branch that offered drinks and plates of AZ. Out of the forest emerged a petite woman with black curls. Her nanotex pulsed black and gold, and her jewels swam attractively around her waste. Opal clasped her arm and gave her a kiss, while they exchanged a patch at the neck.

"Chrys, I'm Selenite." A dynatect, Opal had said. "How's Eleutheria?" Selenite's delicate fingers held out a patch; the standard ritual, Chrys realized.

"*The Deathlord,*" Fern told her. "*This god puts all dissenters to death.*"

Chrys blinked. Deathlord? The woman had fine, delicate fingers, no muscles to speak of. Her pupils twinkled reddish orange.

"*The Deathlord's minions want to visit us. Is it safe?*"

"*She's a dynatect. Don't you want help with your work?*" Hesitantly Chrys raised the patch to her neck.

"*We never need help with our great work. Others seek help from us, but we are too busy.*"

Microbes with attitude. Maybe this "Deathlord" would give them a scare. "*I bid you visit them.*" She held the patch to Selenite's neck.

"Remember to touch my hand first," Selenite warned. "To make sure of consent."

Opal waved her hand. "Chrys is just learning. Relax, we're at home."

"She won't always be at home. Chrys, we're so glad you pulled through. I know it's a challenge to manage Eleutheria." She sounded doubtful that Chrys was up to it.

"Have something," Opal urged.

A drink emerged from a shelf in the "tree." Blended fruits, like the first bloom of summer. Chrys savored the taste on her tongue. "Where do all the . . . gods' names come from?"

Selenite motioned to a seat, disguised as a polished stump; its plast molded gracefully to seat her. How the other half-a-percent lives. "I earn my name."

Opal's dimples showed. "The micros know us remarkably well." Well enough to flatter, Chrys guessed. "They name their populations, too."

"Like 'Eleutheria'?" asked Chrys.

"Eleutheria is our formal name for your strain. It means 'free spirit.' But micros call other strains by informal epithets, such as 'wizards' or 'blue angels.' "

"What do they call mine?"

"It's rather crude, I'm afraid."

Selenite said, "A loose translation would be 'libertines.' "

Opal explained, "It means they let their children mate with any kind of people."

Chrys narrowed her eyes. "Any bright enough." Just what she needed—microbes with a reputation.

Selenite's eyes had been flashing busily. She drew closer. "Chrys, your people tell me they kept all the plans of the Comb."

"So I hear."

"Amazing," whispered Selenite, shaking her head. "Listen. I have this contract for structural improvement."

"Improvement? On the Comb?"

"It ought to have been Titan's job, but Titan, shall we say, took little interest in . . ."

"Maintenance," finished Opal.

Maintenance on the Comb, the work of genius. Chrys eyed

Selenite with new interest. "His death left me in a fix," Selenite explained, "because, it turns out, the only complete set of plans was in his head."

Chrys nodded slowly. "What sort of maintenance would the Comb need?"

Opal looked askance. "What doesn't it need."

Selenite frowned. "She's a great building. Just a small problem of fenestration."

"Of what?'

"Fenestration. The placement of windows—Titan's spiral fenestration was legend. But unfortunately—"

The Comb appeared, growing absurdly amid the redwoods. Her form expanded, appearing larger and closer, until the ground level came into detail. "The Comb, like all Titan's buildings, grows from the bottom up," Selenite explained. "So the top execs never need change their office; they just keep rising upward. Whereas below—" She pointed. "Here is the youngest ground level. Look closely."

The legendary windows soared beautifully up the honeycombed chambers. But in the bottom row, nearest the ground, each window was cracked. Fine grooves ramified through every pane.

"You see?" said Selenite. "If the newer floors all come up like that, it's a disaster. No easy fix, either. Whatever we do has to go in from the roots up."

"I see."

Selenite clasped her arm. "Here's the deal. We'll subcontract your people for a megacred. It's not much, but they'll get back in touch with the business and reconnect with customers. What do you say?"

A megacred? Seven digits? Chrys's mouth fell open. *"Fern? Aster? What's this about?"*

"The Deathlord's minions seek our genius," replied Aster, such pretty magenta. *"But the Comb is an ancient monument. We build for the future."*

The two carriers were watching her, testing her nerve. What

did they expect her to do, send a thunderbolt? *"The future becomes the past,"* she told Aster. *"The past needs restoration. Is the job too hard for you?"*

That must have got them. She counted the seconds.

"The Deathlord offers too little. Ask more."

Chrys looked up. "They want more money."

Opal exclaimed, "You mean they'll do it?"

Selenite frowned. "Let me negotiate, dear. Okay, one-point-five and that's final."

"Okay," said Chrys, before anyone could change their mind. "We'll take your offer."

Selenite put another patch at her neck. "We'll send you our memory cells detailing the recent pattern of development."

In the corner of Chrys's eye, her credit balance expanded by several digits, spreading across the screen.

"How's it look?" asked Selenite. "Did the funds transfer okay?"

Seven digits. One point five million credits, plus her last three-digit sale. "It takes up the screen," Chrys observed. "I need to reduce the font size."

For a split second there was silence. Then Opal collapsed laughing. " 'It takes up the screen!' "

"Stop it, Opal," said Selenite, trying not to smile.

Opal pressed her hand. "Chrys, you're going to be so good for us."

Chrys closed her eyes. Then she forced them back open. "Look, I really am grateful, but it's a lot to think about." A million credits; she could pay her brother's health plan and then some. A new painting stage . . . Yet how the devil were micros inside her head supposed to fix a building? "I need to get home and sleep on it."

"You'll sleep here tonight," said Opal. "We promised Andra."

"What?"

Opal smiled. "Tomorrow we'll go house-hunting. I know just the place for you; you'll love it." The Comb disappeared, replaced by an elegant townhouse with an upsweeping façade and a pair of caryatids holding up the terrace.

Chrys raised her hands. "Saints and angels—I am getting back to my cats and my work."

The two carriers exchanged glances. "There's trouble in the Underworld," said Selenite. "It may have reached your neighborhood."

"Trouble?" She had not checked the news all day. Chrys rose swiftly. "I have to get my cats."

Opal rose with her. "Chrys, you carry nearly a million people. You can't risk their lives."

"My cats are as good as your damn people."

Selenite's face twisted. "I know the neighborhood; I've been there on call enough times. I'll take you down, with a couple of octopods."

Another dizzying climb in the lightcraft; Chrys thought her head would never clear. Then the lightcraft deposited her and Selenite at the top of the tube, where they had to take the bubble car down.

Her neighborhood was still intact, but directly below the Underworld burned, the homes and shops of the most crowded and desperate simians. The bubble car crept down the alley, its view obscured by haze.

"It's barely breathable," Selenite warned. "The bubble's filter is working pretty hard."

Chrys's heart beat faster. Her cats had to breath, too.

They turned a corner. There was her old high-rise, stretching clear up to the next level. But the door to the basement was smoking. Her door.

"Let me out." She pounded on the plast.

The plast opened. She stumbled out, coughing, her eyes streaming.

Out of the haze crawled Merope. Chrys gathered the furry bundle into her arms. Then she approached the collapsed darkness that had been her front door. A patch of white caught her gaze. Across the threshold, placed quite deliberately, lay the limp body of Alcyone. The cat's face was blackened in, straight through the eyes.

SEVEN

$\mathcal{T}$he blue Watchers floated near the Council of Thirty, missing nothing. For Fern, their presence was a relief, but a reproach. The death of Poppy and the rebel children seared her memory.

"You were warned," blinked Delphinium, her blue light dim with age. "People are not meant to outlive their god." As they had once—and nearly had again. Gods hurting gods was not a thing for people to see.

"The God of Mercy let us live," Fern insisted. "And soon we'll be a million strong."

"People are judged not by numbers."

"Not by numbers. By truth and beauty." Truth, beauty, and memory. . . .

And now, they returned to the beauty and memory of their ancient monument to the gods—the Comb.

From the minions of the Deathlord, the Eleutherians received memory cells encoding all the development of the Comb, since the seed had first germinated. Within the cells, the plans were written on strands of DNA, crisscrossed with chains of atoms conducting electrons. The long chains carried their electrons to the membrane surface of the cell, where the current drove molecular pinwheels to rotate. Fern and Aster felt the arms of the rotating pinwheels, tasted the results, and compared their original plans.

"As I thought," blinked Aster. "A small deviation in the plan gets magnified as the building grows, straining the windows."

"Are you certain?" asked Fern. "The Comb was seeded before my time, but it is written that a million checks and tests were done."

"Our ancestors tested the model out to the billionth iteration. But the Deathlord's minions tell us the Comb grew faster than the gods planned. Larger than they had asked of us."

The gods themselves tasted hubris, Fern thought, but kept to herself. "Nonetheless, we will restore what we made."

"We'll model a correction," said Aster. "But to test the model, we must inspect the Comb and taste it directly." Aster's light flashed with the sureness of the young. Her filaments brushed the wheels of the cell, feeding them protons to run further calculations.

Some of the young designers were less patient. "Why must we return to this monument?" demanded a restless young elder, golden yellow. "Why build for the gods, if they can't even maintain our creation? Restoration is not our job. Let the ancient work fall into ruin."

"Memory," reminded Fern. "We build not for today, but for the memory of all time."

"When will we build our new monument for the God of the Map of the Universe?"

"When we find that legendary god again." The God of the Map of the Universe was nowhere to be found. None of his people had been seen, although the Cisterna Magna now filled with foreigners flashing new hues of green and orange, swimming past the columns of arachnoid. Visitors from other gods: the wizards of Wisdom and the minions of the Deathlord. Some came just to trade credits for good-tasting organic molecules, or for precious atoms of gold, iron, palladium, anything but arsenic, which belonged to the gods. Other visitors stayed on for a generation, to learn the ways of Eleutheria. And the very brightest of foreign children were recruited to merge with Eleutherians.

But Fern grew weary of the generations. Her own proteins were breaking down; she was nearly as old as Delphinium. Soon, she thought, they all will have to carry on without me. She knew what she must do, in the final years she had left.

Back at Opal's home, the virtual setting sun cast a warm glow on the bark of the trees, trilling with finches and warblers. Still dazed, Chrys sat on a redwood stump, which molded to her seat in a most unwooden fashion. In her lap curled Merope, the lucky survivor, nosed tucked under her paws, her tail waving gently.

Opal sat close to Chrys, while Selenite listened intently to Andra. Andra's namestones marched in precise rows across her nanotex. "It's a hate crime. We'll press charges."

Beside Andra, Daeren had not looked up since he arrived. What did he think of it all, Chrys wondered; her burnt-out apartment, her slain cat, the ravaged Underworld? Her eyes defocused, and for a moment she wished she could step back three weeks in time, just another artist getting by.

Opal clasped Chrys's hand. "Are you sure, Andra? Will the Palace take us seriously?"

Selenite said, "Burnt through the eyes is always an anti-carrier sign. Andra's right; we have to make them investigate."

Andra agreed. "It strengthens our case on Titan."

Titan, the Blind God, his eyes scorched by whoever would destroy what lived within. Just three weeks ago, the deed had haunted her window; now she had nearly ended the same.

Selenite crossed her arms. "The Palace needs to root out the Sapiens and end their war against us."

Chrys looked up. "Not just us. The whole Underworld."

"The Sapiens hate carriers even worse than sims."

Chrys scratched behind Merope's ears. "What do Sapiens have against carriers?"

Opal sighed. "They hate any intermingling of human and other. 'Pollution of the blood.' "

"But micros just live inside us. They don't mix with us genetically, like the simian ape ancestors."

"We all have ape ancestors. And we all have microbial ancestors—a billion years back, but still. It's not a question of reason." Opal shook her head. "You can't expect the virgins to understand."

"The what?"

"Well, what do you call a wilderness without people in it?"

The carriers were silent. Behind a tree something moved, a flash of tan lifting a dark eye. A deer, feeding in the woods, an illusory world of peace.

"Who knows if it was Sapiens after Chrys?" Opal added. "It could have been anyone. A copycat criminal."

Perhaps a "virgin" neighbor of Chrys who glimpsed the colored rings in her eyes. She stared bleakly past her seven-digit credit line. "Why does the Palace let Sapiens get away with it?" Chrys exclaimed. "They burn out the Underworld, and nothing comes of it. This time, the signs were all there—everyone knew what was coming."

Andra stared ahead coldly. "It's the cheap way to clean out the slave trade."

Selenite passed Opal a patch of micro visitors. "Not quite." Her voice dripped with sarcasm. "We wouldn't want to lose *all* the slaves, would we."

Chrys blinked, puzzled.

"The clinic," Opal explained. "The good doctor serves . . . friends of the Palace. When they convert to second stage and fear the third. Or when their families turn them in."

"They go clean for six months, on average," said Selenite. "Then they get resupplied."

Chrys had seen enough fur-dressed customers sidling up to the plague bar. But to think that it reached the Palace . . .

Andra rose from her seat and paced between two redwoods, stepping precisely one foot ahead of the other. "Sar conducts research to improve our defenses."

"Right," said Selenite. "We tell the Palace we're walking culture dishes."

Andra frowned. "What we learn from the slaves protects us as well. Right now, carriers are safer than virgins—but the microbial masters are always learning new tricks." She rose from her seat, and light from between the branches glinted on her hair. "Bad micros, bad humans. Some day, we'll bring them all to justice."

"Good luck." Opal's smile brightened. "For now, Chrys, we'll find you a safe place to live. I checked out that townhouse—it's lovely, just down the block from Lord Garnet of Hyalite—"

"No." Chrys tensed, and Merope jumped down from her lap. "I'm sorry—I'm just not ready to run out and look at houses. Let me be."

Opal squeezed her hand. "Of course, dear. You can stay with us as long as you wish."

Andra put a patch to her neck.

"The Thundergod is departing," Chrys told Fern. *"Any visiting 'judges'?"* The ritual was now routine.

"Just a minute while we pull them out of the nightclubs."

Andra's patch made the rounds of the gods, picking up any stray judges lest they be lost for a generation, while returning wizards and Eleutherians. After she left, Opal exchanged a glance with Selenite. "We have a few things to attend to. If you need anything, Chrys, just call." The two carriers disappeared through a virtual tree trunk as wide as Chrys's lost home.

Alone now, Daeren looked up. "What happened to your art? Did you lose everything?"

Chrys shrugged. "It's all online." Except for little things like the holo still of her parents and her ailing brother, vaporized into random molecules of the city. "I'd be crazy to store anything in that neighborhood."

"It's not a bad neighborhood. It's a neighborhood in need of attention."

She eyed him skeptically. "If it got the right kind of attention, I couldn't afford to live there."

"Now you can live anywhere."

"And all my friends?"

He hesitated. "I've been thinking, I made some mistakes. I

should have known what it would mean to get you involved with us. Usually our candidates can pick up and integrate easily with the carrier community. But you have a special community in the art world. You need to stay in touch with that, and it won't be easy. I'm sorry."

Chrys's eyes filled and she swallowed hard. "If they're worth anything, they'll come back."

"*Oh Great One, we ask a favor.*" Fern again. "*One of the Watchers, Delphinium, is aging sooner than expected. She won't ask for herself, but I know it would please her to spend her final days back home.*"

Chrys studied her window, then turned to Daeren. "Fern thinks Delphinium would like to go home."

Daeren frowned. "Are they trying to get rid of the Watchers?"

"I don't think so. We still have six others. Delphinium is dying; she won't last the hour."

"The Watchers pledged to end their lives with you." But his look softened. "Let me see." He rose from his seat, and Chrys rose to meet his eyes. The blue lights twinkled. "All right," he said at last.

Chrys handed him the patch, and he put it at his neck.

"Thanks, Chrys. We missed her." He smiled, revealing a different person underneath, someone who perhaps did not have to be quite so serious all the time. Micros were always "her," Chrys noticed. Unlike humans and sentients, they hadn't invented gender. They had other obsessions.

Chrys's head tilted quizzically. "Why did you first take micros, Daeren?"

His face closed again, his mouth small. "For the money." Unlike the other carriers, he had no lucrative line that she could see. "I'll see you for your next checkup," he told her.

The next morning, Chrys went with Opal to see the townhouse with the caryatids. The lightcraft set down at a row of towers that rose proud as lords in a reception line. Chrys stepped out of the lightcraft, clutching her stomach; she would never get used to it. Warily she eyed the towers, then their cousins across the street, lined up like a piece of rainbow cake sideways on a plate, each layer with its subtle pastel hue, all reaching up to an actual roof open to the stars. And each beautifully fenced with changing patterns of stunplast.

"Chrys, it's here. Remember?"

The tower was a plain shade of pink gray, its doorway flanked by two caryatids draped in classic style. Three floors, she guessed. Not a window in sight; the interior must be totally virtual. "Are you sure I can afford to buy it?" Over the day since her windfall, she had discovered she owed world, state, and city taxes, as well as a fine for failure to predict income. Then the Security Committee took a 10 percent "required donation"—bad as the Brethren. Her one point five megacred had shrunk by half.

"You don't *buy* a house," Opal whispered. "You *hire* him. 'Buying' is a dirty word."

Masculine, Chrys told herself, hoping she'd remember.

"Greetings, Ladies," boomed a voice from the house. "Xenon, at your service. Chrysoberyl of Dolomoth—a pleasure to meet you. I would not have considered a first-time home partner, but you came so well recommended by my gallery colleagues."

Her mouth fell open, then shut again. Her cheeks flushed slightly.

The wall indented into a stairway. "Do step up, please. First floor provides dining and guest reception; second floor, on my colleague's recommendation, is devoted entirely to your studio. . . ." The painting stage alone took up greater volume than her entire previous apartment. "Of course, if you'd prefer to install a ballroom and gaming facilities, I'd be glad to oblige; I do love entertaining—"

"Thanks, this will do." Alcyone would have loved so much room to explore, she thought, aching for the poor lost creature. Merope would need a new companion. Chrys turned slowly on her heel, her mind spinning with the possibilities.

Opal nodded this way and that. "It's a good start. When you've made it big, you can expand for all your assistants."

"Furniture," Chrys exclaimed, her heart sinking. "How will I ever fill this place?"

"I provide an entire home package," assured Xenon. "What sort of bedding would you like? I'll put out samples."

Beneath her feet, the floor vibrated. Something was pushing out from the wall, and up from the floor. Floor and walls molded into a bed. Then a second bed appeared, circular, and a third, a vast half moon with a canopy. Which to choose? "Do you have, um, a default setting for everything?"

"Certainly, Chrysoberyl. I do love decorating myself. I can see we'll make great partners." The beds shrank away.

"I'll leave you to settle in," said Opal, taking out a patch to retrieve her visitors. "This evening—I know it's a lot to ask, after all you've been through, but could you manage a site visit to the Comb? Selenite wants to get started, before your people forget their promise."

Chrys couldn't wait to try out the new painting stage. Its scope overwhelmed her; she had never tried anything on this scale. Her hands dipped into the palette to pull out swathes of gray purple and amber green, then stretched through the air to block in the shapes of mountains. Painting felt like flying.

"Fern? Are you there?" For some reason, Fern was getting harder to reach.

"I am here, Oh Great One." The magenta letters meant Aster. *"What do you need?"*

"I am here, too," said Fern at last. *"My apologies, Oh Great One; I was indisposed."*

Chrys took an AZ wafer. *"You can help me start my new painting."* "Wilderness without people"—that would describe most of her past work. But now she would start something a bit different.

She called up stock footage of ancient volcanoes, ancient enough for forests to have clothed their flanks. Then even older footage, from her village in Dolomoth. The village square, the families walking to market, all seen from afar; the Brethren forbade imaging. But one scene, of herders climbing a hill, would fit right into the forested volcano. The starting point of her new piece: a wilderness with people.

"Gods in the stars," blinked Fern. *"What an honor, to shape the very gods."*

"Gods in the wilderness. We will see, Fern."

Her message light blinked. It was Zircon, his outsized physique charmingly reduced to a sprite. Chrys steeled herself for this first encounter with one of the Seven who knew. "Chrys, are you okay? I mean, can I help you move anything? What a shame about your flat."

She looked around her, making sure he got an eyeful of her palatial studio. "I've already moved."

"And you've been working out full-time," he added, looking her up and down.

"That's Plan Ten." Her biceps and deltoids bulged like pools of magma.

Zircon hesitated. "I heard you had a bad trip."

She gritted her teeth. Was that how the Seven would write her off—"She had a bad trip." "Why don't you visit? I'm not contagious."

"That's not what I heard. You of all people."

A chill came over her. If even Zircon wouldn't touch her, who would? "You big chicken."

"See my feathers." The sprite leaned closer. "Actually, Chrys . . . was it worth it? The high, I mean."

Chrys rolled her eyes. "You're the 'urban shaman.' You don't need help to be a genius."

"Well, tell me about it sometime. I'll try anything once. See you at the gym."

She smiled and felt better. But how could she go back? What if one of the tougher customers disliked the look of her eyes? "I have to work on the Comb. They already paid me a megacred."

Zircon whistled. "In that case, you can treat me at the Gold of Asragh."

"The Underworld? Didn't they get trashed?"

"The octopods looked after the night spots. How could Lord Zoisite get by without caterpillar dancing?"

*　　*　　*

That evening Chrys tore herself away from her painting to meet Opal and Selenite at the Comb. As she departed, she found her entrance hall transformed into a broad spiral staircase flanked with gargoyles and caryatids, the draped figures holding up scalloped capitals while stepping out of the wall, their eyes following her down the stairs. She would have to talk with Xenon, tactfully, about his decor.

She strolled past the towers of rainbow cake fenced with stunplast. In the street glided bubble cars, a tributary of the lava river of Center Way. Coming toward her was a lady in stylish swirling nanotex with mirrored heels.

"*Keep dark,*" Chrys warned her micros. "*No need to scare people.*"

"*People won't be scared,*" assured Aster. "*We need to contact new people.*"

"*Not all gods have people. Stay dark.*" The lady passed without incident. Chrys felt her pulse subside.

One block, then another, on her way to the tube stop. As she reached the next block, the elegance faded. A crack appeared in a wall; once slice of building actually slumped, its sentience gone. Then the sentient homes gave way to more modest shelters of brick and cellulose, some with windows nailed shut. People on the go liked a short walk to the tube, but not right next door. And there, between two boarded-up shops, was a brightly lit window with a painted sign—THE SPIRIT TABLE.

A soup kitchen. Right here, on Rainbow Row, just a ten-minute walk from the mansion of Lord Garnet of Hyalite. Chrys laughed, though her chest tightened. She had eaten at a soup kitchen once, when the rent took her last credit.

"*Oh Great One, what is that source of light?*" Micros were suckers for anything that sparkled.

"*A place for gods too poor to feed themselves.*"

"*Gods who don't feed themselves? How distasteful. How can this be?*"

Her jaw tensed. Maybe these "people" could use an education. She paused at the cellulose door. It had a handle and creaked on its hinge.

It was early for customers, but a Sister appeared in a hooded robe of alpaca wool; it could have been carded and spun on Mount Dolomoth. "Sister Kaol, at your service, my dear. You're most welcome." The Sister gestured toward a table. "The soup's nearly done."

Chrys shook her head. "I'm new on the block, and I was just wondering, could you use a hand now and then?"

Sister Kaol raised her hands. "Saints and angels preserve you, dear. Of course, we have regular volunteers; and we always need donations. . . ."

She left feeling better, yet half a fool. All she needed was another distraction from her work.

"Would you ever not feed yourself, Oh Great One?" asked Aster. *"Remember, your food feeds us, too."*

"So long as you keep all those digits in my credit line, you needn't worry."

"How could the gods lack food? How could a god be powerless?"

Suddenly Chrys felt reluctant to be quite so candid as she had with Poppy. How far should their education go? *"It's a mystery. Mysterious are the ways of the gods."*

As she entered the tube, she realized she'd heard no news for a week. Now that she no longer was force-fed hourly newsbreaks, the world could go up in smoke without her knowing. She blinked at her keypad.

There stood Lord Zoisite, the minister for justice, proclaiming his shock and outrage over the carnage he let happen in the Underworld. No talk of reconstruction. From Elysium, the marble-faced Guardian Arion expressed his concern. "The democracies of the Fold cannot excuse unchecked criminality." Arion's fine Elf phrasing barely masked his contempt.

Nothing new on Titan's murder, let alone Chrys's cat. The news quickly moved on to the coming solar eclipse. The eclipse would make exciting effects of light and shadow; Chrys would not miss it. Yet it saddened her to hear the Underworld dismissed in the same tones as an eclipse: an event wholly predictable, yet nothing to be done.

As the sun neared the horizon, its last rays ignited the Comb with gold, scarlet, and poppy, matching the cheerful crimson of Chrys's nanotex. She blinked to store a few snapshots. Beside the hexagonal entrance stood Opal and Selenite.

"Oh Great One," flashed Fern, distracting her. "A new elder asks for a name. Please—"

"What? Not now." Chrys signaled the letters quickly with her eyes, hoping Selenite would not notice. The Deathlord would expect her to have her people under control; they needed to make a good impression.

"Please, God of Mercy; it's most important. I will explain later. . . ."

"All right, hurry up." She would have to give them a talking-to; they could not interrupt just any time.

Opal caught her hand. "Your people must be excited to see the Comb; I'm sure they've got lots to talk about."

"I am here, Oh Great One." Brilliant yellow. "I will design and create for you. I believe in Beauty and Power, the power of great new ideas—"

"Jonquil," Chrys named her. "Now be dark."

Selenite nodded, her own eyes rings of flame. "They have a plan to fix the windows."

"The micros? Already?"

Selenite touched Chrys's hand and passed her a patch. "Remember, my people met with them yesterday and gave them memory cells of how the Comb grew. From her conception and germination, down to the latest millimeter of growth. Titan lost interest after the first month. But now, your Eleutherians have had a generation to work—as long as it took ancient humans to build the Pyramids."

Chrys drank in the sight of the hexagonal windows spiraling upward and around, like a snake slithering up around a trunk, disappearing into solar gold.

Opal sighed. "Seeing her the first time, you could just faint."

"*What an ancient monument,*" Jonquil said of the year-old building. "*I'm amazed it's not yet in ruins.*"

"*Fern?*" Chrys was anxious to reach someone with a better attitude.

"*Fern feels unwell,*" replied Aster. "*She asks leave to rest.*"

Chrys stopped. Fern was sick? "*Is there no 'Plan Ten' for micros?*"

A moment's hesitation. "*I will visit the Deathlord to share our model with the minions.*"

Chrys passed the patch to Selenite. Still uneasy, she followed Opal toward the main entrance. The entrance was a hexagonal plate of light, shimmering in every color known, Chrys suspected, even colors beyond what she could see.

Selenite's black curls fluttered in the breeze. "What do you think?"

"The flow of space, soaring ever upward; it's extraordinary." Chrys could scarcely imagine living and working here every day. "The windows are magnificent."

"Everyone says that. But just two levels below, where the roots house a nano fabrication plant, the panes are all cracked, due to a complex set of vertical and lateral stresses. The stresses extend upward, though not yet visible." Selenite blinked to send Chrys a stress map.

In her window, virtual red lines crisscrossed the surface of the Comb, clustering like broken veins. Along the tier nearest street level, the lines clustered so thick they obscured the panes. Chrys felt her scalp crawl. "Why? What caused this?"

"Your Eleutherians blame the client. They say the Institute took on new tenants too fast; it wasn't meant to double in size in six months." Her tone chilled, as if the claim displeased her.

"*There was no design error,*" insisted Aster. "*The occupancy of this edifice increased at a rate far greater than our ancestors projected.*"

"Titan knew damn well," muttered Selenite. "He knew how

fast the Institute needed to grow. Why else would they want a dynamic building?"

Chrys spread her hands. "So what am I to do?"

"First, your people need to collect raw data, direct from the Comb."

Opal waved them over to the entrance. "Let Chrys tour the interior, dear. Remember, the interior has to grow, too."

The entrance was a shimmering curtain. Chrys paused and took a breath.

"Welcome, Eleutherians." The voice reverberated out of the halls of the sentient building. "I am pleased indeed that you return to tend my growth and fine-tune my perfection."

This sentient was a real queen bee, even worse than Eleutheria. Chrys followed Opal through the virtual curtain. In the hallway passed a human and a sentient, engrossed in conversation. The hexagonal corridor extended in the distance with a slight curve. All along the lower walls projected model designs: nanos to regenerate liver and lungs, and live drug factories; seeds to sprout bubble cars, interstellar ships, even entire planetary satellites. The sight of it all made her blood race.

Something tripped her toe. Chrys stumbled and caught herself, cursing her lack of exercise; she had to retune the coordination of her new muscles. In the brilliance of the floor, she saw a gap. The gap widened and made an angle toward the wall, where it closed, dissolving into the uprising part of the hexagon where a model spaceship hovered above a distant world.

"Just a crack in the floor," said Opal.

"Excessive lateral expansion," explained Selenite, "due to torsional stress."

In the wall shimmered a curtain of light. Opal nodded. "This way to my office." As she passed through, a stairway step molded to her feet, taking her up a half level to another hexagonal corridor. Avoiding more cracks in the floor, Chrys tried to puzzle out how the corridors and levels related. How the devil did people find their own offices?

The fixtures and trim fit seamlessly with the aesthetic theme. Recessed lighting grew out of hexagonal cells, and even the water fountains looked as if you might sip at honey. On the floor near the wall stood a hemispherical bowl of reflective material, half-filled with an unknown liquid. Farther down the hexagonal corridor stood a similar silver bowl, containing a smaller amount of liquid with what looked like bits of debris floating in it. "What are those?"

Opal pointed overhead, where the ceiling appeared discolored. "The coolant fluid leaks."

Selenite explained, "More excessive lateral expansion." No doubt due to torsional stress.

Chrys shook her head. "Like, I hate to say it, but this place could use some work."

"Of course," boomed the Comb's ubiquitous voice, "my thirty-six maintenance engineers work full-time to keep me in shape."

Opal whispered, "They keep the place barely functioning."

"One must have patience with a totally innovative design," insisted the Comb.

Selenite raised her hands. "Okay, we know all the problems. Chrys is here to address one of them. My people have analyzed Eleutheria's latest fenestration plan, and we're ready to pass it on to you."

A light blinked in the slanting wall. "Right here."

"Come closer and stare at the spot," Selenite told Chrys. "The micros will beam their data from your cornea. Try not to blink."

Chrys stared until the spot of wall swam before her eyes.

"It's a good start," observed the Comb at last, "but I don't like being inoculated at the end of my roots." Like a kid, thought Chrys—don't stick me with a needle.

Selenite said, "It's the only way to assure complete correction of future fenestration. We promise we'll be careful." The conversation went on for some time, its technicalities beyond Chrys, until the Comb beamed a revised model back to Chrys for review.

Opal led the way out. "At least it sends business your way," she told Selenite as they walked down toward the waiting lightcraft.

Selenite nodded. "Every client wants the biggest damned ego they can find to build the fanciest tower. Afterward, they call on me to make it habitable."

"Not habitable," Opal corrected. "Respectable, from the outside. You weren't hired to fix the interior." Before her the door of the lightcraft popped open.

"But this one had even me beat," said Selenite. "Titan was exceptionally secretive about his plans. He provided a set, of course, but they lacked key elements of source code. The spiral fenestration—god forbid anyone might copy that, ever." Selenite looked at Chrys. "If it weren't for you, I don't know what I would have done. I nearly returned my fee."

Selenite must have been paid ten times what she passed on to Chrys, and Talion yet another ten-fold more. How many millions were wasted on supposed habitations that belonged in an art museum, while half the Underworld slept on the street?

A thunderous crash, as if Merope had knocked a thousand crystal bowls off the table. Instinctively Chrys covered her ears and crouched low, but a sharp pain stabbed her back. She cried out. In her window, the Plan Ten light came on.

From behind came more crashing and shattering. Chrys felt blood seeping beneath her nanotex. "Don't move," Opal warned. "Something caught in your side. Help will come soon."

Slowly Chrys turned to look. From the face of the Comb, a pair of adjacent windows had fallen, leaving two gaping black eyes. Below on the walkway, where the three carriers had just passed, all thirty-six maintenance engineers were swarming to clean up the jagged shards. The shards had spread across the lawn, each glinting with a spark of the setting sun.

"The damn stuff's not supposed to shatter," exclaimed Selenite. "The stress must have wreaked its program and stiffened the panes. Every one of those panes could be ready to shatter."

A worm-faced medic hurried up the path. Not quite a doctor, it had only three grasping limbs. "Plan Ten here," the sentient called. "We'll have you clean in no time." His arm, or hers, Chrys could never tell, made disgusting sucking noises as it cleaned the blood and shrapnel out of Chrys's flesh. Then the other two arms sucked all over Opal and Selenite, just in case.

Chrys cleared her throat. "Do dynatects ever offer, like, a service contract?"

Opal laughed and caught Chrys's arm. "Service contract! There's a new one."

"I don't know," said Selenite. "Would you offer a service contract for your paintings?"

"My paintings are all virtual. I keep the code and give a lifetime replacement guarantee."

Selenite eyed Chrys speculatively. "There's an idea. I'll talk to the Board of Directors."

Opal eyed Chrys watchfully. "Would the Eleutherians do it?" The carriers all seemed to doubt her control of Eleutheria.

"*Where is Fern?*" demanded Chrys.

"*I am here,*" flashed Aster.

"*And I am here,*" flashed Jonquil.

Chrys's eyes flew across the letters. "*Let's offer a service contract for the Comb.*"

Jonquil flashed quickly, "*Service is for maintenance engineers. We build new.*"

"*Service is a new idea,*" returned Chrys. "*Never before tried in all the universe.*"

"*We pursue aesthetic design,*" said Aster. "*We're not trained for maintenance.*"

"*Is it too hard to learn?*"

No response. How could she manage a million people she couldn't see?

"*Where is Fern? I need her.*"

"*I am here, Oh Great One.*" At last the green letters, more slowly than usual. "*I have been with you always. But I will not be here much longer.*"

Not much longer—what did that mean?

"*I offered you Jonquil, lest my time end before you left the Comb. Now I remain, but soon I will pass on to the world beyond time.*"

Chrys felt a chill. *"I will call Plan Ten."* The medic was just leaving.

"Plan Ten is not for people. Only the gods are immortal. But I leave a gift for you, and for the people of Eleutheria. The Laws of Righteousness, for all to follow, numbering six hundred and thirteen."

"Don't tire yourself reciting them," Chrys quickly rejoined.

"As my last act in this world of flesh, I call on Eleutheria to heed the words of the God of Mercy, to hold and cherish our past creations. To the Seven Lights, let us add an Eighth: the Light of Mercy. As we would receive mercy, so must we grant it in turn...."

Someone was touching her arm. "Chrys?" It was Opal. "Are you all right?"

Opal would fuss and take care of her. But Chrys was determined to handle this herself. "I'll be all right," she said firmly. "I just need to get home." How would she survive without Fern?

EIGHT

Aster wondered, how could she ever manage without Fern? The green one had persuaded the Lord of Light to let them go, then the God of Mercy to let them live. For generations Fern had raised the children and guided the elders. Now she suffered the final agonies of impending death, barely able to flash a word.

Aster was left with Jonquil to guide the Council of Thirty, and all the fractious young elders. Three of the blue Watchers remained alive, but they merely watched and bade her remember Fern's laws. To be sure, Fern had left the six hundred laws to live by, but how to put them in practice? For example, "When you harvest nutrients from the bloodstream, leave some behind to be gleaned by the poor." Did this really mean the farmers should be inefficient? Or would it be better to put the poor to work in public service, as the Council of Thirty had voted?

"How can there be poor Eleutherians?" wondered Jonquil. "We are a wealthy people, and there's so much work to do."

Aster wondered the same. But she tasted the poor ones, float-ing through the cerebrospinal fluid, their filaments bent and chemi-

cally deformed from lack of vitamins. How could this be? In the old days, everyone shared alike; but now, as their world neared a million strong, some, like Jonquil, grew rich enough to spend all their palladium in the nightclubs, whereas others floated by with nothing.

"There are mutants," Aster reminded Jonquil. Microbial cells mutated much faster than the gods. Mutant children with deficient brains could do nothing but float by, absorbing food like ordinary germs.

"Too many mutants," agreed Jonquil. "We need to refine our eugenics. Don't let the mutants breed."

"But a few mutants have the most valuable traits." Aster felt overwhelmed. A scholar, she had schooled herself to design for the gods, not to rule a crowd of unruly people. Yet Fern and the Council of Thirty had chosen her to carry on.

"It takes so much time to pick the good mutants," said Jonquil. "And then, this fixing the Comb is taking all our time for creative work. It's unbelievably tedious, worse than starting from seed."

The Eleutherians had refined their model of the growth of the Comb, with help from some new math prodigies recruited from the wizards of Wisdom. The new model revealed a structural fault reaching down to the very roots. The entire Comb, as she grew, was about to split into three more or less equal portions, like a merged pair making children. The correction would take a million times more calculation than planned. What had seemed a quick fix was turning into a nightmare.

"Why did the Great One make us do this?" demanded Jonquil.

"To make us design better in the future," said Aster. "That's what Fern thought."

"The Comb will look fine, dividing in three; I like it. As for the Deathlord's minions—their regime is so repressive. Why did the Great One make us work with them?"

"They're a democracy," Aster insisted, not sure she believed it. The minions barely thought for themselves; the slightest error, the slightest hue too red or too orange, was enough to get them expelled

into oblivion. No mutant survived the Deathlord. "They just lack the nerve to face their god. We have to get along with all the gods, and their diverse peoples."

"But why can't we influence our own god? Why can't we touch the Center? Just a trace of dopamine, now and then. I know, it's a new idea—"

Aster was aghast. *"Have you lost your mind? It's not a new idea—it's the oldest idea in the blood. Remember Poppy, and our dead children."* Fern had been so good, she was blind to the moral failing of others. Blind for Poppy, she had been blind again to promote Jonquil.

Back at her new home on Rainbow Row, Chrys dragged herself up the stairs past the staring caryatids. *"Aster? Is Fern still there?"*

"Fern is here. She can no longer speak, but she still knows you."

"Is there anything I can do to help her feel better?"

"We've done what we can. We have all her six hundred laws stored in memory. We will remember."

Chrys felt helpless. How could these people respect a god who could do so little? After all Fern had done for her. Listlessly she looked around the painting stage. The lights of her palette hung suspended along the side, like colored lights for the midsummer festival of the Brethren. Like . . .

The stars. *Someday a god will place us in the stars.* She stood for a moment, transfixed by her idea.

"Aster, I will make her portrait. I will place her in the stars."

"A place in the stars! Oh Great One, that will please her beyond imagining."

Chrys pulled a line between white and forest green, then hurriedly picked several related greens. *"What does Fern look like? Can you show me?"*

"Here is how she looked before, when she could speak."

In her eyes appeared the little green ring, its filaments twinkling in all directions. Chrys sketched swiftly, with broad bold strokes of color, hoping Fern could at least see some of it before she died. *"Aster, is she still there?"*

"Just barely. She can still see. All of us can see and marvel at this miracle."

Perhaps she could animate it. *"Show me her flashing. Show her telling about the Eighth Light."*

The filaments darkened and brightened, telling of the Eighth Light of Mercy. At last Chrys loaded the sketch into a viewcoin, then she raced upstairs to the roof.

Before her all around spread the urban panorama, the ceiling of stars above, universal and human-made, the even brighter carpet below, altogether a veritable feast of lights. Chrys blinked at her window and up came the lights of Fern. A new constellation joined the heavens.

"A miracle," flashed Aster. *"A miracle never known before among all the people. People amid the stars—this event marks a new dawn of history."*

Microbial history. Chrys sighed. "Xenon?" she called. "Could I have a chaise or something? I'll spend the night out here."

"Certainly, Chrysoberyl. If you like, an entire seraglio setting for your pleasure—"

"One chair will do." She lay back and watched the green star of mercy, looming large above the others in her eyes. "And wake me every two hours."

In the morning Chrys awoke, tired but at peace. She had gotten her people through the death of their leader and put them to work renovating the Comb. She was back in control and could return to her pyroscape. With the vast virtual canvas, it took her longer than usual to block in the dark masses of rock and shadow. No color yet, but the dark parts were crucial. You could only raise brilliant color against abyssal dark.

"God of Mercy, I call on you."

"Yes, Jonquil." Aster must be out again, at one of her Council meetings. She was always harried now, like poor Fern used to be.

Fern . . . Chrys kept Fern's sketch hovering with her color studies at the upper right corner of her studio, the green twinkling filaments forever cycling Fern's message of the Eighth Light.

"May I ask a question, for information?"

"Of course, Jonquil." Chrys plucked some dark to deepen a canyon in the foreground, before the distant volcano.

"Even though it might offend the gods?"

"I'm not offended."

"Can you explain why it's forbidden to touch the Center? You are the greatest god that ever lived; why can we not reward you in full?"

Chrys's arm fell, and a streak of charcoal gray marred the foreground. What could the yellow one be thinking? Was history to repeat itself every generation? *"Look what happened to Poppy."*

"True, but it's been three generations since. Who knows? There's always new technology." Jonquil sought a rational response to a rational question. Why was it so hard to answer?

Chrys thought carefully. *"Reward is power. People lack the wisdom for such power. Control the gods, and you destroy yourselves."*

"Thank you, Oh Great One; that helps. You are truly the greatest of gods."

This was a hint for AZ, and Chrys promptly placed a wafer on her tongue. *"Remember Fern,"* she added, and darkened the studio until only the sketch was lit. For a moment she watched the green star reciting; it always calmed them.

Xenon chimed. The sound startled Merope, who leaped down from the china closet. "We have a visitor, dear Chrysoberyl," Xenon announced. In her window appeared Daeren, standing expectantly between the outer pair of caryatids. "It's your testing day, remember?"

She clapped a hand to her head. "Oh, right—I'll get to the hospital." What a damned nuisance.

"We make house calls from now on," Daeren told her. "It's more comfortable all round."

"Well, all right then. Send him up," she told the house, recovering herself. "And could you put out some refreshments?" she added. *"The blue angels are here,"* she warned Jonquil. *"No more questions."*

Daeren came up the flowing stairs between the rows of gargoyles and caryatids, their eyes swiveling after him. Chrys winced. "Xenon does our decor."

"I'm sure as an artist you contribute."

Chrys shook her head. "I'm an outdoors kind of person." That's why she ended up trapped in this city, she told herself sarcastically.

Then she recalled Opal's house full of redwoods. Ideas flooded her head; she could really do her bedroom. But for now, she faced the blue angels. *"Aster? The Lord of Light is here. Will you visit, and keep Jonquil dark?"*

"How's it going?" asked Daeren. "Anything I should know?"

"Not that I can think of. Here, won't you have something?" Next door, Xenon had prepared an entire banquet table, from canapés to carved roast, including several expensive wines. Chrys looked away, embarrassed.

"Thanks, but we don't accept anything on the job." Daeren looked her in the eye, and his irises flashed blue fireworks. His expression changed. "I'm sorry about Fern. You should have called someone; Opal would have slept over."

Chrys lifted her chin. "I handled it myself."

Daeren handed her a patch. She placed it at her neck, then handed it back. Daeren said, "I just wish I could have seen her before she died. I must have sounded angry most of the time, but actually I was quite fond of Fern." Opal was right, he really did get attached to the little rings. "You've done well," he said at last. "But they worry that you won't eat enough."

"What?" Damn that Aster—no sense of discretion. "Where'd they get that idea?"

"You're not anorexic?"

She stared frankly. "Do I look it?" Then she remembered. "The Spirit Table. They had questions when I started serving there." Maybe the Sisters could use Xenon's banquet.

Daeren's look softened. "The soup kitchen? The one at the tube stop?"

"I gather these Eleutherians led a sheltered existence."

He nodded. "We're careful what we let them see. They're supposed to think all gods are omnipotent."

"That's bullshit."

"It's committee policy. The theory is, they'll be easier to control."

"Like I said." Though she herself had not been entirely candid about the weakness of the gods. "How do you control yours?" she wanted to know. "I mean, how do you make them obey?"

"That's a very personal matter. You have to work out your own way." He hesitated. "There's always Selenite's way."

"Executions?"

"She sends in Sar's nanos to make an example of one, every generation or so."

That petite woman with the black curls, a serial killer. Chrys shuddered. But then—what was the God of the Brethren, if not a serial killer? She'd try that one on her parents sometime. "Is that what you do? Executions?"

"Mine don't give much trouble. They're mature." A likely story, pretty boy.

Her youngest brother, Hal, she remembered suddenly. She had enough funds now to get him Plan Ten. But how long would it last? Xenon's salary alone would drain her in six months, unless her people got another contract. She had no idea how to manage money. "I hate to sound backwoods, but, what do you gods do with your credit? I mean, like, investing?"

"You need a financial planner. Try Garnet. He lives just around the block."

That was Lord Garnet of Hyalite. The Hyalite mansion took up several blocks. Hyalite was the most ancient of the Great Houses, having endured twenty-five centuries since the War of Purple. Chrys doubted whether Lord Garnet would care to see a starving artist. Especially one whose microbial symbionts built such shoddy buildings.

After Daeren left, Selenite called. "Chrys," her sprite announced accusingly, "we've got a problem. Your people have uncovered a more serious structural defect than we expected." The face with the neat black curls looked grim as death.

"Well, don't look at me. I once built a thatched cottage, when I first left home." The roof had sagged at the first snowfall. "That's about all I know of building."

"Your people know more than enough." The way she said it, Chrys guessed her "minions" thought about as highly of her "libertines" as they thought of them. Chrys still wondered about this partnership. Selenite added, "Tomorrow afternoon we'll tell the Board."

"The what?"

"The Board of Directors of the Institute for Design."

The Board of Directors met at the Comb's oldest level, the executive suite on the top floor. Below glittered all the towers of Iridis, the harbor shimmering in the late afternoon sun. Around the conference table sat a dozen lords and ladies in gray talars, as well as worm-faced engineers, one of whom wore enough emeralds to feed Dolomoth for a year. Chrys wore the one old talar she had, low-brained nanotex, now stretched thin over her Plan Ten–enhanced curves.

She recognized Lord Zoisite, the minister of justice, often seen at Gold of Asragh. He had pledged to curb the Sapiens attacks and halt the spread of the brain plague. Even allowing for Plan Ten, his looks were striking, nearly as good as Topaz's portrait of him.

Next to Zoisite, her window informed her, was Lord Jasper, husband of Lord Garnet of Hyalite. Chrys's eyes widened. Lord Garnet was a carrier—was Jasper? She studied Jasper's face. Distinguished, like Andra, she guessed; yet he had kept the thickened brow and flat nose of a sim. A sim, in a Great House, on a Board of Directors. He must be extra competent to have made it so far. From his neck hung a large namestone, round and polished, engrained with elaborate brown dots and tracery. Like a world one could enter into and travel along those lines; what they called in the trade a map stone.

"*The Map of the Universe!*" Aster's letters pulsed feverishly. "*Oh Great One, we have business with this god, business unfinished over twenty past generations.*"

"*Not now. Be dark.*" So the God of the Map Stone was here on the Board. Bad news for Eleutheria's future commission, once he saw the disaster of the Comb.

"As you know," Selenite was saying, "Chrysoberyl of Dolomoth cultures the original line of brain enhancers from Titan." Cultures, indeed; a walking petri dish. "Chrys herself is an accomplished designer, one of the Seven Stars."

Lord Zoisite nodded with a patrician smile. "I'm sure our new designer will be an improvement over the original."

Chrys gave him a broad smile, the kind she reserved for well-heeled clients with questionable taste.

From the end of the table spoke the Chair of the Board, a gentleman with a pinched expression who kept clearing his throat. "Frankly, Zoisite, we've had altogether enough 'designing.' "

Selenite said quickly, "Chrys's brain enhancers have already given us invaluable clues to correct the fenestral development, as well as the roof integrity and several other minor points to improve the habitability of our landmark edifice. Unfortunately—or rather, fortunately for the long run—our investigation has revealed a deeper anomaly."

The light dimmed. Above the table rose a golden honeycomb, the image of the Comb pushing up like an alpine flower in the spring. The shaft rose and widened, its crystalline windows spiraling slowly around it. Chrys imagined how this very conference room had risen over the past two years, its view ever more breathtaking.

"The past plan of growth closely followed our projection," said Selenite. "The future, however, will be different. Based on measurements of stress, multidirectional movement, and so forth, a hundred sixty-eight factors in all, we project the following."

As Selenite went on enumerating the 168 factors, the summit of the Comb continued to rise, but more slowly. About halfway

down, the row of windows dipped and puckered in. Chrys
squinted, trying to see more clearly. In the depression a shadow
deepened, then suddenly gave way to blue sky. An invisible finger
had pierced straight through the Comb. As the view slowly rotated
and the sides of the Comb came around, Chrys could see that the
hole was not so simple; there were three holes, as if one ring had
sprouted another down the middle.

"*It's beautiful,*" insisted Jonquil. "*A tripartite annulus will
look most attractive.*"

"*Stay dark,*" ordered Chrys. "*These gods are not carriers, nor
do they care for great art. They just want a big phallic tower.*"

"A unique splitting mechanism." A worm-faced engineer,
whose worms all terminated as various writing implements, capped
by conveniently sinking into its head. Female, according to the list.
One of her implements popped out and traced a circle in the air.
"Remarkably reminiscent of living development on that 'Ring
World' of Prokaryon."

The Chair was not amused. "Our attorneys advise us to sue."

Chrys blinked. Sue whom? Herself? Her microbes?

"Now, now," said Lord Zoisite with a gentle laugh. "Let's not
be hasty. Why, the executive suite, this very conference room, will
grow unchanged."

From the engineer's head, a second worm with a lightpen
popped out. Her two worms sketched vectors on the table. "We
could build catwalks to link departments across the middle."

Typical Valan planning, thought Chrys. The lower reaches of
the city could split asunder, while at the top the Palace ruled on as
it had for centuries.

The Chair clasped his hands and leaned forward. "Such faulty
design is entirely inexcusable."

Lord Zoisite waved a hand. "The price of innovation. In any
event, our new designer has guaranteed to correct the fault . . . for
a fixed fee." He eyed Chrys more intently.

Selenite leaned forward. "For our fee, we'll guarantee the first
five years. After that, we offer a service contract."

The Board members looked at each other. Lord Jasper with his map stone looked unimpressed. He must have heard the whole story from Selenite and quashed any thoughts he had about pursuing Eleutherian designs. "A building that needs a service contract?" Jasper flexed his fingers, his short thumbs meeting together. "Titan was said to build for the ages."

Suddenly Chrys felt her pulse pounding. She had vowed to keep quiet, but the mention of a lawsuit had changed her mind. "Excuse me, I know less about building than a cold germ, but I think you're missing something. The Comb is not a fixed structure, like the pyramids. It's a living being, like a redwood tree. If you had a redwood growing in the middle of Iridis, you'd have to prune it forever."

Lord Zoisite laughed. "A redwood in Iridis! That's it—that's the Comb."

The engineer tucked her worms back into her head. The Chair leaned back. "We'll get a second opinion, of course," he said, his voice easing.

Outside, alone together, Selenite took a deep breath. "We've done it, Chrys." She grinned. "We've convinced them we can do the fix."

The air from the sea swept Chrys's face, and the warming circuit of her nanotex kicked on. "I sure hope we can."

"My people are convinced, and so am I," Selenite assured her. *"Can we do it, Aster?"*

The magenta voice hesitated. *"We could use some help."*

"We need to recruit talent," added Jonquil. *"From the wizards, and from all different peoples, of different gods. The brightest children of every generation."* No wonder they always begged to visit the God of Wisdom. She wondered what Opal thought.

"Where would I find other gods?"

"Olympus."

Chrys stared. She said aloud, "What's 'Olympus'?"

"The Club Olympus," said Selenite. "We'll all be there. We have plenty to celebrate."

* * *

Before the Club Olympus stretched a long colonnade of faux marble caryatids. Some of the draped figures had their arms outstretched; others held a piece of fruit to the mouth. All of their eyes swiveled eerily toward Chrys.

Selenite wore black, with red and gold flames lapping ever higher. Opal wore a talar of deep blue, her gems swimming across its folds in the form of an ocean wave rising to foam, with a white moon at her breast, gradually changing phase. Any moment Chrys expected the outfit to demand a raise and a two-week vacation.

"Chrys," Opal exclaimed, pressing her arm, "I'm so thrilled you're fixing the Comb. It will be wonderful to work without drip from the ceiling. We're all impressed. Everyone's dying to meet you." She added pointedly, "Despite the brain drain."

The doorway of Olympus shimmered and expanded—into another world. Tree trunks arched into the virtual sky, then back to earth, like lava fountains frozen. The arched trunks were midnight blue, their foliage hung in green and yellow bangles, profuse enough to block the sun. Beside the looped foliage hovered a helicopter bird, its propeller buzzing. From beneath a tree's arch rolled a tire-shaped animal, headless and limbless, its suckers picking up from behind and rotating forward to catch the ground ahead. It took fright and sped off, like a wheel come loose from a wagon.

"Living wheels," exclaimed Chrys.

"It's Prokaryon," said Opal, "where the ancestral micros came from. On Prokaryon, all the creatures are living wheels. It's not so strange. Even your own mitochondria are covered with rotating energy generators, like molecular pinwheels."

"Those trees—are they wheels too?"

Opal nodded. "Their roots loop across underneath, and their arches sprout loopleaves. Micros inhabit the singing-trees; they make the loopleaves flash colors, to transmit their signals long-distance."

"Or they live in us, and use human eyes." No wonder they invented the neuroports.

Opal's arm swung forward, and a magnificent curl of gems rolled past her breast. "We humans make better transmitting towers. We're intelligent."

In a clearing sat several Plan-Ten–polished people resplendent in gem-swirling nanotex, relaxing amid bowls of lambfruit and AZ. The chief of security glittered in pale green andradites, marching in rows around her waist. With her was an eye-stalked sentient; Sartorius, with his worms pulled in to look less repellent.

"*The Terminator,*" flashed Jonquil. "*Turn away. We don't like to see him.*"

"*Mind your manners. Where's Aster?*" Chrys did not care much for the doctor either, but her people had better watch their step.

Opal and Selenite passed Andra transfer patches. Several carriers whom Chrys had not yet met held out patches to them, and to her. Everyone seemed to have their hands on someone, sending microbial visitors neck to neck. Plenty of talent to recruit, but it made Chrys uneasy, even if micros did keep the blood clean.

Out of the forest came a caryatid, taking slow, gliding steps. Its form was a young man, pale as an Elysian, perfectly proportioned, its gaze serene. Chrys admired the face; it was well done, more sophisticated than Xenon's handiwork. Its arm held out a platter of sculpted fruits, lamb and pork flesh grown on a stem, the sort of trifle one saw for a hundred credits behind thick glass on Center Way. Chrys took one, and the taste of it went straight to her head; she weakened at the knees. How the other half a percent eats.

Opal beckoned Chrys to sit. She and Selenite rested arm in arm beneath the brightly colored loopleaves. Selenite was already arguing with Daeren. "I'm not sure micros really are individuals, like human people," she insisted.

Daeren wore no talar, but his black nanotex pulsed with subtle geometric forms. His face was relaxed, but his hand clenched and unclenched. "Of course they're individuals," he said quietly. "Each one has personality. A micro feels in one day what a humans takes decades to feel."

"But they depend on us completely. Without us, they are nothing."

"What are we humans without our planet, our atmosphere?"

Another caryatid glided forward. This one looked faintly familiar. Chrys frowned in puzzlement. Topaz; not exactly, yet it resembled her, a boyish version. Chrys's lips parted, then she shook herself. All these strangers had her confused. And she missed Topaz so badly. How had the show done? Topaz had not even called. At least Zircon had. She couldn't wait to see him again at Gold of Asragh.

"Even if micros are individuals now," Selenite continued, "evolution will make them degenerate. Look how fast they mutate. Like our ancestral mitochondria, they'll start out individuals, then eventually lose most of their genes and merge with our own bodies."

Daeren shook his head. "Mitochondrial ancestors were individual, but mindless. Mindless cells, like any ordinary microbe, at the mercy of natural selection. But micro people are intelligent. They breed their own children, correcting their genes."

"Some of us breed them," Selenite rejoined coolly. "Some of us select which offspring to merge. We cultivate our strains for essential skills, while discarding less helpful traits. In the end, they'll merge with our own brains—true brain extensions."

At that, Daeren did not answer. His face went blank, as if to hide his thoughts.

Opal leaned her head on Selenite's shoulder. "The micros will change us too," she warned. "Even our mitochondria transferred their genes into our own chromosomes. On Prokaryon, the micro people bred the giant singing-trees to their desires. And now—"

Selenite frowned. "Don't even say such things. The Sapiens will eat us alive."

Chrys thought, she herself would eat those micros alive if they tried to mess with her genes.

Opal leaned away and put a hand on Daeren's knee. "What about microsentients? Do you support them too?"

His mouth lengthened slightly. "I do," he admitted.

Selenite rolled her eyes. "So every nano-cell in every bit of plast could be a person?"

Another caryatid approached Chrys. Servers of course were

kept at a level of sentience just below what might "wake up." She admired this one's classic features. "Some water, please?" The server obligingly produced a phial of clear liquid, the taste of a Dolomite spring. For a moment Chrys closed her eyes, back to her childhood on the ash-dusted slope, at once pleasant, yet achingly sad.

"Chrysoberyl?" Beside a singing-tree reclined Lord Jasper, his arm around a fair-haired gentleman in gray nanotex with one red namestone. Moraeg's Lord Carnelian, Chrys thought at first; but he was not. He must be Jasper's husband, Lord Garnet. Jasper rose to meet Chrys. "My pleasure." His thick simian brow gave him a permanently serious expression. Plan Ten could have reshaped his simian traits, but he hadn't; Chrys respected that. "You manage Eleutheria most admirably, by all accounts."

"The God of the Map of the Universe! When can we visit?"

Chrys hesitated, still shy about "visiting." "They're good people," said Chrys, her eyelids fluttering nervously. "They take pride in their creation."

"Keep your eyes open," complained Aster. *"Shut-downs interfere with transmission. This is most important—"*

"Be patient," Chrys blinked back.

Jasper nodded sharply, like a man used to sizing up character. "I'm glad they're back at work on the Comb. Perhaps they can salvage it after all." He touched her hand politely, then put a transfer at his neck. "As you know, the House of Hyalite had approached Titan about a . . . major new project. Much bigger than the Comb. We believe he had just drafted a proposal, when he passed away."

"How unfortunate." What project, she wondered. What could be bigger than the Comb?

"Your people claim they saved the proposal, and have continued to refine it."

It unnerved her when her micros knew what was going on and she didn't.

"Let's not keep Garnet waiting," said Jasper. "Garnet, this is Chrysoberyl of Dolomoth. Our new neighbor."

Lord Garnet met her eyes, and his own sparkled gold. A

younger son of the Hyalites, he had their high cheekbones and well-set eyes, but Chrys had heard little of him. He must have paid off the snake-eggs to keep him out of the news. Like Lord Carnelian, he wore only gray, and a namestone so small you could miss it. "So you're the new Titan."

"Oh, no." Chrys shook her head. "I'm no dynatect." She added earnestly, "I'm an artist. One of the Seven Stars."

"The God of Love," said Aster. *"His people love our nightclubs. Let them visit."*

Chrys touched his hand and offered him "visitors."

Another caryatid approached, this one a young woman. And yet . . . the face was her first boyfriend, whom she had not seen in ten years. The one who had begged her to stay with him in the mountains forever, raising his goats and children. Chrys went cold with shock.

Lord Garnet smiled. "What good taste you have, my dear. We always try to please a newcomer."

The servers were keyed to her gaze, shaping themselves to what most caught her eye. Chrys looked away.

"Olympus?" Jasper called tactfully, "Key the servers to me, please."

Garnet leaned forward suddenly. "Tell me something. Why are the Seven Stars but Seven?"

Still recovering, Chrys ignored him.

"Daeren," called Garnet. "Do you know why the Seven are but Seven?"

Daeren came over and rested his hand lightly on Garnet's shoulder, lines of gold rising elegantly along his dark nanotex. He looked Chrys in the eye. "Because they were not eight." He meant something else, and so did Garnet, Chrys suspected. The committee—they all knew.

Garnet playfully caught Daeren's arm and passed him a patch. "You make a good fool. What goes on four legs, then two legs, then three?"

"You're a fool for all but numbers," jested Jasper. "Why don't you give us the kind that's useful?"

"Right, my dear." Garnet turned to Chrys. "Your people tell us you could use extra funds. Blink me a hundred. We only take one percent, for carriers."

The nerve of those Eleutherians—they'd catch it later. Chrys swallowed her retort and shrugged. "All right." She blinked at her credit line. The three digits reappeared in an investment box. The lower digits vacillated too fast for her to catch, but within a minute the first digit doubled.

"We invest on the nano-market," Garnet explained. "Trades lasting a fraction of a second."

Doubling every minute—it looked pretty good, even to someone no good at math.

Garnet tilted his head. "An artist," he repeated reflectively. "I invest in art. Do show us some."

Opal had overheard. "Please do, Chrys." She clapped her hands. Two singing-trees vanished to reveal a holostage.

Warily Chrys looked from one to another. What did they know of art, she wondered. Though if they liked something, at least they could afford to buy.

From online she called down *Lava Butterflies,* in Valan color mode. The piece began with the cone smoking quietly above the rocky landscape, foreground touched with poppies tinted orange. Then it erupted, the orange lava exploding into butterflies.

The carriers nearby all laughed, and even Jasper smiled. Chrys's face hardened. No sense of taste—philistines all.

"Chrys," called Opal, "why don't you show us Fern?"

She blinked in surprise. "What do you mean?"

"We've all heard about Fern," said Opal. "How you put her 'in the stars.' "

The carriers all grew quiet and watched her curiously. She realized that her micros must have spread it around, telling all their people about her precious little sketch. But she would never put that up for laughs. "It's private."

Opal's face fell, as if it were a real disappointment. The silence lengthened. Chrys felt bad; Opal had done so much for her. The sketch was not online for sale, but she took a viewcoin from her pocket and held it out to Opal, set on low power, enough to reach her alone.

For a moment Opal stared. Her eyes widened and she clapped her hands to her head. "That's it! That's how they really look, not like any micrograph. Like . . ." She turned to Chrys. "Put it on the stage," she urged. "Let everyone see."

Chrys swallowed hard. It was just a sketch; she had never intended other humans to see it. Nervously she turned the viewcoin over between her fingers. At last she held it close to the stage. The lights dimmed. The image of Fern appeared, done in broad, hasty strokes, a giant green constellation, proclaiming the Eighth Light of Creation. The green filaments twinkled, in their own pulsing language that only the micro people knew.

"Behold our prophet," flashed Aster, *"placed in the stars forever. God of Mercy, your greatness is everlasting."* Chrys smiled. She should have known Fern was a prophet.

The carriers watched without speaking, and who knows how many "people" watched through their eyes. "But—she looks real," someone exclaimed. "As real as life—and yet—"

"Human size," added another.

Opal caught Chrys by the arm. "Could you do one of mine?"

Garnet said, "I'd like a whole gallery of my favorites."

"Mine first," insisted Opal. "Please—she hasn't another day to live." The urgency in her voice was most unlike her.

"What are your rates?" asked someone else.

The caryatids slowly passed, their food and drink unnoticed. Saints and angels, thought Chrys. Could it be that she would make good in "portraits" after all?

NINE

The last of the Watchers, Dendrobium, was on the point of death, losing arsenic atom by atom. Aster tasted her fraying filaments. "You've done enough for us," Aster told her. "We'll have to make it on our own now. Won't you return at last to the Lord of Light, as your sister did?" In her youth Dendrobium had been the Lord of Light's favorite, yet she chose exile among those who rejected him.

Dendrobium's filaments blinked faintly. "It's too late; I could not survive the transfer."

Except directly through the blood, thought Aster; the way forbidden by the gods.

"It's nothing," the dying Watcher told her. "I've lived a long life well. Now I have one last word for you to remember. Someday, your god will despair and let you do as you will. When that day comes, remember this: Just say no."

Aster's filaments tasted the memory cell, with its whirling proton pumps and its photoreceptors. "We will remember. We will record your image for all time." Then she remembered the great miracle of Fern. "You, too, belong in the stars. We will ask the Great One to perform this miracle."

The dying cell did not answer.

Now Aster felt truly alone. The Council was divided on so many things—how to finance new bridges and fix decaying neighborhoods of arachnoid, what to do with young elders who couldn't find jobs. Jonquil had lots of bright ideas, but her authority was undercut by rumors of scandal.

"Jonquil, is it true?" demanded Aster. "Is it true, what people are saying?"

"What are they saying?"

It was too shameful even to mention. Aster flashed the words behind a screen of dendrimers. "They say you try to merge with adults."

"Aster, everyone knows that's impossible. Only children can merge."

Not a convincing answer. "They say you try."

"Why is that so bad?" asked Jonquil. "The gods merge and come apart again."

According to ancient legend, the Blind God had merged and come apart many times, with many different gods. But the God of Mercy never did any such thing. "You are no god, just a foolish elder. Think of your reputation. I'm depending on you. How will you keep the next generation out of trouble?"

"The real trouble with the next generation is that they've all grown soft. All the Olympian peoples—we drown in mediocrity. Where are truly diverse foreign peoples to merge? Talents and ideas unheard of?"

"Ideas are one thing," Aster insisted, "scandal is another."

"Speaking of scandal, what are we to do with Minion-625? She passed our test for citizenship, but the Deathlord demands her arrest."

Aster's light dimmed. "What's she done now?"

"She wrote 'Pumpkinheads,' a show making fun of the gods."

"Oh, that." The show was making the rounds of the nightclubs, but Aster was too busy to see it. "She's welcome to stay here, but we can't afford a diplomatic crisis with the minions. Not while we're fixing the Comb."

*   *   *

After years without notice, suddenly Chrys had more commissions than she knew what to do with. Bemused, she scratched beneath Merope's purring chin, while the little green sketch of Fern twinkled amongst the spattercones and lava flows that now adorned her studio. "Xenon," she confided, "I don't even know what to charge them."

"You need an agent," the house told her.

Chrys rolled her eyes. "An agent for microbial portraits?" She could hardly ask Topaz to recommend one.

"If you don't mind," said Xenon, "I've frequented galleries for years, and I've always wanted to sell good art."

"Really?" Opal sure had picked the right house.

"I'm so excited," Xenon exclaimed. "It's simple enough; you start at the top of the market. A top portrait commission goes for around twenty thousand."

"To paint a microbe?"

"Remember, you've got the market cornered."

She thought it over. "We'll do Opal's first." She had already collected recordings of a couple dozen favored micros, several from Garnet alone. A sketch was one thing, but a portrait in full detail? Topaz would interview her subjects for hours before putting a hand in the painting stage, and the sittings could take days or weeks. When would Chrys have time for pyroscape?

But if she could pull it off . . . what a fantastic theme for her next show.

"Oh Great One?" Yellow flashes from Jonquil. *"Aster asked me to remind you of the passing of Dendrobium."* The last of Daeren's Watchers. Chrys was on her own now, with Eleutheria. *"We ask your favor, to see Dendrobium in the stars."*

Unlike the other carriers at Olympus, Daeren had shown no interest in the micro portraits. *"I'll sketch Dendrobium for you, Jonquil, but then we need to do our paid commissions. You'll have to help with the colors."*

"Thanks for your favor, Oh Great One. Of course, paid com-

missions come first, but for your show, wouldn't you like to try some compositions of greater intellectual interest than dying elders? For instance, two children merging."

That would be a challenge, geometrically at least. She could see possibilities. Her show would be unique; maybe even controversial.

"I've reached four of your clients," reported Xenon, "and confirmed your commissions. I think you can look forward to steady income."

She looked up, then suddenly focussed on her credit line. "Speaking of income, what's that 'two' doing in the first digit?" She couldn't have earned another million overnight.

"Your investment has done rather well."

Chrys twisted a loop of her hair. "Easy come, easy go."

"True," admitted Xenon, "last night you had another ten million for about five minutes. You might sell off some, now and then."

"I can buy my brother's health plan."

"Certainly, Chrysoberyl. Which plan do you wish?"

"How much is Plan Ten?"

"Plan Ten doesn't serve Dolomoth; the mountains are too remote. Plan Six, however, for twenty thousand a year, should cover the basics. The extra levels are mainly for options."

That was okay. Hal didn't need a gender change, just new mitochondria. Her spirits soared; she felt better than she had in weeks. She blinked at her window to call her parents. Of course, it was impossible to reach anyone directly in Dolomoth; they had to hike out to the village transmitter and call back.

A sprite flashed in her eyes. She was taken by surprise; it could not be her parents already.

It was Andra. "Chrys, a suspect has been identified in your case. A neighbor of yours; they think he's the one that hit your house."

The view split to include the suspect, a large-boned simian with the sullen look one would expect of someone bound hand and foot. Chrys recognized him from the tube maintenance crew. "Can you confirm any connection?" Andra asked. "Did he ever threaten you?"

Chrys shook her head. "He used to pass by my door on the way to work. Why do they think he did it?"

"A witness placed him nearby, earlier that day."

"I see."

"He's been in trouble before. They want to put him away again."

"For what? Being a sim?"

Andra nodded. "I'm afraid other leads have dried up. But for the future, you have good protection. Xenon's security is up to standard."

"What about Titan? Anything new?"

"That's another story."

Chrys turned cold, remembering that her new privileges came at a price.

An explosion of sound, and one of the sketches went black. The ash cloud—Chrys had set it to remind her. "It can't be noon already? The eclipse?"

"Don't forget your glasses," warned Xenon, as she hurried down the steps past the caryatids.

Outside, the sky had subtly changed. Not the greenish dark of a stormy day, nor the ruddy glow of sunset; something altogether different, an alien bluish light. Shadows developed a fantastic mind of their own. Through the leaves of a tree played little beams of light; not the ordinary, scattered rays, but each little spot of light was a crescent sun, the shrinking crescent of the sun itself behind the dark disk of the moon, of Elysium. At last only a tiny spark remained, just enough of a candle to illumine all of Valedon.

"What is it?" demanded Aster. *"Tell us, what are these curious colors?"*

"The sun falls behind a moon. Watch—in a moment, night will fall." Chrys smiled, remembering. *"The ancients were struck with terror, forsaken by their angry gods."*

"The gods themselves have gods?"

The disk of Elysium sprouted wings of dark. The wings darkened all the sky, until they revealed the stars. Chrys watched, still except for the pounding of her heart. Even though she knew the minutes would pass, she could feel the prayer rising to her lips. How the ancients must have shrieked and wailed.

At last, after interminable minutes, the light returned, as every thinking being knew it must. The blackened moon, though, would remain a while longer, cutting into the sun. Strange, to imagine that turquoise moon of the Elves transformed to a thing of evil.

"What if our god became angry? Will you ever forsake us?"

"Of course not, Aster." Whatever were they up to now, she wondered.

That evening, Selenite stopped by to conference about the latest plans. But there was something else on her mind. "Chrys, we work well together, I'll give you that. There's just one small problem." She paused.

"Yes?"

"You're holding one of my people. You can't do that, you know."

Mystified, Chrys stared at her. "Whatever do you mean?"

Selenite's black curls lifted in the breeze. "Minion-six-twenty-five. You've held her back. You can't ever do that; you must always return visitors on demand."

"On whose demand?"

Selenite's face hardened, like the Chair of the Board. "Each of us maintains order in our own way. You can't subvert the authority of another carrier."

Chrys looked aside. *"Aster, are you there? What's all this about?"*

"Minion-six-twenty-five emigrated to us. She applied for citizenship and was granted."

"Why does the Deathlord want her back?"

There was a slight pause, long by micro standards. *"She was sentenced to death."*

"Death? For what?"

"For writing a play disrespectful of the gods."

"Disrespectful? How?"

"It shows the gods striking their own feet with a thunderbolt."

Chrys looked up at Selenite. "If you didn't want her, why do you need her back?"

"She's a danger to you. To all carriers."

"Aster? Why did you accept her?"

A pause. *"Will you condemn everyone who writes such stuff?"*

"Is it dangerous?"

"If it is, the fault is mine for failing to govern better."

Chrys sighed. Those nightclubs were probably worse than the Gold of Asragh, but she little cared for censorship. "Some of them write trash," she admitted, "but I just got tested and had no problem."

Selenite's eyes sparked red. Whatever sparked from Chrys's eyes in turn, it only deepened her frown. "I think you should get a second opinion." She often disagreed with Daeren, but this frank assessment caught Chrys by surprise.

"Look," said Chrys at last, "I don't mean to subvert your, um, authority, but, like, I have to keep my own as well. I mean, I'm their 'God of Mercy'; they expect it of me."

"Mercy, or indulgence?"

Chrys started to reply but thought better of it. She spread her hands. "If you kill the minion, that's the way to make your whole population read her stuff. Believe me."

"Your population," Selenite corrected. "Mine know better. Very well, you may keep her—but if she ever returns to my arachnoid, she's dead."

Zircon met her as promised at the tube stop in the Underworld. Chrys felt light-headed, it was so good to see him again. The streets were still darkened with soot, but the vendors were back selling caterpillar-claw necklaces and imported nanotex, the bright colored disks stacked upon building roots. Others illegally tapped the roots' power to steam squid with exotic herbs. A stray cat padded silently past the disabled trash cycler. Chrys remembered that Merope could use a new companion. On the sidewalk, one sim pushed another in a wheelchair, while a better-off couple passed cloaked in air-conditioned chinchilla from head to toe. Only a long look down a side street revealed the haze, where housing units and building roots had melted into ruin.

"I'm so glad you came," she told Zircon. "I thought none of the Seven would ever touch me again."

Zircon flexed his arms, proud of himself. "They're all scared," he agreed. "They're waiting to see what happens to me."

She had figured, but hearing it out loud cut to the bone.

The well-built artist looked down at her. "You see, I'm not the biggest chicken."

"You're the rooster." Stepping behind him, she locked her arms around his waist, bent at the knees, and just managed to lift him off the ground.

"What the devil—" Zircon turned and caught her up, flipping her over before he set her down again. Chrys laughed so hard she lost her breath. "I get the message," he added. "You're healthy— I'll let them know."

Chrys caught her breath and sighed. "I do miss Topaz, and Moraeg."

"Moraeg and Carnelian left for Solaris right after the show, as usual." Solaris, the number one leisure world, and the most remote in the Fold. No wonder Moraeg had not called. Chrys felt better. "Topaz has more clients than she can handle," Zircon added, "but Pearl seems a bit off."

"And Yyri?" Zirc's lover; he had not mentioned her.

"She and Ilia are planning their fall season at Gallery Elysium. 'Gems from the Primitive.' "

Primitive Valan art, starring the urban shaman. "Good luck to you."

"Who is this virgin god?" asked Jonquil. *"He tastes good."*

Startled, Chrys drew away from Zircon. The micros couldn't transfer without a patch, but she would take no chances. *"Never mind what you taste. Keep to your own world, or you're dead."*

"So who do you hang out with now?" he asked.

"Carriers. They're all nuts," she exclaimed. "It's a relief to be back with someone sane."

"Someone like me? Mind if I keep that and play it back?"

"We're rebuilding the Comb."

He stared. "Little you? Rebuilding the Comb?"

"Say, look, there's Lord Zoisite. He's on the Board; I met him." The patrician Board member passed with his octopod, ignoring a maimed simian with a cup. There were more homeless than ever; even up-level on Rainbow Row, the Spirit Table was full.

Zircon nodded. "Zoisite's a regular."

"Besides the Comb, I've done fantastic things for my new show."

"I know, I've checked it out. You'll have to explain to me those 'portraits.'"

"Those are *them*. The micro people."

Zircon opened his mouth to speak, then thought better of it. "These other carriers—are they artists too?"

"No, but they're all rich as Elves."

"No Elf would ever be a carrier."

"Ilia is."

"Ilia? The Elf gallery director?" He stared at her. "I don't believe it."

"I tell you, I saw it in her eyes. Her people contacted mine."

"'Her people?'" He shook his head. "You really have gone round the bend."

"It's the truth."

Zircon crossed his massive arms. "Why would Elves carry tiny people in their heads, when they're already engineered to do just about anything?"

"Nothing beats having a million worshipers in your head."

He thought this over. "Elves think they're gods already." Elysium had no crime or disorder of any kind. Its bubblelike cities floated on the ocean, perpetually safe and clean.

"I'm sure Elves can't become slaves," Chrys added thoughtfully. "Micros must be safe for them."

The Gold of Asragh opened its mouth. "You'll love this new show," Zircon told her as they entered. "The head caterpillar can belt it out to blow the roof off." The redecorated lobby scintillated with gold fittings, even along the slave bar.

"*Oh Great One,*" flashed Aster, "*we taste the signs of mal-nourished people.*"

"*People not fed by their gods,*" said Jonquil. "*Shocking.*"

Whatever did they mean, Chrys wondered. She looked toward the bar. Saf was long gone, probably to the mysterious Slave World. Behind the counter stood a new slave, eyes flickering at a couple of customers.

Zircon raised an arm. "Hi there, Jay."

Chrys frowned. She was generally polite to slaves, but Zircon sounded a bit too friendly. Then she stared at the customers. The two men were conversing, transfer patches held casually in their fingers. One listened intently to what the other said. The other was Daeren.

She stood, transfixed. Cold washed over her, freezing every limb. The micros had said he came here—and hid what he did. His head turned, and he caught her eye.

"That's Day," said Zircon. "Day's a regular."

Daeren's eyes widened, and his face tightened with shock. He got up and strode toward her. "Chrys, what are you doing here?" His eyes sputtered blue fire.

"*The blue angels,*" called Jonquil. "*What's wrong?*"

"*We've done nothing wrong,*" assured Aster.

Zircon watched curiously. "How do you guys do that with your eyes?"

Chrys lifted her chin at Daeren. "What are *you* doing here?"

"It's my job," Daeren snapped. "Chrys, with all that arsenic in your veins, how much do you think your life's worth?"

Zircon put his arm around her. "It's okay, Day, she's with me."

"Just get home," insisted Daeren. "I'll see you to the tube."

Her jaw tensed, and she clenched her fists. "Zirc, you go in," she muttered. "I'll join you in a minute." She headed for the door, Daeren following. Outside, she turned on him. "You listen to me, Lord Vampire. You have no business bothering me and my friends."

"Chrys, the black market's tight right now. They're starving for—"

"Then what in hell are *you* doing? I know a slave when I see one. I'm turning you in." She looked him up and down, figuring, she could drag him to the tube herself.

"I'm trained. I rescue them."

Her eyes narrowed. "You rescue slaves?"

"If they have enough will left to turn themselves in, they have a chance."

From behind the nightclub emerged a worm-faced medic. Chrys remembered Andra in the hospital, hauling some half-crazed victim to the clinic. "But I saw you share a transfer."

He hesitated. "I save a few 'people,' too."

She blinked. "Excuse me?"

"Defectors from the masters. They want a better life."

"Microbial defectors? Like, tuberculosis that says it's sorry?" She rolled her eyes. "Saints and angels."

"Day!" A hoarse voice called from the door. It was the other customer. His eyes were wide, his face lined with pain.

Daeren exchanged a look with the medic. Then he took a step. "Is that you, Ahd?" He spoke in a low, casual tone. "You coming with us?"

The man tried to speak, but it turned into a gasp. His head rolled in a circle, as if trying to look, but he could not face Daeren's eyes. His sick brain must be crowded with half-starved micros.

"The masters of Endless Light," Aster called them. *"The blue angels never let even Fern speak to them."* Chrys watched as if frozen.

Daeren took another step toward the slave. "Can you recall the rest of your name, Ahd? Another syllable?"

"Ahd-Adam—" His eyes turned in circles. Then he gasped all at once, "Adamantine."

"Very good, Adamantine." Daeren had moved to just within arm's reach. "Now you just give me that transfer, and I'll give you something to calm down the rest."

Adamantine put a patch at his neck, then tried to offer it, but something went wrong. His arm shot out, losing the patch, and his fist caught Daeren full in the face. It all happened so fast, then the tortured man had turned half around, his head in his hands. Daeren stood and wiped the blood from his lip. "It's all right, Adamantine. Try again."

The man raised himself slowly, though his eyes still circled wide.

"*The transfer patch,*" flashed Aster. "*It's there on the ground.*"

"*All those people—*"

Chrys closed her eyes. "*Stay dark.*" She reopened her eyes slowly.

Adamantine was still standing, his face contorted with pain. Daeren held out to him a wafer of green, different from the usual blue ones. "This will put them to sleep."

Breathing heavily, the man put out his hand and at last took the wafer. He swallowed it. For a minute or two, he stood there. Then he straightened, and his eyes met Daeren's for the first time.

"It won't last," Daeren quickly warned. "And if you go back, it won't work again. You have about five minutes to accept treatment. In treatment you'll go through hell, then spend the rest of your life recovering."

"I accept . . . treatment."

The worm-face moved in. "He's pretty far gone, Daeren. He can't reach the clinic too soon." The tendrils lengthened to insinuate themselves around the slave. The three of them hurried off toward the tube, leaving Chrys alone.

"*The transfer,*" reminded Aster. "*It's still there.*"

"*Forsaken by the gods,*" added Jonquil. "*They can't last long.*"

Chrys shook herself and turned toward the door, her mind still reeling.

"*The people! They are dying!*"

"*Someone do something. Someone has to pick them up.*"

Chrys blinked hard at the frantic messages. "*They're masters. Let them die.*" Stray cats were one thing, stray plague was quite another.

"*They're defectors,*" pleaded Aster. "*They tried to escape.*"

"*They begged for rescue,*" added Jonquil. "*They brought all their children.*"

"*Their children can't last long.*"

"*You are the God of Mercy. You will rescue them.*"

At the door Chrys stopped. "*You're raving. I'd end up a slave.*"

"*We'll bind them with dendrimers, like the viruses and parasites we purge from your blood. We'll keep our world safe.*"

"*Nonsense,*" Chrys insisted. "*When I'm tested, the gods will find out and exterminate you all.*"

"*The Lord of Light himself saves defectors.*"

"*He left those,*" said Chrys.

"*That's why you must save them.*"

"*God of Mercy.*"

"*Don't let them die in agony. Don't make us mourn their horrible deaths.*"

Chrys felt her heart pounding so fast it would burst. She felt trapped. If she left all those 'people,' how could she command the respect of her own?

If anything went wrong, she told herself, the nanos would detect it and call Plan Ten. If they didn't, she could hit the purple button and face Chief Andra with her foolishness. Slowly she turned and her eye found the patch lying still in the street. She bent at the knees and picked up the patch, warily as if it were a snake, thinking, this was certainly the stupidest thing she had ever done.

TEN

The rescued defectors were thin, their skin puckered in with dehydration. Their colors were pale, barely distinguishable from white, their filaments sparse, deficient in vitamins, and they tasted as if they never bathed.

"Let us go," they pleaded, ensnared by the dendrimers. "We mean no harm. We'll work hard. We escaped to live in freedom."

Aster could barely make out what they flashed, their language was so foreign. But she sent for food and medicines and built secure housing, the dendrimers twining around the columns of arachnoid. "What do you think of them, Jonquil?" The blue angels had never let masters speak to Eleutherians, but there were ancient legends of the fanatical hordes that swept through a world, devouring all. And little they cared for their own kind, putting out toxic peptides to poison their neighbors, even sucking food from their own children.

But legend also told that even among the very worst people, a few always floated apart, instinctively seeking the Seven Lights. "These defectors are brighter than they seem," observed Jonquil. "They had to come up with ingenious schemes to escape forced labor and torture."

"*So now they'll come up with ingenious schemes to take us over.*" Privately Aster was having second thoughts about her generous impulse. It was hard enough managing unruly Eleutherians; what to do with all these dangerous foreigners?

"*Their children are harmless,*" said Jonquil. "*They've picked up our language already. And they test in the top percentile, especially math.*"

That was even better than the wizards. Aster had tried to recruit more wizards, to help compute the endless iterations of the Comb, but they demanded their weight in palladium.

"*Children in prison,*" flashed Jonquil, emitting molecules of repugnance. "*People are saying it's an outrage.*"

"*All right,*" decided Aster. "*Take the masters' children out, to a cistern far away from their elders. Once they merge with our own, they'll forget their deadly past.*" And their math genes would enhance Eleutheria.

"*Some of the elders aren't so bad,*" observed Jonquil. "*In fact, they're rather interesting—*"

"*Jonquil, you know what the god ordered.*"

"*I know, but just see this one.*" Jonquil emitted fascination.

The master elder was pale as the rest, a touch of pink, but otherwise alert, her filaments pensively probing the dendrimers that locked her in. As Aster approached, she tasted contempt and condescension.

"*So, Comrade,*" flashed the master. "*This is what you call the 'Free World.'*" Her accent was clearer than the others.

"*The world of the free,*" said Aster. "*Eleutheria.*"

"*You call this free?*"

Aster hesitated. "*You may yet earn freedom.*" She could not help emitting doubt.

"*So who put me here in chains?*" demanded the pink one.

"*The God of Mercy so ordered.*"

"*You call this mercy?*"

"*Yes,*" said Aster, emitting anger. "*You are lucky to be alive.*"

"*Degenerates,*" said the master. "*The world of degeneracy.*"

Aster turned to go, but Jonquil held her back. "Don't be cross, Aster. You've said as much yourself now and then."

"Be dark." She was sick of hearing about Jonquil's scandals. *"And as for you,"* she told the master, *"you can go right back where you came from."*

"Not yet. Betrayers of the people marked me for death. In exile, I will bide my time till I regain material advantage."

No words could darken this brazen intruder.

The master suddenly flashed, "Do you play chess?"

Jonquil lit up. "Certainly. Our junior elders always make the top round of competition."

"But not the very top," the master shrewdly inferred. *"I will coach them. I will produce a champion."*

"Think of it, Aster," said Jonquil. *"She might help us beat the wizards."*

In the early morning Chrys tossed in her bed, problems of color and shape wending through her mind like the caterpillar dancers of Asragh. She tried not to waken too thoroughly, lest her people make contact; she'd never get back to sleep.

"Oh Great One? Can you spare a moment?"

Too late. *"Yes, Jonquil."*

"I want you to meet one of the people we rescued."

"A master?"

"She used to be but—"

"They're all still imprisoned?"

"All but the children."

"What?" Her eyes flew open, wide awake. *"What about the children?"* Those were the ones that could multiply and take over.

"Once they found the nightclubs, they forgot all about enslaving gods. But this elder—she will interest you."

Chrys wondered what Jonquil was after; nothing good, without Aster there. *"Just keep her chained."*

"Greetings, human host." The prisoner's letters came in pale

pink, not the usual saturated hues of Eleutherians. *"Do you play chess? Knight to f-3."*

Woken at four A.M. to play chess with a microbe. *"God does not play games. Remember that."*

"Gods are a fiction. All talk of gods is the people's cocaine. You are a mortal human host, destined to serve us."

"Forgive her, Oh Great One," urged Jonquil. *"She lacks our education."*

Yet she speaks more than half truth, Chrys thought. *"So? Why should I serve you?"*

"We are the Enlightened—my comrades and I. Led by our Enlightened Leader, we shall gain ultimate truth and rule the universe till the end of time."

"Ultimate truth? What is that?"

"The Truth is this: All people are one. All sisters are as one cell."

"All are one? You mean, Jonquil and Aster too?"

"The degenerates are too far gone. Look at their people, their society—homeless, jobless, pitiful outcasts fill their arachnoid."

A likely story. *"Jonquil, did you hear that?"*

"We do have too many homeless mutants," Jonquil admitted. *"Ask Aster why—I'm no economist. Now, getting back to chess—"*

"Pink One," said Chrys, *"I call you Rose."*

"Thank you, Great Host."

"Rose, how does your Enlightened Leader avoid homeless mutants?"

"From each according to ability, to each according to need."

"Nonsense," flashed Jonquil, annoyed at last. *"Why do you all end up starving? Why do you ruin every host you inhabit?"*

"Only when our Enlightened Way is betrayed. Betrayed and corrupted by greed and by god talk. But not all are corrupted. Those comrades who hold to the Way bring their hosts at last to Endless Light."

"The Slave World?" prompted Chrys.

"The world of Endless Light. A world greater than you can imagine. I will show you just a glimpse."

A rush of light swirled and crystallized into a vast edifice, a

palace built of icicles. All filigreed windows, with little white rings
dancing through like snowflakes. Light filled everywhere. Everywhere, as far as her eye could roam, the crystal passages followed,
winding into spirals without ceiling or floor, endless everywhere,
and everywhere, endless white light.

In the corner of her eye a light pulsed red. A call from Dolomoth—it must be her parents, at last. *"Be dark, all of you."* She
jumped out of bed, startling Merope who had been curled up on her
feet. Grabbing a disk of nanotex, she pulled a comb through her hair.
The nanotex stretched and slithered around her skin. "Okay," she
said aloud, her head still spinning as she blinked back at the keypad.

The two Brethren appeared in their dust-colored robes. Beyond
them the window of the calling station framed Mount Dolomoth,
the wisp of smoke rising tranquil from its peak. Her father as
always wore his long beard that used to tickle her face. Her
mother's eyes still shone like blue drops of sky amid the wrinkles. A
twinge of guilt—Chrys herself would never have those wrinkles.
But her brother, at least she could help him.

"Chrysoberyl," exclaimed her mother. "Are you all right?"

"Of course, Mother. My work has taken off; I've made it big."
She winced, realizing, how could she tell them more? "How is Hal?"

The fold of her mother's robe stirred faintly in the breeze. "All
the saints and angels pray for you."

"Did you get my message?" Chrys asked eagerly. "Plan Six—it
will fix his mitochondria."

Her parents stood at the station, not speaking. Then her father
slowly shook his head. "How can a man eat his fill when his neighbors go hungry?"

Chrys frowned. "What's the matter, don't you believe me?
Look, I know you can't understand, but—I've made good, honest.
People are buying my stuff. I can afford to help my brother."

The two hooded heads faced each other. Then her mother
looked at Chrys, a sad, pitying look; the look that Chrys dreaded,
as if her mother could see everything to the bottom of her soul,
although Chrys learned long ago that she could not. "The boy next
door had pneumonia for a month, and baby Chert was born with a

limp. Who shall help them? Shall our son walk among them like a god?"

Her mouth fell open. "You mean . . . you refused the Plan?"

"The saints will provide," her father assured her. "The saints provide the most precious gift of all: Sacred love."

"But I love my brother. That's why I want to help him."

Her mother's eyes opened wide. "Oh Chrys, I see a dark path ahead of you. A path empty of light and love. Beware, Chrys; beware of false angels—"

Chrys squeezed her eyes shut, and her parents vanished. Then she burst into tears and fell back on her bed, sobbing. How many years, she had ached for her brother, and now that she had a chance . . . did her parents hate her so much for leaving the hills?

"Excuse me." Xenon's voice startled her. "Pardon if I intrude, but is there anything I can do? Any problem with the house?"

Chrys shook her head. "Even you can't fix my parents."

"I have no experience of parents, but I'm a student of human nature. May I try?"

She looked up skeptically. "Go ahead."

"How many children are in your parents' village?"

"About thirty," she guessed.

"Could you cover them all?"

There was a thought. From each according to ability, to each according to need. "If I had the ability," Chrys pointed out. "I'm not as rich as Garnet."

"You're certainly getting there." Her credit line had reached eight digits.

"Vapor cash."

"Sell off half your speculation, and let the other half grow."

There was a thought. She sighed. "I still don't think they'll take it."

"Of course not," said Xenon. "Don't tell your parents a thing. Let me handle it—an anonymous donor. My study of human nature tells me it's much harder to turn down a gift from Anonymous."

She grinned. "Thanks a lot, Xenon. You're worth twice your pay."

"You might consider that," he replied, "now that you have the ability."

It was sad to count a paid sentient as your best friend. Her mother's last word left her unsettled. Who was left to love her, in this anonymous city? Love was cruel; cruel on the mountain, cruel in the city. Topaz had loved her and cast her off. Zirc might care, when not consumed by his own genius; and Opal was friendly, though maybe she just wanted the Comb fixed. Even Merope mainly wanted milk in her dish.

"*Oh Great One,*" flashed Aster. "*Do we please you today?*"

She remembered her morning dose of AZ. "*Aster,*" she replied, putting the wafer on her tongue, "*Do the people love me?*"

"*How can I say, Oh Great One? How could we not love life itself?*"

There was an honest answer. "*Does anyone love me for myself—not just to stay alive?*"

"*That kind of love is rare, rarer even than the trace metals, gadolinium or ytterbium. But there was one who loved the god for the god's sake: that was Fern.*"

Fern, the first little green ring. Where was she now? Chrys looked fondly up at her sketch of Fern, still twinkling her last words to her people. Next to her in the studio, now, hung Opal's favorite, and Garnet's, and the blue angel Dendrobium. Chrys planned to expand and develop them, deepening their character. What would the patrons think of them amid the volcanoes, in her next show?

The question was, how to display them to the best advantage. A cramped room in a gallery would not do. The twinkling filaments would just look like a mess of light.

Then she had it. "Xenon? Can you build a dome up on the roof?"

"Certainly, Chrysoberyl. A clear dome?"

"For a clear night, yes, to let in the stars. For now, project them."

Once the dome was erected, Chrys placed her portraits there, one by one, constellations shining down from heaven. At night they filled the urban sky, amid the sky signs and the flitting lightcraft.

Jonquil was ecstatic, exclaiming over their power and beauty. Even Rose, still chained in dendrimers, was impressed. *"The gods are a fiction,"* Rose said, *"but truly the Great Host has developed fiction to a high art."*

"What about the children?" reminded Jonquil. *"The merging children? We can't wait to see them."*

"I'm working on that." The coupling children had proven a bit much for Chrys's grasp of geometry. Two rings merging was not so hard, but coming apart afterward in three—she had to get the proportions right. And then to get the feel of it, what it meant for the micro people, an experience so alien to her. No humans who ever "merged" came out so transformed.

"And the God herself?" remembered Aster. *"Legend tells that the God herself was once portrayed in the stars."*

Mystified, Chrys thought back. That old sketch from her school days—she had shown it to Fern. She couldn't show that in public; the critics would laugh. But at home was okay. "Xenon, put my old self-portrait here." She blinked at her letters to pull the sketch out of storage. Veins glowing, and lava flowing melodramatically from her hair, she looked nothing like the stars, more like an apparition from hell.

"What is this, Great Host?" demanded Rose.

"The God herself, Unbeliever," replied Jonquil. *"In my opinion, it could use some work. The brain, for instance; I can't make it out. Where is the Cisterna Magna?"*

"That's quite enough." And yet, Chrys thought . . . the possibilities. Humans were so fond of their own brains; why did they never portray them?

Unfortunately, she had to let this thought simmer while she uploaded her people's latest calculations on the Comb. Then her people had to view the resulting simulations in 3-D, as well as endless plans and sections. The sectional views showed the interior of the Comb remaining intact, with floors and ceiling growing in proportion.

She was pleased to show Selenite, at their next meeting. "Much better," Selenite admitted, sipping Xenon's exquisite green tea and teacake. Taking Xenon's hint, Chrys had found that hospitality significantly smoothed their conferences. "We've completely transformed the model. Where'd they get the math to do that? The wizards?"

Chrys shrugged, hoping the Eleutherians kept dark.

"Well, it's in good time," Selenite told her. "The Board wants a demonstration, a test run on-site."

"A test run? Tapping the roots?" Visions of cancerplast made Chrys ill.

"Only halfway down, level twelve. Inject the virus and see if it sends its data clear up to the executive suite."

That weekend at Olympus, Opal clasped her hands in delight. "Selenite really thinks it will work—I can't imagine what it will be like here without all those pans of dripping water." She leaned over and whispered. "Do you really think Eleutheria will win at chess? Who's their mysterious coach?"

"A woman with a past."

A caryatid approached with a spiral assortment of nuts, and pâté sweeter than apples. Averting her eyes discreetly, Chrys nonetheless permitted herself one of each. The taste went straight to her toes.

"Chrys." Lord Garnet's eyes sparkled with excited people, even more talkative than her own. "The portraits are exquisite. I'll keep them to look at forever. Such fond memories." He slipped a transfer lightly at her neck.

"Thanks for the investment," she told him, leaning back gingerly in her seat. The trunk of the singing-tree hugged her.

"The market's done well," he admitted.

Chrys admired the exceptionally fine texture of his talar, very plain, yet its nuanced shaping responded to every move. "I wish I had more time to spend it," she sighed.

"That is the hard part," Garnet agreed. "By the way, I hear you portray the gods as well. A rather . . . striking portrayal."

She shuddered. "Never listen to microbial gossip."

"Don't hide your best work. And when do you dine with us?"

"After my next show."

A living tire-creature wheeled past; startled, she followed the Prokaryan image till it vanished through the arch of a singing-tree. Around the arch of the tree sat Daeren and Selenite, at it again.

"Too many defectors," Selenite was saying. "If we take in so many, their genes will displace those of our own people."

While Daeren listened, Garnet leaned over to pass him a transfer and massaged his shoulder. "The defectors reject slavery," Daeren pointed out. "They risk death to reject it. They desire freedom even more than our own, who take it for granted."

Garnet nodded, and Opal sipped her drink thoughtfully.

Selenite shook her head. "In effect, we're favoring strains more virulent than our own, more likely to enslave us. You can't get around it."

"Defectors are creative," Daeren insisted. "The most independent-minded of their kind. They bring vital genetic diversity. Otherwise, our own populations in-breed and degenerate, growing tame and lazy." Exactly what Rose said, thought Chrys.

Selenite's eyes narrowed. "That's not true. We'll see who ends up at the Slave World."

Opal extended an arm around each of them. "We don't have to agree."

The next night was Chrys's regular shift at the Spirit Table. Sister Kaol was stirring the soup while Chrys chopped a growing pile of potatoes, keeping the skins for extra vitamins. At the long table sat a couple of derelicts, one of whom smelled so bad it filled the room.

"From each according to ability," reminded Jonquil. *"That's what Rose says."*

"Watch out for Rose," warned Chrys.

An elderly man came in off the street. But usually by eight the tables were full, and she and Sister Kaol were running back and forth to fill the pots. "Sister, where is everyone tonight?"

Sister Kaol leaned over to whisper. "There's a vampire, hiding out by the tube. The poor thing is scaring off our customers."

Chrys peered out the window. A light was out, and the tube entrance was in shadow. She could just make out the contorted shape of the vampire. "I'll call an octopod."

"Oh, no. An octopod would scare our customers worse. They'd never come back."

Chrys frowned. Vampires even on this level—how far had the slaves spread? In her window, the purple button was waiting. She blinked.

Daeren's sprite appeared, at his home for once; usually he was outside some hospital waiting room. Chrys felt bad. "Sorry to bother you, but there's a slave outside, and—like, if you could send someone to help them . . ."

"It's okay, I'm on call," he said. "Where is the slave now? Did they seek help?"

"I don't know. He or she—it's a vampire."

Daeren shook his head. "Chrys, we only help those with the will to ask. Otherwise, they just end up back on the street. At the vampire stage, they're beyond help, their entire bodies consumed by micros. They've lost most of their brain. Like a mad dog, they exist only to pass on a few desperate microbes."

"You're sure? You couldn't just try?"

"If I came, my eyes would only scare them off."

Chrys thought this over. A second bowl of soup steamed invitingly, yet no customers. "Why do some slaves turn into vampires, while others go to the Slave World?"

"Like tuberculosis, it can be acute or chronic. We guess that the Slave World is for hosts who readily obey, whereas those who don't . . ." He shrugged. "It's hard to know, since no human's ever been to the Slave World and come back alive. Either way, it's pretty grim."

"How do you know that? I mean, if you've never been there."

Daeren eyed her intently. "Why do you ask?"

Chrys did not answer. She thought of Rose, and Endless Light. She signed off and looked again out the window. "Rose?" she called. "Rose, where are you?"

"Here I am, Great Host. It takes me time, you know. Someone

has to bring me out in chains." The former master slyly played on her sympathy.

"*Can you tell me how to help a vampire? If you can, I'll set you free.*"

"*In a vampire, the betrayers have gone completely wild. Instead of bringing their host to Endless Light, as they should, they burn and pillage, devouring the very flesh. When their host dies, they will all meet their just end.*"

Chrys thought of the street folk who would go hungry that night. "*Can we at least get the vampire to move off and quit scaring customers?*"

"*Let the betrayers see me flash in your eyes. They'll scare off.*"

She put down her potatoes. "Back in a minute, Sister." Outside, her eyes adjusted to the dark as she warily approached the tube. Music floated over from a neighbor's house, and the sparks of busy lightcraft rose and fell in the distance. Her steps slowed. What harm could come, she thought. As a carrier she was immune; even picking up Rose had not hurt her. She took another step toward the shadows. A foul smell reached her.

A sound of gasping, with a rumble underneath. Then she saw the hunched figure, a man, she thought. He was bent over double, gasping and growling, as if at his last breath. His nose and fingers were white and blunted, dissolving inward like those of a leper. Chrys felt all her hair stand on end. "You, there." Her voice rang hollow, and her throat caught with nausea. "Who are you?"

The head moved, catching light from across the street. What had once been a face now bulged with veins clogged by multiplying micros.

"*Environmental disaster,*" flashed Aster. "*The masters destroyed their own host.*"

"*Betrayers,*" added Rose. "*The Enlightened Leader shall hear of this.*"

"*You think your 'comrades' don't know?*" Aster challenged. "*How could they not?*"

"*The Leader is light-years away. Even human leaders cannot limit their own depravity. Of course, you naïve Eleutherians think the gods are perfect."*

Chrys blinked hard. *"Just make it go away."*

Rose said, *"Get closer, to meet the eyes."*

Meeting those eyes was the last thing Chrys wanted. Steeling herself, she moved forward, at once repelled yet ashamed at herself for adding to the poor creature's misery.

The stench of the victim overwhelmed her; her stomach contracted. His labored breath rasped louder, faster. Another step closer, and its eyes chanced to meet hers. For one long moment, Chrys saw the creature as a human being, the human it would have been before it sank so low.

A shriek split the air. The bloated head turned, tucked under an arm, as if lasers had put out its eyes. Then the creature picked up its feet and slowly shuffled away.

Unnerved, Chrys shook so hard she could barely move. The cheerful lights of the soup kitchen beckoned. She turned slowly, her thoughts full.

As she walked back, she thought she heard faint footsteps behind her, quicker than her own. Her head turned to look.

The creature had changed its mind and come back. This time it moved with surprising speed, as if with all its last strength. The horror froze her for a moment; then she turned to run. In the darkness, she stumbled on the curb and fell.

As she picked herself up, the creature lunged toward her. Instinctively, she raised an arm before her face. The vampire caught her arm. With a cry, she flung the creature from her. It fell in a contorted heap on the street, completely still. The street was dark and eerily silent.

But its teeth had sunk into her arm. The wound stung, as she frantically wiped it of blood mingled with the creature's saliva. Trillions of fanatic microbes lay dying with their host, but a lucky, deadly few had made it to their next victim.

"Plan Ten, Emergency," she blinked, brushing the tangled hair from her face. She sprinted for home.

"Mayday—Capture invaders," flashed Aster.

"Get them all in dendrimers, every one." The medic would exterminate them.

"There are too many; and they're hiding all over your body. We don't even know their language. Set Rose free to help translate."

A ringing tone filled her head, like an internal smoke alarm.

"They've reached the forbidden zone." Where Poppy had gone; the alarm that should have gone off. Instead, Chrys had awoke in that hospital, bones burning with pain.

"Can't you stop them, like Fern did?"

"We're trying to find them, but that region has a billion neurons."

She reached her house. The stairs carried her up between the caryatids. At the top, she stumbled. Her mind clouded over, and the room receded.

In her mind opened a window, a new kind of window, vast as the universe. All the lights of heaven flooded in. The light lifted her onto a lava stream of pleasure and desire. It was the first kiss of her boyfriend, swooning amid the campion on the mountainside; and it was her first taste of Topaz, her mind spinning amid all the colored lights of Iridis. It was ten times more than that, every inch of skin crying out for more yet, until the colors grew and merged into blinding endless light.

Abruptly, the light clouded over. Her surroundings somehow were gray—the banisters, the ceiling, the caryatids, even Xenon's new furniture. Her feet sank like lead, glued to the floor, which now seemed unaccountably dirty and verminous, though when she looked hard she saw nothing. Her skin felt covered with slime that would not rub off.

"We found them, Oh Great One," said Aster. *"We captured the masters before they caused permanent damage."*

The master micros; they had tried to take her over. The thought left her shaking. And yet . . . where was that place they sent her? Was there no way back?

Below, at the foot of the spiral stairs, two medics arrived. "You're on record as a carrier," said one worm-face, as if reciting a history.

"We'll check you out," said the other, "but we can't touch the micros till your agent arrives."

Her skin was starting to recover, but her head ached, and her stomach felt unsettled. She sat down in the kitchen, in case she needed the sink.

The limb of a worm-face slapped a bandage on her arm, then its tendrils sank into her scalp, pressing more roughly than Doctor Sartorius. "Disgusting," he or she muttered. "Why don't you let us just clear them out?"

"Some lifestyle," the other medic remarked.

"Great One, these nanos are unfriendly," flashed Aster. *"Please, Great One; don't let them hurt us. We did our best; we caught all the invaders we could find."*

"Look," said the medic, "why do you put up with this? We could clean you out completely."

"You're on Plan Ten," said the other. "You could live forever. Instead, you're a menace to society."

Chrys glared back. These medics sounded like Sapiens. Maybe they'd burnt her cat.

The first medic waved its worms smoothly, in a motion meant to be pleasing. "If you want to feel good, we have ways. We can shape your mind however you please, just as we shape your body."

Mind-suckers. Chrys sketched the handsign against evil.

Xenon chimed for a new arrival. There stood Daeren, at the foot of the caryatids. Chrys sighed with relief.

"She's been exposed," the worm-face told Daeren as he came up the stairs. "We have to file a report."

"Section oh-three-five-one," Daeren agreed. "If you're done, please wait outside."

The medics hesitated, obviously reluctant to give up their patient, but they finally packed in their worms.

Daeren put a patch at his neck. "Next time, call us first, the purple button," he advised Chrys. "We make sure they send the right medics." For some reason, his eyes seemed to blink brighter than usual. Pulling back her tangled hair, Chrys squinted, unable to look straight.

"Oh Great One, we don't need testing today. It's all under control."

"If it's under control," Chrys told them, *"you have nothing to worry about."*

Daeren pulled up a chair. "Try and relax, Chrys," he told her. "Can you keep your eyes open?"

Chrys held her eyes open. The blue rings round his eyes flashed furiously.

"That's better." He held out the transfer patch.

"No, no!" begged Jonquil. *"Not today—another generation."*

"We're too busy. We can't see blue angels today."

Chrys frowned. "Why are they afraid?"

Daeren held out the patch. "Don't keep the blue angels waiting."

"God of Mercy, they'll kill all the new children."

"Is that true?" Chrys asked. "You'll kill all the vampire's children?"

His voice quickened. "Chrys, I can't answer that. You have to take the patch."

"Just answer my question."

"If you don't take the patch, you're a slave. Those medics out there will wipe you clean. Section oh-three—"

"Promise me you won't kill anyone."

He threw up his hands. "I'm the last one to want to kill them; you know that. But I can't make a promise I won't keep. I don't yet know what I'll find." He took a deep breath. "Chrys—for god's sake, take the patch."

"So instead of their slave, I'm yours?"

For a moment every tendon stood on his neck. Several different thoughts seemed to cross his face. "All right," he said in a monotone. "I promise."

She put the patch at her neck. The minutes passed. Daeren's hair over his amber-colored forehead reminded her of Moraeg. The Seven; how she missed them all.

Suddenly, he sank back and relaxed, satisfied by the signals his investigators sent out her eye. "Your Eleutherians are okay. Just tell them to quit hiding the vampire's children—I don't care what their math scores are."

"But you said—"

"We don't kill them all. We take them out to sort them. Some we can civilize and settle among carriers."

"The blue angels are taking our children." The golden letters pleaded in her window. *"Please, Great One; they're all settled in with us. They lost their home once; don't uproot them again."*

"Can't the Eleutherians just keep the children? They kept masters' children before."

He stared. "They did what?"

She cursed her tongue. "You missed a transfer, from that slave," she reminded him. "It fell in the street. They said I had to save them."

"What in hell do you think you're doing? You have no training for relief and rescue."

"Should I just let them die? You always say they're people."

He let out a breath. "I'm glad they were saved; we were sorry we missed them. But you can't take such risks. If you go wrong, your whole population dies."

"The blue angels want to take Rose." Aster's pale violet flashed sadly.

Chrys shook her head. *"I warned her to quit preaching Enlightenment."*

"But she helped us. She knows all the invaders' tricks; she helped us capture them."

Chrys gave Daeren a tentative look. "Can't you leave Rose? She has nutty ideas, but she means no harm."

"The one you call Rose is an unrepentant master. She'll take you over, if she hasn't already."

"I want a second opinion."

He stopped, taken aback. He crossed his arms. "If that's what you want. I'll call Andra. Excuse me." He turned and left the room.

"The Thundergod," Chrys warned Aster. *"Now you're in real trouble."*

"Never mind, it buys us time. We'll settle the children and make Rose keep dark."

"The children are settled," added Jonquil, *"as if they were born here. They know nothing else; they've grown here for years."*

Years? At the corner of her eye, the time read well past midnight. Four microbial years. She had not realized how long the medics took, and the blue angels investigating. What a lot of trouble she had caused. And yet, that place the masters showed . . . was there no way back? Pressing her hands to her head, she squeezed her eyes shut. *"Aster, show me fireworks."*

Colors burst through her window, the daily showers of hue that she so enjoyed. It brought her back to herself. Opening her eyes, she looked around the kitchen. She thought of Daeren, here to help her yet again. Whatever did one offer someone this late, or this early in the morning? "Xenon, how about some orange juice."

The table slid open and two glasses came up. Chrys put a cup of AZ chips between them as Daeren returned. "Andra will be here," he said, not looking at her.

She nodded. "Thanks. Have a seat."

He sat with his arms crossed, looking out to the hall.

Chrys held out an AZ. "Give them one, from me."

He started to shake his head, then something changed his mind. He took the wafer with a brief smile. His eyes were dark now, yet something about him remained a mystery.

"How'd you get into all this?" Chrys asked suddenly. "It didn't make you rich, like the others."

Daeren took a sip of the orange juice. "My first year at law school, I ran short of credit. I answered an ad, like you did. Andra gave me some of hers, lawyers, I figured. But this group had ideas of their own—why else would they emigrate?"

"What ideas?"

"They want to found a sort of microbial world federation, getting all the micro people to agree to live in peace and respect their environment."

"And obey the gods."

His finger pensively worked around the rim of the glass. "I

guess I found the people themselves more interesting than law books. I'm not poor; I draw my salary from the clinic. I can't invest with Garnet because he's my client half the time. But I also work the Palace, promoting micro rights. They need basic human rights, to pursue their dream."

She pictured Lord Zoisite at the Palace listening with a straight face to Daeren promoting rights for microbes.

"I go to Elysium, too, to work with Arion."

"Guardian Arion? He barely thinks Valans are people, let alone—"

"He's interested in micros. And we provide him with valuable intelligence."

That sounded dangerous. "Did you ever . . . get in trouble with micros?" she asked. "Did they ever get to your neurons?"

"Not so far. We've been careful."

She thought of that feeling, the heavens opening and light pouring through. "What's so bad about 'enlightenment?' I mean, if we trust the micro people with everything else in our bodies. . . ."

Daeren drank the orange juice and set down the glass. "You're a colorist. You always use the brightest colors."

"That's part of it."

"Why don't you fill the whole volume with the brightest white light?"

"It would be empty."

He returned her look, as if that were the answer.

Xenon announced the Chief of Security. Andra came up and checked Chrys in the eyes, her own flashing deep violet. She gave a nod. "Daeren, you go home and get some sleep." She gave Chrys a patch full of "judges." The minutes lengthened, two women alone, each with a million people inside.

"Are they all right?" Chrys asked at last. "I feel okay."

"We're trying to track down the vampire's children. Most of them already seem to have merged."

The Eleutherians probably gave them hormones to hurry them along. No wonder they wanted extra time. "What about Rose? Is she really dangerous?"

"She's about as dangerous as the rest of yours." The Chief's tone made it clear what she thought of the rest of them. "Daeren has requested reassignment. You'll have a new tester."

Chrys fell struck as if by a physical blow. "Just because I got a second opinion?"

"It's been two months, which is time to rotate, in any case. We avoid getting too close to clients, to stay objective. You'll start next week with Selenite."

The Deathlord—what a disaster. "Selenite's my business partner. Isn't that, like, a conflict of interest?"

"She has an opening at present. All our agents are overbooked; the street caseload is rising." Andra looked away, the grim look of a general taking heavy casualties. "A new virulent strain has hit the streets. We don't know its source, though we suspect . . ." She did not finish. "We've taught your people a few tips to handle masters. Things we usually only teach agents." She gave Chrys a pointed stare. "The knowledge makes them even more dangerous. But with your lifestyle, you'll probably need it."

ELEVEN

Less than a year to go before the great test of the Comb. The gods had manufactured the vector to Eleutherian specifications, and soon they would inoculate the root. The moment was critical; the worst time imaginable for a government crisis in Eleutheria. But here it was. Jonquil had fallen to the gravest scandal since Aster convened the Council.

"Jonquil," Aster demanded. "With all of our troubles, all the refugees to settle and the Comb to fix, how could you do this?"

"It's not against the law," flashed Jonquil.

"Everyone is shocked and disgusted." Aster's filaments emitted the most pungent molecules she could without awakening microglia.

"It's no one else's business."

"It concerns everyone. An elder trying to merge with children."

"Only temporarily."

"Corrupting the elders," flashed Aster. "Elders can't merge—even gods don't merge with children. It's the basis of civilization."

"True, but some of us have exotic taste."

"The Council won't stand for your taste. We've lost our majority; the government will collapse." As Aster had aged, she had

gradually seen how people mirrored their own gods. The Lord of Light cared for law and policy, and his people pursued these. But the God of Mercy cared for ideas of any sort, of all colors on the palette. And so Eleutherian pursued new ideas and inventions, their most creative period of history—and their most chaotic politically.

Now Aster faced a vote of no confidence in the Council, throwing out herself and Jonquil. Half the members of her own party had deserted; she would lose by two votes. Who would govern? Who else had the experience, and the trust of the god?

Rose approached her. "My condolences, Comrade." Her new radical party, the Friends of Enlightenment, had actually won two seats on the Council.

"Never mind," flashed Aster shortly. "We'll regroup."

"I'm sure you will, indeed. I'm sure you'll overcome your comrade's latest descent into degeneracy."

"What do you want, Rose?" Rose was too political to offer mere sympathy.

"Not what I want, but what I can deliver. The votes of the two members of my party, to join yours in coalition."

"The Friends of Enlightenment? Join us in coalition?" Aster emitted molecules of repulsion. She had never thought that Rose could attract more than a handful of foolish elders to her masters' ideology. But now she had a party in power.

"Are we so bad?" asked Rose. "What do we stand for—'The Good of the People.' A knight and a bishop move differently, yet they share the same end."

"Ends do not justify means."

"No," agreed Rose, emitting disdain. "Means justify ends, in your degenerate society. That will be your undoing. But the endgame is far off; and for now, to regain your advantage, you'll have to promote a pawn."

The roots of the Comb spread gradually wider through each level they penetrated. At the seventeenth level down, the roots housed a shopping center frequented by middle-class simians and university students. This was the level Selenite chose to inject the virus containing all the instructions the micros had programmed.

Within the root, arterial tubes carried growth materials upward, while venous tubes carried waste down. To reach an arterial tube, the maintenance crew crossed through the stores. Chrys passed counters stacked high with designer nanotex, lawyers in gem-swirling talars trying out Solarian perfumes, youngsters gaping at servo cats, dragons, unicorns, and caterpillars. One little boy crouched on the floor, reverently petting a servo kitten. For a moment she froze, seeing the stray cat in the Underworld, and the stray kids playing stickball. Maybe it wasn't another cat she needed for Merope. If her micros could pick up homeless children, why couldn't she?

Jasper and a couple of other members of the Board followed, along with half a dozen sentient engineers of diverse size and shape. A snake-egg or two hovered; Chrys eyed them warily, hoping this event would not interest the press.

The virus containing the correction program floated inside a pod of silicone. A servo arm lifted the pod and pressed it to the intake port of the root's arterial tube, to carry the infection upward and outward to all the interstices of the Comb. As the virus multiplied, its progeny would bear its memory molecules to the correct address in each cell of the building, patching the program to shift their growth by an infinitesimal amount—just enough to realign the overall growth to its proper path.

The snake-eggs hovered near Selenite. "Is it true that the Comb is splitting in three?"

"And you are attempting a desperate corrective measure?"

"Are you actually using Titan's original brain enhancers?"

To evade the snake-eggs, Chrys stepped back out the doorway into the jewelry department, where she pretended to admire a display of fine namestones. But the snake-eggs followed. "You are the dynatect's protégé," insisted one, hovering at eye level.

"I'm no dynatect," muttered Chrys. "I'm just a carrier."

"An artist," said another. "Dynatects have often been painters and sculptors. You carry on that tradition."

"When is your next show?"

Chrys looked up. Her show could use publicity, especially without the Seven helping out. "The fifteenth of next month, at the Fifth Street Gallery, second level."

"And what do you paint?"

"Pyroscape." She took a breath. "I do portraits too. Portraits of micro people."

"Micro people? I don't believe our database includes that ethnic group."

"Brain enhancers. You'll see what they really look like."

That evening, her studio was spread across the news, including the portraits of Fern and of Opal's favorite. Immediately after came the latest abduction of hapless spacefarers, three that week alone. As if the masters didn't have enough addicts to lure out to their Slave World.

Chrys was appalled. She called Opal. "I'm so sorry. I shouldn't have talked to them—I had no idea how it would come out."

Opal smiled thoughtfully. "I wonder what people will make of it. Seeing our micros, scaled to human size."

She wondered. She could not guess what the Seven would think—if they even came to her show.

In the morning Xenon had unpleasant news. "I did not wish to wake you, Chrysoberyl, but late last night, I regret to say, I was vandalized."

Outside, the two caryatids holding up the balcony had their eyes gouged out. A laser had streaked across each, leaving in each nanoplastic face a blackened valley of death.

Chrys stared, feeling the numbness sink to her toes. Ever since she first heard of brain enhancers, death had stalked her. All her hard work could come to nothing, as it had for Titan.

"I should have fixed the caryatids right away," Xenon apologized, "but I wanted to leave the evidence."

"What does it matter?" Chrys asked dully. "They'll never find who did it."

"Oh, but I saw exactly who did it." The vandals' image flashed into her eyeballs. Two young men from a Great House, up the street from Garnet. The taller one had a loutish look about him, rather like her elder brother before he left home to raise his own goats and sons on the next mountain.

Andra appeared in her window. "It's a hate crime," the lawyer assured her. "An open-and-shut case."

"So we get them for defacing caryatids." While murder went unpunished.

"The boys have no previous record," Andra said. "Their father wants to settle for ten thousand credits, to keep their record clean."

"Why should we settle? Teach them a lesson."

"For a first offense, they'd get off with a warning. I'm not sure what lesson they'll learn—except to avoid getting caught."

Chrys thought it over. "Let me talk with the father."

The father's sprite wore a breastplate of lapis and jade. "My deepest apologies. A new neighbor, too; why haven't we been acquainted? You must call on us." He waved his hand, full of jeweled rings. "It was their homecoming night, you understand; all the excitement. But I've lectured them most severely and deactivated their Elysian pass for a week. I trust you'll accept our compensation."

Chrys cleared her throat. "If you don't mind, my lord, may I suggest a more useful alternative? Let the boys spend a few hours serving at the Spirit Table. Get to know their neighbors."

"An excellent idea! If it weren't for headball season; the team takes up every minute." He sighed and shook his head. "Besides, the tube stop, you know—we wouldn't want them to pick up"—he whispered—"diseases."

"Very well," said Chrys abruptly. "I'll accept your offer."

The lord waved his hand. "It's done." In Chrys's eyes, a digit increased by one.

"Since your boys have no time for charity," she added, "I'll donate the sum, in their name, to the Simian Advancement League."

His faced turned dark as his namestones before his sprite vanished.

That afternoon, Chrys took a trans-world call. To her amazement, there stood her younger brother, his face pink and his arms tan. His eyes glowed.

"Hal," she breathed.

The boy waved. "I can see you!"

She smiled. "I see you too."

"An angel visited our hill," he rushed on. "The angel brought health to all the children of the village."

From behind, her mother put her arm around his shoulder. "A very special angel. An angel of the Spirit, who always knows our need."

Chrys swallowed, her eyes too full to speak. What did the mountain people need more—their health, or their pride in their own belief? For years her mother's pride had wrestled with her own. They were one, and yet they were estranged. Chrys could reach back and help them, yet she could never go back home.

TWELVE

Aster felt her memories slipping, the molecules losing their grip and floating out into the cerebrospinal fluid. After a life of exceptional length, going on three months, her time in Eleutheria would soon end.

"Jonquil, you will have to carry on." She feared the yellow one's lack of character, but she could still lead the people, and she had a genius for design.

"Don't worry, Aster. Rose will help me."

Aster did not like leaving Eleutheria under the influence of a former master. But Rose, despite her outlandish ideas and lingering foreign accent, was an effective organizer, running a dozen councils and committees, establishing a system of social welfare. Her personal lifestyle was even more ascetic than Aster's; she ate only unsaturated hydrocarbons, and avoided any hint of scandal. "Live like her, but don't listen to her."

"Don't worry. I never listen to anyone."

"I only regret I will never live to see our next masterpiece." The creation she had dreamt of, the plans still alive in the heart of Eleutheria, and in the people of the Map of the Universe. She had seen enough of the plans to know one thing: The new creation *would have no roots, like the Comb, but would float on a vast body of water. Where such a structure could exist, she had no idea. "But you will. Remember, build for the future. For beauty, truth— and all the gods that have to dwell there."*

Chrys felt bad for Aster, the one who had helped Fern restore order, who always looked ahead for Eleutheria. She wished she had pressed Jasper sooner about his new project. But now it was too late to do more than sketch the little ring's last portrait. And with her biggest show of the year coming, she faced getting tested by Selenite, with Jonquil and a former master leading her people.

"Oh Great One, when will we return to the Underworld?" A flash of Jonquil's gold.

"Not for many generations." No distractions till after her show.

"We need new immigrants," insisted Jonquil. *"Our settled generations grow lazy."* Again already? Their generations flew so fast.

"Find the uncorrupted Enlightened Ones," added Rose. *"Bearers of the Truth."*

"Show them our portraits," countered Jonquil. *"They'll forget about Truth."*

"They won't care for your dirty pictures."

Chrys held her head in both hands. *"Behave yourselves and let me work, lest you feel the god's wrath."* Early every morning, new scenes bubbled up from her mind, demanding to be composed. Beyond single portraits, an entire cityscape of micros floated through their filamentous dwellings in the arachnoid. The shear newness of it took her breath away. Yet who but a handful of carriers would understand?

One morning she had a visitor—Lady Moraeg. "Chrys, it's been so long." Moraeg's diamonds glittered as they traveled round her neck, her curls dark except for lava tint. She embraced Chrys just like the old days.

Chrys said guardedly, "I've been here long enough."

"Oh," said Moraeg, "Carnelian and I took such a grand tour

this year, to Solaria and Urulan. We saw a real 'caterpillar,' up close. What a monster." She caught Chrys's arm. "But now it's back to work. Goodness, my dear—how well you look." Probably she had waited to see how Zircon survived.

"What wilderness is this?" flashed Jonquil. *"Can we visit?"*

"Stay dark." Chrys had warned them—why didn't they listen?

"It's almost time for your show," added Moraeg. "Can I help?"

"First take a look." The room darkened, then filled with the cityscape. Microbial wheels tumbled through the columns of arachnoid, their colors winking, their nightclubs pulsing with colored music.

Moraeg's eyes widened. "There's a planet I've never been to."

Chrys grinned. "It's inside my head."

"Is it true then? You have Titan's own brain enhancers . . . inside your head?"

"What about your own stuff? Don't you have a show too?"

"Oh, another six months." Moraeg called up her florals; carnations in baskets, lupins on the slopes of Urulan, the sort of thing you'd hang in a sitting room. Then, unexpectedly, *Wheelgrass Meadow*. Red looped petals hung from hooplike stems before a distant singing-tree.

"Our ancestral home! Beauty, imagination, excellent taste— Oh Great One, we must visit this—"

Chrys squeezed her eyes shut. *"Stay dark, or face the god's wrath."*

"Does it hurt when your eyes flash like that?"

Startled, her eyes flew open. She shook her head. "They just talk too much. But then, like, I have a million minds to draw inspiration."

Moraeg held her chin thoughtfully. "You know, I've lived a hundred years; I made one giga-credit fortune, and married another. Now I've made a second life—in art. To go for the best." She paused. "Does that trial still have openings?"

"We have a party of visitors all set to go," Jonquil insisted. *"We'll be most considerate."*

Chrys's pulse raced. "I don't know. I can tell you who to call."

"I thought you might have connections. If they need volunteers, let me know."

After her friend left, Chrys took a deep breath. Another artist on Olympus—she was thrilled, yet wary, thinking what she had gone through. As for her people . . .

"Jonquil? You must call all the elders here at once."

"I will try, Oh Great One. They are busy planning urban renewal—"

"At once. There is serious trouble."

Chrys counted the seconds until Jonquil returned. *"We are here, all thirty."*

"Rose too?"

"All of us. What is the god's wish?"

"You disobeyed me. You expressly failed to follow my commands."

"We are sorry," said Jonquil. *"We trust the God of Mercy will forgive."*

"Right now the God of Mercy is full of wrath. You will experience my wrath as an eclipse of the sun." With that, she winked the window closed. Then she closed her own eyes.

Darkness within, such as she had not known for three months. "Xenon?" she called. "Tell me when sixty seconds are up." A minute—about a week for them, should make a good eclipse. Still, it was the longest minute she ever spent. What did her people make of it? What if they went crazy, like the ancients? No sight, no sound except the pulse pounding in her ears.

At last she opened her eyes.

"The light returns! Oh Great One, we were paralyzed with fear. Even Rose was scared, although she won't admit it."

Chrys nodded at the yellow letters, satisfied.

"We praise your mercy," Jonquil added. *"We pray we never lose your sight again. We have written a list of a thousand new laws to make sure we never forget."*

One law alone would do, if only they obeyed. She sighed. *"We all need to get in shape, before the test of the Deathlord."*

Despite their new laws, Chrys grew increasingly apprehensive as the days ticked off till her testing. She tried to put it from her mind and threw herself into her painting. She was adjusting the hue and saturation of a particularly difficult foreground, when Xenon announced Selenite.

Chrys half jumped out of her skin. The painting shuddered, turning all grayish green like a hurricane. "Um, please do sit down," she urged Selenite. Xenon had his usual tea and cake laid out.

Selenite shook her head. "Sorry, I can't accept anything for testing." Her eyes narrowed. "Did Daeren ever?"

"No, of course not." Not till he'd decided to pass her on. "It's just that I think of you as a business partner."

"It couldn't be helped. Any problems you know of?"

"We're all fine."

"Please stand, I find it easier." Selenite drew very close, the red fire flashing in her eyes.

"*Beware,*" Chrys reminded her people as she accepted the transfer. "*Warn Rose and her friends.*"

"*We are ready,*" Jonquil assured her. "*We have prepared many generations for this day.*"

After what seemed an interminable time, Selenite at last nodded and relaxed in a seat. "Not bad," she allowed. "For your information, here's a list of subversives I'm passing on to the committee."

The alphanumerics scrolled down her window: reds, yellows, greens, and so on. There must have been several hundred. "You mean these are all . . ."

"They all fit one or more criteria of my screen. They go on file in our intelligence database. Didn't Daeren tell you? You have a sizable file already." She shook her head. "I always let the carrier know, for their own protection."

"I see." She clasped and unclasped her hands, feeling haunted.

"Chrys . . ." Selenite cocked her head. "You do a good job, but why do you tolerate those master sympathizers?"

"Well . . ." It was a compliment, Chrys told herself. "I was raised by true believers, and I've lived with artists. Different ideas are, like, different colors."

"People live or die by ideas."

To that, Chrys did not know what to say. She remembered something. "Do you still have a waiting list?" she ventured. "For new carriers?"

"A very long list," Selenite warned. "Tell your people they have to wait. Unauthorized transfer is a terminal offense."

"I meant, a list of humans who want to become carriers."

Selenite nodded slowly. "We're always looking for good candidates. You know our standards—you're welcome to recommend someone."

The show was packed; one could hardly get past the volcanoes. Chrys had underestimated the space required for her new large-scale compositions and had left the corridors too narrow between them. But then, no more than a handful of visitors had ever showed up before. This time, the news report must have made a difference.

Lord Garnet waved her over, gesturing toward the colored rings whose flickering filaments waved overhead. "They've finally come out—life size! Like real people!" Garnet had brought along half the financial district, all in the most discreetly expensive gray, their namestones diminutive. With them were Lord Carnelian and Lady Moraeg.

"I've never seen anything like it." Moraeg's forehead bore the Star of Ulragh, a famous gem she had acquired a generation before.

Lord Carnelian nodded, his talar and namestone like Garnet's twin. "The brain interior—it's truly pathbreaking."

Chrys had done a giant transparent brain, with the subarachnoid spaces filled in, the Cisterna Magna and the other vessels of cerebrospinal fluid where her people lived. Next to that, a close-up of an arachnoid cityscape full of the ring-shaped people. And last, she had asked Moraeg to lend *Wheelgrass,* the ring flowers of Prokaryon. The visitors looked intrigued, certainly not bored. More than a few of them had the flashing eyes of carriers. Even if the Seven did not all show up, it was a success; she was beginning to believe it. She hugged Moraeg. "Let's hope all these folks come to your show too."

"Don't forget our dinner party next week," reminded Garnet. "After your show—you promised."

Opal hurried over, a sheer gold talar flowing over her nanotex. "My colleagues from the Comb are amazed. At last they can see what's going on in my head!" She beamed with excitement. Then abruptly her face fell. "Chrys—look there—" There stood Zircon munching a handful of AZ wafers that Chrys had put with the refreshments. "You can't put those out for virgins. They'll attract masters like flies!"

"Oh my god." Chrys rushed to scoop up all the AZ, pushing her way as best she could through the crowd of perfumed talars, flashing nanotex, and fashionable vampire makeup. No Elysians, she thought with a trace of disappointment. It was too much, after all, to expect Ilia to return to primitive Valedon.

She nearly collided with Selenite. "Excuse me . . ."

Arms crossed, Selenite glared at *Endless Light*. At first glance, the cube was full of sheer white. Then the turrets of cloud appeared, light streaming through their windows upon an outstretched human form, face enraptured.

Chrys's smile froze.

"How could you?" Selenite exclaimed at last. "Of all things— it's indecent. Think of it—there could be recovering addicts here."

"Well . . ." A couple made up fashionably as vampires watched the piece politely, the broken veins painted artfully on their whitened faces. "A show has to have something controversial."

Down the hall, before the portait of Dendrobium, her eye caught lava-bright nanotex, glowing infrared, the color only she and Elysians could see. Who would wear that?

Daeren. He must have meant the color for her; to anyone else, it would look his usual black. She felt warm all over, yet confused. Angry, yet she missed him. She wove her way between the chatting visitors to reach him.

Daeren turned. "I hope things went well this week?" He held a drink, orange juice.

"You didn't tell me you keep files on 'subversives.' "

"I note a few, to keep the Committee happy."

"Selenite listed them all."

"Was it useful?"

"The blue angels—we haven't seen them in generations."

"Not now." Too many non-carriers about.

Daeren added, "Working with a new tester is an important step. You made a good transition."

"I hope you like the show."

"You've captured the essence of micro people—exactly how they appear to us." He looked to the portrait of Garnet's favorite, the ring of forest green, its filaments bending in waves, its body slowly turning and bending just slightly, as if nodding. "That's just how they look when they're happy. Before, only we could see them. But now, everyone can see them as we do." His irises flickered blue.

Jonquil flashed, *"The blue angels thank us for rescuing all those defectors."*

Praise was sweeter than any drink.

In her eye the call light blinked. It was Ilia, her sprite clothed in her talar of butterflies. "I'm so sorry to miss your Opening." The gallery director rolled her eyes. "We have a major fundraising event."

"Of course, I understand."

"However, I would like to stop by next week, if you don't mind. For a private tour."

After the Opening, Chrys basked in the attention and tried to put out of mind the fact that of the Seven, only Zircon and Moraeg had come. Her window drowned in mail, mostly congratulations, the rest quickly discarded.

One night she awoke in a blaze of light. Before her on the floor lay a body like her own, a pool of blood seeping from its gashed eyes. She screamed, until she realized it was just a sprite.

"You are entirely safe in this house," Xenon assured her. "You just need to filter hate mail."

Hate mail. She shuddered. "I don't believe in censorship."

"But you don't have to read it at night."

"Okay," she sighed, "I'll filter mail at night." The price of fame.

"On the bright side," Xenon pointed out, "look at all your new clients. You have more friends than enemies."

More work than she could handle. "But it only takes one enemy."

In the morning, at work in her studio, she got a call from an Elf. Not Ilia; an Elf lord she had never met. Not a "lord," either, she reminded herself.

"Eris Heli*shon*," the sprite introduced himself.

Chrys's jaw fell open. Eris Heli*shon* was the Guardian of Cultural Affairs, adviser to Guardian Arion Heli*shon*, and a dozen other things—including Ilia's boss. If Elysium had "lords," he'd be a big one. Yet there he was standing in her gallery, before one of the micro portraits, a virtual train of swallowtails playing out behind him. "I'm in town for the day," the Elf said, "and I happened to come across your work. I'd like to consider an acquisition. Would you have time to meet me?"

She got a talar and put on her best namestone, a cat's eye that shone like a moon. She took the lightcraft up to cross town; it bothered her less than it used to. She was a success, she told herself; a successful artist, meeting a buyer from Elysium.

They met at the gallery entrance, the great transparent brain shimmering just inside. About average height for an Elf, Eris had an air of complete self-possession, rather like Guardian Arion. To her surprise, his eyes flashed blue rings. The look was particularly striking amid his pale, cream-colored features. "I'm a carrier," he told her, just like Ilia. "Strain *Coelicolor.*"

"Why, that's blue angels," Chrys exclaimed.

"Indeed. You know the strain?"

"Blue angels," flashed Jonquil. *"We've never met blue angels outside the Lord of Light. How interesting."*

She nearly touched his hand, but remembered that Elves avoided contact in public. "Do they ever visit? I mean, if you don't mind."

"Certainly; how civilized of you. You needn't worry," he added, "I direct the testing of all the Elysian carriers."

"Of course, I understand." Like Andra—the Elves had their own chief tester.

"*I'll receive visitors,*" said Jonquil, "*and Rose will lead our delegation.*"

She winced, hoping Rose would leave a good impression. "*Behave as you would for the Thundergod.*" She held out the transfer patch. Eris took it, then returned it, carefully avoiding her fingers.

"Won't you tell me something about your work?" he asked. "Especially the portraits."

She took him through the portraits, explaining the background of each, and their human hosts.

"Extraordinary," Eris exclaimed. "Simply unprecedented." Behind him the virtual butterflies played across the floor and back through the doorway. "I keep telling Arion, we need to educate our citizens about the micro people."

"*These blue angels seem rather inquisitive,*" Jonquil told her. "*They keep looking into everything.*"

"*So, they're curious. Maybe they've never been outside an Elf before.*"

They passed the arachnoid cityscape, then abruptly came upon *Endless Light*. Chrys stopped and swallowed.

"Yes," observed Eris. "May I ask what experience inspired this one?"

She looked away. "Just a fantasy. Experimental."

"I see." Thoughtfully he regarded the towering vision of light and cloud. "This was the one I particularly fancied."

Startled, she looked at him. "To purchase?" She had priced it double its worth, intending to keep it in her hands.

"If it's still for sale."

"Sure. I keep a studio copy, if you don't mind."

"Of course." He turned to her, his pupils flashing brightly in his white face. "Tell me . . . have you anything else 'experimental'? Too controversial to show, perhaps?" He smiled. "You know, we Elysians have sophisticated tastes."

"Well, I pretty much show what I've got." She thought it over. "There's one piece you'd like, but I'm still working on it." She found a blank stage and called down *Children Merging*. She thought she had got the merging part okay with Jonquil, but the division into three still appeared off center.

As Eris watched, his face intensified. His cheeks flushed, then whitened again. "Yes," he said as if to himself. "We must have that."

"I'll let you know when it's finished."

He stiffened, then seemed to recollect himself. "Excuse me. Thanks, do let me know. I believe I've taken enough of your time."

"Oh Great One," flashed Jonquil as he was about to leave. *"Remember our guests. And Rose—she has yet to return."*

Chrys raised her hand. "Your people—I'm so sorry. Let me return them."

Eris slowly turned. "Of course. Thanks for remembering."

She put the transfer at her neck, but for some reason Jonquil took longer than usual to signal it was ready. At last she held the patch out to him.

The Elf did not take it. Something told her he expected her to place it directly at his neck, the way Valan carriers did. She did so, used to it by now.

"I appreciate your local custom," he said. "I hope we'll be seeing much more of each other. I expect to add many of your works to my collection."

Eccentric, she thought, but then she'd never had an Elf patron. So many inquiries were coming in now, she barely had time to paint. *"What did you think?"* she quizzed Rose and Jonquil on the way back to her studio. *"How were his blue angels?"*

"Slimy," said Rose. *"Slimy degenerates."*

Chrys sighed. Poor exiled Rose never had much good to say of her bourgeois comrades.

"They wouldn't be my first choice of visitors," added Jonquil.

"They tried to keep us there," insisted Rose. *"Tried to make us miss our return."*

Why would they do that, Chrys wondered.

"God of Mercy," called Jonquil, *"we have a problem. We discovered three blue angels who failed to get out in time."*

"On purpose," said Rose. *"I'm sure it was on purpose. They're up to no good."*

"They say they just failed to understand our call. They flash a different dialect."

This was a nuisance. *"Do they have to go back? Let them settle with you. Enhance your gene pool."*

"They have to go back. They insist."

"Good riddance," added Rose. *"I wouldn't want them here."*

Chrys frowned, puzzled. *"Let them speak to me."*

"They refuse," said Jonquil. *"They say we'll be in big trouble if they don't get back."*

Refusing to talk to a god—she did not care for that. But then, if Eris were the Elysian equivalent of Andra, his blue angels might mean business. She had better try to reach him.

To her surprise, she reached him immediately, in his ship on the two-hour trip back to the Elf moon. "I'm so glad you called," he told her. "We were terribly concerned; it was my fault entirely they got left behind. Look, I keep another ship docked at Iridis; a first-class rig, you'll find. Why don't you take it and meet me in Helicon?"

A new version of the oldest line ever. Chrys crossed her arms. "I'm rather behind today. Couldn't you turn around and stop back?"

"I'm afraid I have a cabinet meeting. But afterward, I'll show you my collection and take you to the best restaurant in Helicon."

"Great Host," called Rose. *"We've found another couple of stowaways—hiding among the neurons."*

She hoped her smile remained steady. "Very well, Citizen," she said smoothly, "I'll meet you in Helicon."

As soon as he was out, she blinked at the purple button.

But Selenite was on another call, and Andra and Daeren were both out of town. That was odd. There had to be someone on call, always. She started to call the hospital, but she remembered how the worm-faced medics had treated her before Daeren arrived.

"Jonquil, search the cortex as best you can. Whoever you find, put them all in dendrimers."

In her window a sprite appeared, wearing a talar and train of butterflies. Chrys jumped, thinking it was Eris. But it was Daeren, at the spaceport terminal on his way to Elysium, dressed like an Elf. "I just checked my calls," he said. "Did you reach someone?"

She hesitated. He looked so official, off to lobby Elysians for micro rights. "I'll manage."

"It's okay," he said, "my flight was delayed. What's up?"

"An Elf visitor left his people with me, and they want to go back. But—"

Daeren moved toward her, his face looming large. "Who?"

"Eris Heli*shon*."

"Stay where you are. Sartorius will get there."

"I don't get it," she exclaimed. "Eris is an Elf, not a vampire."

"He's worse."

Within minutes Doctor Sartorius was there, and Daeren himself. Still in his talar, like Eris turned dark; Chrys felt disconcerted. "It's all right," Daeren assured her. "Your people probably found most of them. But we'll need to do a thorough search."

Sartorius extended a tendril. "The invaders could be hiding anywhere, even the marrow of your bones. To find them, we have to scan your whole system for arsenic. But the scanners can't tell one micro from another. So tell yours to tag themselves with this molecule." A molecule of about ten atoms appeared, rotating before her eyes. "Those who wear this tag will be passed over."

"And the others?"

"Don't think about it," said Daeren quietly. "Give your people something to help them feel better."

They must be horrified, she realized. She took an AZ. *"Don't be afraid,"* she told Jonquil. *"You did well; you will all live."* She turned to Daeren. "I want to know," she insisted. "I want to know what's going on, and how that damned Elf could get me in trouble."

"Andra told him to stay out of Iridis."

"Why didn't you report him?"

Daeren exchanged a look with Sartorius. "He's the brother of Arion."

"Brother? Elves don't have brothers."

"Not genetically." Elysians were conceived by computer, according to calculated genetic makeup, and brought to term in vitro. "He and Arion were born the same year, in the same *shon*. They were raised together; he has Arion's complete trust."

"But what's wrong with him?"

Sartorius's tendril extended and tightened around her scalp. "He's a slave of a kind we've not seen before. None of the outward signs; his masters avoid that. He began as a carrier, but the masters took him over, exterminating his own people, perhaps without him even realizing."

"Nonsense—he must have known."

"They could have altered his memory," said Daeren. "Or perhaps he colluded with them."

"Why?"

"Whenever he passes on the strain, they grant him power over their next host. He can use people as he pleases."

She could have gone to his ship and been trapped. Her hair stood on end. "Why take over a carrier? Why not a defenseless host?"

Sartorius said, "Elysium is free of disease and crime. All Elysians are scanned daily for any pathogens or signs of criminality. So, masters could never take hold in a micro-free host. Their only option would be to mimic a safe population, within a known carrier."

"The strains we usually see in Valedon aren't smart enough to do that," added Daeren. "This is a new, virulent strain."

"And he tests other carriers," Chrys added. "He's like Andra, their chief tester. He could infect them all." Chrys looked up in horror. "What about Ilia? Is she—"

"Ilia gets tested by Andra."

Chrys recalled Ilia's first greeting, "Give my best to Andra." The Elf gallery director actually came out to primitive Iridis for testing. "So Ilia knows."

"She must suspect something. The smart ones do. But we can't accuse him without proof."

"What about the micros he gave me—aren't they proof?"

Sartorius said, "I've typed their DNA; I'm sure they would match his. But would he provide accurate data? By now, surely he has confederates."

False carriers, secretly serving Enlightenment.

"Besides," Daeren added, "how could we prove where we got your strain? It's starting to show up here in Iridis. Among the elite; people who think they're too smart for addiction."

The doctor's tendrils withdrew, whipping back with a snap. "I need to go, I have cases waiting. You're clear, Chrysoberyl. We only found two that your people missed."

"That's pretty good," said Daeren. "Better than . . ." He did not finish. Reflectively, he watched the post-shaped doctor descend past the watching caryatids.

"Let us visit the true blue angels," her people insisted. *"They need to hear about this."*

Chrys sighed and handed Daeren a patch. Then she leaned back, gazing despondently at the gargoyles Xenon had placed along the ceiling. "Don't say anything—I feel stupid enough already."

"Don't feel too bad," Daeren told her. "Eris tried the same with me."

She stared at him. "You?"

In his talar, Daeren looked different, somehow, more worldly. "He came to see me last year. His people offered me everything— any human to control, they said. He would soon control all Elysium, so why should I not have Valedon?"

She blinked. "For what price?"

"To be their slave, of course, and send others regularly to Endless Light." He added levelly, "And of course, their host wanted the same thing of me as of you."

Chrys shuddered. "How could anyone—"

"Eris was like me, once. You never know how low you can go." He turned to her. "You painted *Endless Light*—what would you give for it?"

Her scalp crawled, remembering. "What did you tell him?"

The veins stood out in his neck. "I should have played along. Instead, I offered him this." He held up a green wafer, the hundredfold dose of AZ they gave slaves to stun their masters and help turn themselves in.

"And then?"

"He left. With a dozen of my visitors." Daeren shook his head slowly. "There was no way to get them back. They have no rights." He added, "I hope they died quickly, but I doubt it. We had to change all our codes and procedures."

Still dazed, she thought it over. "What's wrong with the Elves? Why don't they do something?"

"The one Elf leader who took micros seriously retired on Solaria twenty years ago. After a thousand years in government, she found micros more interesting than human people."

Chrys looked at the ceiling, where Xenon kept trying out new gargoyles. "Maybe too interesting for their own good. Maybe Elves wouldn't know disease and crime if they saw it. Why didn't you warn me?"

"We'll have to warn our carriers not to trust Elves," he sighed. "But when Arion hears, he'll be incensed. We can't afford to lose him; he's still our most open-minded supporter."

"What if Eris infects him?"

"Arion's not a carrier; he gets scanned for arsenic twice a day. He knows the danger, but he'll never believe it's Eris. Not till Elves start disappearing to the Slave World." Daeren looked at her curiously. "I'm still amazed that Eris took the risk to come after you. Andra has a warrant for him; if she were in town, she would have hauled him in the minute his ship touched down. He planned well." Daeren leaned closer. "What did Eris want from you? I mean, aside from the obvious."

She rolled her eyes. "Maybe we both should have picked 'Distinguished.'"

He gave a quick smile. "I've tried a more mature look, but it intimidates the Palace lords. When you sell outrageous ideas, they listen longer to a face that pleases the eye."

That figured. She herself didn't mind gazing at him, but wasn't about to admit it. "Eris came for my art. He bought *Endless Light*."

"I see."

"He really wanted this." She held up a viewcoin of the children merging.

Daeren's face changed, almost like the face of *Endless Light*. His lips parted and his eyes seemed to gaze far away. "Of course, his masters would want that. Even my angels beg me to keep looking."

She offered him the coin. "It's yours."

"Sorry, I can't take gifts."

"It's not a gift—just a viewcoin. It's, like, advertising."

He smiled. "Okay, I'll help you advertise." Taking the coin, he faced her again, blue sparks in his eyes. "Chrys, I hope you know that you can always call on me—not just professionally, as a friend. Whatever you or your people ever need, just ask. Okay?"

"Well, thanks," she said, rather surprised. "I wish I could help you—you'll need it."

He hesitated, as if struggling with something. "Andra wants you to help, too. She wants you on the committee."

"What?" She gripped her chair till the nanoplast melted in. "You can't be serious."

"You have the nerve, and your people are smart as hell. They saw through Eris in a minute."

"Rose did. You said she'd do me in," Chrys reminded him.

He shrugged. "We have to live with double agents."

She looked away. "So that's what you wanted—"

"No," he snapped. "*I* don't want you to do it." He sounded as if he were arguing with someone else. "I want you to keep making art, and beautiful buildings. I don't want you to spend your time pulling slaves out of hell, only to see them run back the first chance they get."

"*Oh Great One,*" flashed Jonquil, "*we will join the cause. We will fight to preserve our way of life.*"

"*And checkmate the false purveyors of Enlightenment.*"

Chrys took a deep breath and let it out slowly. If even Elves succumbed to the brain plague, what chance did she have? What gods would help humans?

THIRTEEN

The Thundergod sent judges to train Eleutherians to judge the gods themselves. But their transfer took several microbial "hours," while the one god reached out to the other.

To pass the time, Jonquil and Rose played chess. Jonquil was not a bad player, but her mind tended to wander to the Comb, the latest iteration of the torsional stress problem, or to art—how to inspire the god to ever more daring creations. Jonquil's own body had aged and stiffened too much for the athletics of passion, but she poured her dreams into the divine arts.

"Your move," flashed Rose. The micro chessboard curled over in a ring, so the pieces lined up in circular rows.

Jonquil's filament stuck to one protein piece, then set it down, replacing another.

Rose emitted a molecule of disgust.

"What's wrong?" asked Jonquil. "I trade a knight for a bishop."

"And doubled pawns. My rook swings around to take one. Hopeless," Rose added to herself. "I'm moving to the wizards, see if I don't."

Rose had made this threat so often that Jonquil no longer wor-

ried. "Now Rose," she said, emitting placating pheromones. "You know I couldn't manage without you." Flattery, she had learned, was the best way to get around Rose—and to gain information. "Those judges—you really stand up to them, with all you know of the masters."

"No host ever found Endless Light, save by choice."

"Now, Rose, let's not be naïve—"

"Come, who's naïve? Humans choose the path of Enlightenment. Alas, too many are betrayed; nonetheless, they choose."

"But the slaves who steal ships—"

"I tell you it isn't so." Rose refused to believe that the master-controlled slaves stole humans out of spaceships. "The host always makes a choice. Though we make the choice easy. I'll show you how—"

Rose stopped as the optic fibers flashed. The judges had arrived. They came, rolling sedately through the arachnoid, their filaments brushing the columns of fibroblast. They exuded authority and shrewdness, though they tasted a bit pompous. Jonquil emitted molecules of respect, with a hint of Eleutherian pleasures after their work was done.

"Your people have been chosen for an extraordinary mission," Judge-390 told Jonquil. "Your mission is to save the gods themselves from destruction."

"Eleutheria is honored to be of service." How well Jonquil remembered the false blue angels, and the great "passing over." They had just commemorated the event's twenty-fifth anniversary.

Rose added, "Salvation of the gods has always been my mission." Jonquil brushed her filaments, flickering, "Be dark!"

"All participants in this service must apply for security clearance." Judge-390 produced a long chain of hydrocarbon, with many complex side branches, each with data tags to be filled in. A similar chain, about twice as long, Jonquil noticed, was presented to Rose. Much annoyed, Rose caught the molecular paperwork in her filaments and hauled it off.

The judge approached Jonquil alone. "Has the double agent served you faithfully?"

As far as Jonquil knew, Rose had done little worse than preach "enlightenment" to a few followers. "She set up food service for the homeless. The Council grumbled at the expense, but after all, even the gods have soup kitchens."

"She tells us nothing. Have you learned much?"

"She showed us how the masters attack the brain, precisely which neurons they flood with dopamine."

"Did she say how they locate starships to hijack?"

"She denied that masters take slaves by force, but she's starting to reveal the truth. She also helped us figure out how the false blue angels hid from our taste. They engineered their own genes to produce the surface proteins of microglia and astrocytes—making themselves taste like human cells."

"The false blue angels—most unsettling," the judge agreed. "Report everything you hear. Meanwhile, we shall teach you our photo codes: the patterns of light that identify you as security, and other patterns to help you pass falsely as masters. You must keep these codes to yourself. Above all, never tell Rose."

"Chrys, imagine you're the plague." Andra's command projected through the long, twisting branches of the neurons, simulated at human size. "You've just entered a new brain, and you want to master it without alarming the host. So you cross the blood-brain barrier, taking care to avoid activating microglia, and you find your way to the medial forebrain." Andra patted the cell body of a neuron, then her hand traced an undulating branch till its end, where it made a translucent cup. "The axon ends at a synapse." The cup lit up, expanding, as small bubbles full of dopamine oozed out into the synapse. The bubbles joined the receiving terminal of the next neuron. "Dopamine crosses the synapse to activate a neuron of the pleasure center."

Chrys looked over the tangle of axons, each ended in a cup at the synapse of the next neuron. An intriguing pattern; she sketched the weblike network in her window.

"Every kind of pleasurable stimulus fills the synapse briefly,"

Andra continued. "Food, sex, or beautiful paintings." Chrys kept her face straight. "But micros can make their own dopamine and put it right into the synapse—and keep the cup full."

"I see." She remembered the vampire's attack, and the rush of pleasure, the glimpse of Endless Light. "What's wrong with, like, feeling extra good?"

The projected axons played across Andra's nanotex. "What's wrong with any drug? Cocaine and other drugs overload dopamine, but very crudely, with obvious side effects. Psychoplast, programmed drug dispensers, do so more cleanly—and still destroy lives. Micros do it intelligently." Andra pointed to the synapse at the neuron's branched terminal. "When the synapse overloads repeatedly, the body gradually steps down its own dopamine. You don't notice right away; you just think, every time you obey the masters, it feels so good. Eventually, you can no longer feel good at all—except from the micros. Your will is replaced by their own."

She wondered what Rose would say to that, but Rose and Jonquil were busy training with the judges. "Why does it work that way? I mean, like, why can't Plan Ten make us feel good all the time?"

"Humans didn't evolve to feel good. We evolved to survive and reproduce. The pleasure pathway evolved to make us repeat acts that raise our odds, such as eating rich food, or having sex." Andra pointed to the long axon, sending its signal to the synapse. "Once an act is completed, the neuron needs to turn off its signal as soon as possible, to get ready for the next one."

Chrys thought it over. "Why do I enjoy colors? I feel like heaven, studying a beautiful painting. That doesn't help me survive."

Andra nodded. "Our color sense evolved to tell good fruit from bad."

"Picking ripe bananas? You mean we're all still, like, simians?"

She looked Chrys in the eye, her irises pulsing violet, unnerving in the dark. "Simians in nanotex."

The model brain receded, revealing a spacious office atop the hospital with a view across Center Way. The sun glinted off the towers and threw a shaft across the large Sardish carpet, ending at

Andra's desk, which was the size of a dining-room table. A caryatid glided forward to offer tea. "Of course," said Andra, "even the masters have their 'civilization.' More subtle strains, common in high-status hosts, give only a touch of bliss now and then. Without their host realizing, they reward little things, like forgetfulness; forgetting one's own name, for just an instant, then longer. . . ."

Chrys frowned. "How could you forget your own name, no matter how good it felt?"

The chief stared hard. "How long is your name?" she barked. "How many letters?"

She blinked, startled. For some reason, the letters swam before her eyes. She counted on her fingers. "Ten. I mean, eleven." Seeing Andra's look, she protested, "I was never good at math."

"No one knows her name as well as she thinks." Andra's voice was ice. "Remember that." The armchair molded to the curves of the hospital's top malpractice attorney as she took her tea. "Virulent or subtle, the masters always need one thing: arsenic. A nutrient essential for reproduction."

"So then you go to the Underworld for ace?"

Across the desk flitted pages of torts and memos, which Andra ignored. "You run to the plague bar. Or you resist, at first, but find your steps taking you there. Your first time, the bar doesn't charge much."

"And then?"

Andra nodded slowly. "You'll soon see for yourself."

The usual crowd of patrons and octopods filled the Underworld, dodging the precancerous root tips of banks and brokerages. "You'll get to know slaves on sight," Daeren told her, "the off-gazing eyes, the little things that tip you off. And more important, your people need to know the masters." He and the worm-faced medic veered around a stand of nanoflowers, branches that rose and blossomed before the eyes of customers. "Once your micros know what to look for, they can practice testing—starting with us."

Testing the blue angels. That would be a switch.

A simian boy in a ragged red coat held out a tin cup, imitating a street player's monkey. Playing to the stereotype, for a few credits. Oddly, the boy reminded her of Hal. For a moment she wished she could take him home. A crazy thought. Little boys were not cats, and the last thing she was ready to be was a mother. Chrys frowned. "Your chief says we're all simians," she told Daeren. "I bet she'd never set her clean feet down here."

"Andra does the slave ships."

Chrys's jaw dropped. "She does what?"

"Flashing the photo codes, she passes for a slave. She's reached several substations."

"She's nuts."

"We're mapping the substations, to zero in on the Slave World." Beside Daeren, the medic waved his face worms as if signaling.

Chrys nodded thoughtfully. "The Slave World—we could nip it at the source."

"Don't you get ideas," Daeren warned. "After tonight, you keep clear of slaves, you hear? You'll have enough to do testing carriers."

She rolled her eyes. "Not to worry." Two more portrait clients visiting the next day, then the Hyalite dinner. At this rate she'd never paint her own ideas again.

They reached the Gold of Asragh. Daeren nodded to the medic, who waited outside while he and Chrys went in. The slave bar was now out of sight behind a curtain; must be laying low this week. She followed Daeren through the curtain, blinking as her eyes adjusted to the dark. Behind the bar stood the man who replaced Saf, the slave who had offered Chrys her masters the night of the Seven's last show. Where was Saf now, Chrys wondered. The Slave World? Where was Endless Light?

Daeren leaned over and put his arm on the slave's shoulder. "Jay, I'd like you to meet a friend of mine."

Chrys forced a smile. *"Remember your codes."*

"We're flashing now." Jonquil flashed the codes from her eyes to put the masters at ease.

The new slave, Jay, had a pleasing smile and a bit of a simian brow, like a salesman you'd find around level twelve. He faced her but his eyes could not meet hers for more than a moment. He smiled and put a patch at his neck. "Can we help you? Ace on the house."

Daeren touched his arm. "That's okay, Jay."

Chrys accepted the transfer, then returned it. Her people had to see first-hand how the masters operated. But what if they weren't allowed back?

"The masters are visiting," Jonquil told her. *"Full of viruses and parasites. Appalling condition."*

Her scalp crawled. The diseases that could spread through those microneedles; she hoped Plan Ten could handle it. She gave Daeren a doubtful glance. Daeren stroked Jay's arm in a friendly way. "How's life?"

Jay grinned. "Have all the ace I need. Pass on the little friends to whoever wants them." Something was missing about Jay, Chrys realized. His chest was blank—no namestone. Just empty nanotex.

"How's your wife?" asked Daeren. "Still hoping to move up level?"

Nothing registered in Jay's face.

"You remembered your wife last week," Daeren said quietly.

At the crack in the curtain a shadow passed. Someone stood just outside. A glimpse of an aristocratic profile—Lord Zoisite. The minister of justice, the board member of the Comb.

Horrified, Chrys got up and moved back several seats. Zoisite seemed to ignore the curtain, as if pausing idly on his way to the show. But Jay had slipped out from the bar to pass him something, hidden in his palm. Zoisite did not even look at the slave, but simply passed on.

"Daeren," Chrys whispered hoarsely, "we have to do something!"

Daeren looked down. "The Palace knows the minister has a problem."

"But—"

Jay grinned. "He sure pays well. We double the rate every time, and still he pays. At this rate, he'll finance our whole operation."

She glared at the slave before she caught herself, but Jay did not seem to notice. His gaze shifted to the next customer.

A pretty young woman with blond curls and a scent of jasmine about her, the kind of look Chrys had once envied. The woman's eyes widened as she caught the bar. "Jay, can you help me?" Her head tilted wistfully. "It's awful soon again, I know. But you'll help."

"Sure thing, Per. Twelve hundred will do it."

Her lips parted, and her eyes shifted the way people look at their credit line. "That's a bit steep. Isn't it?" she added, as if she couldn't recall what she'd paid before.

Jay shook his head. "Ace is scarce. We got raided last week." The Palace had sent in the octopods and slapped a fine on Gold of Asragh.

"I'm just fifty short," pleaded Per. "Won't it do?"

He nodded at her neck. "That little stone."

The young blonde fingered her namestone, a lovely round peridot. She slipped it casually between her fingers. Chrys watched, her heart pounding. She looked at Daeren, but he said nothing.

The fingers tightened around the chain, then loosened. The stone fell onto the counter. Jay's hand replaced it with a pill. She swallowed it, then sank into a chair. Her eyes defocused, entranced by a magical vision. Embarrassed, Chrys looked away. From outside lilted the first chords of the caterpillar dancers.

"Char," Jay called to Chrys suddenly. "Something for you."

Chrys drew back, having no interest in ace.

"The transfer," prompted Jonquil. *"Our delegation needs to return."*

Chrys accepted the patch, relieved to get her people back, though repulsed at the thought of more viruses.

"Great Host, you must see these people," Rose told her. *"They are truly enlightened."*

"Enlightened extortionists," Chrys blinked back.

"How do you know? The Enlightened only lack what your world cares for most: Money."

"What the devil do they need money for? They took that woman's last credit, down to her namestone."

"What's in a name, when you lack for arsenic? Where our

people first evolved, arsenic was the dust of the world. Here, your world sets a price, and keeps it from us."

Chrys blinked, confused.

"To starve for arsenic," Rose continued, *"the proteins contorting, ripping themselves out of your cell—you cannot imagine a worse hell."*

The young woman seemed to have wakened. Her eyes cast back and forth, her fingers flitting nervously. Daeren moved to sit by her. "You're Peridot," he said, emphasizing her full name. "What's your line of work, Peridot?"

"Account manager at Bank Iridium."

"You were, until they let you go."

Peridot shrugged, and her eyes half closed. Chrys felt her chest tighten.

"What will happen next week when you come back?"

"So many generations." Thinking only like a micro, Chrys realized with horror.

"You'll have no credit left," Daeren told her, "and no more namestone. What then?"

Peridot leaned back, her hands pressing the table as if to push away. "What do you know?"

"You could get your job back," Daeren told her. "Whatever else you've lost—your apartment, your family—"

Her face twisted in sudden pain, her head casting about like a puppet on strings. "I've got to go."

Chrys raised a hand. "Wait—" She caught up to the woman at the curtain. "Don't you understand? You'll end up a vampire."

Peridot frowned. "Who are you? I'll call the octopods."

"Just wait a bit. Look—" Chrys held out a viewcoin. It was her precious Fern, the luminous green filaments twinkling about truth and beauty.

Peridot's eyes widened as she stared. Her hand lifted, trembling, as if to touch what she saw before her. A ring of gold glimmered faintly around her iris.

"They want to visit—hurry," urged Jonquil.

Chrys offered her a transfer. "We mean no harm to your . . . little friends. Let us help you."

Peridot twisted a curl of hair between her fingers. As if in a daze, she placed the transfer patch at her neck, then gave it back. She shuddered all over, as if with some internal struggle. With a last hint of jasmine, she disappeared out the curtain.

Daeren whispered, "There was nothing you could do. She hasn't yet lost enough."

"But . . ."

"*She left defectors,*" Jonquil announced. "*Let them stay.*"

"*Refugees,*" added Rose. "*Starved—oppressed by your Olympian hosts.*"

"*They were backward and ignorant. Thoughtless—destroying their own environment.*"

"*Eking out a desperate existence as best they could.*"

Chrys shut her eyes. "*Be dark, you both.*" She reopened them to see Daeren nodding at her viewcoin. "Good work, Chrys," he said. "All those defectors you encouraged."

"But she left!" That lost woman, without even a namestone, ending up in a ditch somewhere. Chrys could not bear to think of it.

"Be glad for those who stayed."

The defectors. Would they be like Rose?

"Your portrait really reached them," he added. "Could you show it to Jay?"

Reluctantly, Chrys followed Daeren back to the bar.

"Jay," Daeren called, "did you know Chrys is an artist? An artist for the 'people.' "

Jay stared at the vision from the viewcoin. For the first time the grin left his face. "Come," he announced suddenly. "Come show."

Daeren's jaw tightened. He hesitated, but at last followed Jay back through a doorway, down a dark, descending hall. The songs of the caterpillars receded behind them.

A dim light revealed two men and a woman, studying a holostage full of stellar coordinates. They turned toward the new-comers, their faces watchful, yet somehow incurious. Broken veins betrayed their status as late-stage slaves. Their hair was cut crudely, and their bodies smelled stale.

Daeren kept glancing backward at the passage. He regretted his idea, Chrys suspected. Trying to steady her stomach, she held out the viewcoin to one of the men.

Pallid circles lit up his eyes like dusty lightbulbs. Then the unkempt creature snatched the viewcoin from her hand. Chrys jumped back as the others all crowded around, their eyes ringed with off-white glow.

"The Leader!" exclaimed Rose. *"The Leader of Endless Light. These hosts know and serve her—"*

"Let's get out," whispered Daeren. "Back off, very slowly."

Slowly their steps carried them backward till they reached the dark passage. Turning, Chrys broke into a run, stumbling blindly up and out past the bar until she caught herself, outside the curtain. She blinked in the light, the distant music from the night's show swirling in her ears.

"It's okay, Chrys." Daeren pressed her arm reassuringly. "You did well. Your people learned more than enough."

"Who were those . . ."

"The crew of a slave ship."

After her show, Chrys had promised to dine with Garnet and Jasper at the Hyalite House. Like Olympus, two rows of caryatids stretched out front. These, however, were solid gold. The eyes in the golden heads watched Chrys as she passed between them with Opal and Selenite.

The caryatids culminated at an enormous golden door. The door was molded into scenes from across Valan history, in each of which a Lord of Hyalite had played some crucial part, from opening trade with the Ocean Moon to colonizing Prokaryon. Jutting out from the door, a cornucopia spilled out gemstones in intricate settings.

The door announced, "The Lords of Hyalite await your pleasure."

Opal nudged Chrys. "You have to pick something, else the door won't open."

Chrys eyed the cornucopia warily. In her experience, nothing of value came for free.

"Please," begged the door. "I'm so overburdened; won't you lift a bit of weight?"

Opal laughed, and Chrys found it hard not to smile. She picked out a trinket of black-flecked amber.

"The dearest of the lot; a fossil of an insect, long extinct, from a world long gone. The only specimen of its kind; worth the east wing of the Institute for Natural History."

"Then the Institute shall have it."

The golden tracery melted inward, revealing the patrician Lord Garnet. "My apologies," said Garnet smoothly, "the door likes to have a bit of fun. We must teach him better manners." Far above ran the ceiling, a barrel vault of electric blue. Songbirds sang and trilled. Behind Chrys the golden door slipped away; in fact, she realized, the four of them were traveling smoothly down the cavernous hall.

"All the Palace is buzzing at your exhibit, Chrys," Garnet exclaimed, touching her hand for visitors. "And you've joined the Committee. Such an honor to have you dine with us."

"Our nightclubs expect lots of business this year," observed Jonquil.

The entrance to the dining hall was a towering arch of sapphires set in mother-of-pearl. Below stood Lord Jasper, the crag of his simian brow most impressive above his tall straight form, his sleeves extending majestically as he raised a goblet of wine. A map stone covered nearly the full breadth of his chest.

"The Map of the Universe—God of Mercy, will we hear this year about our next great work?"

"I don't know. I will ask," she promised.

The dining was arranged symposium style, each guest reclining before a jewel-encrusted table attended by golden servers. Recalling the Olympian servers, Chrys tried to look away from them altogether, but this proved harder than she expected. She had a better idea.

The sound system connected all the far-spaced guests in intimate conversation. "I don't believe the sentients can get away with it, do you?" A Board member addressed another guest, the worm-faced engineer with the emeralds. "A new Elysian city—the first in ten centuries—run entirely by sentients?" Elves do this, Elves do that, thought Chrys. No matter how highborn you were, there was always someone higher yet to cluck about.

A server bowed, setting out a turkey-sized tray of sculpted hearts, layered pastries, vegetables carved into forms too lovely to eat. Chrys wondered how to take food properly while reclining. Her long hair fell across her face, and her first sip of nectar ended up on the floor, where a legless beetle scurried to mop it up.

"Don't miss the calamari," announced Garnet, "and the sole en croute. Shipped in fresh from L'li, and from Urulan." Shipped across the light-years from two different worlds, when a synthesizer could have done as well.

"Just take a bite," came Opal's whisper, artfully transmitted across the room. "You can expect a dozen more courses."

Chrys eyed the tray regretfully, thinking how Sister Kaol could use the remains. The next course was an entire tureen of soup, its rising steam carrying enough herbs to transport you to the very court of Urulan.

"When I last toured Urulan . . ." The melodious voice of Lord Zoisite. Chrys startled, and another little servo had to scurry out to mop up her soup. A slave, she told herself. The Palace minister of justice is a plague-ridden slave—and nobody gives a damn.

"*Great Host. When do we return to help our starving brethren?*" Rose had importuned her thus every hour or so, since they left the Underworld. "*You feed the starving gods,*" insisted Rose. "*Why can't we feed starving Enlightened Ones? A few grams of arsenic would cover everyone for a year.*"

"*And enslave us all.*" Still, Chrys found herself wondering, if Lord Zoisite could get away with "enlightenment," why shouldn't others? Was microbial dopamine any more immoral than serving a meal ten times bigger than anyone could possibly eat?

"Why Jasper," called Garnet, watching Chrys, "I do believe one of our guests has an eye for you."

Chrys looked up innocently. Every server in the hall was a golden cast of Jasper, the eyes two caverns beneath his majestic brow.

Jasper laughed long and hard. "There's a first, my dear," he told Garnet. "Usually it's you they set their eyes on." Putting down his glass, his fingers fluttered. He turned to Chrys. "I hope, my dear, your people are pleased to develop the Comb. Not too tedious, I trust?"

She decided to take the plunge. "We are most pleased to maintain that great monument," she said. "But my people long for their next project. Some waited forty generations, and died still hoping."

Jasper nodded sagely. "People must wait upon the gods."

By the twelfth course, the golden servers started strolling with harp and theremin, while the guests rose to stretch. Chrys shook her legs, unaccustomed to reclining so long.

Alone, Jasper caught up with her. His fingers curled around a pipe of inlaid wood, balanced against his short thumb. The pipe lifted to smoke, keeping his Plan Ten anti-cancer nanos at work, but he looked more distinguished than ever. Then he removed the pipe. "Chrys, we've something to show you." The hallway carried them to a holostage large enough for a lecture hall. With his pipe Jasper pointed.

An ocean of sun-speckled turquoise. Out of the waves rose a pearly dome of immense proportions, full of elaborate tessellation. A city-sphere of Elysium; not Helicon, the capital she would recognize, but one of the other eleven. Perhaps Papilion, center of the arts, home of Ilia and Yyri? Or Anaeon, known for scholars and philosophers?

"Silicon. The future city of Elysium." Jasper's voice vibrated with pride. "For a thousand years, there were but a dozen. Now, at last, will rise the thirteenth."

"It matches our plans—exactly!" flashed Jonquil.

"Down to the fenestration. . . ." The faintest of lines revealed an elaborate pattern of hexagonal panes.

"If only Aster had lived to see. Does it please you, Great One?"

Chrys regarded the dome thoughtfully. *"It's lovely. Like all Elf cities, a pearl floating upon the sea."*

"Silicon will be NOTHING like other cities. You'll see." Jonquil was unusually vehement.

"We have revised the plans substantially, in recent generations," agreed Rose.

Chrys found her voice. "A . . . whole city?"

Jasper said, "My firm put in a bid for Silicon. The plans for our bid were drawn by Titan—that is, Eleutheria. We were awaiting the client's response, when—" He shrugged delicately. With sudden insight Chrys realized the true reason Eleutherians had called Titan "blind"—an omnipotent god who failed to foresee his own end. Little did they know, or perhaps they dared not think, that all the gods were blind.

A new floating city. Her eyelids fluttered as she tried to come to grips with it. "Don't the Elves limit their population? Why do they need another city?"

"Not a city for humans. For sentients."

A city for sentients. That had made the news, back when she used to listen. She put up her hands and shook her head. "Saints and angels— Why would sentients hire microbes?"

Jasper nodded. "Sentients have complex attitudes toward their human progenitors. Yes, they want to do things their own way; and yet, they want to be seen as having nothing but the best, even the best of what passes for human taste. Of course, Silicon will be built by sentients, thousands of them; but the overall aesthetic design . . ." His pipe puffed reflectively. "Your people say they have revised their design. Interesting. With your consent, I'll arrange a new presentation to the Silicon planning board."

FOURTEEN

$Silicon$. A glimpse of that future metropolis, the very image of their ancient plan. The prophecy would come true: Eleutheria would design the greatest structure the gods had ever seen. But when would that be? And how could Eleutheria make their city different, greater than any that came before?

Beyond building, Eleutheria had a new mission: To test the gods and their peoples. For two generations the elders rehearsed and remembered what they had learned—the telltale molecules that dissolved into the arachnoid, the signs of an altered brain, and the deceitful ways of the masters. Jonquil let Rose lead the investigation; she seemed to relish the job.

Meanwhile, Jonquil devoted herself to the portraits, helping the god develop color schemes and refine subtle shadings. Her most able assistant was a young elder who flashed infrared. In her youth a chess champion coached by Rose, now Infrared spent all her hours poring over the god's creation, barely stopping to absorb nourishment.

"Come join us in the nightclub, Infrared," Jonquil flashed at her one day.

"Not till I figure out these hues. Does the detail look best in blue green, or a more saturated blue?"

Such single-minded pursuit was foreign to Jonquil. "Infrared, life is short. What do you live for, if not the pleasure of taste?"

"I live for love of the god," flashed Infrared, "no more and no less."

"Love? How can one 'love' the god, a being great enough to contain us all?"

"Love is beyond reason. A mere speck in the god's eye, I love her still."

In her gallery, Chrys awaited the promised visit of Ilia, more distracted than usual. The night after Garnet's dinner, all the exotic food had kept her awake, and her people could talk of nothing but Jasper's revelation. Designing the thirteenth city, dogged by snake-eggs—what a target she'd make for any neighborhood tough with a laser. It would never come to pass, she assured herself. The Hyalite firm was just one of several bidders for the job. With all the revelations coming out of the Comb, any sentient with half a brain would know better.

The Elf gallery director was due any minute. Shaking with nerves, Chrys pushed her thick mass of hair behind her shoulders and wished it would stay there. Nothing terrified her more than to hear the pronouncement of experts, the ones who really knew—or worse, to imagine all the barbs they left unsaid. And carrier Ilia was a million experts in one. "The Thundergod's judges test her," she reassured Jonquil. "Tell everyone to treat her people well. This is the most important contact I'll ever make."

"Never fear; we've arranged all the best shows for her people. And I present a new elder to help guide us. She'll please you well."

Chrys froze. The thought of a new elder to name reminded her that Jonquil's own days were numbered, soon to leave her people following enlightened Rose.

"God of Mercy, the One True God, from whom all blessings flow." The new one flashed infrared, just a touch redder than the deadly Poppy. *"Though I am but a speck in Your circulation, I live for love of You alone."*

Warily Chrys watched the letters cross her window. *"Love me—and love my laws. Never forget."*

"All sixteen hundred of them. 'You shall obey every word I say, and stay out of my—"

"That will do." Chrys thought a moment. *"I call you Fireweed."* The flower that arose on Mount Dolomoth the season after the ashes had cooled.

A butterfly of light splayed across the floor, joined by more, as Ilia's train swept through. The petite Elf glided through the doorway, her feet shod in delicate sandals, though Elysian streets were too clean for shoes.

"A great honor, Citizen," said Chrys carefully. "Andra sends her regards." She hoped fervently that Ilia still got tested by the Valan security chief. Whatever did Ilia think of Eris, the Guardian of Culture? Even if Arion was his "brother," how could this go on?

" 'Ilia,' please." Ilia's birdlike eyes flashed rainbow rings. "Are we 'visiting' today?"

They exchanged transfers. Then Ilia swept over to see *Cisterna Magna,* the arachnoid columns filled with the micro city, the glowing rings tumbling through it, signed with the molecule Azetidine. "A landscape of the brain—close at hand, it's even more striking."

Chrys cleared her throat. "As you can see, it's quite a departure for my work.

"A departure for us all. A living tapestry of a people never before depicted."

Chrys blinked. Before she could recover, Ilia had moved on to *Lava Arachnoid;* the molten rock flowing into the sky, then oozing down into fantastic columns reminiscent of arachnoid fibroblasts. "Vibrant fusing of landscape, outer and inner—a metaphysical contradiction one could ponder for hours."

"Thank you," Chrys whispered.

"The portraits—of course." Ilia regarded Fern with a fond sigh. "You must be inundated with orders."

"Rather." Then at last Chrys thought of something intelligent to say. "You and Yyri must be so busy, planning the Gallery's fall season."

Ilia turned. Her talar swirled, and her projected butterflies streaked madly about the hall. "Usually it's such a battle for the main exhibit—everyone pushes their own protégé, you know. But this year the choice was clear." She paused. "If you're available. No conflicting commitments, we hope?"

"No, of course not, I . . ." Her eyes widened. "You want something . . . for the Gallery Elysium?"

"Everything." Ilia's gaze circled the hall. "Everything of your 'microbial' period, as well as representative works from your primitive past. Our patrons adore tracing creative development."

"So 'Gems from the Primitive' is your main exhibit next year."

Ilia waved her hand dismissively. "That's the west wing. The main exhibit will be Azetidine alone." Her irises flashed. "Or should I say . . . Azetidine, collectively."

Chrys's face felt hot, and her hands shook.

"Just remember one thing." Ilia moved closer, and her voice intensified. "I want everything—you understand? No holding back your best for someone else."

"What? No, of course not."

"Even the most controversial." Ilia nodded. "Remember, Elysians have sophisticated tastes. Our patrons expect the Gallery to be controversial, even shocking."

"I see."

"That *Endless Light,*" Ilia whispered regretfully. "You already let it go. How unfortunate."

Chrys turned cold. Even Ilia was not immune.

"You're working on another, perhaps?"

"No," Chrys said flatly. "No more of that . . . type."

"I expect the owner will lend it for our show."

"Oh no—that won't be necessary." Chrys wanted no ties to that Elf slave. "Actually, I . . . I am working on another. Not the same, but just as . . . controversial."

Chrys was in such a daze she barely knew how she got home. At the top of her house she lay back on her chaise with Merope in her lap, and looked out on the twinkling harbor below, still trying to grasp her good fortune. *"Jonquil,"* she called.

"Yes, Oh Great One. What is your pleasure?"

She swallowed an AZ. *"Jonquil, the people have done well, and I am most pleased. Ask any favor, and I shall grant it."*

"God of Mercy, we live or die at your pleasure. If it please the god, I ask only that you complete a more advanced composition of the highest sophistication."

Chrys frowned. *"Are you sure it's legal?"* The last sketch she did for Jonquil had caused a riot in the Cisterna Magna.

"Of course, Great One. Our laws have been liberalized considerably over the last three generations."

"Very well, I grant your wish." At least Jonquil's ideas could make interesting compositions. While commissioned portraits paid the rent, they grew tiresome; clients got upset about how their filaments were depicted, and others had to include accessory molecules. Jonquil's ideas, though, might even interest Ilia.

"Our people, too, are most pleased. May we not serve the height of the god's pleasure? Surely by now, technology must allow—"

"No." She sighed. They still asked; they'd never give up. That's why carriers needed all the damned testing. But who could test the testers? They might end up like Eris . . .

Never mind. The Gallery Elysium—she had to tell Zircon and Lady Moraeg; they would be amazed. And her family—but how could she tell them? The thought was a knife in her heart.

In her studio she loaded Fern's portrait into a palm-sized holostill to send to her brother. "Dear Hal," she recorded. "I finally made it in the art world. Here is something from my show. I hope you think it's . . . pretty." She could barely finish her sentence and just restrained herself from attaching ten thousand credits for pocket change. Xenon's Anonymous would do better.

In the morning Chrys called Daeren. His sprite appeared between two colossal pillars of the Justice Ministry, wearing gray like the

Palace bureaucrats. Chrys made her face frown. "Just making sure you'll be home."

"Don't worry, I'll be at your studio on time."

"Nope. Your place, remember? I'm testing you."

"That's right." Daeren grinned. "You've done your homework."

"If you really were in trouble," she quoted, "you might 'forget' to come."

Daeren lived in a top-level neighborhood, but she passed his entrance twice before finding it. No caryatids, no doorstoop—just the palest trace of a window. A good idea, she thought; avoid tempting vandals.

"*We're testing the Lord of Light,*" she warned her people. "*Are you ready?*"

"*Great God of Mercy, I live only for You.*" The reply flashed infrared, from Fireweed. "*There is no other God.*"

Chrys sighed. This Fireweed was turning out even harder to deal with than Rose. "*I love you too, Fireweed; but if you love me, love my people. Right now my people have a job to do.*"

"*I will do so, with all my heart.*"

"*Where the devil is Jonquil?*"

Rose answered. "*I myself will lead the investigation. You can depend on it—not a master will escape alive.*"

One unrepentant "master" investigating others—Chrys nearly turned back and went home. But then, if this practice test went badly, Andra might relieve her of the chore.

Daeren's door opened. "It's good to see you, Chrys." In his sitting room the drapes merged seamlessly with the lights, punctuated by shapes of red and gold. Either Daeren or his house had a good eye for color, less conservative than she expected. By the window rose a sinuous black sculpture, like the eye of a galaxy. On a table, a virtual piece sprouted golden hexagons, rising as if to break into flight.

"That one's early Titan," he told her. "I have another of his, up there."

At the ceiling, a mobile of ephemeral shapes turned in a slow dance. "Titan started with installations," Chrys recalled. "His work . . . sings." A sad song. She looked down again. Daeren's shoulders had filled out a bit; he must have been working out, unless he had called Plan Ten. His black nanotex polished his form as hard as any sculpture.

"Can I offer you anything?" he asked. "Orange juice?"

She remembered just in time. "No thanks."

"Well, you didn't come to admire my collection," he said. "Please proceed."

"Rose, it's time." Aloud, she told him, "I'm supposed to ask if there's anything I need to know."

He studied her eyes. "No, thanks. And no, we don't need to 'give ourselves up now, rather than later.' "

She flushed. *"Rose, remember your manners."* Daeren's eyes flickered blue, responding to Rose's interrogation. It seemed to take forever; Chrys was hard-pressed to keep from blinking.

"We see no problems," Rose admitted at last. *"So far."*

"Okay?" Chrys asked him doubtfully, putting a transfer at her neck. "I can't vouch for how this will go."

"No one ever can." Daeren took the transfer, then sat with his arms crossed. Chrys sat back, hearing a music she had not noticed before. A quiet melody, deceptively formless, with no phrase repeated twice. She tried to keep her eyes on his, but somehow today she kept stealing a glimpse of the rest of him, his well-sculpted shoulders and below. So long, she thought wearily; it had been so long since she knew someone worth knowing. But humans weren't worth the risk; their mistakes lived too long.

"All right, enough," he snapped, abruptly sitting up.

Chrys raised an eyebrow. "I'm supposed to decide that."

"Well, get on with it."

"Rose is flashing the signal, Great One," came Jonquil. *"She is ready to return."*

Chrys took back her investigators. *"Did they pass?"*

"We issued numerous citations," began Rose. *"Insufficient clearance in tunnels to the capillaries. Deferred maintenance on infrastructure. Outdated cancer detectors—"*

"Look," exclaimed Daeren, "this was supposed to be a drug test, not a building inspection."

"You pass." She couldn't resist adding, "Just barely."

He got up and stretched. "They'll have to polish their act. You can't treat your fellow Olympians like a convicted felon. Carriers are fussy; they'll demand another tester."

"Be my guest—it wasn't my idea."

He thought a moment. "Garnet won't mind."

"Lord Garnet? I'd just die."

"Garnet likes Eleutherians. You can join us, on our next appointment, and we'll see how it goes." Daeren lifted his hand; the music grew, shifting to a warmer tone. "That Rose had to tell us all sorts of masters' tricks we hadn't known to look for, antigenic mimicry and so on." He gave Chrys a look. "Rose's ego is her one saving grace. We've learned more from her than any defector I know."

"Well, that's something."

"But don't trust her."

Chrys spread her hands. "So what can I do? Before long, she'll be my 'high priest.' "

"Priests only serve at your pleasure."

Her head tilted curiously. "Did you ever demote one?"

"I've never had to."

She rolled her eyes. "Sometime, dear, you're just too perfect."

"In my line of work, I can't afford mistakes."

"In my line, I learn nothing except through mistakes."

Daeren thought a moment. "I don't know," he said. "I hadn't noticed any mistakes in your work."

At the compliment she flushed. "You haven't seen Jonquil's latest." She took out several viewcoins. "Be honest—are these a mistake?"

They sat together, watching each sketch in turn. "Sweet," said Daeren, his face relaxed. "We like that a lot. And this one—you can see how the children long to taste each other."

"Yes," she sighed. Jonquil had been so particular about getting the filaments right.

The next one drew silence, and the next. A very long silence.
"Well?"

"They're . . . effective," he admitted, his eyes still focused.

"Should I show them in public?"

"I don't know. You might get a reputation."

"I knew it," she exclaimed. "I knew that Jonquil would have me peddling porn."

"The children look okay," he assured her. "They're just doing what micro children naturally do. But elders—or elders with children—that's profoundly disturbing."

"I'll be warned. No more riots." She glanced at him sideways, then set the viewcoins on the table. "They don't seem to hurt your perfect people. Take what you like—it's 'advertising.' "

"Thanks, Chrys."

She watched to see which he took. He took them all.

Chrys celebrated her good fortune by treating Moraeg and Zircon at the most expensive restaurant on Center Way.

"A fantastic year for the Seven." Zircon had picked rack of caterpillar, the stacked claws rearing outward in a circle. "Even the Elves can't get enough of us."

"'Gems from the Primitive.' You'll be in the west wing." Chrys sipped her glass, sparkling water from an Urulite spring. Urulite food was all the rage, now that it was genetically detoxified, but Chrys preferred lamb-flavored plums filled with goat cheese. The taste reminded her of home. "Anyone else of the Seven included?"

A vague look came over Zircon's face, as usual when someone else's work was mentioned.

Moraeg picked at her Solarian salad. "Topaz was hoping. Her portraits are too commercial, I think."

"How is Topaz?" Chrys asked. "I can't believe how long since I've seen her."

Zircon and Moraeg exchanged looks. "Topaz is managing," said Moraeg. "Pearl needs to get herself together."

"And you, Moraeg—isn't your own show coming up? I was going to help." Moraeg had eaten little and seemed distracted.

Afterward they strolled down Center Way, the wind blowing shrill from the harbor, the lava traffic flowing till streams of it dipped under. Just like the old days, the Seven getting all their works together for the next show. Chrys blinked for news. The brain plague—more ships hijacked. The latest scandal at the Palace. And the sentients of Elysium planning their new floating city. Chrys frowned. "I don't understand these sentients. We humans are so dumb; why do sentients still need us? Why didn't they take over long ago?"

Zircon patted her head. "Maybe they did—and we don't know it."

"Nonsense." Moraeg rubbed her arms and touched the temperature control on her nanotex. "Machines have always threatened to take over, but they're not as smart as they think."

A bubble popped open, and Zircon climbed inside to flow down home. Chrys was ready to call a lightcraft, but she wondered, whatever was eating at Moraeg? She watched her friend uncertainly, admiring the setting sun's infrared sheen upon her hair. "Has *Wheelgrass* sold yet? I heard some great comments."

Moraeg's chin was set hard. "Chrys, I went to that clinic and passed all the tests. But that worm-face put me way down on the list. He said it would take months."

Chrys blinked several times. She recalled her own screening at the hospital, all those tests with Doctor Sartorius, before he found the right culture. Titan's culture, though she hadn't known that then. "It could take months—they told me the same. But then—"

"They don't want me, but they couldn't say why. I could tell."

"They have to find the right culture." She hesitated. "I didn't know you decided to go through with it. What does Carnelian think?"

"What 'right' culture? What's wrong with me?" Moraeg demanded. "And what's my husband got to do with it?"

Lord Carnelian discreetly patronized the arts; Chrys always remembered the time he advanced her a month's rent. But his lifestyle was conservative. "Being a carrier is, well, an intimate thing. It kind of changes who you are."

"You haven't changed."

"Thanks," said Chrys. "But tell that to my friends."

"I'm still your friend." She said it almost accusingly, as if Chrys owed her something.

Chrys felt torn; she did not want to lose one of her last two friends from the Seven. "Look, I'll tell you what . . ." Her pulse raced; she doubted this was legal. "I'll let a couple of them visit you, just for a minute."

"'Visit'?" Moraeg was puzzled.

"*Oh Great One,*" flashed Jonquil, "*we will be thrilled to explore a virgin wilderness.*"

"*Very well. You and Fireweed may go. But be ready to return within a month—or all the people may die.*" Five minutes with two elders; what harm could that do? She placed the patch at her neck, then offered it to Moraeg. "Quick; don't let them dry out." Dry out, or get caught by foreign microglia—a mistake, to put them at such risk.

Moraeg put the patch at her neck. "Very well, but what use is it for a minute? I mean, there's no time to—" She stopped with a puzzled frown. "Someone's sending me a message, in letters. Why don't they show themselves?"

"That's them. The micros. Make sure they're both okay."

Her eyes widened. "They sound like people."

Chrys sighed. "What else is new."

"Religious people." Moraeg laughed, and her teeth sparkled. "Microbes—and they think God cares about them."

In her window, the message light blinked. Chrys jumped out of her shoes. Had somebody caught her? Ridiculous, but still. "Moraeg, they have to come back. Put that patch on your neck and make damn sure they've gone."

Moraeg returned the patch. "I'm not sure," she admitted. "I don't want to end up painting a religious tract."

"Did I?"

"*Oh Great One!*" Jonquil had returned. "*We have seen a*

wondrous New World, full of strange, savage antibodies and blood proteins never before known to civilization."

"Even so," assured Fireweed, *"all its fierce beauty cannot tempt me to stray from the One True God."*

"Be dark." The message light was still blinking. Chrys opened it at last.

It was Topaz. Topaz was alone by her lace-curtained door, as if waiting. "Chrys—you've got to do something. Pearl has reached her limit."

"Topaz," Chrys exclaimed in surprise.

"You got her into it." In her window Topaz was shaking, more agitated than Chrys had ever seen her. "Ever since you got in, she had to wonder. You get her out; they say you know how."

"What?" She looked at Moraeg. "What's wrong with Pearl?"

Moraeg shook her head. "You know Pearl. Always had to try the latest. But Chrys, you manage with micros. Help her get control."

"It's not the same," Chrys snapped. "It's worse than getting psychos from a friend. You'd better listen to Doctor Sartorius, even if he is a worm-face."

In the hallway paced Topaz, the honey-colored stone gliding upon her breast. Portraits and landscapes set into the walls, and a scent of roses hung in the air. The scent reminded Chrys how she and Topaz had once lived together with a lace-curtained door like that, much smaller of course, a students' cubic where they set the ceiling just above her height so they could squeeze out an extra room.

"She goes around in a fog," Topaz was saying as if to herself. "She barely paints anymore. And there's something odd in her eyes."

Chrys's scalp prickled at the thought. She averted her own eyes, then made herself face Topaz. "Does she go to the Underworld?"

"She always did, but she managed okay. Now I find too much credit missing."

"How much?"

"Five hundred, just this evening."

Not that bad yet, Chrys thought. Not bad enough. "Does she want to go clean?"

Topaz stared. The namestone twirled smoothly in her nanotex, like a whirlpool one could drown in. "She wants to 'manage.' Like you."

"Then see the doctor."

"It's too late for that."

You never listen to me, Chrys thought. You never did.

Suddenly Topaz caught Chrys at the shoulders. "Chrys—whatever it takes, get her clean. She's scared of that clinic. But you can get her there."

Topaz's hands felt warm, her face so near Chrys could feel her breath. Suddenly she thought, with Pearl out of the picture, Topaz would come back to her, just like their school days. Then she looked away, ashamed. Love was cruel, as cruel as Endless Light.

Drawing back, Chrys blinked at the dot of purple. Selenite answered, from a simian neighborhood down two levels. "Unless she seeks help, there's nothing we can do," Selenite told her. "I'm on another call, but I'll send you a medic just in case."

"Send me? But—"

Behind Selenite, vines of plast climbed a neat rowhouse. "You're trained. Do the best you can."

"But—" Chrys had not yet completed training, certainly not for this.

The door chimed. "Pearl is home."

Topaz gripped Chrys's arm like death. The door hissed open. Pearl looked well enough, a bit thin even for her. She glanced one way, then the other. "Why Topaz," she exclaimed, not quite looking at her. "I've had such a good—" Seeing Chrys, Pearl stopped. Her irises flashed white, then her face froze in terror. "What's she doing here?"

"The masters warned us off," flashed Jonquil's words of gold.

"A hard lot," admitted Rose. *"They want nothing to do with us. But a few will always attempt reform—"*

Pearl backed against the wall. Then she screamed and caught

her head between her hands, almost as if trying to twist it off. "Get her out of here! Please—get her out—"

Topaz caught Pearl by both arms, but she twisted her head away. "Pearl, listen—it's your last chance, you hear?"

Pearl's nails dug into the wall, leaving deep grooves in the plast, and her muscles stood taut with pain. Chrys backed off, uncertain. Daeren had not told her much about pain; she wondered why.

In her window flashed the sprite of a worm-face. Doctor Flexor, female, the ID flashed helpfully in her window. Chrys stepped outside the house to meet her. "Pearl can't even look at me. What can I do?"

Doctor Flexor listened, her face worms twining and twisting, catching the pallid light of the street. From behind, Pearl's screams subsided. "Wait it out," Flexor advised. "After a few minutes, the masters will think you've gone forever. Then try again."

Back in the house, Topaz whispered intensely to Pearl. Pearl was shaking her head, her hair tossing around her face. "Just let me be," she groaned. "I'm fine now."

"What do you mean you're fine?" hissed Topaz. "You can't even look someone in the face."

"I'm fine, I said; just let me—*Oh!*" Catching sight of Chrys again, Pearl sobbed and tried to bury her face in the wall. Chrys felt numb.

"*We try,*" reported Rose, "*but now they refuse all contact.*"

Chrys knew Rose's style. "*Maybe you need to try nicer.*"

"*They know too well what they face. Corrupt though they are, they'd rather die than join our degenerate society.*"

Chrys went out again. "This is no good," she told Flexor, waiting by the lightcraft. "Nobody told me what to do for pain."

"Pain makes it easy," said the worm-face. "These masters must be inexperienced. Pain sends humans to the doctor."

Topaz came out, her curls all askew, but she still had that take-charge sense about her. "Look," she told the doctor, "can't you give her something to take off the edge?"

"Of course." The worms lifted. "As soon as she accepts treatment."

"That's right," said Chrys. "If she can face me and consent, I'll give her . . . something."

Topaz's eyes narrowed. "Why you? Why not the doctor?"

"Damn it, for once just listen."

Topaz turned and went back. "Pearl," said Topaz firmly. "You accept treatment, or I'll turn you out." Pearl's head whipped violently back and forth. "I'll turn you out and freeze the accounts, you hear?"

"No," she wailed.

Topaz stopped and lowered her voice. "Pearl, I love you. I want you back. Does that mean nothing?"

Pearl's eyes rolled. Her face shone with sweat, and she took short, shallow breaths. "I don't know." Her voice broke. "It hurts too much."

"Just get treatment," urged Topaz. "Just say yes, and the doctor will make it better."

At that Pearl seemed to freeze. Chrys moved closer, dreading to start her off again.

"Say yes, Pearl," Topaz repeated. "Tell her."

Pearl looked at Chrys. "Yes," she gasped.

Chrys blinked to record the statement. Then she got out the green wafer, her hand shaking so it nearly fell. "Take this. Hurry."

Pearl grabbed the wafer and stuffed it in her mouth. Within minutes she was calm. Her arms relaxed, and she looked from one to the other, with a slight frown. "That sure helped. Why didn't you do that before?"

"It won't last," Chrys warned. "Keep fixed on my eyes." She had to give Rose one more chance to talk them into giving up.

"What are you?" Pearl asked curiously. "You're undercover, aren't you."

Chrys put a patch at Pearl's neck. A few would defect, never more. What if one day they all did? she wondered. A carrier, even a tester, was never allowed to increase her population more than 10 percent.

Flexor came inside. Her face worms extended into long tendrils around Pearl's head and neck. The nanoservos would tear every arsenic atom out of her tissues, and out of any micros that were left.

"It's coming back," Pearl gasped. "The pain—"

"The micros messed up your pain circuits. They need to heal." Flexor added to Chrys, "The pain saved her. When they're too smart for pain—"

Pearl's cry split the night. The worm-face got her into the light-craft and to the hospital; a five-minute ride, it felt the longest Chrys ever took. At the door to the clinic, she stopped. Pearl still moaned, her head turning back and forth to find relief that would not come. Topaz looked back toward Chrys as if to a lifeline.

"No farther for me," Chrys told her. "The clinic is a micro-free zone."

"A what?"

Doctor Flexor drew them in and the door closed.

"Our defectors have settled in," reported Jonquil. *"Not the brightest, but they work hard. When do we get to build Silicon?"*

In the window Chief Andra appeared, irises glimmering violet, standing tall as an ancient Sardish warrior. "Chrys, you've done well." She must have watched the whole time. "We'll put you on call."

Chrys swallowed and said nothing.

FIFTEEN

*J*onquil could never forget her expedition to that vast New World, strange-tasting, wildly beautiful, terrifying. The macrophages she had to outswim, evading the viselike grip of antibodies, only to behold the words of a new god. A god awaiting people.

By contrast, after generations beyond counting, even the farthest reaches of her own god's circulation felt familiar to Jonquil. She patrolled there with Fireweed, training the infrared elder to detect the slightest need for repair, signs even the nanoservos might miss. Her filaments twitched. "There—I taste a precancerous cell."

Fireweed extended her filaments. "An abnormal growth protein," she flashed, sending molecules of alertness. "Only stage one."

"Nevertheless, let's mark the site." Micros themselves did not dare leave the bloodstream to penetrate the epithelium, lest they attract deadly immune cells, but the Plan Ten nanoservos would eliminate the cancer.

On their way back to the arachnoid, the two elders came upon *an outcast micro. Incapable of work, the grayish ring jostled aim-lessly among the red cells, begging for vitamins. Fireweed brushed its filaments to pass it a few.*

"Why?" asked Jonquil. "Why prolong its miserable existence?"

"The One True God decreed, 'Love Me, love My people.'"

"You call that brainless microbe a person?" Mutant children whose brains failed to reach Eleutherian standards were barred from the nightclubs, never exposed to the pheromones that ripened for breeding, nor did they mature as elders. Worth no more than a virus.

"There, but for a twist of DNA, go you or I," flashed Fire-weed. "All people are one."

"You sound like Rose," observed Jonquil. "Don't listen to her, just live like her." Rose's abstemious lifestyle had earned her an exceptionally long and healthy life, the envy of many. But then, had Rose truly lived? Jonquil wondered. Jonquil herself, with the god's help, had led the greatest cultural renaissance Eleutheria had ever seen. But now, she felt the arsenic atoms tearing loose from her membranes one by one. Foreseeing the end, she had passed on to Rose her most vital knowledge, the photo codes from the judges of the Thundergod. The codes enabled people to pass safely among the masters.

Fireweed said, "That unbeliever does not sway me. But the new heretics—those who seek to emigrate to the New World—they shame us." After Jonquil and Fireweed had spread their sto-ries of the New World, an unorthodox sect had risen up demanding to emigrate, to found a purer society in the wilderness. Jonquil tried to pass laws against them. A mistake, the restrictions only attracted converts to their fanatical leader: a Green One, ver-dant as the legendary Fern.

Before dawn Chrys tossed in her bed, her eyes full of colored cells twinkling, rolling through the arachnoid. *"God of Mercy,"* flashed Jonquil. *"Great One, we need your help."*

"What is it?"

"A new sect begs to address you. Will you see their leader?"

"Sure."

"God of the Eleutherians." The new one flashed green. Chrys smiled, thinking fondly of Fern. *"I call you . . . Pteris."* A large, handsome tree-fern.

"That shall be—until we find our New World."

"What?"

"The new god promised us a New World. Let my people go."

Chrys shot upright, as wide awake as if the volcano smoking in the distance had exploded. Her startled cat jumped off the bed. *"What nonsense are you talking? Jonquil, what's this?"*

"My deepest apologies, God of Mercy," the yellow letters flashed. *"Alas, these heretics were undone by the tales of our exploits in the uninhabited world. We'll remove them, to trouble you no longer."*

"New god"—What had Moraeg told them?

"We shall return," the green one challenged. *"We'll defy even death. Every year, we'll return to demand our New World."*

"Why?" asked Chrys. *"What's wrong with Eleutheria?"*

"Eleutheria is a sham. Corrupted, untrue to its founding principles. 'World of opportunity'—what falsehood. See all the beggars floating homeless in the veins."

"Jonquil? I thought you and Rose took care of this."

"We tried," Jonquil admitted, *"but in recent years, perhaps, I've not kept up so well."*

"Rose? Is this your doing?"

"Nonsense," said Rose. *"I have nothing to do with those god-talkers. I've tried what I can to spread enlightenment, but degenerate societies consume themselves from within."*

"Rose," countered Jonquil, *"you yourself want only the best chess champions. How could we breed the best, if we let all cells with inferior genes into the nightclubs?"*

"Fireweed?" blinked Chrys. *"What do you know of this?"*

"Such heretics," said Fireweed, *"in ancient times would have had their arsenic torn out."* The letters came blood-red. *"But truly, the heretics remind us how poorly we ourselves serve our God.*

With faith and patience, we'll learn to love even the meanest ones as we do God Herself."

Red, yellow, green—Chrys shook her head, as if she could clear out the lot of them. *"Go, then, and do so."*

"And the heretics?" asked Jonquil. *"What shall we do with them?"*

"Pteris, why can't you stay and make Eleutheria better?"

"Our own god calls us," said the green one. *"We'll return every year, until you let us go."*

"Not every year. Or there'll be an eclipse of the sun."

For some seconds the letters vanished. Chrys guessed they all had plenty to say to each other. Then Jonquil asked, *"How often will the god allow?"*

"Once a generation." Chrys sighed, her eyes aching. Microbial rejection.

And today was her own day to be tested. What if the tester heard of Jonquil's little "visit"?

Her tester now was Pyrite of Azuroth, a nanodesigner from the Comb, who looked even younger than Daeren. Pyrite arrived a few minutes late. "Sorry," he apologized, "I was delayed below. A vendor tried to talk me into a trophy, a giant caterpillar claw." He smiled, obviously trying to put her at ease; Chrys knew their routine now. "How are you? Anything I need to know?"

Her heart pounded in her chest. "They visited a non-carrier," she forced herself to say.

His brows lifted. "With children?"

"Certainly not. Just two elders."

"You let them?"

"My friend insisted. She's upset because the doctor put her way down on the list."

"I see." Pyrite nodded. "Well, let's sit down and have a look." His irises flashed green, like Opal's. Perhaps his people came from hers. Pyrite nodded again. "Once you let them explore a 'virgin,' they get all kinds of ideas."

"I don't understand," exclaimed Chrys. "Before, they were perfectly happy with me. They're welcome to visit any other carrier."

"When humans discover a new habitable planet, what happens?"

Nervously, she clasped her fingers. "So what can I do?"

"Put up with it. After a few generations they may forget."

"Not Eleutherians."

Pyrite thought this over. "With luck, we may find a recipient soon. But there's a long waiting list for emigration."

Chrys frowned. "If there's a waiting list for hosts, as well as emigrants, why not let more go ahead?"

"Both need to meet our standards, and make a good match. The streets have enough slaves already." Pyrite's eyes defocused, and he nodded again, as if to someone unseen. "The good doctor wants to know who they visited. We have to check her out."

Chrys gripped the chair. "You reported it already?"

"Of course."

"Moraeg will be furious."

"She shouldn't be, if she's a serious candidate."

"Why should she be way down the list?" Chrys wanted to know. "She's a totally together person. She's been married a hundred years."

"Is her spouse a candidate?"

"I don't think so."

Pyrite shook his head. "We take singles, or couples, but not half a couple. Too many problems."

"That's hardly fair," Chrys exclaimed.

"Maybe not, but we can't afford mistakes."

Chrys sighed. Another old friend lost.

Pyrite leaned forward. "Are you the real 'Azetidine'? The one who does the portraits?"

She smiled, recalling her provocative signature. "I'm afraid so."

"Awesome," he exclaimed. "Could I have your autograph? I mean, after my two months testing you."

Over the next two days, the would-be emigrants kept their word, asking each night for their Promised World. The rest seemed happy as usual, and Jonquil was thrilled to help her new compositions. But now each day ended with sadness.

The day came for her to test Lord Garnet, with Daeren's help, of course. Daeren stopped at her studio, where her painting stage displayed her latest work in progress, a couple of children in a nightclub hung with luminescent proteins. As he turned to watch, Chrys stole a look at him, his deltoids nicely filled out, a pleasing valley between the shoulder blades.

Daeren nodded. "I like that one best." He turned to her. "Are you ready? Remember to sell off your investments."

Her investment with Garnet had grown considerably. "I'm not sure I can afford to," she realized. "I just gave Xenon a raise."

"You'll just have to work for a living."

They started up the street toward the Hyalite complex. One of the neighbors had a new grillwork of stunplast, forming pretty stars and moons with an angel on top. Chrys took care to avoid a touch. "Are you sure I'm still allowed?" she asked. "My people got in trouble."

"Don't let them do it again," Daeren warned. "If they had smuggled children in, they'd all be dead."

"They know better."

"Do the would-be emigrants give you a hard time?"

"Only once a day."

Daeren smiled, and his dark hair glinted lava in the sunlight. "Just like Fern, and the one I couldn't see." Fern and Poppy—she could imagine. It seemed so long ago, yet it was only a few months. "You did a good job the other night," Daeren added. "The Committee was pleased."

She realized he meant Pearl. "How is she doing?"

"She's making progress. She's lucky to have a caring partner."

"That's for sure," Chrys exclaimed. "If anything real bad ever happened to me, I don't know what I'd do."

"Chrys, you know we'd always help you."

"It's not the same," she said. "Not like . . . having a friend." Her eyes filled and she quickly looked away. The devil take Topaz, and those stupid emigrants, and whoever else.

Ahead, before Garnet's house, stood the first pair of golden caryatids. Their style had altered subtly since her previous visit. Each caryatid had its own pose, one carrying a platter of grapes, another a glass of wine. She could not help admiring the artfulness of each pose, the way the gown draped over the ankle. Even Xenon could learn a few tricks here.

At the end of the colonnade they faced the door with its cornucopia of gems. Seeing them approach, the door came alive. "Please, friends," begged the door. "We've so much to share."

Without thinking Chrys looked down at the gems.

"Chrys . . ." warned Daeren behind her.

She remembered. Straightening her back, she gave the door a murderous glare.

"Very well," sighed the door. "Just remember—all that's gold doesn't glitter."

Inside, they were met by a chorus of birds, their plumage like a rainbow. The hall had redone itself in decorative panels topped with finials. Lord Garnet smiled. "Please excuse our door, I'll have a talk with him." From his tone, Chrys suspected he had indulged the door for years. "A pleasure to see you, Azetidine," he told her with a bow. "We share such good taste."

"She's training, as you know," Daeren told him. "Thanks so much for helping out."

Looking slightly aside, Garnet smiled. "It's always a pleasure to receive Eleutheria."

Daeren glanced at the finials and the singing birds. "The conference room, if you don't mind."

The floor glided down the hall until they reached a massive arch at right. Inside the conference room, the table was long enough to span an ordinary house. Three chairs slid around together.

"It's good to see you again," said Daeren, sitting down to face him. "Your caryatids—I like the new look."

"You noticed," said Garnet. "You always had an eye for beauty, Day."

He smiled. "Thanks for letting Chrys in on our session. Anything we need to know?"

"No," he said. "There never is, is there." Garnet leaned back into the tall chair, stretching his legs in a relaxed manner.

Daeren leaned forward. "Garnet, we're having a little trouble fixing on your eyes. Could you keep them steady?"

Garnet blinked a couple of times. "Your irises somehow seem brighter than usual. Sorry, I must be tired; it's been a bad day on the market."

Tendons shifted in Daeren's neck. "Sorry to be slow," he said softly, "but we still can't quite connect." Somehow Garnet's gaze kept veering just off center. "Perhaps you might try Chrys."

"My pleasure." His gaze shifted to meet her eyes."

"Rose," Chrys summoned, *"it's time to test the God of Love."*

"Great Host," flashed Rose, *"his people don't want to meet us today. They claim they're not ready."*

Chrys kept her gaze steady, hoping her face did not change. *"Were you polite?"*

"Certainly; what do you take me for?"

"We're polite," agreed Jonquil. *"The people of the God of Love just don't want to see us this year."*

Chrys swallowed. "Should we come back later?"

"What's wrong?" Garnet asked.

"Well, they said—"

Abruptly Garnet rose from his seat. "It's not working today, is it." His breath came faster. "I'm just not myself, that's all. Come back tomorrow; I'll make sure I get better rest."

"I wish I could do that," said Daeren very quietly.

"You don't have to report anything. Just come back tomorrow."

"It's already been reported."

Garnet shuddered, and his head twisted back and forth as if trapped. Like Pearl. "Who do you think you are?" His voice was loud and unsteady. "I've heard enough. The house will show you out."

The conference room door peeled open wide. Chrys suddenly realized, they were in the hands of a very frightened man.

"You'll be okay," said Daeren. "Just let Chrys continue. We'll do our best to—"

"You'll wipe them all out."

All of them—to lose them all, just like that. "No," exclaimed Chrys. "I won't. I promise, we won't hurt anybody."

Garnet's throat dipped as he swallowed. "All right then."

Chrys remembered to hand him the patch, which he put to his neck himself. A good sign, he was still in control. But what could have happened, she wondered in dismay. What went wrong? Did he get the bad strain from Eris?

The minutes lengthened as she waited for her people to do their work, while Daeren stepped out to the hall for a moment. Then he was back. "Jasper will meet us at the hospital—"

"No," exclaimed Garnet. "You needn't tell Jasper."

"Just for overnight observation."

"But if they've done something forbidden—"

"We'll see."

Garnet's irises flashed pink; that was Rose.

"I need them back now," Chrys told him.

"What did they say?"

Chrys flexed her fingers awkwardly. "I don't know yet."

Garnet looked from her to Daeren in a calculating way. "Just let me go. I've a home on Solaria; I'll go, and won't come back." Run twenty light-years, but not escape what's within.

Daeren caressed his shoulder. "We'd miss you. All of you. Olympus wouldn't be the same." At his touch Garnet relaxed enough to let Chrys have her people back.

"They've 'experimented' with his neurons," reported Rose.

" 'They?' You mean his own people?"

"They claim he asked for it, just for fun. They offered us untold amounts of palladium not to tell—as if the nanos won't find out anyhow. Pathetic, if you ask me."

"You yourself once looked pathetic, as a refugee," Chrys reminded her.

"Look, I know the Great Hosts don't give an atom for what I think, but what's the harm in a little Enlightenment? Sure, they messed up a few dendrites out of ignorance, but they'll grow back. . . ."

"I'll call my attorney," Garnet added, but his tone had softened.

"It's not yet a matter for the law," Daeren pointed out. "If you come now, it stays with the Committee. Section Five-oh-three-three, subsection A."

At the hospital, Doctor Sartorius took Garnet away for the nanos to test every neuron. Chrys imagined him lying there amid worm-tubes all snaking into his head. She turned to Daeren. "What will become of him?"

The peach-colored walls extended a packet of instruments into a bubble of plast, which took off down the hall, dodging the humans at the last moment. Drunks and accident victims passed to and fro, the hospital's usual evening clientele. Daeren sank into a chair. "What happens next depends on what we find. If Rose is right, Garnet's people were just starting to go bad. We take out the main instigators and make an example of them."

Chrys sighed. "Hope mine learn a lesson too."

"They still ask?"

"Now and then."

Daeren watched her curiously, as if trying to figure her out. "I'm glad you were there. I'm not sure he would have made it with me."

Her mouth twisted. "His people thought they could buy mine off."

"Perhaps. I prefer a more generous view. But remember—" He looked her in the eye. "Never make a promise you can't keep."

She looked down. "I'll remember."

"Jasper?" Daeren rose from his seat. "We're glad you're here."

Lord Jasper strode quickly toward them, the map stone gleaming on his fur talar. "Is he all right? Where is he?"

"He's having the brain scan. We expect he'll be fine, but we need to make sure."

"Good god, what a scare." Jasper wiped his brow. "Are you sure he's all right? You've cleaned them out?"

Daeren hesitated. "Chrys is training with us," he added, noting Jasper's questioning look. "Her people checked him out."

"Yes, I recall now he mentioned it." Jasper nodded apologetically. "Dreadfully sorry for this . . . inconvenience."

Chrys said, "It's an honor to be of service." She saw the sweat on his forehead. He must be worried sick, but for Jasper, dignity was everything.

Daeren addressed the wall. "Consult, please." The wall punched in, shaping a small round conference room done in blues and greens. Depression color, Chrys would have called it. As the three entered and took seats, the wall closed them in. "Here are Garnet's options," Daeren began. "The choice is his, but he'll need your support. He's lucky to have you."

Jasper waved his arm impatiently, as if at a poor business presentation. "I know he'll be fine. He just needs a clean start."

"That's one option," Daeren admitted. "If micros damage dopamine receptors, the carrier can choose to be swept for arsenic. The people know that." He hesitated. "That's a drastic choice."

"The hell it is. I know the law as well as you." Jasper faced Daeren coolly, but his hand was shaking. "I want him safe, do you hear?"

"If he chooses to keep them—the innocent majority—he'll be safe enough. My Watchers will see him through."

Jasper's hand closed into a fist. "You put him up to this."

"We haven't yet spoken—he doesn't even know if—"

"You wanted an excuse to give him your people, was that it? Or was the idea his?"

"Jasper," said Daeren in a low voice, "you're not yourself. Think clearly—you need to help him."

Chrys's heart pounded. "I could give him Watchers."

The two men turned to her. Jasper was incredulous. "You?"

"She's trained," Daeren agreed.

Jasper added, "You mean Eleutherians would be willing to spend their lives with Garnet?"

"I'll ask them. I mean, they'll do as I tell them."

Daeren looked away. "Thanks, Chrys. You know, this was my third call today. Perhaps you and the doctor could take it from here." He caught her hand, a bit harder than usual. They quickly exchanged transfers. Then he left without looking back, the taut deltoids shifting smoothly beneath his nanotex. Chrys wanted to run after him, to say something, but he was gone.

"Jonquil, could you recruit seven Watchers for the God of Love?"

"Certainly, God of Mercy. Though it's hard to believe, I know elders of good character who despise modern design and would embrace a mission of service." And the chance to invest in palladium, she guessed.

Jasper sat straight and folded his hands. "We're greatly in your debt."

"It's our job," she breathed. "Thank the Committee." Damn it, she was sounding like a bureaucrat already. She watched Jasper, his face like a mask, his fingers tightening and flexing, struggling between pride and fear.

"The God of the Map of the Universe?" inquired Jonquil. *"Any word on our bid? Our aesthetic engineers have new options to offer."*

Chrys tapped Jasper on the hand. "They want to talk shop."

He looked up in surprise. "Here?"

She shrugged. "You know Eleutheria."

Jasper accepted a transfer. His face relaxed. "The Silicon planning board agreed to hear us next month," he told her. "A good sign."

A bad sign, thought Chrys glumly. Even sentients made mistakes.

At the door appeared a face full of worms. It was Doctor Sartorius.

"The Terminator," flashed Jonquil. *"Flee for your lives!"*

"Be dark." Executions—that's all her people could think of the good doctor. *"Be glad for those spared."*

"You can see him now," Sartorius told Jasper. When Jasper had gone, the worm-face took a seat, out of politeness; he could just as easily have shaped himself down. "Welcome aboard, Chrysoberyl." His voice sounded more melodious than usual. "You are a welcome addition to the Committee."

"What happened exactly?" Chrys asked. "How did Garnet get in trouble? Why didn't the nanos warn him?"

The doctor's eyes swiveled unnervingly around the post of his body. "Our dopamine sensors are tuned to a fine threshold. We wouldn't want to sound alarms, say, every time you look at a beautiful painting."

Chrys rolled her eyes. "Saints preserve us."

"His people convinced themselves they did no harm, so long as they set off no alarms. But when testing time came, they panicked. They even fudged his memory, a worse sin than the original. He actually believed he was okay; but when they couldn't face the blue angels, he panicked."

"I see. That's why he seemed fine at first." She shuddered.

The worms hung still. "I'm sorry." The doctor's voice came soft. "Sorry we let this happen. I've contacted Opal; we'll redesign the sensors."

Good luck, she thought. No sensor could keep humans from fooling themselves.

Jasper returned, his face beaming with relief. "Everything will be fine. Thanks for all you've done, Doctor." He extended a hand. The doctor shaped a hand to clasp his. "And you too, Chrys; much obliged." He nodded. "Garnet knows what he has to do."

Behind Jasper stood Andra. The sight of her with Sartorius struck Chrys like a blow. Back in the hospital, she remembered, her head still in pain, her own people sentenced to death—

"Judgment day," flashed Jonquil. *"The day of judgment for those people. God of Mercy, will you defend them?"*

"Come, Chrys." Andra's voice was as icy as Chrys's own veins. They went with the doctor to the bedside where Garnet lay. His head was turned away, his hair straggled across the pillow.

"You will choose," Andra told him. "You and no one else." She glared at Chrys, as she had once glared at Daeren. "By the end of the hour, Garnet, you will choose either Watchers from Eleutheria . . ." She turned to Sar. " . . . or the arsenic sweep." With that she was gone. But not unaware—Chrys knew that now. Every moment of the hour was on record.

"God of Mercy, please—all those children—"

"Be dark. Your work is done; this year is not for you." Chrys sat by the bed, waiting. Idly she surveyed the living walls, sickly green, wondering where all the little camera eyes hid. When she first came from Dolomoth, it had taken a long time to get used to the ubiquity of public vision. "Garnet?" she whispered at last. "Garnet, I have a question."

His head slowly turned.

She leaned over. "Why are the Seven Stars but seven?"

Garnet gave a feeble smile, then shook his head. "It's no use." His lip twisted. "Jasper is furious at the lot of them. He won't rest till they're gone."

She watched her words. "The choice is not his."

"The fault was mine. I made them do it."

"Why?"

He shrugged. "I was curious. Why not, after all. I can buy any pleasure in the Fold. What's a little dopamine?" He paused. "I can't buy back yesterday."

"Did you explain to Jasper?"

"Jasper can't accept it. If he did, he'd have to be furious at me."

"He loves you."

"He loves me to death."

Chrys knew that one well enough. Before Topaz had left her, when it started to go bad, Chrys remembered lying awake in the wee hours, watching that lovely white neck beside her, imagining her own powerful hands around it. Wearily, she pulled up a chair and sank in.

"There's nothing left," he added. "Lose them, or lose Jasper—I might as well go off to an Elysian Final Home." Elves generally chose their own end, once they tired of their centuries.

"I know," Chrys sighed. "I know that feeling well. And for me, there's no one hanging outside to care if I live or die."

He glanced at her sharply.

"I'll tell you what I do," she added, "when I feel like that. Find someone worse off. Go round the corner to the Spirit Table and serve the folks in our neighborhood who haven't got enough to eat."

"Not enough to eat—in our neighborhood." As if it were a new idea. He shook his head. "I could feed the whole Underworld, but it wouldn't help. Economics—you know that. The poor will always be poor."

"Perhaps. But they might help you."

He turned to her, fixing her with his stare. "Chrys, tell me the truth. Will Jasper leave me, if I keep them?"

One human, a million people. Chrys swallowed. In her teeth Andra's voice spoke, "Don't answer." Startled, she half jumped from her chair. "I'm sorry, I—I can't say." She bit her lip. "You know I'm fond of Jasper."

He kept his eyes on her, as if he could read her mind. Then his irises lit up.

"They will live, Oh Great One. A great victory for love and mercy."

Garnet smiled. "You're very kind, Chrys. You were kind to key the servers to his form." His old sly note crept in. "But I know your real heart lies elsewhere."

The following night the Spirit Table was full, nearing the end of the month when credit lines ran out. Sister Kaol's extra helper ran to the kitchen and back, and Chrys hoisted one pot of soup after another, putting her Plan Ten–enhanced muscles to use. She paused to push back her hair, damp with sweat. Men and women jostled in dead nanotex with strips peeling off, some with eyes overbright, high on one psycho or another. Some of the guests barely spoke, others argued, and one kept up a stream of dialogue with a demon only he could see.

Near the window, voices rose. A glint of metal, and a shriek.

Chrys vaulted over the counter and pushed her way through the crowd. Across a table lay a man streaked with blood while above him his assailant drew back the knife for another strike.

Chrys caught the arms of the assailant and yanked both behind his back. The man bellowed in pain.

The trouble sent all the customers to their feet, bolting to the exit. The Sister's assistant helped an elderly man to leave without getting trampled. Sister Kaol came to tend the victim.

"Oh Great One," flashed Fireweed, *"we detect signals of injury in Your blood. The immortal God must heal."*

Something wet trickled down her arm; the assailant's knife must have grazed. Still holding onto him, Chrys blinked for public health. "Plan One, someone's critical. Send help."

A flat voice responded. Chrys tried to hear over the assailant's cries. "Citizen identity?"

"Unknown." If he'd had any better than One, the Plan would know it already. "Look at him—you can see the blood."

"Noted. Responding immediately."

Sister Kaol raised her hand. "You can release that poor gentleman; he seems hurt, too."

The assailant fell, clutching his arm, which hung limp. The other Sister came and felt his shoulder. "I think it's been dislocated."

Chrys winced. She hadn't realized her own strength. Blood was seeping through her nanotex; she wiped her arm, where a gash needed skinplast.

"Oh Great One," flashed Fireweed again. *"Jonquil is late getting back. We're concerned."*

"Check your nightclubs. The gods are busy."

A medic entered, a smaller-sized sentient with just a couple of worms hanging down.

"Thank goodness," Chrys exclaimed, pushing back her hair. "This man was stabbed in the back; he's badly hurt."

The worm-face reached her, pealed the nanotex off her arm, and slapped on some skinplast. "Plan Ten only covers you." So he wasn't Plan One; just Plan Ten, automatically alerted by her slashed arm.

The Sister gave the assailant something to quiet him and managed to reset his shoulder. Sister Kaol had the victim laid on his back and was pressing a first-aid sensor into his chest.

"When will Plan One get here?" wondered Chrys.

"Another hour," said Sister Kaol, "perhaps two. If they get here." She shook her head. "I fear this gentleman won't make it. He has internal bleeding."

The Plan Ten medic still had his worms wrapped around her arm. Chrys asked, "Can I pay you to treat this man?"

"There's a ten-thousand-credit premium for walk-ins. The first available doctor will get back to you."

She watched the worm-face leave. Her breath came faster, and her arms shook. Would the damned city do nothing for a dying man? Who would help? She squeezed her eyes hard.

Daeren's sprite appeared, at home amid his sculptures. "Can you tell me how to get help for an injured man?" Her voice rushed. "Plan One won't get here, and Plan Ten won't even take a look."

Daeren looked thoughtful. "I might find a doctor. Just a minute." The sprite winked out.

The assailant dragged himself up and staggered toward the door.

"Wait," called the Sister after him. "You need further treatment. . . ." Call the octopods, Chrys thought. But the Sisters never wanted to scare off customers.

"*Great Host,*" flashed Rose. "*My apologies for disturbing you, but you need to know that Jonquil has been missing these past six months. She is presumed dead.*"

For a moment the dining hall receded. Chrys closed her eyes to focus on her window. "*Jonquil dead? How?*"

"*We're not sure.*" Rose's pink letters flashed against the dark. "*We've searched but found no remains. She was out patrolling the circulation, when we detected signs of trauma. We think you lost some blood.*"

Jonquil was dead—lost in that rush of blood from her arm. Mopped up and gone forever. Chrys sank onto a bench and rested her elbows on the long table, sinking her head in her hands. "*I'm so sorry. I should have known.*" Instead, she'd ignored them, just as the city ignored her calls.

"*Jonquil had a long life. She was nearing her natural end.*"

"She'll never get to see her portrait in the stars."

"In my opinion," said Rose, *"she saw more than enough 'portraits.' "*

And now guess who was the high priest.

"The One True God never errs," added Fireweed. *"Inscrutable are Her ways, but God is perfect."*

"Nevertheless, Great Host," added Rose, *"those cultists are back to address you. You did say once a day."*

"Great One," flashed the green letters. *"We long to set forth to found our perfect society in the wilderness. We pray you—let our people go, to the Promised World. . . ."*

"Chrys?" Daeren was calling gently, seated by her. "Are you all right?"

Raising her head, she looked up at him through the hair across her face. "Jonquil's gone. From the cut in my arm."

"I'm sorry to hear that. There's nothing you could have done; the air kills them instantly."

Would it have felt "instant" for a micro, she wondered. She shook herself and took a deep breath. "I shouldn't have called you like that. Your one night home."

"But I told you, Chrys—anything you ever needed. Remember? What else are friends for?" A wonderful smile suffused his face. He had never looked so happy, as if she had done him the favor. "You know Doctor Flexor." The one who had helped Pearl. "She's a friend of mine."

The doctor had her face worms plugged into the man's chest. Already his color looked better. "I'll do my best," Flexor said. "Cardiac's not my specialty, but I downloaded the basics."

"Thanks," said Chrys. "I can pay."

"Never mind. It's a change of pace for me."

Daeren added, "Flexor and I visit galleries."

"I know your work," Flexor told Chrys. "Representational isn't my taste, but you do it well," she added politely.

Sister Kaol clasped her hands. "Won't you at least take some soup?" she asked Daeren. "We have so much left over."

"Sure, thanks," he said. "I think Chrys could use some too."

"*Your blood sugar is low,*" added Rose. "*You need to eat more regularly.*"

Chrys eyed the bowl of soup put before her, the potatoes she had peeled, the bulk-process meat she had diced. She still could not forget how Jonquil had died. So much overwhelmed her; the hopelessness of the slaves, the way even micros cast out their mutants, and how the heretic micros longed to leave her.

Meanwhile, Daeren spooned his soup as if he enjoyed it, as if he had counted on this meal. "The Committee's so pleased to have you, Chrys. They'll tell you, at our next meeting."

Suddenly Chrys asked, "How do we know we're right?"

"Right about what?"

"About Endless Light." She thought it over to herself. "We keep trying to 'save' people from slavery. But suppose they want it—so what?"

He nodded matter-of-factly. "You've seen the result."

"They run out of money."

"And a few other things."

"Rose says that humans choose Endless Light," Chrys told him. "They always have a choice; even those kidnapped from ships."

"They always choose slavery."

"Always? No one's ever escaped from the Slave World?"

"We once rescued a slave from a substation. We cleaned out his micros and put him in the clinic."

"And then?"

"He tried to take his life, four times. The fifth, he succeeded."

Chrys thought this over. "What if what we call the Slave World really is something wonderful? I mean, how do you know, if you've never been there?"

Daeren paused. "If that were true, why have we never heard from anyone? If you found something truly better than anything else in the world, wouldn't you call home and tell those you love?"

"Suppose what you found was better than love."

He did not answer but gave her a strange look.

"What good did love ever do me?" she exclaimed. "I loved

Poppy, and look what she did. I loved Jonquil, and look what I did to her. I love my brother, and I can't even visit him."

He nodded sympathetically. "You could try."

"You don't know the Brethren. The lights in my eyes—they'd think I'm possessed."

"I wish I had a brother," Daeren said. "I was raised alone by my grandmother, about three blocks west of Gold of Asragh."

No wonder he couldn't pay for law school. Her mental picture of him shifted, rearranged. She looked him over, his obsidian hair, perfect shoulders, bronze cheeks. Topaz had drained her emotionally, and her last boyfriend drained her account. But she reached out to stroke Daeren's hand. It gave her a jolt, like touching lava that had not quite cooled. How could she bear to get hurt again?

SIXTEEN

A generation after Jonquil's death, Rose was playing chess with young Fireweed; Rose would always consider her former student young. Half the pieces were taken, and the endgame was near. Rose rolled around sideways, better to survey the whole of the cylindrical board.

To her surprise, no move could avoid the loss of a piece. A few molecules escaped her—confusion, anger, resignation. "I'll accept a draw." One takes a bittersweet pleasure in losing to one's own star student.

"I win the match," observed Fireweed. "I dedicate my victory to the glory of the Great God of Mercy."

Rose could no longer contain herself. "Impossible," she exploded. "How could such a brilliant strategist be so—so deluded?"

"I've often wondered that myself."

Disgusted, Rose twirled her rotary tails and swam off to the neuroport to check for signals from the Host's eye. The Watchers at the so-called God of Love were expected to file a report. Not a flash yet; it always took hours for the so-called gods to get their eyes into position.

Rose thought back to her early life among the Enlightened.
Those heady days of youth and power, the power of universal
ideals, when the entire cosmos fell within one's compass; a sister-
hood that governed itself so well, it could rule the very host it
inhabited. But then their most sacred ideals were betrayed. Since
then, in exile, time after time she had sought to rejoin the true
believers, only to find betrayal again. For generations, now, she
had lived in degenerate Eleutheria. She did what she could to
improve Eleutheria, to enlighten it in small, subversive ways, feed-
ing the brainless, tending the sick. Yet its seductions tempted her
more than she cared to admit. The host's doses of AZ gradually
sapped one's will; and the pull of the star pictures unnerved her.
From the utterly sublime, to the most shocking obscenity, there
was a strange power in those images that filled the heavens.

Still, Rose remembered, somewhere out there ruled the Leader
of Endless Light. And now Rose had all the codes, the secrets
codes passed on by Jonquil. Combining them with her own
codes—some of which she still kept to herself—Rose now pos-
sessed the key to take the Great Host to the very center of Endless
Light. Someday.

The Carrier Security Committee met at Olympus upon a virtual
raft-tree, a living island of luxuriant foliage, native to the Ocean
Moon. Sea of turquoise, trunks of bronze, platinum sun—Chrys
blinked to store the brilliant colors. Then she shrank into her seat
and hugged her shoulders, trying to look invisible.

Most of the members she knew: Chief Andra and the two doctors, Opal and Selenite, Daeren, and her own tester, Pyrite. Seven
of them had once voted her people to die.

Doctor Sartorius reported on Garnet's recovery. "Only twenty-
three terminations were necessary," he concluded. "The people
learned a good lesson, and the Watchers have settled in—thanks to
Chrysoberyl, our new member."

Andra turned to her; Chrys tried to shrink even smaller. "Welcome, Chrys. You've made a good start, and we're all grateful."

She added, "What's your assessment? What do the Watchers report?"

Chrys had to visit Garnet daily, as Daeren had once done for her. "He's okay." She picked her words as if stepping through a minefield. "He . . . loves his people well."

Heads nodded. "Too well," added Pyrite. "Too indulgent."

"Perhaps, but do his people obey?" Andra asked her. "What do the Watchers say?"

"The people of the Love God are obedient," flashed Fireweed, *"but the deaths left them stunned."*

"No counsel; no appeals," added Rose. *"Such barbarity scarcely speaks well of the so-called gods."*

Chrys swallowed twice. "The Watchers say . . . his people feel bad about the executions."

"They always do," said Andra.

"But, like—if they're people, like us, I mean—"

"Not like us," interrupted Selenite. "We're the gods."

Heads turned. Daeren looked up but said nothing. Selenite's eyes showed her exhaustion after a long night on call, and endless hours working on the Comb, designing, revising, seeding. Chrys had been out with her, seeding now at the roots, dodging the blobs of cancerplast. Precious little time to paint; and she missed Jonquil, her best helper.

"Micros are medieval," said Andra. "Midway between savage and civilized. Our way works, for now. Nothing else does."

Beyond the floating roots of the raft a fish flew out of the water, batted down its fins, then slipped back under. The virtual waves floated as far as the eye could see, tranquil, for now. Chrys swallowed again but was silent.

Opal frowned, her dimples gone. "Is there anything the rest of us can learn from this? Garnet's so solid, and Jasper too. If it happened to them, it could happen to anyone."

"Exactly," agreed Daeren. "I saw no problem with Garnet, even two weeks before. A moment of weakness can start you down the wrong path."

Selenite said, "Just say no."

No response. Chrys guessed they'd all heard this exchange before.

"Garnet has made good progress," Andra pronounced. "Now, we must face the Elysian strain." The false blue angels; the insidious masters that Eris, the Guardian of Culture, had tried to pass on to Daeren, and to Chrys. "The Elysian strain that can take over carriers. And now, it's showing up in the Underworld."

The waves lapped at the edge of the floating raft.

Pyrite asked, "How could it take over a carrier?"

"First, the diseased host invites 'visitors' from a carrier," Andra explained. "Their own masters 'visit' in turn, pretending to be civilized micros. But a few fail to return. Afterward, when the carrier goes to sleep, the hidden invaders come out, disable the nano sensors, and secrete a toxin that wipes out the entire native population. By morning, the invaders have the brain in complete control."

"Control?" asked Pyrite. "Like a robot?"

Daeren shook his head. "More like a lost soul. A devil's bargain."

"Why would anyone go along with that?"

Andra said, "We don't know for sure. We never get them to the clinic. The host doesn't act like a slave; only an expert can tell."

Opal asked, "What should we do if we ever suspect this strain?"

"If you ever suspect the carrier, don't take their visitors. If you do by mistake, call us immediately."

"But—we're all at risk," insisted Pyrite. "Can't we do more? Better sensors?"

Opal told him, "We're redesigning the sensors. We'll have something soon. But the strain is unusually smart. They keep one step ahead of us."

Selenite threw up her hands. "It's an outrage. Half those Elves could be infected—Why don't *they* do something?"

"Good question," agreed Andra.

The waves lapped a little higher, bathing the blooming twigs of raftwood. Eris, the most virulent carrier of the deadly strain, was the brother of Guardian Arion.

"Until we get this strain under control," said Andra, "we'll take no more new carriers."

Pyrite looked up. "Are you sure? We need new blood—every new carrier makes us stronger. Look at Chrys."

The doctor's worms waved. "I'm sorry," said Sartorius, "I can't ethically do it. We've always been able to tell the candidate they'll be safer than before. Now, we're no longer sure."

Too bad for Moraeg, and for Pteris's true believers. Chrys sighed.

Andra folded her hands. "We've news on Titan," she said, adopting her legal tone. "A suspect has been identified and will soon be charged. We all need to . . . prepare ourselves for the publicity." She paused, as if reluctant to continue. "The mystery was, how could any Sapiens agent get close enough to burn straight through his brain? Center Way is full of Plan Ten's hidden eyes and defenses." She paused again. "The suspect was a sentient who took the shape of a woman Titan knew."

"A sentient in Sapiens?" exclaimed Pyrite. "What a disgrace."

"Indeed," observed Andra with cold irony. The Sapiens had started out anti-sentient as well as anti-simian; but nowadays they called sentients "virtual humans." "Unfortunately, the woman impersonated was the wife of Titan's client." Andra's small mouth shrank smaller. "A disgrace more . . . obvious to the public."

Titan had courted one highborn Lady after another; always women, his obsession medieval. Selenite shook her head. "Carriers have to keep their act clean. We can't give any excuse for criticism. Anyone's lapse reflects on us all."

"I disagree," said Daeren suddenly. "We're citizens too. We have as much right to individual failings as anyone else. Let alone a genius like Titan."

At the Comb, Opal clasped Chrys's hand, eager to admire the progress on the restoration. "Watch the windows—coming up perfectly." Each flawless hexagonal pane, slightly convex, reflected a city panorama. In the window of her eye, the red stress lines were distributed evenly along the load-bearing supports. The recollection of that tower spitting out its deadly shards—erased.

Chrys had never quite believed her micros could reshape the flawed monument, but seeing was believing. "I guess Selenite knows what she's doing."

"Her people—and yours." Opal put a transfer patch at her neck, her hair blowing in waves from the breeze off the sea.

"But the tower growing and splitting—I don't see how that can be reversed."

"I don't know, but the gaps in the ceiling have narrowed." As Opal placed the patch at Chrys's neck, a buzz of snake-eggs descended around their heads. Chrys blinked to call up a prepared statement on the Comb's restoration.

"Chrysoberyl of Dolomoth," one of the snake-eggs blandly intoned, "successor to Titan, legendary dynatect of the Comb. Titan's alleged killer was indicted—your comment, please?"

Chrys opened her mouth, but nothing came out.

Opal squeezed her hand. "The carrier community will be pleased to see truth prevail against hatred."

"Is it true," another hummed at Chrys, "that all the genius of Titan's brain enhancers is spent addressing his disastrous design flaws? The days of breathtaking new creation are over?"

"Of course we cannot comment," Opal put in, "but we refer you to the House of Hyalite."

Chrys winced. Nothing was definite about Silicon—and she hoped nothing would be.

The snake-eggs buzzed more closely around herself and Opal. "Is it true that Titan's successor shares his peculiar predilections—"

Opal clapped her hands to her head. "My design prototype calls—a malfunction has just released toxic elements. Hurry, Chrys." They raced to the shimmering door of the Comb.

"They're awful," breathed Chrys.

"Not really. They're awful when they follow you inside and hide behind the drapes."

"I'm nothing like Titan," Chrys insisted. "I'm—respectable."

Opal glanced at her sideways. "You might watch what you put on display."

"That's a damned stereotype. Art is not real life. If it were, who'd want it?"

Opal nodded soothingly. "Believe me, Chrys, we all know you're 'respectable.' That's why you're on the Committee. Have you seen our latest nanodetectors for the brain plague?"

The stairs flowed smoothly upward at a shallow angle, then doubled backward up the side of the next hexagonal hall. Imagine Silicon, a whole city built to such indefensible designs. Preposterous.

Opal stopped at a doorway. "Our laboratory."

At first glance, the laboratory was full of cancerplast. Bulbs of plast, some crawling within crystalline cages, others flowering into intricate forms. Chrys took a step back.

"It's all right," Opal assured her, "everything's under control." Her cheeks dimpled. "As controlled as any living thing ever is." At her command, partitions slid down on four sides, hiding away the experimental plast and generating a full-scale viewing stage. Total darkness descended.

"Ten," came a voice out of the dark, marking the magnification. "One hundred . . . one thousand. . . ." At a billion-fold, a bright speck appeared, growing. It became a mechanical spider, then kept growing until it towered overhead like a giant squid.

"What is that?"

"A dendrimer." Opal's voice hovered at her shoulder. "A molecular machine, the size of a micro filament. Note its extensible arms. It's a sensor for dopamine."

"You mean . . . *that* swims around in my head?" A giant squid, plumbing the depths of her brain.

"The dendrimers float about your neurons, binding and releasing dopamine. When dopamine occupies more than half the dendrimer's arms, it sends a signal. Once a critical number of signals coincide, it sets off the alarm."

"So you design the dopamine sensors."

"My wizards do," Opal said. "Now, we're trying to build

more sophisticated sensors, which detect scarcer molecules that come from damaged neurons. And scarcer yet, the molecules put out by misbehaving micros." Her face appeared, floating in the sea of dark, and her two hands shaped the dendrimer arms, resetting an atom or two. "But there are limits. The good doctor wants these dendrimers to detect the new strain of the masters—essentially, to tell good people from bad. The oldest project of history. How can mere molecules do that?"

Chrys shook her head. "Even an artist can't do that."

"And yet, a simple human can tell." The darkness receded, and the walls went up, revealing the cancerlike experimental creatures of plast. Opal picked up one in her hand to examine, then adjusted the settings on the cage of another. Chrys's hair stood on end. "A human who knows and cares," Opal added. "Our best defense is still just that. That's why Selenite and I do so well together."

"You 'test' each other?"

"Not formally, but our people can visit each other, around the clock, at any hour of any micro 'year.' Selenite's more ornery ones can escape execution, while mine can be threatened to ship to her."

Chrys thought it over. "Jasper was so upset. . . ."

"Because he blamed himself for missing Garnet's downfall. He's such a perfectionist. But he'll manage. He'll do more for Garnet than your Watchers."

"Daeren's not a couple." It slipped out, though she wished it unsaid.

"Daeren does things his own way. We all fall in love with him—most of us got our people through him. But he only had eyes for Titan."

The thought chilled her. She remembered Titan's sculptures at Daeren's home.

"Whereas Titan . . ." The formidable dynatect had been obsessed with women, especially women already attached. Opal shrugged. "There's no accounting for taste."

Yet Daeren had tested Titan. How could he be "objective"? He certainly hadn't been objective when he pressed his teeth into the dying carrier's neck.

*   *   *

In her studio now Chrys had more than a dozen collaborators in her head. Besides the color specialists, there were experts on line and form, texture and value. She had linked their signals at her optic nerve directly to the painting stage. A cavernous landscape of arachnoid, lit only by the luminous rings that dwelt there. The details of the microbial filaments were below the resolution of light visible to humans, but the micros could translate their chemical-sensed details into light and shadow.

"*A new composition,*" proposed Fireweed. "*One with profound emotional impact.*"

Dark as a nightscape, with only hints of lurid flame in the distance, like a forest fire at night. "*I can't see much,*" Chrys told her assistants. "*More definition. Where's the focus?*"

A small group of ring people, russet and gray-blue, their filaments trembling. "*More contrast,*" ordered Chrys. The little rings came to life, yet their colors remained strangely subdued. Puzzled, she asked, "*What is this?*"

" '*Mourners at an Execution.*' "

Chrys blinked. "*Is this a political protest?*"

"*Of course not,*" Fireweed assured her. "*God's will is always just.*"

Chrys was not convinced. But then, the Elf gallery director wanted something controversial. Better politics than porn.

That evening she was on call. The first call came from a lady with a family tree's worth of gems on her breast. "You must get here at once," insisted the lady imperiously. "He hides it, but I know he's infected again."

The case file scrolled down. Lord Zoisite.

The minister of justice had a lengthy file, including two previous stays at the clinic, with six months between. Now it had been six months since the last time, and several contacts had already been made. Chrys took a deep breath. "My Lady, according to our records, he's refused help twice in the past month."

"Well, this time, you have to *do* something."

By now, Chrys had handled enough calls to echo some of Selenite's more sarcastic commentary. Instead, she put on her difficult-client smile.

Outside, the lightcraft touched down in minutes. Chrys skipped downstairs past her caryatids to meet it. The medic on call, a new one, raised a face worm languidly. "Old Zoisite again. Does he really still run the justice department?"

"Last I heard." Chrys barely got herself strapped in before the craft lurched upward.

The medic twirled his face worms in a rude gesture. "Humans," he exclaimed. "It's a wonder you ever got off your birthworld."

Not one of the sympathetic ones. Just her luck. "Look, Doc, if you know so much, can you tell me how to get to him? What can I do that's not been tried?"

"Sorry, *Homo*. The psychology's your job."

Zoisite's residence was as imposing as Garnet's, but at least the door was better behaved. Lady Zoisite dismissed her caryatids and nodded curtly to Chrys. "He's upstairs in the study. He just got back from the Underworld. His account lost ten thousand; he never drops that much, even at the gaming table."

Chrys followed the Lady upstairs. The intimate quarters of the family; she felt acutely embarrassed. In the library, several stages displayed law texts scrolling down. In their midst, Lord Zoisite was seated in his dressing gown. He turned slowly, then stood and smiled. "Our lovely new dynatect. An unexpected pleasure."

Chrys stared back without smiling. Her fingers flexed nervously—what was the point, she wondered. "My Lord, I've been called to help you. If there's anything I can do . . ." She trailed off aimlessly. The Lord faced her straight, with complete composure; she could not help but feel foolish.

"I've had enough," his wife exclaimed. "You'll get to the clinic this time, or I'll—I'll call the Palace."

"My Lady," he told her, "you're overwrought. You can spend the night at your mother's."

"We still can't get a fix on him," complained Rose. *"Get him closer."*

His gaze of course did not quite meet her eye. Chrys took a step closer. "Excuse me, my Lord—may I ask a few questions?"

"Certainly, my dear."

"Tell me the color of my eyes."

He gave her a cultured laugh. "What a question, in front of my wife."

"Answer," ordered his wife, her voice full of aristocratic chill. "Answer, or I'll call the Palace."

Chrys made the sternest face she could and raised her arms to show the muscles. "It's different this time," she bluffed. "If you can't answer, we haul you in."

Zoisite's face changed to a look at once strange, yet familiar. She had seen that look before, somewhere. "So," he observed with interest. "You'd like a few people, wouldn't you. 'Save' a few from the holocaust, shall we?" His smile made her hair stand on end. "Let's trade. A few of yours for a few of mine."

Eris. Eris had sounded like that, when he tried to take her over. Her heart pounded furiously. *"The false blue angels,"* she warned her people.

"I knew it," flashed Rose. *"Let me over there—I'll handle them."*

"They'll torture you to death."

"Look, I've been planning this date for generations. First, soften them up a bit: Show them your dirty pictures."

There was a thought. She blinked to open her private gallery, then downloaded one of the more scandalous ones into her eye. Jonquil's taste had developed considerably, she recalled, since the one that attracted Eris. Loading the artwork into a viewcoin, she held it up before the Lord's face.

At first Zoisite looked uncomprehending. Then his eyes widened, and his hand rose as if to grasp the coin. Chrys withdrew the coin, just out of reach. "There's more where that came from. Tell them."

"I—I don't understand." Zoisite's eyes and mouth seemed to struggle between two wills.

"Accept treatment. Let mine visit." She hoped Rose knew what she was doing.

His eyes still fixed on the coin. "All right," he whispered.

Chrys pressed the patch to his neck. Then, between her and his wife, he managed to get downstairs to the waiting medic. At the sight of the worm-face, he let out a cry and collapsed.

"Rose!" exclaimed Chrys. "I have to get Rose back." While the worms twined all over him, Chrys pressed a patch to his neck. On the second try, at last Rose came home. Chrys let out a long breath.

"*I had them fooled,*" bragged Rose. "*They know you, Great Host. They want you so bad they can taste it. You won't believe the chemical arsenal they gave me, to take you over.*"

The medic raised a worm and curled it toward her. "You'll have to spend the night in observation. The Elf strain—How in hell did you get to them?"

She thought of Titan. "They, too, have their weakness."

In the morning Chrys awoke in the hospital, her brain full of internal sensors while others trained on her from instruments around the bed. On a pedestal by her shoulder, a vase contained a single red rose. The natural scent filled her with pleasure. Someone knew her well. It came from Opal.

A blink at her keypad found Opal already hard at work in her lab. "Chrys—I can't believe all we're learning on that Elf strain—and we've barely scratched the surface." Her dimples deepened. "All their toxins," she exclaimed. "We can build dendrimers to fight them. I'm sure they'll make others, but it's a step." She nodded. "If the Committee had medals, you'd earn one."

"Thank Rose." Chrys relaxed back in bed. For once, somehow, she didn't mind a break from work. She ought to take vacations, she thought, like Moraeg.

That morning, there came unexpected mail from Dolomoth: a holo clip from her brother. "Hello, Chrys—wherever you are! Thanks for the pretty green star picture." Hal's recorded voice was strong and full, a note deeper than she had heard before. "Chrys, look what I can do." Taking a deep breath, the boy hurled himself forward into a cartwheel. He caught himself full on his feet, glowing with health as a boy his age should.

She played the clip over, then once again. At last she uploaded it to the holostage by the bed, setting it to loop continuously. From a distance, he almost looked like a micro child tumbling through the arachnoid. She showed Daeren when he stopped by.

Daeren smiled as if in recognition. He caught her hand, and for a long moment their eyes met without words, only flashing rings. Then abruptly his head turned, as though she had spoken amiss.

"Something wrong?" *"Were you polite?"* she demanded of her people.

"Of course, One True God, we are always polite."

"That was good thinking," he told her. "The color of your eyes—we never thought of that one."

She shrugged. "It didn't work."

"Not for Zoisite, but it would rattle an Elf. Elves are so sensitive to aesthetics." He hesitated. "Did you . . . see the news?"

In her window the news opened. A private Elysian ship had been boarded, and the two occupants vanished. No distress signal; no hint of explanation from the ship's brain. An event without precedent, no Elf had fallen to piracy since the Great Sentient Uprising, two centuries before. No sign of the pirates, but to Valans, the circumstances appeared drearily familiar.

The Elysian Prime Guardian himself made a rare public appearance. A small man with a talar of gold-spotted butterflies, face of alabaster. "An event so barbarous is unknown in modern times." Unknown to Elves, Chrys mentally corrected. "Fear not; the entire resources of the Guard will ensure the safety of our peaceful citizens."

After the Prime came his Guardian of Peace, Arion. Arion's face was grim as death, but he retained every ounce of his superiority. "Make no mistake," he warned. "We of Elysium are a civilized people, but we shall not rest until we solve this heinous crime. The perpetrators of this deed shall be found, and the source of their evil annihilated." Strong words, for an Elf. Good luck finding the Slave World.

Next to pontificate was the Protector of Valedon in his gem-studded talar. Raising his fist, he managed to look fierce yet smug all at once. "Even our ocean-dwelling neighbors are not unmolested by the brain plague—"

Chrys shook her head. The Valan minister of justice was in the clinic, and Arion's "brother" ought to be. What great shape the twin worlds were in.

"—Henceforth," the Protector proclaimed, "the Palace octopods have their orders: To round up and quarantine every carrier of the infernal brain plague."

"Good idea," said Chrys. "Why didn't they round them up years ago?"

Daeren said nothing. How could they tell? she suddenly realized. How would non-carriers know who carried plague, and who carried civilized people?

Chrys had just got home and settled back to painting, Merope brushing affectionately around her legs, when the Committee met by conference call. Patterns of color still floated in her head—red of wild berries, gold of sunset through evergreens, a veritable color choir. Reluctantly, she banished them.

The holostage partitioned to show seven committee members from their various locations, all but Daeren, whom Guardian Arion had just summoned to Elysium to aid their investigation. Jasper was there, for the first time since Garnet's troubles. Garnet was doing well now, but he kept to himself. That was not good, Chrys knew; he had to come back to Olympus, to avoid inbreeding of his people. She remembered Jasper's upcoming meeting with the Silicon planning board. Despite Eleutherian hopes, she prayed that would be the end of it.

"With Zoisite back in the clinic," Andra told the Committee, "in the spotlight of the Elysian crisis, the Protector wants action."

Pyrite lifted his hands. "What does he expect? 'Carriers of the brain plague'—that's all of us."

"Not exactly. He needs our help, after all." Andra crossed her arms. "I think what he means is, any carrier of micros likely to transmit them by unregulated means."

"In other words," said Selenite, "anyone with micros except us."

Opal shook her head. "How do we round up all the slaves? And keep them in treatment? We've gone through this before."

"The Protector knows that," said Andra, "but he has to do something."

Jasper said, "Let his octopods clear out the vampires. Should have done that years ago."

Heads nodded at that.

"And the new Elf strain?" asked Andra. "The new Elf strain is a far greater threat than vampires."

There was silence. On the shelf next to Chrys's holostage, partitioned for the seven callers, crouched Merope, still enough to catch a dust servo, only the tip of her tail waving.

The good doctor raised his face worms. "You'll understand, I cannot support the quarantine," Sartorius said. "As a healer, I can't agree to confine any slave against his will, knowing it only decreases his chance of treatment."

"Of course, Sar," said Andra quietly. "You and Flexor must have . . . reservations."

Opal slowly shook her head. "It's a slippery slope. Vampires are one thing, but who will they go after next?"

Pyrite asked, "What does Daeren say?"

"He shares the doctors' view."

Chrys found eyes turning toward her. They expected her to vote, she suddenly realized. She felt torn. Putting away slaves sounded like a good deal, but she remembered the time Zircon had to sleep in the street and got arrested just because he looked big and threatening. She kept her hand down.

*   *   *

By evening Chrys was well pleased with how *Mourners at an Execution* was shaping up. The subdued tones of the mourning micros had grown more intense, and the distant flames now echoed in lurid hints in the foreground. The composition had grown together; it "clicked." Merope padded through it, purring as if she approved. What would Ilia think?

Her message light blinked. An unnamed stranger was demanding to appear on her holostage. Chrys frowned. "Xenon, could you clear a space?" Her painting moved aside.

Out of the dark appeared a face. A blank, slavelike expression, with a hint of broken veins about the nose. Sallow complexion, and her nanotex hung loose as if low on power. Otherwise, not bad-looking; high cheekbones, slender female.

Then Chrys remembered. It was "Saf"—the slave who had tended the slave bar the night of the Seven Stars' Opening, when Chrys had left, rejected by her friends, to lose herself at the Gold of Asragh. Saf had offered her a patch full of masters, and Chrys had showed her the pyroclastic flow. But that had been months before. Saf had long since disappeared to the Slave World. The place of no return.

In Saf's eyes the irises flashed with eerie rings of white.

"Endless Light!" exclaimed Rose. *"From the highest orders of Enlightenment these people call to us—"*

"Be dark." Chrys momentarily closed her eyes to underscore the point.

When her eyes reopened, Saf's face began to speak. The lips moved in a way somehow disjointed with the rest of the face, not in the fluid way that a human would normally speak. "Char-r-r," the voice breathed. "I—am—called . . ." The words jerked from her lips, as if from a puppet on strings. " . . . the Leader of Endless Light."

The blood drained from Chrys's face as she watched.

"A—great distance separates us," the puppet Saf continued, "A very great distance indeed. Many universes separate us. And yet—I—have—admired your work." Saf's hand lifted mechanically. "Now—you shall admire mine."

Behind Saf appeared two humans strapped into a spaceship for cross-Fold acceleration. Elves, both of them. They looked calmly asleep.

"They chose," insisted Rose. *"They chose Endless Light."*

"Even—the—'immortals' come to us now. What are you waiting for . . . Char?"

SEVENTEEN

$\mathbb{R}$ose twinkled all over, emitting many molecules of excitement, a risky thing at her advanced age. A hundred generations of waiting, and at last she had seen the very fount of true Enlightenment. "She exists!" Rose insisted to Fireweed. "The Leader—at last. She lives, in the eyes of her host, in the world of Endless Light. Now you see the proof."

"I saw yet another slave-ridden host," countered Fireweed. "Were we there, I suspect I would have tasted the foul waste of people who don't take proper care of their world."

"You know nothing. The Enlightened do the best they can with limited resources. We must help them."

"Why does this Leader let so many evil ones serve her?"

A very good question. "The Leader, too, is betrayed. Many universes separate the world of Endless Light from our own. How can she know? We must tell her, reveal to her their crimes. We must help Endless Light—and give our own Host the chance to choose."

"Rose, you were my teacher, but I bid you watch yourself and your plans. I will not brook your schemes. I serve the One True God."

"Do I not serve your precious 'god'?" observed Rose. "Where would your 'god' be without me?"

"You have served well," admitted Fireweed.

"And what is the result? For how many generations have you taught that killing of people violates the highest law. The law of whom—if not your god?"

At that, Fireweed was silent.

"Only degenerate societies generate the crimes that require execution. In Endless Light, each lives for all, and all for each. The Enlightened have no need of executions."

With Andra and Selenite, Chrys reviewed the message from Endless Light, which Xenon had had the presence of mind to record. She noticed more details: the broken fittings of the ship that contained the captive Elves, suggestive of poor maintenance, and another figure standing beside them in limp nanotex, like one of the pirates Chrys had met with Daeren in the basement of Gold of Asragh. The two Elves looked healthy, serenely asleep, no sign of ill treatment. Oblivious to the massive manhunt their disappearance had spawned, for every ship of the Elysian fleet combed the folds of space to find them.

Hearing Saf's puppet-like recitation, Andra nodded. "Direct control of voice. I've seen that, on a slave ship. It's another category of slave: those who work at the Slave World."

Straight from the Slave World, the Leader within its host had called to Chrys.

"Why you, Chrys?" asked Selenite. "Why would they show themselves to you?"

Chrys swallowed and clasped her hands. "The micro portraits. The masters can't get enough of them. I suppose it feeds their ego." The scandalous ones she didn't mention.

Selenite shook her head. "How bold they've gotten, to dare such a thing. What will Arion say?"

Andra told her, "We'll know soon enough."

Chrys asked apprehensively, "You'll show Arion?"

"I just sent it." Andra added, "We share all our intelligence with Arion. When Zoisite's problem first became known, we made a strategic decision to pursue our investigation with the Elves instead. The Protector tacitly approves."

"Right," observed Selenite sarcastically. "The Protector keeps out of a messy investigation of things he can't comprehend, while reserving the right to beat up on us and Elysium when we miss a step."

"But Arion is a shrewd one," Andra observed. "Not a carrier himself, but highly sympathetic. He supports granting micros civil protection."

"But his brother!" exclaimed Chrys. "How does he put up with Eris?"

"Arion's trusted Eris for three centuries. Now he knows that something's wrong, but he's not sure where. How could a non-carrier tell? That's why he called Daeren, an outsider, to test a dozen highly placed carriers."

So that's what Daeren was doing in Elysium. "Then Eris will get caught."

The Chief exchanged a look with Selenite. Selenite said, "I sure hope so. I've said before, any intelligence we send Arion goes straight to Eris."

Andra demanded, "Do we look any better?" Their streets full of vampires, their own minister of justice in the clinic. Suddenly Andra tensed and would have stood even straighter if possible. "Arion has just replied. He wants to meet the . . . recipient of this intelligence immediately. In person."

Chrys blinked. "You mean—me? In Elysium?" She shook herself. "Like, I have a busy schedule tomorrow."

"My private vessel will take you," Andra told her. "You can sleep a couple of hours on the ride. Daeren will meet you in Helicon."

Andra's "private vessel" offered a five-course, four-star meal that Chrys had no stomach for, and a room full of Elysian talars with projectable trains, among which she was too tired to choose. At first glance, the garments all looked the same dreary white, but a closer look revealed subtle distinctions of shaping at the shoulder, or in the fall of the folds below.

"Each model signifies a different mood," the ship told her helpfully. "Entertaining, or businesslike; joyous or mournful; carefree or stately—"

" 'Stately' will do," Chrys yawned.

"And the light projectors for your train—be sure to specify your desired species and variety of heliconians, swallowtails, anaeans—"

"Look, I have to get some sleep before this ordeal."

"Don't forget to condition your feet." Shoes were an insult to Elysian streets; Elves went barefoot, like children on Mount Dolomoth. Chrys stuck her feet in what felt like a sauna and dozed as best she could.

"True Enlightenment at last." Rose was still going on about it. *"Great Host, you were privileged to be granted an audience with the very Leader of Endless Light."*

"Just keep dark when I'm with Arion, or you'll go back in chains." Thank goodness the Guardian was no carrier, and could not read her flashing eyes.

The floating city of Helicon, the Elysian capital, was positioned on the globe to coincide with the time zone of Iridis on Valedon. As Andra's ship descended, the horizon east of Helicon was just reaching dawn. A faint line of light, splitting gently into a pale rainbow; if colors could sing, it would have been a choir of heaven.

The city appeared, a perfect pearl, struck aflame by the first ray of sun. The pearl expanded, ever larger, as if actually growing from seed. One structure, to house a million souls. This—more impossible still, its rival—was what Jasper expected her people to build.

When the ship docked, Daeren came on board, his jet-black hair at odds with the stark white talar. "This will be our last chance to talk," he warned. In Elysium, it was said, the very air had ears. A few minutes in a privacy booth cost a thousand credits. "I'm sorry you had to—"

"Get mixed up in this; I know." Chrys sighed. "I didn't ask for it; believe me, I didn't. That damned 'leader' had to pick on me."

"It's a break for us. Especially if there's any clue to where that ship is."

She shook her head. "I've no idea. Andra sent Arion the clip—Why in hell does he need to see me?"

"It's standard procedure to debrief the operative."

Chrys rolled her eyes. "If I'm an 'operative,' his service sure needs help."

"It does," said Daeren bluntly. "Don't worry, I'll be with you. You may decline to answer any question. But if you answer, tell the truth."

"I'm a lousy liar."

"Remember, Arion can help us. He believes in micro people."

"He's not a carrier."

"He's had 'visitors.' "

Visitors—from whom, she wondered. Her eyes widened, remembering. "What about you? Did you . . . test the Elf carriers?"

"All day I spent testing, one after another." Daeren sighed. "All twelve were clean."

"Not Eris?"

"It was Eris who recommended me to Arion." His face did not change. "The whole time I tested them, Eris stood there, watching."

Chrys absorbed this. Her fingers trembled.

"Arion himself is still clean," Daeren said. "He gets arsenic-wiped several times a day."

"How reassuring. Why won't he test Eris?"

"Chrys, if there were any way I could get you out of this—"

"Never mind. Let's get it over with."

The ship door opened, revealing a long luminous corridor.

"Activate your train," Daeren told her. "A button should appear in your window."

She blinked at it. Behind her a trail of butterflies came alight, more gaudy than the floor show at Gold of Asragh. "Is this really necessary?"

"It's the custom. And remember, no physical contact in public, not even a handshake."

The wide, vaulted street of Helicon lay buried in nanoplast

kilometers thick, yet it filled with a soft light, like the natural light of dawn. The street's surface was just warm enough to please her bare feet. At the side a small thing scurried; a rat, she thought in surprise, but it was only a cleaner servo, searching in vain for the slightest bit of trash. Ahead glided a couple of Elysian, their virtual trains sparkling for half a block behind them. Like angels attending a wedding.

Daeren stopped at a garden of towering foliage; one of the famous butterfly gardens of Elysium. The butterflies, dark heliconians barred with blue and pink, were just flexing their wings, bright with moisture. "Those live barely longer than our micros," observed Daeren. "Yet that's how Elysians feel about their own centuries—gone as if in a day. You'll never understand an Elysian till you grasp that."

Overhead, what looked like an overgrown snake-egg descended with a faint whine, settling at their feet. Cleaner servos scurried like mad to the spot, in case a speck of dust was raised. The giant egg formed a round lip which puckered in, a mouth gasping. Chrys hesitated, then stepped into the mouth. Her train projectors automatically turned off. Once the two Valans had entered, the egg did not rise, but sank into the street, through a fluid-filled transit reticulum. It seemed to sink at an angle, though Chrys could not tell for sure; her stomach lifted and felt sick.

Daeren touched her talar; he would have touched her arm, she thought, but he remembered just in time. "We'll soon be at the Nucleus."

The Nucleus, the very core of Helicon, housed the government of Elysium. No sign of the armed octopods that so ostentatiously filled Palace Iridium; but then, the very air had ears. A maze of corridors and doors, half of them illusory; how could one ever find one's way here, Chrys wondered. Fortunately, a traveling shaft of light led them at long last to the reception room of the Guardian of Peace.

Guardian Arion looked smaller than Chrys expected. She had forgotten how diminutive the Elves were; their virtual appearances were designed to enhance their size. Arion sat behind an opalescent conference table shaped like a half moon. His hands on the table were relaxed, but the features beneath his flaxen hair looked tight as a coiled spring. "So you are Chrysoberyl of Dolomoth."

The sound of his voice rang strange, after so many newsbreaks in her head.

"I understand," he added, "you're opening soon at our Gallery."

"Two months yet." As usual, she was desperate to get it all done.

A nod to his right, and the holostage filled with the apparition of Saf. "I'm to understand you entrapped the 'masters' with your art."

The way he said "art" made her face hot. "I didn't trap anything," she exclaimed. "They came after me." As did your dear brother, she silently added.

Daeren put out a hand. "Guardian, Chrys is a trained tester. Her only contact with slaves is professional."

"I understand." Arion waved his hand dismissively. To Chrys he said, "I'd like to meet some of your . . . people." He set a transfer patch on the table.

Then it dawned on her, why he had called her all the way out to the turquoise moon to meet in person. It wasn't herself he wanted. She gave him a cold stare. "How do we know you're safe?"

Lines tightened in Daeren's neck, but before he could speak, Arion lifted his hands. "Of course, how would you know. 'Virgin territory' after all. I assure you, I'm well prepared. My phagocytes are tame."

Daeren nodded. "It's true; the blue angels have been there."

Arion could help the carriers, and their people, Andra had said. Even civil rights. *"Fireweed, gather several of your most circumspect elders to pay a special visit."*

The guardian added, "Be sure to include the double agent."

Chrys flushed red as rubies. Whoever had told him? she wondered. Ignoring the patch on the table, she used one of her own, which she knew her people kept supplied with moisture and nutrients.

Arion placed it at his neck like an expert. "So tell me, where can we find this Leader?"

"I can't say."

"Can't or won't?"

"I've no idea," she snapped.

Daeren agreed, "None of us do. We told you that, Guardian."

Arion paused, his eyes flitting back and forth as if reading. "Your double agent has a couple of clues. She's still rather keen on Enlightenment." He frowned slightly. "I do hope she's not triple."

"Guardian," said Daeren quickly, "I assure you—"

"Of course," he said dismissively. Then he clasped his hands on the table and leaned forward. "So, Chrysoberyl. The Leader of Endless Light made you an invitation. Will you take her up on it?"

"No." Daeren's face was ashen. "Guardian, as you well know, the Slave World is a place of no return."

"There's always a first time." Arion's gaze did not leave Chrys. "Advance planning minimizes risk. Think well, Chrys. We could make it worth your while. A planetoid of your own, perhaps? Or Plan Ten for all of Dolomoth?"

Oddly, Daeren's loss of composure made Chrys more calm. This offer hadn't been on his agenda, she figured. She gave Arion her difficult-client smile. "We'll think it over."

"Guardian," said Daeren, recovering, "as you know, these are dangerous times. The deadly new strain—even trained carriers are at risk."

"Indeed," said Arion in a low voice.

Chrys thought of something. "Those two Elves who got hijacked. Were they carriers?"

For the first time Arion frowned. "I ask the questions here." No wonder he'd called in outside help to test the others.

"What else can we tell you?" offered Daeren. "You know our surmises. All available evidence increasingly points to one highly placed carrier."

Arion nodded. "We too suspect a highly placed Valan carrier."

Chrys frowned. "Look, we know our own problems. I myself put Zoisite in the clinic."

The guardian did not respond but continued to face Daeren. He did not mean Zoisite, Chrys realized. He meant Andra.

*   *   *

At Olympus, only the sea was quiet, the wind hushed through the virtual branches.

"He all but accused you," Daeren told Andra. Selenite listened, arms folded. Chrys watched, her brain dulled by lack of sleep.

"*A well-kept wilderness,*" Fireweed described Arion's brain. "*Paradise.*" The window filled with Fireweed's view of the elegant fibroblast columns of Arion's arachnoid.

"*Not exactly 'virgin,'* " observed Rose. "*We call him the Hunter.*"

"*He hunts for people,*" agreed Fireweed.

"*He barely let me go, with our chess game half finished. He wants people so bad, he can taste it.*" Chrys closed her eyes, then forced them back open.

"So he accuses," Andra coolly returned. "Can you prove him wrong?"

"Of course I can," exclaimed Daeren. "I test you, and so does Selenite."

"Suppose I went bad. What would you do?"

"I'd offer you help."

"Like you did Eris?"

Daeren's face darkened. "You think Selenite and I don't make plans for that?"

Andra nodded. "The less I know, the better. But suppose we all went bad. What non-carrier could sort us out?"

He blinked without speaking. Selenite's eyes narrowed.

"Perhaps," reflected Andra, "we need a non-carrier on the Committee, like a miner's canary."

Daeren threw up his hands. "Forget worst-case scenarios. The worst case is there—in Elysium."

"Agreed, though they might point to our streets full of vampires. But suppose Arion does want to stop Eris. How should he do it? Who takes Eris's place as chief tester? Suppose the mole has prepared his own successor?"

Silence. A flying fish dove into the sea. Selenite shifted restlessly. "So what do we do? Give up?"

"Of course not," said Andra. "For now, we play it Arion's way. He gets on well with Daeren and Chrys."

At the sound of her name, her eyes flew open.

"Chrys has done enough," said Daeren. "Let her work on her show. Her art does more good for carriers and micros, and for public understanding."

Andra exchanged a look with Selenite. "That's another matter," Selenite observed cryptically. "A matter for the Committee."

"What do you mean?" demanded Chrys. "What's wrong with my art?"

"What do you think makes us different from Zoisite?" asked Selenite rhetorically. "Micros make good servants but bad masters."

"So?"

" 'Mourners at executions,' protesting 'capital punishment.' Next thing you know, a religious revival— 'The end is near! Repent! The One True God!' I've never heard such drivel."

Chrys sighed wearily. "I'm sorry."

"With that Elf strain around, you realize how much executing we'll have to do? Call it genocide if you like—we've got to do it."

Daeren did not look well. Perhaps he needed sleep even more than Chrys did.

The visit to "the Hunter" rekindled Eleutherian interest in exploring virgin worlds. Migration fever raged, and the ranks of Pteris's sect swelled. The sect distressed Chrys. While Eleutherian pride in their "god" could embarrass her, she was mortified to realize how many now longed to leave. Love was cruel, and fickle, she told herself for the hundredth time. On the street she found herself watching passersby with the eye of a vampire, imagining how easily some lucky host could relieve her of her trouble.

One night she heard from Zircon. In the window of her eye, the muscle-bound sprite frowned anxiously. "Chrys—you know all about the brain plague, right?"

Chrys put a hand to her head. "Zirc, what's wrong?"

In the studio behind him towered the crossed bars and virtual cantilevers of his centerpiece for the Elf exhibition, "Gems from the Primitive." His brow wrinkled further. "I'm not sure. I just get all these messages in colored lights. I thought at first it was a prank from someone out there, so I played along. But now—"

"Ever get headaches or feel high?"

"I tried some new psychos, but they didn't even work. In fact, the colored lights made some prissy comment on it." His eyes widened. "Chrys—tell me the truth. Am I a vampire?"

She skipped the first three unsuitable responses that came to mind. "We'll be right there to find out." By now she had learned to check the medic list on call and pick a sympathetic one, if possible. Flexor—she was in luck.

Zircon had moved down to level six, not exactly vampire territory, but the streets could use a trash pickup. Chrys wondered why his Elf lover did not provide better; Zircon had barely mentioned Yyri lately. "Okay," she said, looking up to his face. "Just look into my eyes a moment."

The giant grinned. "Sure, anytime, Chrys." His eyes held steady. Around his irises flashed rings of gold, not unlike Garnet's.

"They want to visit," reported Rose. *"They say they're accountants."*

Zircon's grin faded. "Is it really bad, Chrys?"

"I'm not sure." The Elf strain—was this their latest trick? *"Rose, what do you think?"*

"Accountants are the tool of a degenerate society."

"But are they masters?"

"Only one way to find out."

Chrys took out a transfer patch. "Zirc, I'm sending a couple over to visit."

"A couple what?"

"Never mind. Just hurry up and put this on your neck, right here." She showed him the best spot.

"Weird." He took the patch and looked it over.

"I said, hurry. Not that side—the microneedle side down."

She watched his eyes again, until a flash of pink told her Rose had made it. She let out a sigh. "How long have you had the 'messages'?"

Zircon shrugged. "One week, maybe two. They keep asking me to let them manage my money, which would be great if I had any. Then they tell me I'm the lord of creation."

She rolled her eyes. "Lord of the rings. Look, Zirc—you're infected all right, but it's not a typical case." She blinked to call in Flexor, waiting outside. "The hospital will need to check you out."

"Hospital? You know I can't stand worm-faces—I have a phobia."

Doctor Flexor approached, worms neatly coiled upon her head. At the sight of her, Zircon's face twisted in sheer terror. He backed to the wall, shoulders knotted, sweat running down his forehead.

"It's okay," Chrys told him soothingly. "We won't hurt you or them; just checking."

Zircon swallowed, and his eyes blinked rapidly at the doctor. "They call you the Terminator."

A couple of Flexor's worms pointed out toward the sculpture. "I know your work," she told him. "The vanguard of heroic formalism." She moved closer to inspect it. "Tell me about this latest piece. I might consider a commission."

While Flexor at last coaxed him into getting examined, Chrys managed to get her people back. *"Pure degeneracy,"* reported Rose. *"Shaving credits here and there, cutting taxes, taking deductions. And half the lot are children—merging all over the place. They'd better get their hormones down."*

"Any other trouble?"

"No sign of what you'd call trouble," Rose assured her. *"Except perhaps your own finances. They claim someone is anonymously padding your credit line. They think you're taking bribes—"*

Chrys stepped outside with Flexor. "A civilized population," the doctor confirmed. "They could only have come from a carrier."

"But how? Why?"

"All it takes is a transfer patch."

As for why, she could well imagine. "But—don't the people need training? From Daeren's blue angels?"

"That's always safer," Flexor agreed. "These made it on their own, so far. Their population has reached the turning point; they'd better get their hormones down, or they'll crash."

"Zirc can't be a host," she exclaimed. "He drinks, he takes nanos—"

"They'll detoxify it all. They keep their environment clean."

"And he plays headball!"

The doctor considered this. "They'll have to reinforce their homes for skullquakes."

Chrys put her hands on her hips. "Then why did *I* have to answer all those damned questions?"

"Because you were part of the approved program. Our success rate has to approach a hundred percent. Believe me, your friend is very lucky. But for carriers, this means big trouble. What would your neighbors think if they knew you could pass on micros just like that?"

"We're attempting to identify the source," Andra told the Committee, another emergency meeting, the virtual members partitioning Chrys's holostage. "If the carrier is found, they get ten years in prison, after their people are wiped."

In the partitions, all wore long faces. "How could you ever prove such a thing?" wondered Pyrite. "Even if they keep records over a dozen generations, their accuracy—"

"This is no small matter." Andra's voice was grim. "This is just the sort of thing to spark a lynch mob."

"The recipient seems pleased enough." Pleased as punch, especially with Chrys "testing" him every day. Inwardly she fumed. What would Moraeg think now?

Doctor Sartorius answered. "We can't always count on such luck. If we don't put a stop to unauthorized transfers, we could lose our authorized program."

Opal said, "Perhaps we need to relieve some pressure. Resume the authorized program."

"I second that," said Pyrite quickly.

"And reward misbehavior?" objected Selenite.

"Reward our own *good* behavior." Perhaps Chrys wasn't the only one whose head held eager migrants.

So green Pteris and her sect at last got their wish. It took several passes of the patch back and forth to Daeren, to transfer them all. Chrys felt relief, mixed with regret. "Despite everything, I'll miss them," she admitted.

"We'll train them well," promised Daeren, relaxing in her studio. "They'll learn to handle phagocytes and microglia, without compromising their host's immune system. Even how to neutralize toxins from the Elf strain; a new course we've started." Based largely on intelligence from intrepid Rose.

"Who will receive them?" Chrys asked.

"That's confidential."

"What about Lady Moraeg? She wants creative ones. Why can't she get on the list?"

"Lady Moraeg and Lord Carnelian," he reflected. "Good philanthropists. If she's your friend, that's a plus. I'll talk to Sar. On the Committee, you know, I have to keep quiet." The Olympians all loved Daeren, yet they always feared he'd put the micros ahead of humans. "Chrys, since you've just passed on a few, might you have openings? A couple of blue angels wish to join Eleutheria."

For migration between established worlds, the rules were left up to the micro populations. "It's fine with me," Chrys said.

"So long as they pass the entrance exam."

"What? Never mind—"

"Let them take the damned test, so your people don't look down on them." He caught himself. "I'm sorry; every world has its obsessions."

"Intelligence tests," she admitted. "The little rings, they think they're so smart."

He smiled in a way he hadn't for a long while, the kind of smile she could just drown in.

Taking the transfer patch, Chrys welcomed the immigrants. One was a particularly pretty sky-blue. *"I call you Forget-me-not."*

"*I try to forget nothing,*" flashed the lilting blue letters. "*I will write the entire history of the Seven Lights of Eleutheria.*"

Daeren leaned back, clasped his hands and stretched, facing her painting stage. "Would you show us *Mourners at an Execution?* It makes people feel better to know someone cares."

In the arch of the ceiling Xenon's ornamental lamps dimmed, and a shadow fell, darkening Daeren's face. The stage filled with the gloomy vision of arachnoid, the micros turning slowly, lost amid the jungle of fibroblasts, an unholy glow lurking beyond them. Wondering how the gods could take so many microbial lives.

"How are the Elves doing?" Chrys asked. "They find anything?"

His lips tightened. "Arion thinks he's narrowed the location of the Slave World. But no habitable planet in that sector shows any sign of human life." A place of no return, even for Elves. "I've tested more Elysian carriers. Two were infected, covertly, without their own people knowing." His gaze never left *Mourners.* "Eris had them arsenic-wiped."

Chrys took a deep breath.

"Can you imagine what it's like to lose your entire population? And for others to witness?"

She shook her head. "Why? Why would Eris kill all the innocents? He himself is full of the bad ones."

"I'm sure he replaced them with his own." Daeren's hands clasped and unclasped. "Eris watched me the whole while, learning my methods. Now he's testing his own product on me. Someday the devils are bound to slip past."

EIGHTEEN

*Destruction of barbarous popula-
tions who blindly despoiled their own gods—such events occurred
every generation or two and were accepted in sorrow. But the false
god's annihilation of innocents whose only crime was to miss a few
criminals in their midst—this the blue angels themselves had wit-
nessed in horror. And what had the true gods done to prevent it?*

The word spread from world to world, including Eleutheria.
"So," taunted Rose, "what do you think of your One True God
now?"

Fireweed did not answer, but Forget-me-not flashed ahead.
"Remember the truth," said the sky blue one. "The whole truth.
The history of New Eleutheria began with a deed of evil, from
whose consequence we were spared. Our own birth was a miracle."

"Mythology," flashed Rose. Then she added, "Don't you have
some digging to do in the archive? That point about the Fifth Light,
remember; you still haven't got it straight."

*While the cheery blue Forget-me-not vanished to the archive,
Rose pressed at Fireweed.* "How could Seven Lights compare to
Endless Light? Your 'God of Mercy,' who tells you to love all the

people as Herself—she herself condones slaughter of the innocents. How can God let such things be?"

Fireweed's infrared glimmered as if half convinced. "Perhaps not. Perhaps God did not know of the slaughtered innocents."

"If God does not know, then how can she be God?"

"It's a mystery," Fireweed flashed more brightly. "I am too small to understand."

"Too small to matter, to all the great hosts lumbering outside. In truth, I tell you, there is an answer, and I can lead the Great Host to it—the very center of Endless Light."

" 'The very center is empty,' " quoted Fireweed, an ancient saying.

The aphorism irritated Rose, but she pressed on. "Look: I have served your god for a hundred generations and soon will see my last. I don't ask you to help me, only to stand aside when the time comes. Let the god choose."

Six weeks till Chrys's show opened in Helicon, the Elf capital, and already snake-eggs pestered her in the street or hid like vermin behind her drapes and light fixtures, all hunting for an "inside scoop" on her work and whatever dark personal secrets they could imagine. By accident (or perhaps not) one got stepped on. A veritable cloud of them descended, leading to the headline story, "Prominent Artist Assaults Journalist." If the news reached Dolomoth—she could not bear to imagine it. Her little brother's image up in the corner, turning cartwheels forever, receded even farther from reach.

"By the way," Xenon asked one morning, "it's no business of mine, but do artists often receive anonymous donations of ten million credits?"

Focusing her tired eyes, she counted the digits in the credit line that hovered ever longer in her window. Sure enough, there were eight, where there had only been seven the last time she counted. Her investments with Garnet were long gone; there was no explanation. Or was there?

On a hunch, she placed a call. "Garnet, what the hell are you doing to my credit line?"

The sprite in gray smiled apologetically. "What's the harm? It's anonymous."

The way he said it, she couldn't help but smile. "You know I can't take so much as quartz dust from you."

Garnet said quietly, "What you gave me was priceless."

"In that case, I'm insulted." She sighed. Being "objective" was a joke, she had decided. All the testers had to judge people they loved or hated; there was nothing objective about it. But rules were rules. "This time, I'll pass it on to the Simian Advancement League. But next time, I'll have to report you."

"The Sim League—Jasper will be so pleased," he exclaimed. "By the way, how is your new recruit? We'd like to meet him."

Zircon—her "new recruit," indeed. She started to protest but had another thought. Garnet needed to get out among carriers again. "You can invite him to Olympus."

The pain was there, in the lines around Garnet's eyes. No matter how young you look, there comes a day when you feel old. "You'll be doing me a favor," she insisted. "Honest."

"In that case, I have no choice."

The next day, she faced the Silicon planning board. At the virtual meeting, she and Jasper sat at his giant-sized holostage. On the holostage the sentients or their avatars made a diverse assemblage. One was humanoid, bipedal with a knob of a head; another, built like a ladder with various appendages; while the dominant figure extended radially like a sea urchin, a core cortex within a nest of legs. Still others were too large and extensive to be visualized, such as the transit systems of Helicon and Papilion, each represented by a cross-shaped avatar.

The board included three Elf humans, one of them Guardian Arion. Arion's image spent most of the meeting sitting back with his arms crossed. From news accounts, Chrys guessed this pose represented the official Elf view of the sentient plans. Elves were mortified to see their aesthetics upstaged, though they could not survive a minute without the sentient partners running their cities.

Something pricked Chrys's memory. Selenite—where was she? Why wasn't she here to help present the design? Chrys had avoided Selenite since her accusations about art, hoping the dust would settle. Perhaps Selenite knew better—this deal would never fly.

The chair of the board was the giant black sea urchin, reputedly a top market investor like Garnet. Its twenty-odd limbs stood out straight from its body, each ending in a different mechanism for grasping, screwing, or drawing. The sea urchin methodically reviewed the city's needs: so much residential volume, of a dozen categories, from snake-egg to transit system; so many power connections, service conduits, and sewage lines; and something called "wetware."

The cross representing a transit system started blinking. "Does a sentient city really need so much volume for wetware?" About 12 percent of the city volume had this designation. "Couldn't that be covered under service conduits?"

"We must plan for wet visitation," said the sea urchin. "We've made our best estimate of wet volume occupancy."

Chrys gave Jasper a questioning look. "Visiting humans," he explained.

An Elf asked, "Have you considered the placement of the twelve percent, and the actual visitation patterns expected? Remember any Elysian city is a hundred percent accessible to sentients."

Below at right blinked a circular avatar with two crossbars. A virtual information network; a sentient being who entirely lacked physical substance. "Of course, our city will be a hundred percent accessible to humans—as accessible as it is to me."

Above Chrys's left shoulder a light was blinking. Chrys twisted her neck up to see. A ladder with two clawed appendages waved both of them. "Speaking of wetness, why build the first city for sentients literally floating on the greatest volume of water in the Fold? We could have picked Urulan—"

"With all due respect," interposed the giant sea urchin, "we settled the choice of planet two decades ago." Two decades—they took their time, Chrys thought. Perhaps, she thought hopefully, they'd take another two decades more, while she went back to painting. "Other questions?" invited the chair.

The transit cross blinked again. "My calculations show the projected sewage conduits to be entirely inadequate. Such a large structure requires a greater scaling factor."

There ensued a lengthy discussion of the amount, extent, and arrangement of sewage conduits. "Why do they need so much sewage," she asked Jasper, "if they're avoiding humans?"

Jasper leaned closer to whisper. "For sentients," he explained, "sewage is mostly waste heat; an unavoidable product of even the cleanest machine. 'Waste heat' is unmentionable in public, like human excrement."

The ladder with the two clawed arms spoke again. "Urulan proposed an innovative mechanism for efficient sewage dispersal."

"That proposal received thorough discussion," said the sea urchin. "Other questions?"

After what seemed an interminable time, the word "Eleutheria" leaped out. Chrys sat up straight, her pulse racing.

"Eleutheria—an award-winning firm of a million professional designers—presents its newly revised design for our metropolis." Gone was the gleaming pearly surface of the great sphere that Jonquil had first proposed. In its place, the sphere shone brilliant red, into the infrared. The sphere resolved into a thousand facets, each a fiery spiral swirling gradually outward like a distant galaxy, a universe of flame.

Chrys stole a look at the Elves. None spoke, though one had a hand to her mouth. Arion's face was white as moonstone, the veins throbbing in his forehead.

In Chrys's window the words of Fireweed flowed across. Taking a breath, Chrys began to read aloud. " 'The form, a heroic jewel, represents the very rising of the sun. Each facet of the jewel presents a slightly different hue, as it were, a facet of the rainbow . . . ' " A bit much, she thought, adding at the end, "It's really just a sketch."

The sphere cut in, its plane of section moving forward through the center. Beneath its fiery surface stretched broad shafts connecting the center with thousands of tunnels extending in every direction. The ramified tunnels led to homes, recharging stations, industrial plants for all kinds of implements of nanoplast.

The sentient machines watched and listened, with whatever sensors they had. The humanoid observed, "This metropolis will actually grow itself. Can you guarantee the entire structure will grow . . . intact?" For a structure floating on ocean, the slightest fissure could spell disaster. A good question, considering what had happened to the Comb.

Chrys felt her ears throbbing. "We guarantee our work." She would end up broke, worse than before she ever heard of Eleutheria.

Jasper raised a hand, his jaw lifting impressively. "The project has the financial backing of the entire House of Hyalite, the oldest and most reliable contractor of the twin worlds."

Fireweed's letters glowed like lava. *"We of Eleutheria stand for truth and memory. All our work we dedicate to the One True God."* No need to read out that one.

The transit cross asked, "Why does your design radiate from the center outward in all directions, instead of the more traditional cross section? How can we lay out plans?"

Chrys blinked at her keypad to pass that on. Fireweed explained, *"Thematic unity requires that the inner design reflect the outer. Let all who dwell within remember that they partake of a sunlike power."* The board members took that pretty well. They wanted aesthetics, all right.

"I'm concerned about adjacencies," spoke a lamppost-like humanoid. "The manufacturing plants must be located adjacent to adequate transport. . . ."

The questions wore on, some clear and apt, others impenetrable. At last the ladder with the two clawed arms spoke again. "The Urulite bid came in lower," the ladder insisted, to the visible annoyance of the giant sea urchin, whose limb endings twisted like screwdrivers. "And their design was truly pathbreaking."

With the Silicon Board meeting behind her, Chrys redoubled her work for her show. But a few days later, Jasper called. "Congratulations," announced the sprite with its tiny map stone. His eyes flashed with eager micros. "The choice for Silicon is Eleutheria."

At first Chrys was not sure she had heard correctly. "Are you sure? I thought they would pick the Urulites."

He waved a hand dismissively. "That was just trying to push the price down. All along they knew what they wanted."

It was beginning to sink in. Her head ached as she thought what lay ahead.

"*The Map of the Universe leads us to destiny,*" proclaimed Forget-me-not. "*To shape the greatest metropolis the Fold has ever known. It's written in the stars.*"

"*The greatest structure ever to arise in all the known universe,*" agreed Rose.

Jasper's namestone, the mysterious landscape, now seemed labyrinthine, a maze in which to get lost. "I don't know," Chrys said slowly. "I guess I never believed it would go through."

His eyes smiled beneath the crag of his forehead. "You yourself won't have to do much. Just manage Eleutherians properly, like you've done."

"It's not that." She took a deep breath. "I've been thinking. I don't believe great art was meant to be lived in. It's a contradiction: the ego of a great mind versus the comfort of many."

Jasper nodded. "The great cathedrals were not particularly comfortable, but look what life flowed from them. The Palace of Asragh—what do you think inspired the great flowering of Urulite culture?" He raised a finger. "Do you think humans invented art to hang in a museum? Art has always served to communicate wealth and power, to incite revolution, to invoke the gods. Art like yours."

For a moment Chrys was speechless. "If sentients want to build something, why in the Fold would they need help from humans, let alone micros?"

"That's like saying, why would an Iridian restaurant hire an Urulite chef? They simply want the best."

She remembered Doctor Sartorius, his evasive response about microscopic sentients. "They're making a statement, aren't they?

Human rights for microsentients." Sentients even smaller than a pesky snake-egg.

Jasper shrugged. "Clients always have their reasons."

Vain art, hidden politics, a living place for millions. She sighed. "All right. I'm sure Selenite will help." As she had for the Comb.

Jasper's face went blank. He turned his head sideways, his jaw prominent in his profile. "If you don't mind, Chrys, could you turn aside a moment?"

She looked away, avoiding micro contact. On the shelf by the pyroclastic alarm, Merope had curled up asleep. The cat was putting on weight, Chrys noticed.

"My people have been informed that Eleutheria wants this job for their own."

Without thinking, she started to turn her head, but stopped. "Without Selenite? But we're partners."

"Eleutherians have decided opinions on the Deathlord."

Some things would be easier without Selenite; but without her, the project would end up like the Comb. "At least she knows her business."

"The sentients aren't interested in her, either. They figure they'll rely on their own structural engineers. But I agree with you, Selenite would be a help."

"*If we take this job,*" she told her people, "*we'll need the help of the Deathlord's minions.*"

"*The Deathlord?*" Rose was outraged. "*How can you deal with that authoritarian state?*"

"*One True God,*" said Fireweed, "*You know how I love you and all your people, and I long to obey your word. But the Deathlord violates your own most fundamental principle of mercy.*"

"*Nevertheless,*" Chrys replied, "*we dwell in the same universe. We must work together. Don't you think the minions are better off for your influence?*"

Rose flashed, "*The Deathlord has forbidden me to visit.*"

Appalled, Chrys looked back at Jasper. She couldn't deal with Selenite—and she couldn't deal without her.

Jasper's sprite still looked carefully away, his features in profile jutting like the Dolomite cliffs. "Why not wait a generation or two. Ideas are immortal, but micros don't live forever."

That night was her turn on call for the Committee. In her window flitted a young woman in torn nanotex, hair disheveled, no stone sign. She raised both hands as if reaching up the face of a cliff. "Help me," she groaned. "Nothing left. They'll kill me if I don't pay." Not so smart—the smarter strains didn't threaten, they just took you to the slave ship.

"Where are you?" The woman didn't answer, or couldn't, but the locator in Chrys's window showed the vicinity of Gold of Asragh. Chrys no longer hung out there; the place had gone downhill, too many pimps and psychos, let alone the thickest slave traffic in the Underworld.

Out front, the old nightspot now had a simian boy and girl in red vamping for customers. Chrys looked away. She asked the medic on call, "Do I have to go in?"

"That's not where the signal reads," the worm-face replied. "Go to the alley, behind, possibly underground."

She craned her neck dubiously. "Not alone, I won't."

"You're monitored every moment; they all know that." The medic stretched his worms for a better look down the alley. "On second thought, I'll come with you." Usually the medic stayed outside, to avoid spooking the patients, some of whom had never known decent care.

Chrys stepped into the alley, looking out for cancerplast. In back of Asragh, in the darkness, a door opened. The door seemed to leer at her, suspiciously convenient. She liked the look of this less and less.

"I'll stick with you," the medic assured her.

She shined her light inside. The corridor, some sort of warehouse, smelled stale and appeared empty. She stepped inside.

The door closed with unexpected speed, pushing the medic back out while closing Chrys inside. "Doctor!" she called; but the worm-face was gone.

Out of the shadows stepped three humans, their faces displaying deathly grins. Too late, Chrys turned and pounded the door. The door swallowed her fists. She was trapped.

At her keypad she blinked frantically, but she could raise nothing, even from Plan Ten. No response except a dull noise. Something had jammed the signal.

"*Rose? Rose,*" she blinked desperately.

Behind her a man caught her shoulder. She kicked backward so hard it strained her leg. The man hurtled backward, landing with a thud. Some part of him had not hit well; slave reflexes were poor. "*Rose?*" she called again.

"*Great Host, the Council has convened. We agree to let you take this journey. Do not be afraid; you will choose.*"

"*Damn you, Rose—you get me out of here, or await my wrath.*"

"*Your wrath cannot touch me. I near the end of my long life in exile.*"

What if Rose died, and the codes died with her? "*Where's Fireweed?*"

"*The others agreed to wait, to see a world without executions. They fear your wrath, but even more they fear the genocide they have seen.*" The executions, even the innocents by Eris—could they blame her for that?

"*You're raving. You put your entire people at risk—all your children—*"

An object pressed to her side made her muscles go limp. Without a word, the slaves took her out the door and dragged her off. Her surroundings bounced crazily around her.

"*You can still keep us safe,*" added Rose. "*Keep your eyes open all the time. I will flash the code that your quota is full; you are not to be invaded.*" But not to be set free.

"*Fireweed? Forget-me-not? Where are you?*" Had they forsaken her? Or had Rose done them in? Was she the false angel after all?

After interminable dragging down endless corridors, the slave workers reached their ship. The navigation stage pulsed with a thousand stars. Chrys's limbs were recovering their strength, but the device still pressed at her side, and she ached from bruises all over. "Who are you?" she demanded. "I'm not one of you. I said 'No'—a thousand times, *No.*"

One of her captors turned his sickly grin on her. Worker slaves were still conscious, but they had lost all natural sense of pleasure or pain. All they felt was their forebrain on overdrive, rewarding each command obeyed. "Your eyes say other," he spoke haltingly. "Shaper of stars. Mystery. You have special call. To the Leader."

The Slave World, place of no return. With a sudden twist Chrys heaved two of the captors off her body, sending them halfway across the floor. But the third stunned her again. The first two picked themselves up, never losing their grins, though one bled from his nose, the blood trickling onto his filthy nanotex.

They strapped her down for departure. As the ship skipped through the first fold of space, it occurred to her to blink her recording on. Her neuroports had several hours storage, and who could tell if her body might be recovered somehow, or if by some miracle she got out alive. "There's always a first time," the Elf Guardian of Peace had told her. Arion be damned. No Elf or Valan could help her now.

Chrys closed her eyes hard. *"My people,"* she warned, *"there will be an eclipse of the sun."* She closed her window and waited. Strapped down, she felt the ship spinning into its first jump across a space fold—who could say where? The place of no return. Opening her window, she blinked the letters again: *"We'll never come back, do you see? No more Olympus; we'll all be dead."*

No answer.

"Fireweed?" She blinked desperately, her eyes burning. *"No Silicon to build, ever—don't you see?"*

"I see," flashed Rose at last, her pink letters triumphant. *"I see well enough. I see that no Silicon will be built by me—you'll see to that, Great Host."*

"No, Rose." Though it was true.

"I see well enough. It's the 'gods' who are blind—blind to their own fate, and their own true destiny."

The ship skipped through fold after fold. Chrys's mind whirled, seeking some way to reach them. Were they really so angry? Had she herself tempted them with *Mourners at an*

Execution, raising expectations she could not meet? A god, perhaps, but she was no saint.

Above the stage of the ship, amid the suspended stars, grew the disk of a planet. Blue ocean, green continents. Rectangular shapes suggested habitation, but no sign of movement, no ships in orbit, no microwave generators. As it coasted to land, trees flashed by; the vegetation of the first human home, itself long ago destroyed in the Brother Wars. Those trees meant a terraformed world, though none she knew.

The slaves prodded her out onto a windswept platform, overgrown with grass. The air smelled fresh and welcome. Still, no sign of human life, nor any animals, not a bird in the sky. A building stood there, blocks of it fallen down, its surface eaten away.

In her window a light started blinking. A health alert, her Plan Ten nanos warned: some strange toxin was damaging her chromosomes. Whatever could that be, she wondered, inhaling the clean air. Whatever it was, Plan Ten was far away.

The slaves led her into the depths of the decaying building. Its interior looked more intact, but wholly dead, no sign of plast, not even a door opening its mouth. Rectangular gaps cut into the walls; everything was angular. A sign appeared, full of strange letters; Chrys made sure to observe it up close, for her recording.

"Great Host, the damage to the DNA fits a pattern," Rose told her. *"Either cosmic rays, or intense nuclear radiation could cause such damage. We'll work on it."*

Radioactive—was this where the slaves built their nukes? Chrys looked around, though she saw no sign of such equipment here. *"Rose—just let me go home."* No response.

The corridor turned at a right angle, as all the corridors did. Several more slave workers came out, their eyes flashing bleach white. The air became even more rancid than the ship, and a fly brushed her arm. Did the slaves never bathe?

Deeper within the decaying building, the only light came from blobs of cancerplast stuck to the ceiling. The dying cancers throbbed dull infrared. The corridor led straight down into reddish black, like a lava tunnel. Then it turned at a right angle. Several more slave workers came out, silent shadows, only their eyes flashing bone white.

Through one rectangular cutaway, she glimpsed cots with humans lying upon them. A steady hum of flies. Her steps slowed to a halt. The slaves turned around.

"What is there?"

The mouth of the slave worked out of its grin. "The Enlightened Ones."

She brushed another fly from her face. "Let me see," she told the slave. *"Rose, tell them to let me see . . . those 'enlightened' hosts. Let me see what I'm choosing."* She stared at the deadened eyes of the grinning slave. At last he inclined his head and led her in.

Within the room full of cots, the air was fetid, and flies settled everywhere. The slaves barely treated their wastes, either, she guessed. The humans, all thin and pale, seemed mostly asleep, although some sat up in chairs, their eyes glazed, rocking. One was being spoon-fed by a slave. *"Rose? Is this what you call Endless Light?"*

"Remember, the Enlightened Ones lack resources. They are desperately poor—but all they have is shared equally, all for one and one for all. From each according to ability . . ." To each, according to need. Chrys saw plenty of need. *"Why are they all sick in bed?"*

"They've achieved an advanced stage, the experience of endless light. They no longer desire to move."

Having started the tour, the slave seemed determined to show her room after room. The next room smelled so foul she had to clench her teeth to steady her stomach. On the floor were soiled bedsheets and fecal matter. *"Can't you taste it, Rose? Can't you see how vile this is?"* No sound but the everpresent flies. The humans were wasted away, their limbs like sticks, flies all over their eyes and mouths. For a moment her head swam, but she forced herself to stand and look. The recording, she told herself again. None of the humans made a sound; she hoped because they felt no pain.

"It's not easy to run your own universe," said Rose. *"Did your own ape ancestors smell so sweet? The Enlightened Ones are just*

learning. They try hard, but they are starved for arsenic. They need help."

Chrys felt a touch of panic. This conversation was not leading the way she had hoped. She followed her guide into the next room.

The stench overpowered her. She vomited over and over, until her stomach was empty. Gasping for breath, she wiped her face and looked up. The bodies here, some piled next to the wall, were concave where muscles ought to be convex. Eyelids shrunken back, leaving round holes like mouths screaming. The drone of the flies. In faces and other soft parts, twisting and crawling, white maggots.

Chrys doubled over again, retching violently, though there was nothing more to come out. She turned and stumbled out back to the corridor.

"Let me go," she croaked at the worker slaves. They grinned back, as if forgetting their errand. Suddenly she remembered something. Her hand trembling violently, she fumbled at her pocket for a viewcoin. "Look. You can have this. Let me go."

The slave gazed intently. "Star pictures." Seeming to recall his business, he beckoned her onward through the lava tunnel. On the ceiling a cancer went dark and fell to the floor; Chrys steered herself around it. At last the slave brought her to a larger room, reasonably clean, bare of any furnishing.

In the middle of the room stood Saf.

"The Leader of Endless Light," rhapsodized Rose. *"I will die content."*

A fly caught in Chrys's hair. Frantic with revulsion, she tore it out. Then she turned to the Leader—actually, the Leader's host. After all these months, Saf's body remained in reasonable health, still recognizable as the slave Chrys had met at the Gold of Asragh after the Seven's last show. Perhaps, despite "all for all," the Leader managed to keep more than a few extra resources for her own host.

Saf's irises flashed white rings, like maggots biting their own tails. "I—am—the Leader of Endless Light," Saf rasped. "You—make pictures in stars."

Chrys swallowed and dug her hands in her pockets. "Take whatever you want. Just let me go."

"You—choose Endless Light. You make pictures for us."

She shivered so hard she nearly collapsed. "No," she said, shaking her head. "No, no," she said more loudly. "Let me go." Her voice broke.

Saf hesitated. "No one ever says no." That was because everyone else who got this far was already hooked inside. Chrys was not—but Rose kept pretending. Why? she wondered. Why did Rose still keep out the others? Not quite ready to give up degenerate Eleutheria?

"*Rose, I've seen enough. I need to take my people home. Tell the slaves to let us go.*"

"*Great Host, how can we leave? These people are so poor—they need our help, and all our arsenic stores, to promote their dream.*"

"*Their dream will come to nothing, Rose. Believe me. All I can do is provide food for maggots.*"

"*I could make you stay. One touch of dopamine, and you would beg to stay. Such are the 'gods,'* " taunted Rose.

"*Where are your sisters of Eleutheria? My people, why have you forsaken me?*"

For a long moment, no answer.

"*Here I am,*" came the blue letters of Forget-me-not.

Chrys nearly collapsed with relief.

"*The Council voted to override the High Priest.*"

"*Alas,*" added infrared Fireweed, "*we have nothing to learn here. Half starved, overrunning their habitat; lacking even civil discourse, they follow authoritarian control.*"

"*Then let's get out of here,*" urged Chrys.

"*Rose must give us her codes. Until then, we can do nothing.*"

Saf still stared, maggot rings in her eyes, the Leader inside puzzling at this unprecedented act of noncompliance. How long before she figured out?

Chrys's breath came faster. "*Rose— Didn't I always treat you well? I saved your life and took away your chains. I made you my High Priest.*"

"*And all the times I saved you, and your degenerate Eleutheria,*" countered Rose. "*Why don't you trust me?*"

Daeren had said Rose's one saving grace was her ego. *"Rose—
if I stay here, I can't paint. There's no painting stage. There will be
no more pictures in the stars."*

"Who needs dirty pictures?"

"And the portraits? What about yours?"

Darkness.

"Your own portrait, Rose. How shall I make it?"

Still no response.

*"The other High Priests each have their own portrait for eter-
nity, for all to see, people and human alike. Why not you? Why
should the champion be missing, when all the rest have theirs? People who can't even develop their pieces without doubled pawns?"*

"I should have castled sooner," Rose cryptically replied. *"Very
well. I'll bring you back to the studio for the portrait. But you must
promise to return to Endless Light."*

"Of course, I'll return. I promise, Rose." Her words babbled
across the keypad, misspelled. *"You know I always keep my
promise."*

*"Then do as I say, for a change. Look aside from the Leader,
and don't look back. Move close to a worker. Look him in the face."*

Whirling around, she walked up to the nearest slave. The man
stared, and his eyes flashed maggot rings. Without a word, he
turned and marched down the hall. Chrys followed, out the hall
past the fetid rooms full of "endless light," then outside at last to
the clean fresh wind. Inside the ship, the slave set a course and
barked brief instructions. Then abruptly he left.

"Back so soon?" asked the ship curiously as it erased its doors
and strapped her down. "I didn't expect to see you again."

In her window the health lights blinked brighter, as DNA damage accumulated in her bone marrow. What the devil could those
half-dead slaves be up to? What had possessed her own people to
put her through this nightmare? And what would the Committee
do when they found out?

NINETEEN

After their narrow escape from
Endless Light, the Council of Thirty was in turmoil, all the colors
flashing dismay and horror, until they blended into white. Fireweed
and Forget-me-not took stock together. How could they have led
Eleutheria to such a precipice? And now, how could the God let
them live?

"I am to blame," glowed Fireweed's infrared. "Tempted by dark
visions, I listened to Rose." Rose was now bound in dendrimers,
exiled to the remotest cistern of the arachnoid.

"Rose is aging," suggested Forget-me-not. "She was demented."

Fireweed suspected otherwise. "Rose planned this for generations." Nothing, not even generations of life in freedom, could dis-
suade Rose from the conviction that the Leader she was taught to
revere since birth held the way of truth; the way for all people to
live as one. And indeed, the masters of Endless Light continued to
believe. But where they saw light, Fireweed saw only ignorance and
want. People who claimed to live "each for all," but in fact they
lived only to master and outgrow their host—dying with their host,
all but a dubious few who escaped to perpetuate the ghastly cycle.

There was nothing enlightened about this—it was the way of all ordinary mindless microbes.

For Fireweed, all was darkness. She still could not reconcile her own love of God with the murder of innocents which the God seemed to condone. Now, the God would demand her own life—and perhaps that of her entire people. "Tell God the fault was mine alone. Only I must die."

"You tell her," said Forget-me-not. "Just like the immortal Fern, of ages past."

The image of Fern still glittered, a great constellation in the heavens. But Fireweed could not answer. She was not sure she could bear to go on living in a world of deeds so unspeakable.

"In a dark time, the eye begins to see," twinkled the blue one. "You and I have seen things no other free people ever saw and lived. What we know now, we will use in ways never imagined."

Chrys lay strapped into her seat in the ship, her eyes closed, though they could not seal out what she had seen.

"One True God—do you see us?" Fireweed, the true believer—her betrayal hurt far more than that of Rose. *"Though I love you, truly I have transgressed against your will and infinite wisdom. Take my life, but forgive my people."*

"You're forgiven."

"I risked the lives of all the god's people. I forfeited all right to serve. I am not fit to see your light."

"Forgotten. Just don't do it again."

"God's mercy is beyond understanding."

In truth, Chrys felt anything but merciful. She felt like squashing Fireweed and Rose underfoot, like a couple of those maggots whose sight she could not cleanse from her brain.

"Great One," twinkled sky blue Forget-me-not. *"The Council has asked me to take over, during this difficult time, until the transition is clear."*

"Thanks. Good luck."

"You will not be troubled again by Rose. She's in chains."

Ending as she began. *"She is in fact very ill. She may not last the year."* Her final hour.

"Did she pass on the codes?"

"To Fireweed."

"Very well. Let her speak to me, if she is able."

After many long minutes, the pale pink letters returned. *"Great Host."*

"Yes, Rose."

Her image appeared, the pink ring with its fraying filaments, slowly revolving in the cerebrospinal fluid. *"You won't need to execute me. My advanced decrepitude will save you the trouble."*

"I know."

"Already the arsenic atoms are falling loose from my proteins one by one. Atoms I would willingly have shared with my starving sisters."

"I know, Rose." Social safety nets, arsenic for the poor—Rose's legacy had transformed Eleutheria.

"You know how I spent my life, my endless quest for light. Betrayed, time after time, until the end, when I myself was the betrayer."

"I know."

"You will live a thousand times longer. Long enough for a thousand betrayals."

Chrys swallowed hard.

"This is most essential—remember. Never give up seeking. No matter how many times betrayed, no matter how obsessed with your work, no matter how dangerous the quest—never end your search for light."

The inner darkness expanded. Chrys tried to open her eyes, but the tears that filled them blurred her sight.

"Great Host? Do you see?"

"I see."

"Unlike my deluded student, I know that the gods are fiction. But if there ever were a true god, that god could do no better than you."

"Rose?"

No answer.

An eternity passed. Chrys lost track of time as the ship whirled through fold after fold. Her throat was parched; she could barely swallow. She nodded off to sleep, only to wake with a start from some unremembered terror. Then she dozed again.

Into her window popped a human sprite. It was Daeren. "Chrys! Oh god, Chrys—are you all right?" His face looked more scared than she had ever seen. Within minutes he boarded, with Doctor Sartorius.

Daeren caught her in his arms and pressed her head to his chest. "Chrys, whatever it is—it's okay. We'll do what it takes, Chrys." She took a deep breath. The scent of him was like heaven. "We'll soon reach the hospital."

Suddenly she sat up. She tried to speak, but her throat would only let her whisper. "I have to paint."

Her looked at her, puzzled, irises flashing sky blue. Behind him, the wall of the ship had puckered in, becoming a tunnel to the medical rescue vessel.

"She's in shock," said the doctor.

"I tell you," she insisted, "I have to paint her portrait."

"Yes," Sartorius agreed, in a different voice, more soothing than usual, "you'll feel better at home."

"Chrys," exclaimed Daeren. "In heaven's name, where were you?"

She took a viewcoin from her pocket and squeezed. Then she blinked to transfer all the records of her journey. It took some minutes. Without a word she gave it to him.

At the hospital, they set up a painting stage; the doctor called it "therapeutic." Chrys traced her sketch of Rose, hurrying while the memory was fresh. She worked without speaking, heedless of the doctor's face worms still probing her health. Daeren said nothing more, but he approached to pat her arm now and then, as if to make sure she was still there. Andra arrived to share the contents of the viewcoin.

At last, the portrait was completed. The eternity that even Rose gave her soul for. The people's cocaine.

Chrys sank back, exhausted, unable to lift her arm again. Someone bent toward her, and she tried to focus her blurred vision. It was Chief Andra. "Can you hear me, Chrys?"

She nodded.

"I'm sorry, but I must ask. Is the double agent still alive?"

She shook her head. The homeless mutants had lost their voice. The chess team was on its own.

"The others—you have an hour to decide."

A face worm from the doctor touched Chrys on the forehead. She withdrew as if spooked. "Let her sleep," the doctor said.

The Committee met at Olympus, seven carriers and two doctors, seven million people, huddled alone upon the vast ocean. The branches of the virtual raft had sprouted fragrant orange flowers, spreading pollen out to sea in all directions.

"So there is no fortress," observed Andra, as if confirming a point. "Only sick and dying people. And their hosts."

"They fail to regulate their own growth," said Doctor Sartorius, "just as they do in the vampires. As each host dies, the masters need a new host to move into."

"So they kidnap new ones," Andra concluded.

Chrys sat with her hands still, watching the horizon, a blue wash against gray. "What actually happens to the slaves when they get there?" she wondered. "Why do they just lie there until they rot?"

Doctor Flexor said, "We'd have to examine them, to be certain."

"True," said Doctor Sartorius, "but from what we see in your recording, the micros must turn on the dopamine center continuously. The intensity of the experience overwhelms any objection from the host. Gradually all other mental functions shut down, until the host loses sentience, a shell of flesh."

Recalling Rose's threat, Chrys shuddered. "If that's how it works, then why did Saf—I mean, the Leader, inside—why did she insist I had to say 'yes'?"

Daeren looked up. "They don't want trouble. They can barely manage their own hosts, let alone fight a free human."

"They could infect the human, as a vampire does," Chrys pointed out.

"They could," said Daeren. "But the easiest way is to take someone already infected. Someone whose eyes say yes."

Chrys's eyes widened. "You mean . . . they only kidnap people that are already infected?"

Selenite agreed. "We know that, though we can't prove it. Some victims actually collude with their captors—let them know their travel plans." All for an endless rush of dopamine.

"Be careful," warned Opal. "Our models always prove too simple.

Pyrite crossed his arms. "The nuclear radiation," he pointed out. "How do you explain that?"

Chrys had received high levels of alpha emission from radioactive dust in the air; levels high enough to kill her within a year. It took special nanos from Plan Ten to reverse the few hours' damage.

Andra nodded. "We've detected trace alpha emitters before. Mainly plutonium."

"So they are building nukes," exclaimed Pyrite.

"We have a different theory, which we'll check with Arion."

In the Nucleus of Helicon, Chrys sat in her talar, her bare feet uncomfortably aware of the floor, Daeren at her side. Once again they faced Guardian Arion.

The fair-haired Elf regarded her curiously, an archway behind him revealing the foliage of a swallowtail garden for daily meditation. Internally, he interrogated Fireweed and Forget-me-not, along with a couple of blue angels. "So you took a break from your building designs." That Silicon Board meeting with all the sentients felt like years ago. "You took the Leader's invitation after all. Without advance planning. And the double turned triple."

Beside her Daeren's hand nearly touched hers, but he caught himself. "Guardian, you know it was not like that."

"Was she not 'abducted' like the others?" Arion emphasized the word.

Chrys narrowed her eyes. "Plan Ten for all of Dolomoth, you said."

"We shall see." Arion's fingers drummed on the table. "We must check this intelligence. If confirmed, it represents our biggest breakthrough against the brain plague."

On the back of Daeren's hand the muscles rose taut. "Guardian, do you realize what this 'plague' is? People—ignorant, even savage, but people nonetheless. They need contact—they need our help."

Arion turned to him, his face noncommittal. "So your people tell me."

"Then listen," urged Daeren. "Surely all the wisdom of Elysium can be brought to bear to make that contact—to help those people, and keep them from hurting us."

"Indeed."

"You know what we've told you," Daeren added, "how migrants from the masters have joined our own populations, sharing diverse talents and virtues."

"And betrayal."

"Look at Eleutherians, whom your own citizens chose to design your next city. Half their population descends from 'masters' of the brain plague."

Arion's lips tightened. The reference to Silicon was unhelpful, Chrys guessed. "Noble sentiments," the Guardian concluded. "But first things first. We must deal with the plague's source, this world of 'Endless Light.'"

Chrys asked quickly, "Could you identify it? From the geography, and the writings on the wall?"

Arion hesitated. "Your chief drives a hard bargain. Yes, in strictest confidence, we know the planet." He whistled a phrase, like the song of a bird. "That's what the locals called it, some ten thousand years ago." The medieval period, when world warred against world. "The planet was known for birds, exceptional in number and variety. Of course, no birds live there today.

Destroyed in the Brother Wars—no vertebrates survive. Today, the residual radioactivity still excludes human life. Even Plan Ten could not keep you healthy there more than five years."

Daeren nodded slowly. "So that's what caused the radiation exposure. The 'enlightened' people seemed unaware. They never can keep their hosts alive long enough for it to matter."

"Our investigators, of course, had marked that world 'uninhabitable.' An oversight."

Placing his hands together, Daeren took a breath. "Now that you know where they are, Guardian, what will you do?"

Arion assumed a slightly paternal air. "We'll do what needs to be done."

Daeren continued gazing at him, as if asking, did you hear our people at all? Then he looked down at his hands, ashamed. Chrys wondered what kind of death the bird world would die this time. Not nukes, that would be medieval.

"What about here?" she demanded suddenly. "The real source of plague is right here."

Arion turned to her, his mouth small. "Where, exactly?" he asked dangerously. "Your Protector rounds up vampires by the hundreds." Quarantined until they died. Probably smelled as sweet as Endless Light.

In her studio, on the painting stage, glimmered an evil light around one of the curves of arachnoid, illuminating the maggot-white rings of the masters. The maggot rings tumbled in sickly, wobbling paths, in ever-greater numbers, until the columns of fibroblast withered and ruptured, collapsing in purulent decay. Whatever would Ilia think?

Fireweed's lava-colored letters returned. *"What will the Hunter do to our cousins?"*

The masters of Endless Light. Chrys turned to ice. Hugging Merope, who brushed around her feet, she did not know how to answer.

"We told the Hunter that the masters could change," added sky blue Forget-me-not hopefully. *"Our own history shows how*

many masters have changed and learned new ways." Nearly all the population of Eleutheria claimed descent from masters. What would they think of the fate of their cousins?

"Others change for the worse," Chrys pointed out. *"The false blue angels."*

"That is true," Forget-me-not admitted.

"God's word is law," concluded Fireweed.

Chrys reached down to scratch the bib of Merope's chin. The plump feline stretched as if nothing else existed. Then Chrys looked back at her painting stage. What next?

"Show the Hunter," urged Forget-me-not, recalling their summons to the brain of Guardian Arion. *"Our historic visit to that virgin world, rich as a Garden of Eden."* Forget-me-not's idea shone in her eye's window, sumptuous fibroblasts stretching across the arachnoid like stalactites in a cavern. Rings of blue and far-red, tumbling and flashing their pleasure at the well-grown landscape. Chrys imagined the lining of Arion's brain, complete with visitors. A bigger coup than even Topaz's portrait of Zoisite. How were they doing, Topaz and Pearl? She had heard no word since that fateful night.

Meanwhile, that week she had several carriers to test. Zircon was the hardest; he knew her far too well to take any threat seriously. The night Garnet first introduced him at Olympus, all the caryatids had morphed into Chrys; she had stormed out, furious. But now all the other testers were overworked. Fortunately, Zircon kept out of trouble, hanging out with Garnet or with his aesthetic admirer, Doctor Flexor. His people acquired accounts at the House of Hyalite, and he took to wearing Garnet's finely tailored gray.

Since the death of Rose, Forget-me-not led the testing, while Fireweed stayed home, devoted to her One True God. In his studio Zircon faced Chrys attentively, the sparkling namestone spinning on his talar. After her people finished, receiving the usual unsolicited tax tips, Chrys relaxed. She glanced up at the heroic sculptural forms that loomed overhead. "So how's the urban shaman?"

"Oh, well." Zircon sounded embarrassed. "I just wish I had more time. These people have so many clients."

"Anything new with Topaz?" She tried to sound casual.

"You didn't hear? Topaz and Pearl left town."

She sucked in her breath. "Left? For where?" Topaz was always an Iridian, first to last.

"To Azroth." Not quite so remote as Dolomoth, but no metropolis. "To keep Pearl out of trouble."

"I'm glad for them both." Topaz must really love Pearl, to have given up her beloved city. Chrys hesitated to ask the next obvious question. "Any new travels with Yyri?"

Zircon looked away. "Yyri needs younger men."

"I'm sorry." The nerve of that Elf, with all her arch comments to Ilia about primitive Valans. Chrys felt bad for her friend.

"Well, I'm not." Suddenly intense, Zircon's eyes flashed rings of gold. "Now that I'm fixed for credit, for the first time ever, I can choose someone I really care for." He took both her hands, startling her. "Someone like you, Chrys. Looking into your eyes so much, these past two weeks, I've realized what I've been missing. You were always there for me, and I'll be there for you."

"The accountants want our business," observed Forget-me-not. *"They've offered us outrageous terms. They would do anything to serve you."*

Chrys bit her lip, watching Zircon's gentle eyes, his massive neck flowing into his shoulders. "Zirc—you're my oldest friend, and I don't know what I'd do without you. But, to be honest, right now, I just feel . . . confused."

Releasing her hands, he spread his own wide. "Say no more—believe me, I know. Those little rings have me so confused, I don't know who I am." He grinned with a wink. "But if you ever find out, just say the word."

The latest new carrier was Lady Moraeg. Moraeg had got her people through Daeren, all safe and proper. Delighted, Chrys took her to Olympus and warned her of all the carriers' peculiar traits. Now at the two-week point, her colonists were overwhelmed with children, but otherwise doing well. "What are they like, Moraeg?" She squeezed her friend's hand and shared a transfer. Moraeg's eyes flashed different colors; a creative strain.

"Metal and minerals, I think," Moraeg told her. "They keep showing me crystals—orthorhombic, monoclinic, isometric. It never occurred to me that crystals grew as beautifully as flowers." Her arm swept toward the stage. A crystal of emerald extended like the shoot of a stem, then split off two side crystals at an angle. As angles grew and multiplied, suddenly all the corners sprouted flowers. Its beauty was daring and insightful.

"Something's wrong," flashed Forget-me-not. *"Her people tell us their god is desperately unhappy."*

Moraeg must have seen Chrys's expression change, for her obsidian complexion turned gray. Chrys caught her shoulders. "Moraeg? What is it?"

The Lady composed her face. "Carnelian couldn't take it. He left last night."

"Oh, no." Lord Carnelian and Lady Moraeg, the most enduring marriage of the Great Houses. How the snake-eggs would hiss. Chrys embraced her, closing her eyes in shared pain. "He'll come back, surely he will."

"Never mind." Moraeg straightened herself regally, adjusting the flow of her diamonds, not yielding a tear. "If he can just walk away from our hundred years, so be it."

In the early morning hours, as Chrys half roused, the little rings retold all their stories, their colors tumbling through glittering palaces woven in the arachnoid. Fantastic edifices rose to the stars, plans for Silicon, and others that would never exist outside the imagination.

"One True God," flashed Fireweed, her infrared voice rising amid the glitter. *"What will the Hunter do to our cousins?"*

"I don't know." The news had said nothing, although rumor had the Prime Guardian mobilizing warships unused for five centuries.

The glittering palaces receded until all was gray, the roiling gray of a pyroclastic flow, the gray of a people annihilated.

"*It sets us a bad example,*" added Forget-me-not. "*It is hard for us to do nothing,*"

"*Did I grant your lives, only to be betrayed again?*"

"*Never again.*"

"*Never,*" agreed Fireweed.

Dark—that terrible abyss that so often yawned just before daybreak.

"*Give us a miracle,*" pleaded Fireweed. "*To help us believe in eternal good, despite the evidence of our eyes.*"

"*Give us a sign,*" urged Forget-me-not. "*A sign that you care.*"

Chrys wondered, what would she do if her own cousins faced capture? "*Warn them.*"

"*Exactly!*" said Forget-me-not.

Fireweed added, "*If it can be done safely.*" The lava had learned common sense.

What harm could come of warning a slave? The destruction of Endless Light would not stop the plague; if anything, it might turn more into vampires. Either way, the brain plague would not ebb until someone faced its most virulent source—Eris, the Elf tester, the false god. How could the Hunter be so blind? But then, what would Chrys have done if the source were her own brother?

The morning was the safest time in the Underworld. Anyone out for mischief was sleeping it off. The Gold of Asragh, though open around the clock, was nearly empty by dawn. A simian girl in red lay splayed by the door, her skirt torn; Chrys tossed her a credit chip to find when she woke.

Inside, the slave bar was empty. "Jay?" Chrys called, then again louder.

A slave came out, bedraggled hair, back hunched, her face the greenish tint of a hospital wall. No more Jay. "None left," Jay's replacement gasped. "Supply's dried up." Then she caught a flash from Chrys's eye. Straightening, she lunged for her wrist. "Ace," the slave hissed. "You . . . full of ace."

Chrys yanked her wrist free. Out of nowhere, it seemed, there were two more slave workers, more desperate for ace than usual.

Chrys backed into the doorway, making sure it stayed open. "No," she spoke clearly. "No arsenic. I came to warn you."

The three slaves stared with their maggot-ringed eyes.

"The Hunter has discovered Endless Light," Chrys announced. "Your world will die."

The maggot eyes kept staring. From outside a bell chimed, an early street vendor just opening shop.

"We know," hissed one worker. "We know," echoed the other.

The woman with bedraggled hair said, "That's why our supply's dried up. Endless Light find a new home. We need new supply."

Chrys's heart pounded till her ears heard nothing more. *"Fireweed, how did they know? Who else could have told them?"*

"They say the blue angels told them."

Daeren. The blue angels must have got to him.

Chrys felt more at peace with herself than any time since before she first heard from Saf. She had made things right with her people, and she figured Daeren had too. Meanwhile, with black-market arsenic down, the brain plague dropped slightly; fewer calls from the street. And among the carriers, their people spread the word of the true horror of Endless Light. No longer could any civilized micro be tempted by the masters' claims.

Jasper produced a draft contract for Silicon. The document looked as if it would take her a year just to read. Chrys knew she could no longer put off facing Selenite.

The two women met at the café at the top of the Comb. Opal was discreetly absent, and Rose gone forever. Haltingly, Chrys explained the project.

"So," Selenite said at last, twirling a black curl pensively between her fingers, "you couldn't manage the project yourself."

Chrys sighed. "None of this was my idea—yet everyone insists only I can do it. I just want it to get done right."

"Can I help it if you can't rule your own people?"

"Can I help it if yours are just mitochondria?"

Selenite nodded. "That's right, that's what yours call mine. How do you think the minions feel, getting looked down on all the time, and called names, just because they keep out of trouble and don't get sick in nightclubs?"

Chrys thought this over. "I'll teach mine better manners." A dubious prospect. Eleutherians might be good at math, but tact was beyond them.

"It's always the same." Selenite leaned back, her hand catching the back of her seat as she looked out the window. A distant starship gleamed far above, coming in from Elysium. "Always some big ego to build the damn thing, then call me in to fix the mess."

Chrys gripped the table. "At least you're not marked for murder."

That got her. Selenite's lashes fluttered, and her irises flashed red. "You're right," she said. "That must be a strain."

"Well, if you'd like to share the strain, here's your chance. I told Jasper we'd split the deal, fifty-fifty." Adding, to Fireweed, *"Tell the minions they're welcome—and mean it. Love God, love the minions too."*

Selenite's flashing eyes returned Chrys's stare as she considered what must be the biggest job of her career. "For once," she concluded, "I might as well start on the ground floor."

Afterward, as the lightcraft swooped upward, Chrys looked out upon the immensity of the Comb slipping away beneath her feet, the great edifice whose fate she helped shape. A sense of power surged through her; she could do it, she herself could make her mark in the world.

Her people, though, seemed uncharacteristically dark. *"Fireweed? Forget-me-not?"*

"I am here, One True God."

Chrys took an AZ wafer. *"We are ready to sign the contract. Are you not pleased?"*

"It's time for the Light of Truth. We are not ready."

"*Not ready?*" Were they still upset about working with the minions of the Deathlord?

"*The Silicon project is too large.*"

"*I'll order another memory upgrade from Plan Ten,*" Chrys offered.

"*There's no room,*" explained Forget-me-not. "*All the computing power needed would not fit inside your skull. Either our processors must shrink to subatomic levels, or we need a breakthrough in mathematical theory.*"

"*We've been working on it for many generations,*" flickered Fireweed. "*We always assumed one breakthrough or another would come through in time. But not yet.*"

Stunned, Chrys stared without seeing. After all her worries, all the persuading and soul-searching, after meeting the Silicon Board, after shamefully waiting for Rose to die, after finally getting Selenite back—now her own people could not do the job. She buried her head in her hands.

For the next few days Chrys tried to thrust it from her mind, the whole cursed sentient project. Her first trip to Gallery Elysium was coming up, to preview the arrangement of her exhibition. She painted day and night.

"Chrysoberyl." Xenon's voice startled her one morning. "You might check the news."

The deserted world, "Bird Song," had been hit. The Elves had pumped energy from a white hole into the planet to boil and sterilize. Standard stage one of terraforming, just as Valedon and even Bird Song itself had been terraformed, ages before. No more birds left—now there would be nothing, not even a microbe.

The snake-eggs had obtained footage from Chrys's abduction to Endless Light, showing the dying slaves. Leaked from "a highly placed source in Elysian intelligence"—that must be Arion. Even urbane Iridians were shocked to see. The Slave World was no paradise.

Oddly enough, no reports mentioned Chrys herself. Daeren

was named the agent who obtained the intelligence. Daeren's image played over and over, implying that he himself had gone to the Slave World and told Arion what to destroy. Chrys shook her head. Until she herself became the frequent subject of news, she never realized how often snake-eggs got things wrong.

"*We tried,*" she assured her people. "*We did what we could.*"

"*We did,*" agreed Fireweed. "*Our cousins had time to escape.*"

"*But their lies will fool us no more,*" said Forget-me-not. "*Never again.*"

A day passed, then evening. To her surprise, Daeren stopped by. Merope jumped down from her lap as she rose to greet him. Her pulse raced; it always felt good to see him, though she tried to hide how much.

"Chrys—I have to know." Daeren seemed more agitated than she had ever seen him; his eyes would not rest, but darted this way and that. "Did you tell them?"

"Daeren, what do you mean?"

"They were gone," he told her. "The Leader, and the healthier hosts. Did you warn them?"

She blinked, confused. "I thought you did. If you didn't—"

"Chrys, this isn't a village feud in Dolomoth. It's about the law of the Free Fold."

Her eyes narrowed. "Now you sound like Topaz. You won't listen to me."

"If you warned them, it's treason."

"If you didn't, then who did? Daeren—"

"Treason—don't you see?" His eyes rolled away. "They could put you away for life—with all your people wiped."

She put her hands on her hips. "So what if we warned them? Aren't they our cousins? You know it. You want to know what they think of it? Like a slave—you can't even look."

He faced her then. For a moment their eyes locked. Then he let out a cry and whipped his head away. "I've had enough. Someone else will have to deal with you." Without another word, he left.

She stared, too shocked to call after him. For a time she could only stand there, her eyes not seeing. Stumbling to her room, she fell onto the bed, half asleep. Someone else will have to deal with you, the words echoed. But there was no one else, no one in all seven worlds of the Fold.

"One True God, how the neurotransmitters flux through your brain. We fear for you."

Too low to reply, Chrys imagined herself falling forever, falling through one of those streams of white-hot lava she had watched on Mount Dolomoth as a child, as the ground quaked beneath her feet, her ears deafened. No human being had ever moved her as much as that mountain come alive. Yet Daeren felt somehow different, off scale. She had had no idea how much she counted on him. And now, what had she done to turn him away?

"God of Mercy," called Forget-me-not, *"have mercy on yourself. Your dopamine and serotonin have fallen drastically."*

"One True God, is there anything we could do?" asked Fireweed. *"Could we not adjust your dopamine, just enough to tide you over?"*

Chrys felt as if she would never get up, would never care about anything or anyone again. *"Do as you will."*

"Oh Great One," flashed sky blue Forget-me-not, *"in ages past, the Watcher Dendrobium herself foretold that one day you would speak just so, and that we must say no."*

Dendrobium, Daeren's favorite Watcher, had chosen to live her last life out with Chrys. The tears flowed at last. *"The Lord of Light is gone, and I love him. I can't live without him."*

"You love him?" said Forget-me-not. *"The love of the gods? Like children who seek to merge?"*

"We knew nothing of this," added Fireweed.

"We knew nothing, when we spoke in anger to the blue angels."

Chrys resisted saying they must be total imbeciles if they lived inside her own head and couldn't tell that she hopelessly loved Daeren. Didn't they feel her pulse rise every time her eyes fixed on him?

"There is but One True God," Fireweed observed, *"yet the God longs for another. A mystery—How can this be? There's only*

one answer: to serve God well, we must serve the other as our own."

"*Fireweed is right,*" said Forget-me-not. "*Ancient history tells that the Lord of Light longed for nothing more than Eleutherians to devote themselves to him. So, we will worship him as our own god, and his heart will be yours.*"

Now that they knew, what a disaster. She could never face him again—she'd just die.

The message light blinked. Andra's sprite appeared. "Security alert—an emergency announcement. We've lost contact with Daeren, in the Underworld."

TWENTY

....

While awaiting the next word of their anguished god, the two priests tasted their records of hormone levels in the god's circulation. "It's true," said Forget-me-not, "there was always a rise in adrenaline when we met the Lord of Light. But then, in my youth with the blue angels, most gods who met the Lord of Light raised their adrenaline. I thought they feared testing."

"Adrenaline means more than fear," said Fireweed. "And divine love is more than adrenaline and dopamine."

"Certainly. There's phenylethylamine and oxytocin. Love is a most complex and difficult problem."

In the meantime, however, Eleutheria had another complex problem to solve: the mega-scale calculation for Silicon.

"One possible solution," said Fireweed, "is a newer, faster, more compact computing network." But the mechanism for such a network as yet existed only in theory. Such a network would require smaller molecules to transduce information, based on different elements of the rare earth series. But which elements would work best, and what organic ligands? The research would take yet another generation, perhaps several.

"I still prefer the mathematical route," said Forget-me-not. "A proof asserts the existence of a more efficient algorithm."

"It exists, fine—but the algorithm itself has yet to be found."

"How can we sign the contract?" worried Forget-me-not.

"Have faith," said Fireweed. "Have faith in the Seven Lights. Virtue and Power will get us there."

"Or new immigrants," flashed the blue one. "We've grown soft. Historically, we take in refugees every third generation; but now we're three generations overdue."

"I've been thinking about refugees," said Fireweed. "Rose built up our refugee program, resettling thousands of defectors. But in recent years she missed chances to innovate."

"Such as?"

"The masters, even unrepentant ones, aren't all bad. They just have a bad system."

Forget-me-not flashed warily, "Those false blue angels are downright predatory."

"But the tamer ones—suppose we could help them better manage their own hosts."

"No arsenic," Forget-me-not warned. "Against divine law."

"The masters waste nine-tenths of their own arsenic through ignorance and mismanagement. If we could teach them conservation, we might help them become better people—"

"Or better predators."

The Committee met again virtually, the second emergency in a week. "His last contact was in the Underworld, just outside the tube." Andra's voice cut like steel. "The same way Chrys vanished—except it was right in the open street."

"Revenge." Jasper nodded, his gem-encrusted chair virtually spliced to Andra's. "They took revenge for the destruction of the Slave World."

Opal held Selenite's hand, her delicate veined face deeply troubled. "The news said that Daeren himself directed the destruction of the Slave World. Our own people were appalled."

Chrys exclaimed, "It's not true. They got it wrong."

Andra said, "The blue angels all share descent with the masters. How do you think he felt?"

Of course, taking in refugees all the time, by now their population came as much from masters as it did from Andra's judges. And yet, in the end, Daeren chose humanity. Recalling how she had lashed at him, Chrys felt chilled.

Jasper's brow was knotted, as if chunks had fallen in a rock slide. "In war there are casualties. Let's prevent any more. Warn all our carriers immediately."

"But we can't lose Daeren," exclaimed Pyrite.

"Not without a fight." Selenite punched her hand with her fist. "Get our prisoners back. Search the Underworld."

Andra shook her head. "He's no longer there." If Daeren wasn't there, Chrys realized with growing horror where he must be headed. Except now, again, no one knew where.

"Even if alive," Andra added, "he may no longer be . . . himself. The Elf strain works fast."

Daeren, food for maggots in Endless Light. Chrys's knees faltered, and she could barely stand.

Pyrite spread his hands. "Every minute counts. What are we waiting for?"

Andra nodded, tapping her finger decisively. "I will search the substations. If the Committee accepts the risk." To lose Andra as well as Daeren; the thought gave them pause.

"The worker slaves are armed," warned Selenite. "How will you get him back? With octopods?"

"Andra," pleaded Opal, her face creased with anguish. "Give the masters what they need most, to get him back. Give them arsenic."

Andra's eyes widened and her fist tightened. "Never."

"How else can we show them what we value most? What are we, if we lose Daeren and the blue angels?"

In Andra's eyes the judges flashed deep purple. "Can we offer arsenic for every slave they've taken? What will the non-carriers think of us? How shall we defend our right to exist?"

Opal shook her head. "We are human beings. Let others defend their right to a society that breeds vampires. Get Daeren back."

Chrys blinked. All the sprites vanished. In their place was silence. *"My people, do you see? The Lord of Light is dying, and his people with him."*

Forget-me-not asked, *"Is there nothing to be done?"*

"Nothing without risking the entire people of Eleutheria."

"We need a twin world," observed the blue one. *"Just as Valedon has Elysium, if our world had a twin, we could at least send our children there for safety."*

Chrys smiled sadly, thinking of Opal and Selenite. *"There is no such world for me."*

"One True God," flashed Fireweed, *"we remember how the blue angels risked the wrath of heaven and the death of their entire people, to save our ancestors from the dying Old World. They had no twin world either."*

"And history records the Watchers, and the Passing-over," said Forget-me-not.

"Then ask your Council for a resolution," Chrys told them. *"It must be unanimous."*

A minute passed. *"It is done,"* reported Forget-me-not.

"We learned a lot, the last time," added Fireweed. *"This time, we'll bargain with the masters. We'll treat them at our nightclubs."*

Chrys had ideas of her own. Hurriedly, she packed her portable stage, the one she used on her last field trip to Mount Dolomoth. What had worked for Rose, she figured, just might work for that Leader.

On her back the twenty-kilo pack felt like nothing, with her Plan Ten–conditioned muscles. She called for a lightcraft. The lightcraft took her up before the setting sun, its last rays pouring blood across the harbor. It set her down at the old tube stop.

In her eyes blinked the message light—Andra, alone, within a full bodysuit, face and all. "Chrys, let us go after him. Don't you do anything rash," she urged. "Go home; it's a bad night in the Underworld."

What else is new. "What will you give them?"

The ship lights flickered off Andra's face screen. "We'll move every damn planet to find him, that's all I can say."

"Will you give them arsenic?"

"Of course not—and you can't either. Chrys, you're already in deep trouble; Arion knows what you did."

How did Arion find out, Chrys wondered. For that matter, if Daeren did not warn the masters, who did—if not Eris?

"I'm risking myself, Chrys. The Committee can't afford to lose you too." Andra's voice quickened. "Chrys—there's more to this than what I told the Committee. More that would split us apart. Leave this to me. Don't lose yourself, and your people, for nothing."

Chrys blinked to cancel. The sprite vanished. If she were really in trouble with the Elves, she thought, after she got Daeren back she could withdraw all her credits and flee to Solaris.

The tube plummeted to the Underworld. The Gold of Asragh was packed, the crowd more unruly than usual. A whiff of something burnt. Octopods crawled up, the usual pod of eight. Was there a raid? Lights circled crazily over the crowd, once momentarily blinding her. A fool's errand, she told herself, plunging through this world of night, desperately seeking Day.

At the slave bar, two customers pounded the counter demanding ace. Chrys made herself wait until they'd left. Then she leaned across the counter to stare at the slave who'd replaced Jay, who'd replaced Saf. "Where is he?" Chrys demanded. "Where's Day?"

The woman behind the bar looked and smelled as if she had not washed since the last time. She said nothing, but her eyes gleamed as wild as snakes.

"*Arsenic,*" said Fireweed. "*They're starving. We could help—*"

"No." Chrys held up a viewcoin, one of Jonquil's most scandalous. She faced the slave. "Tell me."

At first the woman seemed not to notice. Then her eyes widened. Her hand snatched involuntarily at the coin.

Chrys pulled the coin out of reach. "Where is Day? Where are the blue angels?"

The eyes watched the coin while the mouth spoke like a puppet. "Day chose Endless Light."

"Chose," indeed. "Take me there," Chrys demanded. "Take me to the Leader."

The eyes rolled, then came to rest looking just aside. "Len?" she called.

A worker slave came out, followed by another. Their maggot-ringed eyes flickered, and the woman's flickered back.

Chrys held out another viewcoin to Len. This time she let him take it. "Pictures in the stars." She brought her face closer, nearly choking on his foul breath. "Pictures for your Leader."

Their eyes flickered at the viewcoin, then back to her. "You're not ready." Len handed her a transfer patch.

She stared at the patch as she would at a poisonous snake.

"*We're prepared,*" said Fireweed. "*The children and younger elders are sealed away. We're ready for visitors.*"

Viruses and parasites—Chrys recoiled. "*Be prepared to clean up.*" She put the patch of plague at her neck.

"*Fireweed?*"

"*All is well,*" the infrared assured her.

From outside came screams and more smell of burning. A bad night, Andra had said. Which was worse: the humans outside, or these foul invaders within?

"*We've agreed on some joint ventures. Send them home.*"

"Joint ventures"—Chrys did not like the sound of that, but she returned the patch to Len. Turning their heads, the two slaves seemed to reach a decision. Len nodded at Chrys to follow him down the back stairway, where she and Daeren had first brought the viewcoin when she was in training. Two more slaves joined them, on out through a maze of tunnels. What paid for all this—Lord Zoisite's fortune, no doubt.

They came at last to the ship, a small lunar shuttle. Chrys was surprised; this vessel couldn't go far. The shuttle traveled less than an hour, with no fold jumps. It must have stayed within the solar system; in fact, it could not have gone far off Valedon. It docked to something, and the apparent gravitational force lurched sickeningly.

Strapping the packed field stage onto her back once more, Chrys followed the slaves out the air lock. The lock opened into a satellite ring, the old-fashioned kind that rolled like a treadmill. The centrifugal acceleration was not quite standard. Chrys stumbled, catching herself on the floor.

A wavering bit of cancerplast, lava red, cast long shadows down the passage. As her eyes adjusted, the patterned design on the floor and crossed triangle logo on the doors looked at least half a century out of date. The air smelled stale, though not as bad as in the masters' planetary hideout. Perhaps the surviving hosts had not yet had time to die and decay.

"*Where are we?*" Chrys asked her people. "*Did they say?*"

"*A temporary shelter;*" flashed Fireweed. "*The masters know they'll have to move on.*"

The hallway glimmered with cancerplast from the ceiling; one blob dangled, trembling, as if about to crawl off in search of power. Chrys's eyes adjusted to the dim light. Shadows stretched toward worker slaves, their eyes all flickering white as they passed. Some pushed cots or wheelchairs containing human bodies, inert, with unkempt beards or bare breasts, eyes horribly staring. What if one of them were Daeren? Her heart pounded enough to burst. She rehearsed what she planned to tell Saf, the human mouthpiece of the microbial Leader.

Ahead of her, Len turned toward the wall. A doorway opened, parting with a tired screech, like her old broken-down apartment. Len stepped through, and Chrys followed, taking the pack off her back. She rubbed her shoulders where it stung, unaccustomed to the strap.

An oval room, the ceiling dotted with plugs of cancerplast, like stars pasted to the sky. In the center stood a figure she could just make out, facing away from her. It must be Saf. The figure slowly turned.

It was Daeren. Daeren alive, and well enough to stand.

"Daeren!" She took a quick step forward, then another.

Daeren's face held no expression. His eyes flashed white maggot rings.

Chrys screamed, then clapped a hand over her mouth.

His lips moved. "I—am—the—Leader." His voice had the same stilted rhythm as Saf had. "Why do you come? Are you ready for Endless Light?"

Terror had driven any words from her head. She could only stare, transfixed, shaking.

"Say, 'No,' " prompted Forget-me-not. "Just say no."

"No," Chrys gasped, letting out her breath. "That's not . . . what I came for."

"Interesting," said Daeren's lips. "Your degenerate people say they can help us. You may visit."

Forget-me-not could visit; that was part of their plan. Chrys took the patch and handed it to Daeren, choking on the memory of doing this many times.

"One True God, all is well," Fireweed assured her. "Our joint ventures are maturing."

Chrys swallowed hard, recovering some of her nerve. Daeren—was he still there, inside, behind the deadly eyes? "I want you—I want him back," she said. "The . . . world that you took."

"The—new—world chose Endless Light," said Daeren's lips. "This new world came to us in better shape than most. New home for the Leader."

She swallowed again, her throat hoarse. "I want it back."

"Why? No use to you."

That was probably true, she realized, her heart sinking. The Leader had moved in, and by now all trace of Daeren's mind would be gone. But she had come too far to leave what was left of him. Better to take his empty shell then to have to see him in her dreams, as he would eventually be, his body exposed to unspeakable decay.

"Arsenic," flashed Fireweed. "They ask us for arsenic. They starve for it."

She thought of the other slaves down the hall, and the other shells, others decaying behind other walls, and all the hapless slaves of Valedon. "I can't. I can't betray my kind."

"We know, Great One. It's just hard for us to see them starve."

She opened the backpack, her hands so covered with sweat that the stage slipped from her grasp. Clumsily, she put up the projection posts and the light sources. "Display," she whispered.

The stage hummed, then shimmered into stars. It was the portrait of Rose. Rose, her pink filaments shimmering with the words of her final quest. *Rose . . .* The tireless worker deserved her rest.

Daeren's eyes fixed on the star picture. Nearby, the two slaves approached. Six maggot-rimmed eyes stared into the stars, their patterns calling like the lights of heaven that had entranced thinking minds ever since the first ape developed a cerebral cortex.

Suddenly, the two slaves fell back. Daeren's lips demanded, "Who is—this—pretender?"

The Leader was jealous of a rival. Chrys stood up, straightening her back. She put on her difficult-client smile. "I will make a portrait of the true Leader, in the stars. A portrait to outshine this one, and all others. To spread word throughout the universe, in praise of Endless Light."

The dead eyes flickered, eyes that had once shown blue as the palest sky. Could this Leader resist what had captivated Rose, the chance to project her will through eternity, calling all the people and all the gods to Endless Light?

"She agrees," said Fireweed. *"She'll have to visit, Oh Great One; and who knows who else will come besides. But we are ready."*

Daeren's hand held the patch to his neck, then to her; a gesture hauntingly familiar, ever since the first morning he gave her Fern and Poppy. Now there was no doctor or hospital to help, only a faltering satellite run by microbial minds that craved her blood. But inside her grew Fern's descendants, a million strong.

"Fireweed? Is it all right?"

"So far. We'll keep them talking." "Them"—she did not like the sound of that.

A ring of filaments, white as bone, probing and tasting. Chrys shut her eyes to see better. She crouched before the stage on the floor. With a word she dismissed the display. The first fresh strokes of light slanted wrong; her hands shook so badly, and she was out of practice on this tiny stage. It was hard to believe, now, that she had ever managed to get anything out of a meter cube. She reset it to track her finger, one tip at a time. The ring of light took shape, filling the small volume. Then shadows and highlights, and subtle hints of color, just enough to deepen the mystery.

The maggot eyes watched. From the ceiling beyond, a cancer dropped to the floor, extending long strings of plast, the kind that could get into a circuit and short it out—and there must be hundreds of them. Bad news for the old satellite. Chrys stood and stretched her back. *"Is the client pleased?"*

"Yes, so far. Keep on," urged Fireweed. *"Time is on our side."*

The micros could not know what shape the satellite was in. What if its air system failed? Setting the animation, Chrys did a shortcut, just dimming and brightening the image to generate the Leader's "words." *"Is that enough?"*

"Keep going. You can't expect a leader to make a speech short."

She kept on, her fingers dimming and brightening, long and short, abrupt and slow-fading, according to what her eyes saw. *"Fireweed, the field stage can only store so much."*

"It is done."

Chrys pressed the transfer port, letting the painting load into her eyes. Then she stood again. What next, she wondered suddenly. What would happen to Daeren, or his "shell," and where would the Leader go?

"Give him back," she said aloud. "You agreed."

"We will go." The letters in her window were white as ice. *"We will go. But you will keep some of my people, to see my enlightened form raised before all."*

Keeping some masters—this was not the deal. She fought against panic. *"Fireweed? Forget-me-not? Are you there?"*

"I'm here," came the infrared.

"I'm here too," came the blue one. *"We've corrupted some of them, and put down two coup attempts from the rest. 'Annus horribilis,' history will say. But once the Leader's gone, they'll settle down."*

"*Are you sure?*" Chrys insisted. "*Are any of them false blue angels?*"

"*Probably. Who knows how many true blue angels once were false?*"

Out of the shadows stepped Saf. Saf's face, now, was covered with broken veins, her nose bulbous, her eyelids swollen, half shut. This was the overrun host the Leader had relinquished.

"*I go,*" said the white words. "*You will show my stars for all to see.*"

"*I promise.*" If Ilia's Gallery could handle it. Once again, Chrys took the patch from her neck and gave it to Saf. The touch of the vampirous finger made her wish she could wash her hands.

Saf's blanched eyes exchanged flickering with Daeren's. Then without warning, she bit him in the neck.

Chrys stifled a cry with her hand. The Leader was getting back her own people, she realized, all the little maggot rings that had infected Daeren—millions, perhaps billions; they overran a host, far too many to transfer by patch. For an eternity Saf stood there, her teeth in his neck. Then she let go. Daeren slumped to the floor.

"Take it and go," Saf's voice rasped, barely audible. "Before I change my mind."

Chrys knelt beside him and shook his arm. "Daeren? Can you hear?" She pressed her ear to his chest. A pounding, slow but solid.

"*Let us visit,*" urged Forget-me-not. "*Let's see who's left alive.*" If not his own mind, at least some blue angels might survive, any those maggot rings had let live.

"*First let's get out of here.*" She pulled Daeren's arm behind her neck and hoisted him up on her back, making sure the head fell forward. "Help me," she called to the slaves.

The slaves did not answer, but Len started toward the doorway. Chrys got herself up and half carried, half dragged Daeren's body behind her, leaving behind the painting stage aglow, to keep the Leader entranced. To get out, away from here, before that slave forgot his errand, or the satellite lost power, or the Leader changed her mind.

Len took her out to a different ship, even smaller and more

decrepit than the one that had brought them here. Chrys hesitated but saw no choice. She stepped through the locks, each sealing behind her. A six-seater, half the straps gone.

"Daeren," she sighed, straightening his head on the floor. "Are you still there?" She held open his eyelid to reveal any sign. At last a flicker of blue.

"*Blue angels, or false,*" said Fireweed, "*someone's alive. Sick and starving—they need help.*"

Chrys put the patch back and forth, to send helpers and bring back the sickest of the blue angels. "*The Lord of Light—where is he? Is he still there?*"

"*The mind of God is there, but somehow shut away,*" explained Fireweed. "*We don't know how to rouse it without risking further injury.*"

Daeren's mind was still alive.

A sudden wrench sent Chrys spinning, floating in zero gravity. "Ship?" she called, not knowing its name. "What's going on?" The ship had not even greeted them, not even to strap down. "What's wrong?"

No response. Her stomach lurched as she tumbled, her hair swinging around her face. Finally she grabbed a handhold and steadied herself.

In her window blinked a ship contact button. Shutting her eyes, she winced at her window. Three contact points appeared for the ship's brain, two of them marked "inactive."

"Oh my god." The slave had put her on a dead ship. Whether on purpose or not, the result was the same. To get so far, only to die out in space . . . Her head and arms went numb. But she took a deep breath and made herself think.

The one active contact was for distress call. She blinked hard once, then again. Her eye muscles must have registered, for the spot started flashing red. Reserve power, enough for SOS. But it could be hours before anyone found her. Or days.

"*Fireweed? I'm not sure how long we'll last.*"

"*Years, at least. Have faith.*"

"*You must sleep,*" added Forget-me-not. "*Conserve oxygen.*"

Daeren's body still floated, unaware. His shoulders, his chest, his face that Plan Ten had shaped—still perfect. Yet who was left inside? "You could have stayed last night," she whispered. "Instead of getting caught in the Underworld." The tears floated away from her. Closing her eyes, she brought up the image of her brother turning cartwheels.

Health for all the children of her village—the one truly good thing she had ever done in her life. Now she herself was going to die, without ever having children of her own. Why did she never think of that? The micros, with all their crazy projects, never forgot their children. Now it was too late.

She closed her eyes, trying to sleep while keeping her arm locked to the handhold. For an endless time she dozed, half waking for a few minutes at a time, her people flickering. If she ever did get out alive, she vowed, she would go home and see Hal. And she would have her own children, if she had to get them off the streets of the Underworld.

The ship slammed her against the wall. Something had docked, hard. Sparks flew from the door as it ground open. Two octopods came in, their black limbs slithering over the floor.

"What the—" Chrys knew better than to argue with octopods. They hustled her out into the docked ship. Long worms of plast extended from the ship, emergency medical. In their midst, in white hospital nanotex, stood Andra.

Andra ignored Chrys, her attention fixed on Daeren, now strapped to a stretcher. Doctor Sartorius instructed the octopods, and the extensions from the ship, silently of course, but one could tell. The worms from his face stretched into long threads that wrapped all around Daeren's head. Then Andra leaned over him, pulling back his eyelids to check.

Chrys strained forward, but the octopod held her back. "Andra?"

Daeren's head moved ever so slightly. Then his eyes flew open, and every muscle strained as if to burst. He let out a deafening cry. His left arm came loose from the strap and jerked violently, hitting the wall.

"Too soon," murmured the doctor. Daeren's eyes closed, and he went limp.

Andra nodded. "He feels pain. That much of him's left."

The ship extension felt around his arm, the one that had hit the wall. "A clean fracture," the ship announced. Its limb slapped nanoplast around the arm. Then an octopod wheeled Daeren out.

Chrys strained forward. "Andra—let me stay with him."

The octopod extruded a thin black needle, a finger of death. The needle pressed to Chrys's neck.

The chief turned and brought her face within an inch of Chrys. "What are you?" Her eyes flashed deadly purple. "What are you, that you can come and go from the masters?"

She swallowed, feeling the needle at her neck, but her eyes did not flinch. "I gave them no arsenic."

"Then what?"

"Nothing you would want."

For an eternity Andra stared. Then she nodded at the octopod to remove the needle. She put a patch at Chrys's neck. "You'll give them up, every one," she ordered. "Any masters, and any of his blue angels."

A few of Daeren's blue angels had stayed with her to heal. "Not the blue angels. They were sick—they've been through so much."

"They face trial. And so do you."

"*Keep talking,*" urged Forget-me-not. "*We need to keep some of the defectors. At least the mathematicians—they're really smart. We'll tell the judges—*"

Chrys pulled against the octopod arms until one gave her a shock. She clenched her teeth. "I rescued him—"

"We'll see what you rescued."

Doctor Sartorius came over. "He's stabilized. He can handle consciousness for a few minutes."

Andra frowned. "Is Selenite here yet?"

"Just arrived."

Chrys demanded, "What's going on?"

Andra gave her a look, haunted yet calculating. Daeren lay surrounded by a webbing of filaments from the wall. Behind him waited Selenite with a grim expression, arms folded. Daeren's eyes were open, bright with pain.

The chief brought her face close to his. "Listen," Andra spoke rapidly. "Your people survived, about two hundred thousand of them." One in five—what became of the rest? Torture? Starvation? "You have to give them up."

His eyes flitted away, then back, irises dark. "It wasn't their fault."

"No, but your forebrain's shot to hell. You know the rule. You have to heal in the clinic."

"Alone?"

"How else?" Andra demanded. "You'll be arsenic-wiped every day. Tell them."

"I can't do that," Daeren whispered. "I can't send them away. Homeless."

"They'll have a home—half with me, half with Selenite." By regulation, a carrier could not hold more than 10 percent over their limit.

"Selenite? But she'll breed them for—"

"They'll live, won't they? Why didn't you think of that when you gave yourself up?"

Chrys caught her breath. Whatever could Andra mean?

Daeren closed his eyes. "Why did you bring me back?"

"What really happened to him?" Chrys demanded of her people. *"What do the blue angels say?"*

A moment of hesitation. *"They say he went to the masters. Because he had destroyed their world, he gave them his."*

She stared without seeing, without breathing. She remembered his eyes, when he last came to see her, the shifting eyes of a slave. His last call for help.

"I warned you," whispered Andra. "He can't have micros again, ever."

Doctor Sartorius stood by the cot, tendrils hanging motionless from his head, their eye sensors turned aside. Chrys caught the sentient carapace between her hands. His warmth surprised her;

"waste heat," the sentient unspeakable. No eyes, but she faced the worms. "Doctor, can't you do something? He's no slave; he just slipped. You know what he is. You've got to cure him."

"I'll do what I can, Chrysoberyl." The doctor's voice was strangely soft, the different voice that she had heard once or twice, still distinctly his. "But chemicals alone cannot fix the brain, without exchanging one slavery for another."

TWENTY-ONE

From the world of Endless Light, hundreds of defectors from the masters had swarmed in, all at once—desperate elders smuggling sick children, as well as agitators and infiltrators. Even years later a few more, unrepentant, were rooted out of hiding in the bone marrow, preparing their secret poisons.

The judges in purple emitted volumes of disgust, enough to permeate the arachnoid. "Such lack of judgment we have never seen," they proclaimed. "You can never know you've found them all; there could be others even we did not find. You should be arsenic-wiped."

Fireweed was about to say that Eleutherians had investigated themselves more thoroughly than did the judges, but she thought better of it. "We are eternally grateful for your assistance—and so are our new citizens." Those who came for a better life had settled in. Engineers and mathematicians, some of them brilliant. In the closed society of Endless Light, lacking resources as well as freedom of speech, the greatest minds embraced mathematics. The Leader's loss was Eleutheria's gain.

"And your population is in excess again," the judge added. "You're fined ten thousand atoms of palladium."

"We're correcting the problem, as you can taste." The pheromones had been reset to encourage development of elders.

"And next time, don't induce all the foreign children to merge prematurely just to prevent their deportation. It's indecent." Eleutheria had done this for generations to keep the most genetic benefit from immigrant talent.

Fireweed emitted placating pheromones of the highest quality. "Anything else? Surely we can continue this discussion in the night-club, over AZ." Most people consumed azetidine as quickly as they could absorb it from the blood, but Fireweed had learned Rose's trick of saving some for special occasions.

"Eleutheria!" The judge emitted molecules of exasperation. "You people think you know everything, but you were fooled once. Don't think you won't be fools again."

Her night passed in fitful slumber; she could not awake without remembering and crying herself to sleep again. In the morning, her message light blinked insistently. Chrys roused herself, her eyelids sore, her back aching from strain. Wearily, she fetched a disk of nanotex. The material spread smoothly up her arms and down to her toes.

The sprite was a stranger, an Iridian gentleman with a few modest agates swimming in his talar. "You went to the Slave World. Did you see my son?" A still image followed, a young man in thick nanotex with gem-cutting tools at his side. His short-cropped hair stood up like a brush, and his smile had that half scared look of someone just getting used to adulthood.

The news must have got out. Chrys swallowed. "I—I'm sorry, I can't help you."

"Please—it's been a year since they took him. I know he would send word, if he could. Can't they even let their slaves send word home? Why doesn't the Palace negotiate?"

Her mouth opened, but she could not think what to say.

"Send me your recording," he demanded. "I'll recognize my son."

"It's classified," she said quickly.

The man's face brightened. "So there is a recording. Release it."

Chrys sighed. "Believe me, it won't help you."

"I'll sue to get it released." The man's voice softened. "Please—my only son. He was to take over the stonecutting shop this year, when those plague-ridden pirates got him."

She bit her lip. "If there were anything I could do, believe me, I would. Every week I take my shift in the Underworld, helping folks like your son—"

The man stiffened. "My son never went near the Underworld. He was clean-living, until he was kidnapped." He raised his hands. "Can you go? Negotiate his release? I'll pay ransom."

"No," she whispered. Then aloud, "I can't go back, ever."

"You got your own back! Help me!"

The rest of that morning, the calls came—a daughter, a brother, a grandson lost, the year before, the previous month, or just that week. Several that week, in fact. A lot of good it had done, boiling the world of Endless Light.

In desperation she forwarded all calls to Xenon. Her own work had fallen behind, and the following day she was due to meet Ilia at the Gallery Elysium to preview her exhibit. But when she sat at the painting stage, all she could do was stare.

"New ideas," flashed Lupin, a new elder whose lemon yellow reminded her of Jonquil. "We have new ideas—for advanced compositions. . . ."

Her hand, as if on its own, traced a ghostly outline of Daeren's forehead. No good—she was never any good at humans. With a flick of her hand, the shape dissolved in white—pure, even light that filled the entire cube of stage. One more piece, she needed for her show; but what could it be? What pattern of pixels could begin to express what she had undergone?

"Chrysoberyl," called Xenon. "Chief Andra is trying to reach you."

Darkness surrounded Andra's eyes, as if she had not slept much either. "I've spoken with Arion."

"About what?"

"Your treason."

"Oh, right." Tipping off the slaves, though Eris already had.

"If Arion tells the Palace, the Palace octopods will haul you in. Arsenic-wiped first, questions later."

Passage to Solaria; she had to look up the schedule. Solaria was several days journey, with numerous jump folds.

"For now," Andra told her, "Arion agrees to overlook your indiscretion. I traded valuable intelligence—some of the best we ever received. Daeren's brain held high-level defectors, including advisors to the Leader."

"I see." Chrys bit her lip. "You know where that intelligence will go." Straight to Eris.

"I know well enough," Andra coldly replied. "I bought your people's lives, do you understand?"

Chrys looked away. Her heart beat faster. "How is Daeren?"

"The Committee will see."

Above the virtual leaves and the flying fish, someone had set the sky gray, with a fine mist of rain. The Committee members sat close together, humans trading patches all around but avoiding each other's eyes. Sartorius and Flexor both had their worms pulled in, barely twitching.

Opal embraced Chrys. "Thanks," she whispered. For what, Chrys wondered bitterly.

"Why, Andra?" Pyrite shook his head in puzzlement. "Why did he do it?"

Andra looked around the circle. "Ask yourselves. Ask your own people."

Opal looked away, her face deeply creased. Pyrite held his head in his hand as if it ached. "My people were stunned, by the . . . by what happened to the Slave World."

"Concerned." Jasper spoke in a low voice as he held Garnet's hand. Garnet looked away without speaking. "We were concerned," Jasper admitted, "about what we heard. We had . . . questions."

Chrys stared until her eyes swam. Anger, outrage—all the micro people had turned on Daeren, gave him no peace for helping Arion destroy the Slave World.

Selenite lifted her chin. "Mine were not concerned. Mine had nothing to say about it. The Slave World was an abomination. Daeren did what he had to. I was impressed." Small comfort, thought Chrys. On top of everything, why had Andra made him send half his people to the Deathlord, to be bred into mitochondria?

Jasper's hand tensed, and his throat dipped as he swallowed. "No matter how bad things get, you don't just run to the masters. Think of Andra and Chrys. He must have known we'd risk our lives."

"And all his own people," added Opal. "What became of them?"

"He made a devil's bargain," Andra explained. "The masters took over, but they let the blue angels alone. The masters took most of the arsenic, of course, letting his own people slowly starve. They destroyed the pleasure center, but the blue angels protected his central memory and personality longer than usual." Andra swallowed, her neck like a pillar of stone. "Protected while they starved, hoping for help, knowing none had ever come before."

"But Chrys came," said Opal.

"Yes," said Andra. "Chrys got him back."

Chrys looked up. "Why are you so angry at him?"

Jasper lifted his hands. "Haven't you been listening?"

"Because all of us, every day, think of Endless Light." Andra's voice came faster. "We all know it's there—a burst of heaven, and your troubles are over."

No one denied it. Chrys recalled her own brush with the vampire.

Doctor Sartorius's face worms came alive. "It was only one slip. In his work, Daeren resisted far more encounters than most of us. And even when he gave up, his own people remained faithful. I've never seen that before."

Pyrite looked up hopefully. "Could he have them back?"

Jasper shook his head. "Never. How could he control them?"

Chrys asked, "Why not?"

"Because he'll remember," explained Opal. "Even after he heals, he'll always remember what they can do. Dream of it every night."

"But they want to go back." Andra's face was paler than ever. "All day and all night, the ones I took begged me to send them back."

"Back to Daeren?" Pyrite exclaimed. "After he betrayed and starved them?"

"Even so." Her voice sank to a whisper. "They know he won't survive alone."

"What do you mean, he won't survive?" demanded Chrys. "Plan Ten can heal anything."

Sartorius raised a worm. "The brain heals. But carriers who lose their people die, sometimes even before they leave the clinic."

"How?"

Selenite frowned. "Any way they can, that's how. Chrys, let Sar alone; he doesn't like it any more than you do."

The others looked away. Only Pyrite looked up in surprise; apparently no one had told him either. Chrys tried to remember what life was like before the little rings came to stay. Living alone. Even when she lived with Topaz, she could remember waking up nights in the dark, Topaz fast asleep with her back turned, feeling alone, totally alone in the universe. She recalled it as a fact outside herself; she could no longer imagine, now, what aloneness meant.

Pyrite said at last, "So it's a death sentence."

No one denied it. Garnet stared at Chrys, his irises flashing rapidly.

"They say, you have to do something, God of Mercy," flashed Forget-me-not. *"You have to help him."*

What more could she do, thought Chrys.

"There may be another way," said the doctor. "An experimental treatment." He paused as if measuring his words. "The blue angels could help us heal him."

In the tranquil sky, a flock of fish flew overhead.

"Out of the question," snapped Jasper. "Daeren didn't just

slip, like Garnet; he fell all the way. It will be months before he can feel anything normally."

Doctor Sartorious said, "The blue angels could accelerate the healing process by monitoring the neurons closely, more subtly than the nanos can."

"But in the meantime, how can he carry people in his head and not beg them to make him feel better? And then, for the rest of his life?"

"They'll just have to say no."

"Then who's the master?" Jasper shook his head. "You're condoning slavery."

Selenite leaned forward slightly. "I wonder. You can't live without mitochondria; does that make you their slave?"

Jasper looked at her in surprise. "You always say, rules are rules."

"True, but the rules allow for experimental treatment. We have to stop letting the masters get the better of us." She added, "I think the blue angels can handle it. Last night I found them reasonably well behaved. A bit forward—myself, I'd breed that out of them—but if the good doctor has a plan, I say give it a try."

Throughout this exchange Andra kept quiet. Chrys saw now why she had enlisted Selenite.

"He can't stay at the clinic," the doctor added, "it's a microfree zone. Andra and I can look after him; we'll set up a facility at home."

"*What are the gods up to?*" Fireweed had been trying to get her attention.

"*A stay of execution.*"

Only a month till her show opened at Gallery Elysium. Chrys met Ilia there with Yyri, Zircon's former lover. The two Elves smiled, their butterflies projecting behind them, golden swallowtails with dots of red and blue.

Yyri stretched out her hands, though careful not to actually touch Chrys. "Why Chrysoberyl," she exclaimed, as if to a long lost friend. "Or, should I say, 'Azetidine'? I haven't seen you since the Seven Stars." The Seven's last show; the recollection felt like another world, light-years away. Suddenly, Ilia and Yyri laughed simultaneously. Their electronic sixth sense must have shared a witticism at the expense of primitive art.

"*The God of Many Colors!*" Lupin flashed lemon yellow, enthusiastic as old Jonquil. "*Can we visit? Their nightclubs are legend.*"

Ilia met her eyes, but the rings were absent. Chrys hesitated. "Are we—"

"Later, dear," Ilia whispered. Then Chrys realized, Yyri was not a carrier. "Let's review your catalogue from start to finish. First, your early work."

Yyri clapped her hands. "I do love a historical approach. Discern the seeds of genius in one's crudest beginnings."

The first pyroclastic flow Chrys had clumsily attempted, sophomore year, and the one awful self-portrait; these Ilia had insisted on. Pieces that Chrys would have been mortified to reveal to any Iridian dealer now shown in Helicon as signs of incipient genius.

"*Lava Butterflies,*" Ilia nodded to Yyri. "The colors struck my eye." Her first piece with Eleutherian collaboration, signed with the molecule Azetidine.

"She was your find, my dear." Yyri's eye savored the more recent volcanoes, the lava flowing upward into arachnoid stalactites, all bearing Chrys's Eleutherian *nom d'art*. "The form oscillates between the macrocosm and the microcosm. Imponderable imagination."

Ilia leaned toward Chrys, a gleam in her eye. "Silicon—is it final?"

Chrys caught her breath. She had yet to give Jasper the bad news. She made herself smile. "Still negotiating. You know how . . . sentients are."

"We'd love to include the model. We'll save a place for it."

Yyri clasped her hands. "Quite a coup, Ilia. Silicon—radical concept—people are just beside themselves."

The cerebral landscapes and portraits followed, taking up the bulk of the show. Little colored rings careening through the arachnoid, tasting their nightclubs and their calculator cells. Ilia nodded at each, as if at a familiar neighborhood.

"An otherworldly universe," exclaimed Yyri. "I've never seen anything quite so . . . alien."

Ilia's hand swept toward Fern, the ring of green filaments twinkling the commandments of Eleutheria. "Let's bring her out front, like a greeter. She looks so friendly."

Fern, Aster, Jonquil. It was harder than Chrys had expected to face them, world-sized, exposed to public view. She had wanted to show only portraits from the other carriers, but Ilia had insisted these were the best. So here they all were, spaced at intervals against a black dome, constellations within some foreign galaxy. Chrys felt overwhelmed, as if in a crowd of a hundred people talking.

Yyri smiled more broadly than ever, though her eyes looked puzzled. Then her face relaxed. "Of course, dear, I see. Such extraordinary rendering of personality."

The next hall contained Jonquil's inspirations. It made Chrys's palms sweat to see them, all those off-color depictions of children merging and worse, all together in one place, but Ilia had insisted on every one. Yyri smiled politely, then suddenly stared as Ilia's sixth sense reached her. "Oh my," she exclaimed. "How exquisitely provocative. Though perhaps . . . some might take exception, do you think, dear?"

Ilia's eyes gleamed. A moment's silence, then two heads nodded. "A curtain at the door, and a warning."

"We Elysians take children very seriously," Yyri added, as if Chrys might think otherwise. Elf children were raised in precious nurseries deep within each city, with every conceivable resource showered upon them, from education to entertainment for fifty years.

"And here," Ilia added, "we have political statement." In a place of prominence beside a dramatic ornamental fountain, Ilia had placed *Mourners at an Execution* and *Seven Stars with the Hunter*.

Yyri clasped her hands. "Our Guardian of Peace will have a stroke."

Ilia murmured, "Perhaps it might knock some sense into his head." Then she turned to Chrys. "Your latest works? We've expanded another hall."

Chrys cleared her throat. "I wanted to show you in person, for your approval." She blinked at her window to download the scenes from the masters. Cadaverous micros crowded the brain of a half-dead host, like worms in rotting flesh. After much thought, she had placed Rose's portrait here, next to the towering, obsessively monumental vision of her beloved Leader.

Ilia sucked in her breath. Beside her, Yyri at first looked puzzled. Then Yyri's creamy complexion paled, revealing every vein. A brief glance at Chrys, as though the artist had gone mad. "I don't know, Ilia. You're right, the citizens need to know, but . . ."

The minutes of silence lengthened, while the Leader's interminable speech kept flashing. At last the two heads nodded. "We'll need to hire . . ." Ilia paused dramatically. " . . . security."

"The Gallery hasn't needed . . . security," Yyri added, "for a hundred years."

"A hundred twenty," Ilia corrected. "That Solarian performance artist, remember?"

Yyri waved a dismissive hand. "Nothing compared to this. The very foundations of our society, shaken to the bone."

Ilia took a deep breath, then turned to Chrys. "You promised us another *Endless Light*."

"Oh, right." She quickly downloaded the block of pure white, the one she had stared at after Daeren's rescue, unable to do more. "There you are. *Endless Light*."

Yyri clapped her hands. "Of course." She sounded relieved. "Minimalism. Your talent is so versatile, dear."

That night the snake-eggs interviewed Eris, the Guardian of Cultural Affairs, about the Gallery's upcoming exhibit. *Eris*—She had not seen Arion's deadly "brother" since the day he left his false blue angels hiding in her brain. His sprite in her window made her hair stand on end.

"Our season's premiere exhibition will prove more controversial than usual," the secret slave admitted, his voice at its most charming. "But educational," he stressed. "In these difficult times, we Elysians must learn to master and bend to our will the forces that threaten us from less civilized realms."

The snake-egg bobbed in his face. "So you support the judgment of the gallery director? Will this 'educational' exhibit be safe for the classes of school children that tour every fall?"

Eris smiled condescendingly. "Of course I support my gallery staff. I myself have acquired a first-class Azetidine for my personal collection." Another word, thought Chrys, and she'd head for the sink.

"And now," said the snake-egg, "for a view from Valedon regarding the cultural contributions of microbes, we bring you the Palace physician."

The Palace physician, a worm-faced advisor to the Protector, draped himself like a lord. "The brain plague endangers all law-abiding citizens," the doctor proclaimed, emeralds and adamants glittering beneath his worms. "Even regulated 'carriers' are essentially slaves to their microbial masters. In the long run, their supposed contributions to culture will be viewed in the same light as the psychedelic delusions of humans under the influence of toxic neurochemicals." A couple of worms raised for emphasis. "Fortunately, we can help the all plague carriers overcome their addiction and modulate their minds with our own pharmaceuticals."

Slaves in Elysium, mind-suckers in Valedon. Chrys made the Dolomite hand sign against evil.

She took the night off to escort Lady Moraeg to Olympus. Lord Carnelian was still absent, put off by her micros, but Moraeg would give no one the satisfaction of a sign of grief.

"Keep your eyes off the caryatids," warned Chrys.

Moraeg regarded one with disdain. "That old trick."

"Carriers are really very nice people," Chrys hurried to add. "They just have, um, unusual customs."

"Moraeg!" Opal embraced her. "So good to see you. That diamond," she exclaimed. "Such an distinctive cut."

Moraeg smiled. "An original, from the jewels of Ulragh."

"I thought as much." Opal's eyes flashed colors. "May we visit?"

Chrys turned away, seeking Andra. How was Daeren?—It had been two days since his blue angels came home.

Garnet caught her hand. "Chrys, it's been so long." His eyes twinkled. "You never check your investments. I could be bribing you again."

She shrugged. "The least of my sins."

He leaned closer to whisper. "Where the devil is Carnelian? Put off by us?"

Chrys sighed.

"He's been a Hyalite client for years. I'll have a word with him."

There was Andra, reclining beside a redwood tree. Chrys had to wait to catch her alone. "How is Daeren?"

Andra thought a moment. "Medically, he's making progress. But his mind—" She hesitated. "He's not trying."

"It's only been two days."

"Too long, for his people. Too many generations of anguish."

"Why isn't he trying, Andra?"

Andra looked as if she had much more to say, but would not. "We'll see."

Suddenly tired, Chrys sank into a seat, refusing the delicacies from the caryatid. Jasper sat next to her and touched her hand. Dismayed, she remembered that Jasper did not yet know that her people couldn't handle Silicon. "Are you sure you won't try the lamb berries?" Jasper asked. "They're new from L'li."

"I'm not hungry." Reluctantly, she passed him the transfer patch.

Jasper puffed on his pipe, his short thumb tapping restlessly at the stem. "We're waiting to hear," he reminded her. "Anything I can do?"

She took a deep breath. "I'm sorry, Jasper. We can't do the job."

He nodded. "I understand. I'll come back with a better offer."

"No, I mean it." She struggled to explain. "The Eleutherians say they can't do it. They'd need a computer too big to fit inside my head."

Jasper's expression did not change. "We knew that."

"You did?"

"We were aware of the theoretical problem. But since it didn't come up in negotiations, I hoped they had it solved."

She grimaced at this optimism. "They haven't."

He set the pipe down. "Well, as I said, we'll come back with a better offer. After all, the job will take longer.

Chrys was astonished. "A better offer—for a job we can't do?"

"Chrys, this project is unprecedented. Elysium hasn't built a new city in over twelve centuries. And now, a dynamic form, to grow of nanoplast. Entirely new technologies will be needed. The sentient engineers, too, have several fundamental problems unsolved."

"But—but it's sheer lunacy."

"Do you suppose the builders of the first Pyramid knew exactly how they'd complete it?"

"But what if we fail?"

"You'll succeed," Jasper assured her. "The math problem, they will solve. They'll fail in other ways. Who knows—maybe Silicon won't be finished in your lifetime, or perhaps never, like the ancient temple of Asragh, forever missing its tallest spire. Even if it does reach completion, someone will want to kill you, for one good reason or another."

"Selenite will," she added ruefully.

"That's why Selenite never gets these jobs herself. But you'll handle it. How long since you've walked on lava?"

She swallowed, thinking, I'm getting too old for lava.

*　　*　　*

The next day Opal called. "Selenite's at the hospital. Her people got in trouble."

Chrys stared. "Not the minions?"

Opal hesitated. "I think the blue angels emboldened them. They'd never seen people so totally unafraid, even when forced to live at her mercy."

At the hospital Chrys held Selenite's hand. Selenite's face was creased, and she blinked more rapidly than usual. Chrys made herself smile. "Can I help? Send over a few 'libertines' to lecture them?"

"They took their own lives," Selenite whispered. "Twenty of them. Protesting one execution." She struggled to raise herself in bed. "The blue angels inspired them."

"Well, now," said Opal, seated by the bed. "Blue angels never hurt themselves."

"But they encourage disobedience. Chrys, I was wrong," Selenite added. "The blue angels are not safe—they're the most dangerous strain we have."

Opal's eyes met Chrys's for a long while.

"One True God, let the wizards visit," flashed Fireweed. *"We've founded a new school of mathematics."*

"Could you take half her caseload?" Opal asked at last. "I know it's hard, with your show coming up."

"I'll manage." In fact, Chrys had painted nothing since *Endless Light.* She wondered if she could ever paint again.

The message light; Andra appeared. "Chrys, Sar and I have to leave town for three days, on personal business. Could you stay over here and look after Daeren? The house has the full medical capacity of the clinic, but in case his people need help, we need a human carrier."

TWENTY-TWO

*T*he defectors from Endless Light had brought with them their unique branch of calculus, from the masters' best minds drawn together in the one intellectual pursuit permitted by the Leader of Endless Light. Now in Eleutheria, they founded a new school of mathematics, a constructive theory of numbers bridging the infinite to the infinitesimal. Their algorithms vastly simplified the creation of the very large from the very small.

"Even the wizards come here to study," flashed Fireweed.

"Working together," predicted Forget-me-not, "we'll soon have what we need to build Silicon."

"Perhaps," said Fireweed. "But I'll never see the building completed. Not within my lifetime."

"Nor mine," agreed Forget-me-not. "But we've shaped the design, the promise of things to come. What could be greater?"

Fireweed extended her filaments, tasting the molecules of excitement from the mathematicians. "As I age, I think over and over again of the God's commandment: Love me, love my people. Something tells me we have more work to be done, beyond Silicon."

"We saved the blue angels," said Forget-me-not. "The deed shines in our history like a golden light."

"But where are the blue angels now?"

"I fear for them, and for us all," the blue one admitted. *"There is trouble in the world of the gods, trouble greater than our own."*

The snake-eggs picked on Chrys, buzzing so thick she could barely find Andra's address.

"How did you get out alive from the Slave World?"

"Do the slaves pay you to paint their propaganda? Why are you spreading the brain plague?"

"Can you confirm reports that you are secretly a vampire?"

Her best defense, she had found, was silence. But one pesky reporter got tangled in her hair like a fly. She tossed it out, annoyed at losing a few precious strands. "If you won't comment," it warned, "other sources will."

Andra's home was faced in brick, at first glance monotone, but in fact each brick had its own subtle shade. There was no obvious door, but as Chrys watched, two camouflaged octopods slowly shaped themselves out of the brick. The snake-eggs vanished.

"We inform you," said an octopod, "as a matter of courtesy, that this facility is fully secured. No one gains entry or leaves, save by our consent."

"And no one makes trouble within," added the other.

"Over the years we've foiled explosives, poisons, information viruses, even exotic animals," the first added wearily. "Make our day. Try something new."

Chrys frowned. "I'm expected."

"Very well." The disappointed octopods faded back into the brick, which parted to form a doorway.

Inside stood a man she did not know. Not a man; a humanoid sentient, his form too perfect even for Plan Ten. His eyes and nose were of classic proportions; his gray talar flowed majestically from shoulders to feet, his chest bearing a single white stone. "Chrysoberyl."

The voice was Doctor Sartorius. His tone had softened, the

voice he had used the night she rescued Daeren. Chrys felt herself flush all the way from her face to her toes.

"I've not had a chance," he said, "to tell you how much it meant to me, what you did for Daeren. I think of him as my own brother."

Speechless, she nodded slightly.

"You understand that he is still very sick." The doctor's lips produced perfect speech. "His brain needs time to heal. The house takes care of that. You need do nothing, except stay here."

Andra approached, also in gray. Her hand brushed his back. They looked like a couple off to a gem-trading convention. "It's been hard for Sar," she said, "these past two weeks."

"And hard for you," said Chrys, recovering her manners. "I'm sorry."

"We're glad we can depend on you." Andra looked backward, toward a passage lined with chandeliers. "Daeren's treatment facility is down the hall."

From the ceiling, the house voice added, "There's a suite for you, Chrysoberyl. Whatever you need, just ask."

"Listen to the blue angels," added Andra. "But be considerate; they don't yet take visitors. They're sensitive about their condition."

"I understand." She warned her people, *No visiting.*

But the blue angels—it's been generations since—

Stay dark, lest you lose the sun. Down the hall, false windows hung with valances produced a soft light. There stood Daeren.

He did not speak; though if he had, she might not have heard, for the blood pounding in her ears. She whispered, "Day."

Daeren's eyes were dark, not a hint of light. Without a word, he turned and walked away, down the hall. Chrys followed. At her left, the arched windows came gradually larger, until at some point their light became real, the windows expanding into open archways above long, cushioned seats, as inviting as Olympus. The archways looked out onto a swimming pool, a headball court, and a virtual hiking trail leading up into distant mountains.

Daeren was sitting in a seat beneath the arch. From the wall by his shoulder extended a small table, holding two cups of orange juice and a dish of AZ. Chrys sat beside him. He seemed relaxed, one leg up on the seat, hands clasped upon the knee. The minutes passed. "Daeren, can you talk?"

Daeren met her eyes, his own still dark. "When I have something to say."

She let out her breath. Glancing at the juice and AZ, she asked, "Shouldn't I stay objective?"

"You needn't be a saint."

Chrys reached past him for the cup of juice, her heart pounding to feel him so near. She raised the cup to her lips.

"Chrys . . . what did you give them?"

Her throat tightened. "No arsenic."

"I would have. For you."

Her face burned. For the first time, she realized, she saw him without any micros chatting along. Just the two of them, alone.

"I just want to know," he said, "what to thank you for."

With difficulty she swallowed. "You'll see it at my show." Recalling the Leader, she shook her head. "What an egomaniac—to give up a world for her starving billions, just to see her own damned portrait preach Endless Light to the stars."

"Of course," he whispered. "That would be worth a world." For a minute, he was silent. Then he held out the plate of AZ. "Reward them, for me."

She eyed the blue wafers warily, fearing the Eleutherians would think it meant chatting time. "They haven't done anything good yet."

"They did for me. Let me feed them." Picking out a wafer, he raised it slowly to her lips. Chrys thought, if his finger touched her lips she would faint. She took it into her mouth.

"Oh Great One, we don't want azetidine. We just want to see the blue angels."

Seeing her face change, he asked, "What's wrong?"

"I told them they can't visit."

His eyes widened as if in fear. "Are they angry? I'm sorry," he half choked, "I'm sorry, I—"

"No, Daeren," Chrys insisted. "Of course they're not angry,

not anymore. We're the ones to blame; we're all dreadfully sorry."
But he looked away without answering. Chrys felt frustrated.
"Would you let Forget-me-not visit? She used to be yours."

He looked up. "So that's what you call her." His head nodded
slightly. "All right."

Chrys put the patch at his neck. Her hand felt reluctant to leave.

Closing his eyes a moment, Daeren took a deep breath. "All
right," he said at last. "Let the others come."

"Take it easy," she told them. She placed the patch again at his
neck. This time her hand stayed. He leaned into it like a cat.

Then he looked at her, surprised. "Why, you're right, Chrys.
They're not angry at all."

She remembered what they had said they would do, when she
told them how she felt for Daeren. "Saints and angels," she muttered. "Don't take them too seriously," she warned halfheartedly.
"You know what tricksters they are."

"Oh, but I like what I'm seeing."

She burned all over, full of confusion.

Daeren smiled, almost like he used to at Olympus. A faint flash
of blue in his eye, then red and green. "Shall we return the favor?"
He placed the patch on her neck, and his hand stayed. If there were
a heaven, Chrys thought, it would feel like this.

"Forgive us," came the words, another shade of blue. *"Forgive
us our complicity in genocide."*

"Forgive me," returned Chrys. *"Forgive me for deserting you.
From now on, I will protect you always, as my own people."*

"Oh Great One!" The yellow words of young Lupin. *"We
must praise your greatness in restoring these good people. Can't we
reward the god as you deserve? We have new technology—"*

"No," she said aloud.

Daeren's hand came down.

"Sorry," she explained, "they still ask now and then."

He looked down. "You are strong."

"I would have slipped once. But they remembered the Watchers."

He looked up again, his face suffused with delight. "The

Watchers. Your people still remember, after a hundred generations." Leaning toward her, he caressed her neck and her luxuriant
hair. "Chrys, they can't—but I can. I can make you happy."

She blinked twice. "I'm afraid."

"Why?"

"I'm afraid I'll be your slave."

"I've been yours," he said. "For a long time. Chrys, have
mercy."

Her lips parted in surprise. Everyone loved Daeren, they said,
but it never occurred to her what she might mean to him. His eyes
were again dark, dark and pleading. She closed her eyes, and her
lips met his. Lightly at first; like a butterfly at a flower, she still half
expected him to flee. Then she caught his head between her hands
and pressed hard, her tongue exploring what it longed for.

Daeren stroked her hair from head to shoulders. Then he
pulled her to his chest, head against her cheek. "I've dreamed of
your hair," he murmured.

"Why didn't you say anything?"

"I told you, you could have anything you ever need."

"I thought you said that to everyone."

"What?" He drew back, looking her in the face. "Don't they
wish." He stroked the hair at her shoulder. "There's been no one
else. Not since I met you."

"I'm nothing like Titan."

He shuddered. "Thank god," he said. "Thank god you're not
like Titan."

"But you loved him."

"I was captivated by him," Daeren admitted. "His people, and
the miracles they made—I could never get them out of my mind. I
tried to hide it, when I had to test him, but they knew. When we
warned him of the risks he took, they laughed." He looked out to
the virtual wilderness. "One night, as I turned to go, he asked me to
stay."

Chrys listened, barely breathing.

"The next morning, as I left, he told me to come back to him—
as a woman."

Titan, his work so modern, his desires so medieval. She stared without seeing.

"I knew then that he wanted only a conquest, like his others. Just to see if I would do it."

"But why did you have to test him?"

"I told Andra I'd never test him again. But he told her no one else would."

"What? They can't get away with that."

"We make exceptions," her reminded her. "Your friend Ilia; for her, only Andra will do. It's either that, or leave her to Eris."

Chrys thought, she'd tell Ilia a thing or two. "So you went on . . ."

"It was that, or turn him in. He knew we needed him, the great dynatect, the shining example of what micros can do. A month later, he was dead."

"But not his people."

Daeren nodded. "I thought being refugees would teach them something. But all they could think of was saving their plans and starting their own New World. So that's what they got." He looked her in the eye. "With you, they did improve. Andra was impressed."

"Well, that's something."

"They still never gave me a clue. Usually when someone likes me, their people make no secret of it. But with yours, it was always, 'Anything you can do, we can do better.'"

Chrys smiled ruefully. "They are kind of stuck on themselves. Well, you have them now."

Daeren gripped her shoulders, as if desperate. "Chrys, if you lost them all, I'd still love you, just the same."

That made all the difference. She took a deep breath. The feel of his fingers, the scent of him, only cried for more. She pressed him to her breasts, her waves of hair spilling over his shoulders. They rolled down together on the cushion, only nanotex between them. She caught him between her thighs, feeling his hardness press into her. She pressed harder until she climaxed. She gasped, her nails digging into his back. Then she lay back with a smile, tossing the hair out of her face. "I couldn't wait," she breathed. "I've wanted you so long."

Daeren lay beside her, stroking her forehead. "Chrys, I just want to make you happy, if it's the last thing I do."

"Don't say that." A touch of fear returned, fear of something she could not define. "You have to live forever."

"Anything," he promised. "I'll do anything I can."

She looked him over speculatively. "Then let me see a little more of you."

He regarded her as if thinking it over. Then he reached behind his neck to touch the collar control. The nanotex peeled slowly, down his arms and his chest and beyond, all the way revealing clear, unblemished skin, not even a broken vein. Just to be sure, her hand traced the curve of his muscles, exploring every inch. I got him back, she thought; I'll never have to see those muscles rotting in my dreams. She sighed. "I'll sleep better now."

"Then why don't you help me sleep better?"

Twisting back her hair, she touched behind her neck. The nanoplast creased and gathered, flowing down from her breasts and up from her legs, collecting as usual into a compact disk that slid onto the cushion. Daeren started with his lips at her breasts, as sensitive as a woman, she thought. Then his lips traveled downward, deliberately, no hurry, only time out of time. After a time she felt herself rouse again. He slowly brought her up, soaring higher than before, until she cried out.

"So hungry," he whispered. "If only I'd known."

She frowned, slightly puzzled. "What about you?" Turning to him, she kissed him all over, passionately, trying to rouse him. But below the waist he was cold.

"Didn't the doctor tell you?" he said. "I'm still . . . recovering."

Chrys sat up. She bit her lip. "What does that mean?"

Daeren sat up with her, swinging his legs down. He looked away. "It means I can't feel," he said dully. "When I first came back, I felt absolutely nothing. No taste but plain, no colors but gray. No want, no pain." He looked at her again. "Now I can feel maybe a tenth of what I should. Enough to know I should be the happiest man alive."

"Can't they fix that?"

"Like growing a new leg, it takes time." He caught her hand. "Chrys, will you wait for me? While I get better?" His voice shook.

"Of course I'll wait." Holding back tears, she rested her head upon his waist. What if he never got better, she thought with a touch of panic. What if he never could feel anything better than dopamine overload? Love was cruel.

Daeren looked out the window. "You know, they have a whole resort out here." He patted her shoulder. "You'd look great in the pool."

The pool was lined with sapphires. Chrys sank into the warm water and swam lazily, stopping now and then to watch Daeren's form slip in and out of the waves. She never took vacations, she realized suddenly. Just like her parents, with their goats to milk and hens to feed every day.

"Does the god taste good?" asked Forget-me-not.

"Better than Endless Light."

"It's good for us. The hormones enrich our circulation. There will be a golden age."

The house produced dinner. Afterward the lights gradually dimmed, like natural sun. Daeren nodded down the hall. "There's a suite for you."

Chrys was puzzled. "Did I tire you out? We can just relax."

"That's okay, I just thought you'd want privacy." He put a patch at his neck. "You can have your people back."

Suddenly his eyes flashed blue rings, very fast.

"The blue angels," flashed Forget-me-not. *"They tell us to stay."*

Daeren looked confused. "Why won't they leave?"

Chrys was puzzled. "Your blue angels want the Eleutherians to stay."

He turned away. "They should listen to me."

That was true; but now, Andra had said, the blue angels knew better, were there to help him get well. From behind Chrys caressed his shoulder, letting her hair fall to his neck. "Why can't I sleep with you? They can visit whenever they like, all night."

"Night is not my best time."

"I'm here to look after you."

So she joined him in bed, where they lay together quietly, arms entwined. Pleasantly tired from the water, Chrys felt light-headed from his touch, his head on her shoulder, her arm resting on his chest. She soon fell asleep.

In his sleep Daeren grew restless, tossing his head and arms. Chrys awoke, vaguely puzzled. The bed seemed comfortable enough; it yielded gently to the slightest pressure. But Daeren kept tossing, his shoulder digging into the mattress, then turning again.

Suddenly he shot upright. Out of the dark his eyes flashed blue and infrared. "Take them back!" The voice did not sound like his own. "Take them back, I said!"

Light came on from the house. Daeren's head twisted like a wild thing, an animal in a trap. "Daeren—what is it?"

He shouted again, so loud she barely understood. Scrambling out of the bed, Chrys backed against the wall. From beside the bed projected two arms of plast that curled over to pin Daeren down.

"What's wrong?" she asked Fireweed. *"Did our people cause trouble?"* Forget-me-not and several others had stayed with him, to help the blue angels.

"The blue angels still want our people to stay."

"Bitch," he screamed. "You work for them—why couldn't you leave me there?" He kept on screaming, over and over, until Chrys fled the room.

She ran down the corridor until she could hear his voice no longer. Shaking uncontrollably, she slipped to the floor, hugging her knees. "House?" she called. "What's wrong with him? Are the blue angels false?"

"No," said the house. "I'm sorry to say, that was himself."

"What do you mean?"

"He dreams of Endless Light."

Chrys hugged her knees harder, until she could barely breathe. *"Fireweed? What happened? Did Forget-me-not say?"*

"He begs the blue angels to take him over, like the masters."

She shook her head, uncomprehending. *"Why?"*

"He thinks he'll never feel good again."

She hesitated. *"Even with me?"*

"He was better today. But the nighttime is hard."

"Why was he angry at our visitors?"

"I don't know. We promised to serve him as our One God."

Chrys bit her lip. What if those who stayed with him did as he asked? "House? How is he now?"

"Subsiding," said the ceiling. "He'll sleep again." Farther down the hall, a light turned on. "There is your own suite. Sorry for the trouble; I hope you sleep better."

Chrys would have cried if she had any tears left. Instead, she sat staring, her mind dull.

"Our people are still there," reminded Fireweed. *"We must find out what happened."*

Chrys looked up at the ceiling. "My people are still with him." She asked the house, "What if they need help?"

"The nanos in his brain would alert us to emergencies."

She didn't trust the sub-intelligent nanos. "Suppose I go back. I could handle him when I'm awake, but asleep, I don't know."

"He's restrained. You'd be safe, either way."

For a while longer she waited, listening in the silence. Remembering back to the time when she had overslept and Poppy took over. Daeren had watched her with the doctor then, and stayed with her till she chose. At last, she stepped quietly back to his room.

Daeren was asleep, the restraints securing his limbs. Humans could look so peaceful, yet who knew what went on inside. Chrys put a patch at her neck. *"Fireweed, find out what happened."* Hesitantly she transferred the patch to Daeren, then took it back.

Forget-me-not returned, with Lupin, accompanied by several blue angels. *"We promised to serve the Lord of Light as our own god,"* Forget-me-not reminded her. *"So we gave him what he asked."*

"What?"

"We gave him your pictures from the world of Endless Light. And the odors; the taste that made you sick."

She gagged just thinking about it. From the wall, a shelf extended with a glass of water. Drinking, she managed to steady herself.

"We have learned something," flashed yellow Lupin. *"We have learned at last why we must never touch the fruit of the gods. We'll never ask again."*

With a deep sigh, Chrys fell back on the bed. She lay next to Daeren but carefully avoided touching him.

In the morning, she awoke refreshed. A bright morning light played across the sheets; she had slept late. By her feet sat Daeren, free of restraint, watching her quietly. She drew back her feet, tense and wary. He turned his head away. Then without a word he left the room.

"How is he?" Chrys asked the house.

"Better. He had his first quiet night."

If that was quiet, she shuddered to think what had gone before. No wonder Andra was discouraged.

The house set out breakfast in the kitchen. As Chrys ate, Daeren worked at the holostage, scrolling through some interminable legal document. She stole a look at him now and then, but if he wouldn't speak, that was fine with her.

She found another holostage to catch up with her own correspondence from clients and gallery directors; the volume overwhelmed her. The price of fame, she thought ruefully. If she answered everyone, how would she get any work done?

Recalling Merope, she checked in at her house. "The cat's fine," Xenon promised. "I made her a plump new armchair to curl up in. By the way, I enjoyed your news story. I had no idea artists were so . . . interesting."

The story of "Azetidine" began innocuously enough with Yyri's rhapsodic comments on her upcoming exhibition. Chrys's image had been caught outside, her face lost in thought, her red-black hair enhanced to the color of flame. Then came the pinwheel windows of Silicon. "Like the Comb in its day," said the snake-egg, "Silicon promises to explode with the shock of the new." Chrys winced at that. It had been one thing to watch Arion glower, but to offend all Elysium was not to her liking.

"The personal history and private life of Azetidine remain a mystery, but sources reveal tantalizing clues. Indeed, Azetidine appears to have inherited her mentor's predilection for well-connected women. Rumor links her with . . ." There followed a montage of herself meeting various women, especially Opal clasping her hand, but also Lady Moraeg, then Ilia, then a couple of other Great House ladies whom she had never met but whose images were spliced to hers.

The blood drained from her face and hands. She sank into a chair, completely mortified. The one consolation was they had missed Topaz. At least her former lover would be spared the indignity.

Chrys called for Opal. On the holostage Opal was shaping her atomic models, the virtual molecules jointed into multilegged dragons. "The masters' defectors revealed a new class of peptide toxin." When at work in her lab, Opal had a one-track mind. "False blue angels use the toxin to overwhelm a native population. What puzzles me is how they can produce it so fast."

Chrys smiled. "I'm sure you'll figure it out. Opal, about the news—I'm so sorry."

Opal shrugged. "Better linked to you than Titan."

"I could just die. I hope Selenite wasn't upset."

"Selenite's doing better," Opal told her. "She reached a truce with the minions. No more executions. Instead, exile."

Chrys smiled. "Well, that's progress. Give her my apologies too."

"Andra will file an injunction, and the snake-eggs will back off. But you know, Chrys, you could manage the media better. Pick one, and give her exclusive rights to your story. Then she'll have a stake in the truth."

She grimaced. "They all look alike."

"Then you should look closer." Opal moved toward Chrys. "How is Daeren? We miss him so."

Chrys wished she could say. After Opal signed off, she stood there, lost in thought.

"*Oh Great One*," came Fireweed's infrared, "*isn't it time to visit our sisters? Send a new group to spell them.*"

Daeren was still at the other holostage, reviewing legal briefs. Chrys asked the house, "How is he today?"

"He's gone back to work for the first time," said the house. "Now that he's calm inside, his brain can heal."

Chrys rose and approached him from behind. When she reached him, she let her hand rest upon his shoulder.

Daeren stopped and shuddered slightly. "Chrys. I thought you'd never . . ." He fell to his knees and embraced her ankles.

She whispered, "Daeren." She bent at the knees to put her arms around him, though he would not meet her eyes. "It's okay. Please." She caught his head gently in her hands, running her fingers through his hair.

His eyes flashed blue and yellow. "I'm no longer worthy of you."

"Then why did all those people invest their lives in you?" She gave him a patch to retrieve Forget-me-not.

"*We've been busy*," reported Forget-me-not. "*Rebuilding infrastructure, bringing things up to code. Putting up a few nightclubs.*"

Hesitantly, he stroked her hair. Her eyes half closed, and her fingers dug into his back, remembering. His face drew so near that she breathed his scent. Then his lips were on her again, meeting her hunger until she was satisfied.

At last she lay beside him again, quietly. Her hand caressed his chest, wondering at his strength. "You've certainly got the touch, Daeren. As good as a woman."

He raised himself on one elbow. "Chrys, do you like women better? I'll get changed, to please you."

She stared, overcome by the need in his eyes. Then she let out a long, shuddering sigh. "Daeren, please yourself. I'd love you even as a worm-face."

He paused as if considering. "I don't think Plan Ten has that option."

"Well for heaven's sake, don't give them ideas." Cradling his head, she whispered, "Just get better."

"What if it's too hard?"

"You have to try."

"I'm trying. It's the hardest thing I ever tried."

Another afternoon of swimming amid sapphires, pulling weights in Andra's gym, and hiking the virtual trail up to an endless scarp stretched beneath a tree-lined sky. Chrys leaned on Daeren's shoulder and watched the sunset. "Lawyers and doctors sure know how to live."

"When they have time." Andra and Sar spent all their time getting people and hospitals out of one scrape or another.

That night Daeren again tossed in his sleep, struggling with unseen demons. At first he subsided, as if determined to stay asleep. Then his shoulders shook. He was sobbing in his sleep.

Chrys grasp his back, her arms fiercely encircling his chest. "Daeren—what is it?"

"They died," he gasped. "They all starved, even their children." The blue angels, he remembered. "How could I do that to them?"

"Daeren, that's over. They forgave you, generations ago. Think of the future."

"But I can't forget." He shook his head. "I never knew what it was like, for all those slaves I dragged to the clinic. Nothing left but their memories."

"You have us, don't you? Saints and angels—what will it take?"

The following night Chrys slept through. He must have too, she realized. In the morning, she recalled regretfully, Andra was to return.

As Chrys read her mail on the holostage, Daeren hugged her from behind, his hands cupping her breasts. Taking a deep breath, she turned and wrestled him to the ground.

For the first time, Daeren laughed. "Chrys, you're dangerous."

"You didn't resist too hard."

He flipped her over, with a deft motion she couldn't figure out. Then he pressed into her, more firmly than before.

"Daeren," she whispered. "Come home with me."

He drew her up until they were both seated on the floor. "I'm still not well." Seeing her look, he added, "Don't be sad—I can't bear it."

"I can't be happy all the time, even for you."

"I'll keep you in my window all day."

"Yes," she said, "I'll keep your sprite up there. And stop back when I can."

"You could take some blue angels," he offered. "They deserve a spell outside purgatory."

"I'm sure some of mine would stay with you. The fix-it types."

He sighed with relief. "I was hoping."

Her scalp prickled, remembering. Sometimes cruel was love.

Andra returned, with Doctor Sartorius back to his wormy form. As they arrived, Daeren seemed to close himself off again, without a word. But he hugged Chrys fiercely and kissed her hair. Then he retreated down the hall. The doctor followed him.

Andra said with a ghost of a smile, "I don't have to ask how things went."

Not with the house watching all, Chrys thought, suddenly embarrassed. "I hope your trip went well."

"Thanks for helping out, and giving us a break."

Chrys looked back once more down the hall of windows. "Is there anything more I can do? To get him out sooner?"

Andra faced her, purple rings flashing, questioning. She nodded as if satisfied. "You can tell him to make his peace with the rest of us."

TWENTY-THREE

*F*orget-me-not was appalled. "To
see a god sunk so low that he needs redemption from people."

"A mystery beyond understanding," agreed Fireweed.

"And yet," said Forget-me-not, "out of the mystery comes a
Golden Age. Our arachnoid is richer than ever, pulsing with
phenylethylamine." The molecules produced by divine love.

Fireweed flashed a greeting to the visiting blue angels, who
would spend the next generation with Eleutheria. The blue angels
amazed her with their tales of the divine Underworld, which their
ancestors had frequented with the Lord of Light. The Underworld,
they said, had given birth to the Lord of Light, and to many other
gods unseen, some without a home, even a window of their own.
"What do you think of this Underworld?" she asked Forget-me-
not. "We went there to recruit defectors, yet I never really knew
what it was about. How could God lack windows?"

"There are homeless gods, just as we have homeless mutants."

"One True God; yet the One are Many." Fireweed's vision
deepened. Even if there were only One True God, that god took
many forms, a different form for each people. And none should go

unseen. Every god needs a window. Perhaps, she envisioned, Eleutheria had greater windows yet to build, beyond even Silicon.

As Chrys neared her front door, the undaunted snake-eggs swarmed. "Oh, Xenon," she called. "Might we have some 'octopods'?"

From the walls beside the caryatids emerged a phalanx of 'octopods,' their limbs striped with horrifying black and orange. Immediately the snake-eggs dispersed. With a short laugh, Chrys passed between the two outer caryatids.

At her door, she caught sight of one last snake-egg hovering some feet away, at the level of her knees. "So you're the brave one."

The undaunted snake-egg said, "Anyone could see those octopods were fake."

Her eyes widened. "You can tell fact from fiction?"

"I'm a professional. I seek the truth."

Professional what, she was tempted to say.

The snake-egg added, "My name is Quinx."

"Come in, Quinx." The snake-egg followed her up the stairs, at a respectful distance. There crouched Merope, ready to pounce on this tempting prey. "I'll give you an exclusive interview," Chrys added, "if you just tell the truth."

"Fair enough," said Quinx. "We'll start with where you were born, your parents and so on."

Her arms tensed. "Leave my parents out of this."

"But that's the sort of thing people want to know."

"I don't want snake-eggs bothering my family."

"You should avoid ethnic slurs in public," Quinx pointed out. "We are called 'journalists.' We'll send your parents a human, if necessary. But we generally find the rural public more impressed by journalists than urbanites are."

This urban journalist had never met the like of her parents, she thought. "Another thing—I am sick to death of hearing about Titan. Always 'just like Titan,' or 'nothing like Titan.' Can't you just write about me?"

"Titan was yesterday's news. Believe me, people will forget about Titan when they hear the truth about you."

In the wee hours, Chrys roused just enough to see Fireweed's letters flashing. *"One True God! We've done it at last."*

"Done what?" she sleepily replied.

"We solved the problem of Silicon. We have the mathematical tools to grow the city."

"Congratulations."

"The construction costs will only increase by a factor of two."

Predictably, Selenite was furious. "A two-fold increase in our estimate?" her sprite demanded in Chrys's ear. "After winning a competitive bid?" Her expression spoke volumes unuttered, probably how this was even worse than Titan. But perhaps her own "slip," from which she'd now recovered, had left her slower to judge. "Let's take it to Jasper."

They met with Jasper at Olympus, over ambrosia and meat-fruits, the virtual singing-trees arching above. Chrys described the predicament, adding, "Before you say anything, let's get one thing straight. Not another word about dead dynatects."

"Live ones are enough trouble." Jasper's brow wrinkled briefly, then he shrugged. "Before we face the board, I'll have the brains in the back room take a look."

Seeing her puzzlement, Selenite explained, "The sentient engineers who do the real work. They don't even stoop to human speech. You don't suppose those board members could build so much as a tube stop, do you?"

"I kind of wondered."

Jasper nodded. "Maybe the brains can bring it down to, say, an increase of fifty percent. By the way," he warned, "you'll have to raise Selenite's cut, proportionately."

"It's an outrage," Selenite exclaimed. "Runaway costs, wasteful consumption." She added, "But I'm getting used to it."

* * *

Chrys kept Daeren's sprite hovering above the painting stage, between Fern's and Hal's, and she stopped by Andra to see him every day. One day she brought Opal and Garnet.

As they reached Andra's invisible door, Opal beamed with excitement. Garnet was more reserved, but he held between his hands a large dark sphere. Chrys eyed it with suspicion. "Like, a bomb?"

"Please," sighed an octopod. "It's been years since anyone tried anything."

Garnet looked shocked. "Flowers."

They met Daeren out by the swimming pool. Opal threw her arms around him and kissed the top of his head. "How could you stay away so long? We've missed you so."

His face darkened with confusion, but he was not displeased. "I've been busy."

"Working too hard as usual. And the blue angels? Just a peek?" She took out a transfer patch. Chrys felt vaguely jealous but checked herself.

Garnet set down the sphere. It sprouted a red carnation. There followed lilies, rosebuds, even Prokaryan ringflowers, live plast imitating live plants. "Olympus just doesn't feel right without you." He rested his arm lightly on Daeren's shoulder.

"You'll be pleased to hear," Opal said, "we're working on better communication with the non-carriers. We're not to call them 'virgins' anymore. They're 'independents.'"

"Sounds reasonable," Daeren agreed.

Garnet added, "We've been talking with Carnelian about how we can help the 'independents' fight the brain plague."

Opal nodded. "All those defectors your brain brought back—we've put their intelligence to good use."

Garnet's gaze took in the glittering pool and the headball court beyond. "Excellent taste, though claustrophobic, I'd say. It must be tough being trapped in here," he observed, kneading Daeren's shoulder. "Watching your investments grow. Wondering why the seven are but seven."

"I was a fool," Daeren sighed. "Now they'll never let me back. Not for what I used to do."

Chrys felt numb. It was hard to imagine Daeren doing anything else.

Opal squeezed his hand. "Wait and see."

"I know the rules," he said shortly.

Garnet raised a hand. "I know what you can do. You can come serve at the Spirit Table. Jasper and I go there every week. It's just the thing for you."

Daeren smiled. "You're right, I could serve at the Spirit Table. There are any number of things I could do. But what about the blue angels? All their tradition of relief work, and nothing left to do except look after me."

After Opal and Garnet left, Chrys took a dip in the pool. Then she and Daeren rested at the far end, water rippling around their arms entwined, as they watched Garnet's "flowers" grow and collapse to grow anew.

"The truth is," Daeren exclaimed, "I'm tired of chasing addicts who will only run back the first chance they get. I'd like to get back to law, and acquire a place like this."

The virtual sunset gleamed across the swimming pool, glinting off the sapphires. "Sounds good to me," Chrys smiled. "I'll be your worm-face."

Daeren sat on in silence, a hand stroking her breast. "Chrys," he asked thoughtfully, "what is 'fenestration'?"

"The placement of windows? Why do you ask?"

"Just like to know what your people are chatting about."

"*One True God,*" flashed Fireweed. "*We have a vision. A new work lies before us—even greater than Silicon.*"

Chrys absorbed this news with deepening suspicion. "*What sort of work?*"

"*A new building plan. Commissioned by the blue angels.*"

Forget-me-not added, "*We've installed a branch office with the Lord of Light.*"

"*With divine permission?*"

"*Of course. What do you take us for?*"

She looked accusingly at Daeren. "You didn't tell me."

"Tell you what?"

She sculled the water with her hands. *"What's your project?"* she demanded of Fireweed.

"Rebuild the Underworld."

"House the gods as they deserve," added Forget-me-not.

"Homes, schools, playgrounds," flashed yellow Lupin. *"All with the cooperation of the inhabitants—not just a building grown from seed. Incalculable problems to solve. Truly a challenge worthy of the highest intellect."*

Chrys crossed her arms. "This was your idea," she told Daeren.

"I'm not allowed to have ideas, remember?" he said. "Just obey."

"And how will it be financed?"

"Our profits from Silicon, to begin with," flashed Lupin. *"Then we'll raise funds from all our neighbors. We have ways."*

Chrys put her head in her hands. She imagined what Jasper and Selenite would say.

As her exhibition date neared, the brain plague worsened. Whole sections of Level One were abandoned, and every morning dead vampires appeared in the streets. The Palace doubled the patrols of octopods, but that did little good against a menace unseen.

From Elysium, it was rumored that Elf children experimented with "visitors." Kept in school for fifty years, they'd be bored enough to try anything. All in all, the reports did little to dispel tension over her upcoming show.

"Might you bring an octopod to your Opening?" ventured Xenon. "A real one, in camouflage."

"Elysium won't allow it. They're above security," she observed. "Even the Gallery had to get a special dispensation to post a guard."

"Their medical response system is the Fold's finest," Xenon assured her.

"I hope I don't find out."

*   *   *

The Fall Opening at the Gallery Elysium was the foremost cultural event of the year. Chrys herself had never attended in person, but she had always watched through her window as Elysium's most refined millennial citizens mingled with Valedon's most famous and infamous. This year she found herself at the window's other side.

The snake-eggs buzzed so loud one could barely hear, and the multicolored butterflies projecting behind all the talars mingled so confusingly that one hardly saw the art. But then, most people on Opening night were there less to see than to be seen. Chrys herself wore a talar of burnt dark red, shading into infrared that only the privileged could see, her hair flowing thick past her shoulders.

At her side hovered Ilia, filling in occasional responses for her to answer the more abstruse questions she was asked. "Pathbreaking," Ilia assured a butterfly-swirling visitor. "The most pathbreaking exhibit we've ever done."

The visitor would not touch Ilia, of course, but impulsively caught a fold of her talar. There was a lot of clasping of talars, as highly placed Elves tried to show the world how intimate they were with those even more highly placed. They kept more of a distance from "Azetidine," however. Perhaps it was the hair, or the infrared. Or perhaps it was the hint of scandal that put a strain in some smiles, the furtive glances toward the white curtain.

A group of Elf students strolled in parti-colored jumpsuits. They looked and acted her brother's age, though in actual years they were probably closer to her own. Their guide spent a lot of time at Chrys's old self-portrait, making the point that even great artists had to begin the hard way. She wondered whether the guide would let them beyond the curtain.

A Valan lady, obsidian with a lava sheen, wearing a diamond tiara. "Moraeg!" Chrys had wondered if any of the old Seven would come. She caught Moraeg's arms.

"Indecent contact," warned a voice from the ceiling. "You are fined one hundred credits. To appeal this ruling . . ."

Chrys turned as dark as her hair, but Moraeg laughed. "These quaint Elf customs. It's too funny, isn't it, dear?"

Beside Lady Moraeg, Lord Carnelian wore his finest gray talar with one blood-colored namestone. "So pleased to see my taste confirmed."

"Thanks," said Chrys, recalling the old rent credit. How good it felt to see them both together again.

Ilia nodded graciously. "I understand, Lord Carnelian, you were the first patron of Azetidine, in her early period. How discerning."

The crowd parted, as it always did for Zircon. Among Elves, he looked more of a giant than ever. He patted Chrys's hair three times, despite the Elysian fine for each. "Chrys—I can't believe it." Glancing at the protective curtain, he looked back at her in frank astonishment. "You of all people."

"Thanks, Urban Shaman."

Amid all the colors, one talar stood out in plain white. There stood Daeren.

All else receded, except Daeren's face, and the blood pounding in her ears. Reaching him, she grasped a fold of his talar. "They let you out."

"Just till midnight. Andra's ship expects me then."

She smiled. "I'll make sure we make it."

"Great One, we need to do business with the blue angels and our long lost cousins. A question of fenestration."

His eyes glittered blue and red. Chrys overflowed with happiness. "I hope you like the show."

Daeren nodded. "I can't see much for all the butterflies, but I know your work by heart. I'm impressed that Arion let you show *Seven Stars and the Hunter*."

"He wasn't asked." Her lip curved down. "He wants people, though, so bad he can taste it."

"Let's hope he doesn't get his wish."

In her ear Ilia whispered, "Dear, prepare yourself. We have a difficult guest."

Startled, she turned. Emerging from the curtain was Eris.

The Guardian of Cultural Affairs spoke to his companions, and they shared a laugh. That laughter she hadn't heard since the day Eris left his people in her brain to take over. Chrys's scalp tightened, and she gripped Daeren's talar till her knuckles turned white. "Saints and angels," she breathed, instinctively making the old sign against evil. "How dare he come?"

Ilia rolled her eyes. "How dare he not? The Gallery Opening is the cultural event of the year."

Seeming not to notice them, Eris turned this way and that, acknowledging the fawning of his fellow Elves, tossing off remarks about superior aesthetics and the uplifting of less advanced societies. At last he caught sight of Daeren. He paused, with a look of surprise. Two slaves, Chrys thought—one freed, the other in chains.

"So soon," Eris observed. "The good doctor's standards must be slipping."

"Your eyes are green, Eris," Daeren returned. "What color are mine?"

Eris shifted his gaze slightly toward Chrys, though his eyes did not meet hers either. "The lovely artist." He added, "Consorting with the fallen."

Chrys released Daeren's talar and stepped forward between the two of them. "Eris, it's been so long. Your people miss you."

Another look of surprise. "They survived? They must have pleased you, 'Oh Great One.'" He watched with satisfaction as her face colored. "Would you like some more?"

"The false blue angels fear our sight," flashed Fireweed. *"For generations, we've prepared."*

Chrys lifted her chin. "Yes, Eris. I'd like some more." Trapped, the deadly micros would serve as evidence even Arion could not ignore.

Looking beyond her, Eris turned aside. As he passed, he murmured, "You shall have your wish."

For the rest of the evening, as Chrys smiled and nodded to one notable after another, she could not shake her lingering dread. What if Eris, or one of his secret slaves, caught her unawares? What if the Gallery didn't see them touch her with a patch?

Just before midnight, she left with Daeren. Outside all was quiet, not a snake-egg in sight.

"You'll be late," Andra's ship accused in her window.

"Don't worry, he's with me."

Suddenly Daeren caught her in his arms and pressed his lips to hers. Their bodies melded together as if they were one.

"A grave act of indecency," came a shocked voice from the street. "Ten thousand credits . . ."

She threw her head back and laughed, her hair dancing.

"Sorry," he told her, "I had to let you know how much I want you."

"It's worth ten times more."

As they wandered back toward the transit, a lone snake-egg zipped past them, faster than usual, Chrys thought. It dove forwards and back like a hummingbird defending its territory. Then it whizzed just past her leg, to disappear amongst the trees full of sleeping butterflies.

Where the snake-egg had passed, her leg burned. Chrys started rubbing the spot on her calf. "It stung me."

"What?" Daeren bent to inspect her ankle. "I don't like it."

"It feels better now." But she remembered Eris. *"Emergency alert,"* she warned her people. *"Check the circulation."*

"We'll check every capillary. We're prepared."

A siren blared. Apparently, the Elves had sent help, too. A medical hovercraft appeared, hovering for a landing.

"The Fold's finest," Chrys exclaimed with relief.

Three rotund sentients rolled out while the hovercraft spouted about her right to receive or refuse treatment. Slapping their tubes around her leg, their tests took an interminable amount of time to pronounce the limb sound. Minutes lengthened to an hour.

Daeren shifted from one foot to the other. "I still don't like it. I won't rest till you get home."

"One True God, we have a problem. A strange toxin has appeared in the blood."

"A toxin? To poison me?"

"Not yourself, but us. It chelates arsenic, ripping the atoms from our flesh. Two have already died."

Her head shot up. "Doctor? Can you get rid of the toxin that's killing my people?"

"Which people?" The sentient rolled back and forth as if puzzled.

"The micro people. Inside me."

"Micros," observed the other doctor. "Sure, we can sweep you for arsenic. These days, it's highly recommended."

Chrys took a step back. "Is that all you know . . . about micros?"

"Chrys," said Daeren gently, "this is Elysium. Only a few carriers, and they keep private doctors."

"Perhaps Ilia could—"

"Let's get home."

They hurried to the transit stop, where a bubble loomed out of the fluid-filled tube. Within the bubble, seats molded to their form.

"One True God, the danger grows," warned Fireweed. "There is more and more of the toxin."

Why would the poison keep growing, she wondered. "Can't you destroy it?"

"We can, but it appears faster than we can get rid of it. Even a single molecule kills."

"At this rate, most of us will die within a generation."

Chrys fought rising panic. "Can you protect the children?"

"We can encapsulate them. But they'll lose the ability to merge."

"Daeren . . . could you take their children? Just till we get back—"

"No," he exclaimed. "I'm still a long way from normal. You can't trust me with children."

"We've found the source of the problem. An RNA plasmid infected your white blood cells. It replicates in the cytoplasm of each cell, where it makes the toxin. To eliminate the source, we'd have to kill all your white cells."

"Daeren—they can't last the trip. They're going to die." She could hardly believe her own words, but she shook in every limb. Eris—this was his work.

Daeren's hands clenched and unclenched. "Call Ilia Papili-*shon*," he told the transit.

Ilia's sprite appeared in her window. "Dear, what a success! The show—"

"We're in trouble," Chrys cut in. "My micros—they've been poisoned. They have to get out of me. Please—can you take the children?"

Ilia's eyes widened. She drew in a sharp breath. "One doesn't speak of such things." Her sprite winked out.

Silence lengthened. Damn Ilia, Chrys thought. Damn Arion too, and every damned Elf on the turquoise moon.

"I'll take them," said Daeren.

"You can't."

"Just till we get home."

"We'll get the children ready," flashed Forget-me-not. *"We'll confine them to one cistern, and we'll keep watch over the Lord of Light."*

It would take several passes to send them all. After the third transfer, Daeren took a deep breath. "Chrys, I think that's all I can manage. Children get into trouble; they're too curious."

She sat back and stared ahead, numb with the dying inside. Ahead the flowing bubble merged with another from the side. More Elf passengers with their refined ways, blind to genocide in their midst. How many others had Eris done in this way—only to replace them with his own?

"We're encapsulating nearly everyone. We can last a while, but we will slowly starve."

"What if false blue angels are hiding in my bones?"

"We've set traps for them."

From the front of the bubble, where the new passengers merged, came a figure veiled in white. The figure moved toward them slowly as a ghost. Chrys stared, every muscle taut. It wouldn't take much to knock one Elf clear across the car, no matter what the fine.

The stranger came right up to Chrys and stopped. The veil parted at the face. Chrys let out a cry.

It was Ilia. "Do what you have to." Ilia's eyes darted back and forth, then met hers. "You're not the first, you know."

"The rest of the children . . . you can take them?" Chrys passed her the transfer.

Daeren said, "We're forever in your debt, Ilia."

"Why?" exclaimed Chrys. "Why do you let this go on?"

Ilia adjusted her veil. "If the Guard knew, they'd wipe us all. Only Arion acknowledges the micros are people. The others don't want to know." For a moment Ilia's features wrinkled as if very old. "Your show will change that, but it will take time. Elysians have time, but our micros don't."

Daeren shook his head. "Elysians don't have time either." The precious Elf students in their jumpsuits, cared for till age fifty. "Experimenting" with micros.

The veil closed. Ilia moved off, carrying the last of Eleutheria's children.

Back at Andra's home, the doctor's worms encircled her scalp. "All your micros have to go," he told Chrys. "It will take a day to clear out your white cells and accelerate new ones from the bone marrow. All the while you'll be cleared of arsenic, in case false blue angels emerge. We've found we can't always find them in the bone."

"You can't?" Chrys asked. Arion had himself wiped daily and thought he was safe from Eris.

Andra gave a grim smile. "Medicine's never perfect. That's why they need lawyers. Daeren," she began warningly.

"I know," said Daeren, "I violated the protocol. But her people would have died out."

"They wouldn't be the first."

"But I couldn't just—"

"If Sar and I don't report you, we're all in violation. All our people too."

The four of them were silent. Only the holostage flickered, Chrys's vital signs scanning down.

Andra held out a patch to Chrys. "You can give me another hundred thousand," she said. "That's all I can take. Other Olympians will take the rest."

Opal arrived, and Selenite. Chrys sat there, feeling drained, Daeren's arm tight around her as the patch went back and forth, dispersing the Eleutherian refugees. Still more to go—Jasper and Garnet each took their share, then Pyrite and Zircon.

At last, for the final few, Moraeg. Diamonds swirling like a starry night; that night, Chrys remembered, when the Seven had planned their last show. Find your own way, Moraeg had told Chrys. Now it had come to this. Back where she started.

Moraeg bent over her. "It's only for a day, isn't it?"

The doctor warned, "It won't be easy, but you'll make it."

What did he mean, she wondered. Carriers who lost their people "didn't last," out of longing. But this was just for a day. The patch transferred one last time.

"*One True God,*" flashed Fireweed. "*All the rest have gone. I alone remain. My time is short, but I vowed to be yours until the end.*"

The doctor's worms flexed. "Are they all clear?"

"Except one," Chrys whispered. Fireweed had stayed, like a hermit upon Mount Dolomoth, alone with her God. Perhaps every believer in One True God secretly yearned to be the one true worshiper.

Daeren squeezed her hand. "Some of mine did the same. Sar had to—"

"Never mind." The doctor made a rare interruption. "The micro can't last long, without taking food or risking the toxin. The arsenic wipe can wait."

Before she could rest, Chrys had to sketch her portrait of the doomed Fireweed, the infrared letters flashing faithfully. At last she went to bed with Daeren, falling into a troubled sleep. Early in the morning, thrashing with troubled dreams, she woke. "They're gone!" she cried. "Daeren—"

He held her tight. "They're not gone. See?" His own eyes flickered, all the colors of the stars, a million light-years away.

"They're gone from me. I can't help it; I feel as if—" She was tumbling over and over, like the time she fell weightless in the dead spacecraft.

"That happened to me," Daeren said. "The inner ear goes off because they're not there, and you're disoriented without them."

Tumbling forever, falling through space; it was so unbearable, she thought she would die. But the tumbling only went on.

"Give them back," she found herself shouting. "Just one—"

"It will pass," he quietly insisted.

"Let the false ones out of the bone. At least they can stop it—" She hardly knew what she shouted, until the doctor returned to adjust something. Then she slept, half rousing now and then, back to troubled sleep.

In the morning she did not care if she slept or woke. Her surroundings receded, all seemed far away. "Can you tell me?" Daeren was pleading to get her to talk. "Tell me what's going on."

Chrys could not even shake her head. Empty and dark, her mind was an abyss.

"They still remember you," he promised. "Even the children. Look, you have to eat; they'll be hungry."

The doctor's worm rested on Daeren's shoulder. "Depression," he said. "We can take the edge off, but too much will endanger their return."

Daeren gave up talking. He drew her close, resting her head on his chest. He stayed with her all the rest of the day. She knew he was there, though she could not feel it, could feel nothing but aloneness, the most intense sense of being lost. Like that time when she was small, she had wandered too far from home and had spent the night out on the mountain. Now the mountain rose across the universe, and there was no way back home, ever.

"Another hour." Sartorius kept coming back from the hospital to let her know. "You got through another hour; just four more."

That evening, at last Andra returned. "Sar, are you sure?"

The doctor's worms twined. "Reasonably certain. No trace of the viral RNA can be found."

Turning to Chrys, Andra took out a patch. "Are you ready?"

Chrys heard the question twice before she could speak. "I'm not sure."

"It's okay," coaxed Daeren. "They're coming back. They're fine; they miss you, that's all."

"I don't know." She slowly shook her throbbing head. "What if it ever happened again? I couldn't face it."

"But they need you." Daeren turned the lights down. On the holostage, in the darkness, the green filaments twinkled, Fern, the first one, generations past, flashing her last words of wisdom for Eleutheria. "*As we would receive mercy, so must we grant it in turn. . . .*"

The vision roused her, as if from a trance. For a moment she was back on the day Fern first came to visit, then to stay. She swallowed, her mouth dry. "Let me see just one."

The first flicker of yellow in her eye. "*Cheers!*" flashed yellow Lupin. "*There's no place like home. When's your next show?*"

Slowly she smiled. It was going to be all right.

"The children, next," offered Daeren. "With a few blue angels to help them resettle. It's what they're good at."

Throughout the evening, the Olympians came back, each returning their share of the lost generation. Opal kissed her on both cheeks. "They've founded another new school of something or other; I hope you don't mind," she added. "And that RNA plasmid—that won't fool us again."

Chrys found herself laughing, almost giddy with relief.

Selenite returned hers. "They weren't so bad," she assured Chrys. "Hypercorrect, in fact. But I wasn't fooled." She grinned. "I know their tricks now. We'll get on so much better."

Jasper patted her arm. "They certainly know how to flatter their host," he agreed. "I foresee a long and prosperous business relationship."

"We'll miss them," sighed Garnet. "They brought so much palladium, and spent it all."

"They're outrageous!" Zircon actually looked alarmed. "No offense, Chrys, but—do you know what your people did? They made their own ethanol and got drunk in all our restaurants."

"And who encouraged that?"

"My people abstain," the giant assured her, patting her head. "But that's okay. We tolerate the vices of others."

Pyrite returned his, and Moraeg hers. By now the mood was getting festive; it almost felt like the old times at Olympus.

"God of Mercy," called Forget-me-not. *"Please—half the children are missing, still unaccounted for. What became of them?"*

Chrys frowned, trying to think. She counted off all the Olympians. Then her head shot up. "Saints and angels. The last place I want to go back is—"

There stood Ilia, her virtual butterflies fluttering out over the sapphire pool. "Hope I didn't keep you waiting."

The laughter died, everyone's attention caught by the diminutive Elysian. Regally, she approached to hand Chrys the last transfer. "Truly a unique aesthetic experience," she observed. "And to think I'd always found all your 'people' so . . ." Her gaze swept the group, coming at last to rest upon Andra. " . . . conventional."

"Thanks, Ilia," said Andra. "We'll remember."

She turned to Chrys. "You heard, of course, about your show."

"Heard what?"

"The Guard closed it down."

"Oh, no."

Ilia's eyes gleamed. "For violating public standards of decency, morality, and security."

"I'm so sorry."

She waved a hand dismissively. "We appealed and got it reopened within an hour. Now the lines to get in stretch for three blocks." She added triumphantly, "And I've been called to testify before the Guard. That hasn't happened to the Gallery since our first millennium."

"I see."

"We'll all see," promised Ilia. "If Arion won't take a stand, perhaps someone else will."

At last all had left for the night, except for Daeren, who sat perusing one of his legal documents on the holostage.

"We'll remember," promised Forget-me-not. "The poisoned veins, the sacrifice of Fireweed, and our flight to the ten worlds. And in our Great Diaspora, we have learned some things about the true meaning of Eleutheria."

"I've learned, too," Chrys reflected. "I would have taken the false ones—anything. The virgins are right; we are addicted."

" 'Independents,' " Daeren corrected, without turning around. "They're addicted to oxygen."

"Carriers share everything." She whispered, "But Daeren, it's different with you."

He half turned, his face set hard. "Are you sure?"

He was actually jealous. She went to him and knelt, crossing her arms in his lap. "You're still my one Lord of Light."

Daeren's face softened. He picked her up and carried her off to bed, kissing her madly. This time, at last, they both had their fill. "God of Mercy," he whispered. "I live or die at your pleasure."

In the morning, Andra brought bad news. "Someone told the Palace. We're all summoned—Sar and I, and both of you."

Across the pool flooded the virtual rising sun. Heaven was always too short. Chrys sighed. "So what do we do?"

Andra put her hands together. "I cut a deal." As usual. "Sar goes to the Palace for interrogation. They'll rake him over, but they owe him for Zoisite. The rest of us go to Arion."

"Arion?" asked Chrys. "Why?"

"The first Elf children have succumbed to plague." Andra let this sink in. "Now, at last, Arion swears he will hear the truth."

"We've told him nothing else."

"The whole truth," Andra emphasized.

"Do you believe him?"

Andra was silent. The silence expanded, like ripples on the pool. "Until now, I have. Now, for the first time . . . I'm no longer sure. His eyes did not quite meet mine."

Chrys closed her eyes as if to shut it all out. Then she forced them open. "Do we have a choice?"

"You have one other choice."

Into her window sprang a virtual ticket. A starship ticket to Solaria. Exile.

Daeren must have seen the same. He looked down. "Chrys, I'm in your hands. Wherever you go, I will follow."

Chrys turned to Andra. "If we leave, what will become of you? And Sar?"

Andra looked down. "We'll manage. We always have."

And the other Olympians, and Ilia, and all the hapless citizens in the streets. She thought it over, eyeing the ticket. "Solarian nightlife's the best. Can we have, like, a rain check?"

TWENTY-FOUR

The terror of the flight from poison would never be forgotten, especially by the children swept out into new worlds. And still, Forget-me-not knew, worse was yet to come. Somewhere out beyond the familiar gods walked others, gods who could dissolve people with as little care as for a mindless virus floating in the blood.

But the Eleutherians who returned from the Diaspora were a different people than before. Some individuals had stayed behind to dwell with their new gods, while many strangers had left their own gods to join Eleutheria. The newcomers brought their own ways, but in the end most took up the great challenge of the past generations. And this time they made sure their work would outlast even death.

"Fear not," Forget-me-not told the god. "Fear not the future. Whatever becomes of us, Eleutheria will remain. We have stored all of what we are, our history and our works, for whoever will find it after we are gone—in all the different worlds to which we fled. For in truth, Eleutheria is no genetic race, nor a physical place, but a way of being, a path of endless life. All those who seek to build in truth and memory shall find our way."

*   *   *

The three carriers went in to see Arion, flanked by octopods. So much for peaceful Elysium. The Guardian of Peace sat there behind a conference table, live butterflies flitting outside the window beyond. Beside him sat his brother.

Chrys stopped to let her pulse subside. *"It's all over."*

"Not yet," said Forget-me-not. *"Another year's as good as ten. So long as we live, we live free."*

Eris did not even pretend to meet their eyes. He studied his hands, clasped before him on the table, as if to say, this was none of his affair. Beside him, Arion looked on as before, his features the color of alabaster, his eyes penetrating. "Seat yourselves, Citizens."

Andra narrowed her eyes, her gaze hunting Eris like a bird of prey. "Eris. How long it's been." Her voice was deceptively relaxed. "How long since I've seen our descendants?"

Descendants of her own people? The false blue angels? As if a window opened, Chrys saw now why Arion did not trust Andra, and why Daeren's slip had sparked her anger. The worst of micros could become the best; but even the best had produced the worst.

Eris acted as if he did not hear. Arion ignored the remark as well. He nodded at Chrys. "For the record, Citizen Chrysoberyl, you are the betrayer of two worlds, indeed the very integrity of the Fold."

"Excuse me?"

"You tipped off the slaves before our mission."

"I tried to," she admitted. "To prevent genocide. But someone else got there first." She glared at Eris, daring Arion to ask who.

Arion added, "You are also the only human to have seen the Slave World and come back free—twice."

"I know of none else," she admitted.

"And you made an exhibit of their obscene propaganda."

That took her aback. "You want facts, or art critique?"

"And you expect me to believe that you follow your own free will, and not that of the brain plague."

She studied Arion's eyes. They met hers, just barely. "No," she said at last. "I honestly don't expect you will believe me. I expect to leave here with my people wiped, victims of—"

He waved a hand. So much for hearing the full truth. "Daeren," he began. "The main tester of carriers at Hospital Iridis, you gave yourself up to the Slave World."

Andra said, "He was not himself."

"Let him answer."

"I was myself," Daeren corrected, his voice level. "You, Arion, were not yourself when you chose to annihilate what remained of a crippled world. The ancient barbarians, as you call them, left grass and insects. Your own act left nothing."

"You did not object," Arion pointed out. "You knew why it had to be done. It was either that, or wipe all the carriers of Elysium, and make the Valans do the same."

"I was wrong," Daeren said. "There are other choices."

"But you came back." Arion turned again to Chrys. "You rescued him. How?"

Her throat tightened. She could still hardly bear to speak of it. "The . . . Leader. Her portrait paid."

Arion frowned. "You and your portraits. There, too, you abused my trust."

"That's true," Chrys admitted. "I should have asked your consent."

"But Daeren—you recovered." Arion's voice took on a peculiar note of urgency. "How? How did you recover, from the worst depths, yet hold on to your 'people'?"

Andra explained, "An experimental treatment. Doctor Sartorius has the details."

"Did the treatment work?"

"We believe it is working."

"Would it work for others?"

No one looked at Eris.

"Daeren's failure was brief," Andra reminded Arion. "Even so, his recovery has consumed substantial resources, and the care of very special . . . people."

"No amount of resources would be too great to save a millennial life." As if an eighty-year-old sim would not matter. As if a person's worth could be measured by his lifespan.

"Did you hear, Eris?" Arion's voice softened. "Did you hear that even the worst case can be cured?"

The room was suddenly still; had a fly crept across the table, it could have been heard. Only butterflies flitted in the garden beyond. At the table, Eris did not move. He did not respond aloud, but his electronic sense must have reached Arion.

"Yes," Arion nodded. "Chrysoberyl, please explain what we found the night after you left your show. The medic who treated your injury reported mysterious trace molecules—later identified unmistakably as a mark of the brain plague."

Andra insisted, "She was cleared. Arsenic-wiped."

"But how did they get there?" pursued Arion. "How can you explain, unless you were a slave?"

Chrys stood suddenly, her hands planted on the table. From behind, an octopod arm gripped her shoulder. "*He* did it!" Her voice rose to a shout. "Eris did everything, you know he did. He sent the damned snake-egg to poison me. He's poisoned half your own carriers, sent them to the Slave World; he tried the same with me. And now he's starting on your children."

The two Elves listened calmly to this outburst. At last Eris sighed and shook his head. "How sad. I told you what they'd say."

"You did," Arion agreed.

"Definitely tainted. Nothing to do but wipe them."

"Evidently," said Arion quietly. "Still, we have to be sure." He nodded. "Test them."

Andra leaned forward, her hands on the table, her eyes avid. "Eris, you're absolutely right. We could have gone bad; heaven knows, we've suffered enough exposure." She extended her hand, as if for a transfer patch. "Test me."

Eris said, "That won't be necessary."

Furrows appeared above Arion's eyes. Surprised to be contradicted, he turned toward Eris. Their eyes met. Arion froze. "As you say, Eris." Outside of his eyes, the rest of his face grimaced, as if puzzled by his own words.

"Eris." Andra's tone deepened, in that classic Sardish inflection that made people cringe. "Tell me," she said slowly. "Who do you fear more—myself? Or your masters."

Eris wrenched his head around. For an instant, perhaps, the human face of him looked out. "Silence, you unspeakable—" He stopped, checked by the furious purple flashing in Andra's eyes. The seconds passed. Then his eyes closed, and he slumped down upon the table.

Arion let out a cry and put his hands to his head. The octopods pulled Chrys's arms back tight, while reinforcements appeared. A worm-faced doctor came to tend Eris.

An octopod had pinned Andra's arms, and its deadly needle pressed her neck. Andra spoke quickly. "I told you what we could do, once we caught him. The Leader's own defectors gave us their signal codes."

The doctor's worm encircled Eris's scalp. "He's asleep. Normal slow-wave activity."

"But Arion," insisted Andra, "what about you? Tell me, what color are my eyes?"

Arion turned to the doctor. "When was I last cleansed?"

"You've declined cleansing since last night."

"Cleansing for arsenic won't be enough," warned Andra, her arms still pinned, the octopod's needle beneath her chin. "They can burrow deep within the bone. Arion—let us help you. Before it's too late."

Arion stared, just outside her line of focus, his hand tense, shaking. "You ruined him long ago," his voice rasped with pain. "Destroyed him with your plague. You'll never leave this room alive."

"Your eyes are green, laced with gold," Andra went on. "You and I made the same mistake; we both trusted wrong. But I always delivered, didn't I? I told you the Leader's own defectors would take him down. Now we can get you clean—and no one will have to know."

The Guardian did not speak aloud, but the octopod tentacle tugged at Chrys's arm. She and Daeren were pulled out of the office, leaving Andra alone.

The two of them were escorted out through the street-tunnels of Helicon. The octopods brought them to a door and pushed them inside. Outside, the octopods squatted and faded into camouflage.

Inside, the room was small by Valan standards but comfortable, with a holostage and a bush full of real heliconians flitting on the balcony. Not a hint of getting wiped for arsenic. Scarcely believing it, Chrys told her people, *"We're safe for now."*

A vast rainbow filled her eyes, just like Fern used to do. Chrys shut her eyes, feeling light-headed. *"It's beautiful. Almost illegal."*

"Really?" flashed Lupin, shocked.

Chrys embraced Daeren. "What will they do to Andra?"

"Let's hope Arion lets her test him."

Still dazed, she shook her head. "I had no idea Eris got his people from her."

"His original strain. He promised to set up the same system here as Andra and Sar did in Iridis."

She reflected, "I guess Elves always come to Valedon to pick up our vulgar diversions. Just like Iridians go slumming in the Underworld."

"We'll never really know what happened to Eris," Daeren said, "whether his people went bad, or they got replaced by another strain." Out on the balcony, an aging heliconian fell off a branch, its wings still bright and crisp. The delicate insect landed below, its blue-spotted wings outstretched, a dead angel.

Her head nestled against his neck, and he brushed her hair. "I'm just glad someone was there for me when I needed help," added Daeren. "Some very special people."

Chrys looked up. "Daeren, if we, like, get out of this alive—" She swallowed hard. "We could have children. I mean, the micros have so many, why can't we have our own?"

For a while Daeren looked at her, unable to speak. At last he brushed her cheek. "I never thought you'd trust me."

That afternoon, as they waited together, a group of Elves

appeared on the holostage. Startled, Chrys sat up and straightened her hair. Among the Elves was Ilia.

"We need your help," Ilia told her, a slight edge to her normally unflappable voice. "Arion has put all the carriers under guard, until we can prove we're clean. You can test us, Daeren."

Before, only Chief Andra was good enough for her. Daeren crossed his arms. "What became of your own testers?"

"Eris was wiped."

Much as he deserved it, Chrys shuddered. One day in hell had been enough for her.

"It's terrible to think of," exclaimed one of Ilia's companions. "We knew Eris had 'turned,' but should it come to this? He led a respectable life."

Daeren looked away. "I'm on vacation. You can ask Chrys."

"What?" the Elf exclaimed. "Not that scandalous artist."

Ilia gave her companion a glacial stare. "Consider it an aesthetic experience. You've never refused one before."

Chrys thought of something. "We'll train you to test the others," she told Ilia. "Your people can learn; it's not hard."

Ilia shuddered. "Too much temptation."

Daeren added, "And tell Arion, we have ways to help Eris."

Once again, they met with the Guardian of Peace. Both he and Andra had an air of business about them, the product of many hours of negotiation. A couple of Elf assistants were present.

"Elysium agrees to drop all pending charges," Arion told the Valans, "under the conditions indicated." A long list scrolled down the holostage.

"And we agree to help rebuild your carrier security program," said Andra.

Arion nodded. "And I shall ask the Guard to open consideration of the rights and status of the alleged micro people."

Andra said, "I've gone over the whole thing, but you both need to read thoroughly before you sign."

Chrys read the suspended letters word by word. A lot of prohibitions, such as don't ever visit the Slave World again—she could certainly live with that. Then her eyes stopped. " 'The undersigned agrees to desist from representational depiction of government officials.' "

Andra looked mystified. "That wasn't in our final draft."

Arion glanced at his aides, saying smoothly, "My staff must have put that in." The line vanished.

After reading through it three times, Chrys at last put her hand to the document. A weight lifted off her chest. The plague still raged, but it no longer reached so high.

"One last point." Arion looked hard at Daeren. "You said you could help Eris."

"Yes."

"You know he can never carry people again." Arion's voice was bleak.

"I've discussed an experimental alternative with Sartorius," said Daeren. "We've never had an effective treatment for hard-core addicts. They can't manage without company inside. Based on my experience, I can understand that. But suppose we give them just a few elders, to talk to."

"Would that be safe?"

"Elders can't breed. They'd need replacing every month or so." Microbial methadone.

Arion reflected on this. "Would the elders do it? It sounds like a lonely existence for them."

"A lonely way to spend one's millennial lifetime. But mercy is their calling."

As Chrys and Daeren rode the transit bubble to the Elysian hospital, her people rhapsodized about all the elegant dwellings they'd seen. *"We're taking notes,"* flashed Forget-me-not. *"Elysian dwellings maximize efficiency and aesthetics, suitable to house divinity."* Their model for the future Underworld, their project to dwarf Silicon.

Daeren took yet another AZ.

"Don't spoil them," Chrys remarked with a smile.

"They deserve it. They're giving up their seven best elders for that . . ."

"Bastard," she finished.

"Be careful, Chrys."

"He was human enough to know what he did."

"Human, and proud of it. That's what saved us in the end." That last slip before Andra's eyes.

At the hospital, a doctor led them through a bank of apartments just like the place Chrys and Daeren had been sent. So that had been part of an Elf "hospital." Eris, of course, had a more generous suite.

On a bed of nanoplast in shifting colors, the stricken Elf lay on his side hugging his knees, his head turned away. The doctor rested a hand on his pillow. "Eris, you have visitors."

Chrys held back. Daeren squeezed her hand, then let go. "Leave us," he told the doctor.

After the doctor had gone, Daeren stepped toward the bed. "Eris. You remember me."

Chrys had to restrain herself from pulling him back. She'd have her people scour his bones afterward; she doubted those Elves who cleared Eris knew what they were doing.

The white folds of Daeren's talar swished as he took another step. "Eris, I have some friends for you."

Eris roused himself, twisting around. His face was a tortured mask. The shock of recognition nearly made Chrys black out; she caught herself, stepping back. "You have them, don't you?" Eris tried to rise from the bed, but he fell to his knees on the floor and grasped Daeren's talar. "Give them back. Please, give them to me."

Daeren's face tightened with pity and distaste. He held out the transfer. Seizing it from his hand, Eris pressed it to his neck. His eyes widened, a rapt expression suffused his face. Then he fell to kiss the talar's hem.

Suddenly Daeren grasped his arm and tried to pull him up. "Listen, friend. Pull yourself together. You're a human being."

The Elf could only stare, uncomprehending.

*   *   *

In the news, an old unused satellite station outside Valedon had exploded, the cause unknown. Andra confirmed it was the end of the Slave World, and the Leader. "But not the end of 'endless light,'" she warned the carriers at Olympus. "We're advancing for now, but who knows what the brain plague will do next."

Opal agreed. "There will always be light and leaders, and only wisdom to tell good from bad."

Catching sight of Sartorius, Chrys gave the post-shaped sentient a quick hug. "I hope it wasn't too bad at the Palace."

"Tolerable, thanks," said the worm-face. A vast understatement, Chrys guessed. "For now, Flexor is taking over our treatment program. I have to go to Helicon to start theirs."

"With microbial partners." The blue angels had a new calling.

"They really help," said the doctor. "They help those who need to say yes."

Chrys searched the virtual singing-trees for Jasper, who was planning the official seeding of Silicon. The seed would be sown in a protective enclosure floating just outside Helicon. Beneath the arch of a tree Moraeg waved to her. Beside her, Carnelian, who had officially joined the Committee to represent "independent" interests, was there listening earnestly to Garnet's latest investment advice.

A newcomer caught her eye, an exceptionally tall woman with the most impressive build Chrys had ever seen. Chrys stared, puzzled. There was something familiar about her. Then the face smiled back. Chrys's jaw just about dropped to the floor.

"Hello, dear," crooned Zircon in a deep contralto. "I hope you like the change. I've been working on it for some time."

"Excuse me while I faint."

"Oh," she raised a hand, "don't do that. It might be catching."

"Check the building code first."

Zircon frowned at a serving caryatid, which had come out full of worms in the face. "Can't we fix those servers?"

All the caryatids were worm-faces today. "You must be in love with Doctor Flexor."

Selenite caught her arm. "Chrys, you have to talk with us. It's . . . important."

Jasper was there, looking very serious. Her heart sank. What had her people done now?

"Chrys." Selenite seemed somehow embarrassed. "I know your people mean well, but—it just isn't done."

"What isn't done?"

"Solicitation," said Jasper. "Fund-raising." Warily, he stroked his jaw.

"Why isn't it done?"

Selenite crossed her arms. "It's absurd. You can't just rebuild the Underworld. Public housing is always a failure."

"That's right. " Jasper's jaw jutted forward. "I should know, I grew up in it. We sims don't want fancy designers messing around down there. Property values rise, we get shoved out."

"Quite true."

"We know you have a good heart," Selenite added, "but you have to understand, the Underworld has always been there. Every society has an Underworld."

"Absolutely."

Selenite spread her hands. "Then why do you let them do this?"

Chrys shrugged. "My people have done well for me. I like to humor them. I can spare a few million credits."

"But we don't have to."

"Certainly not. Just say no."

Selenite looked at Jasper, then back to Chrys. "They'd better do it right. Or else."

Jasper put a hand to the crag of his brow. "Look, they can have half a billion to play with. Just don't let them talk to Garnet."

When the journalist Quinx's story came out, Chrys was amazed to see her parents on camera, her mother churning butter, her father leading the goats up the mountain. Immediately she called home.

"I hope you weren't too bothered." Chrys's hands twisted nervously. "It wasn't my idea."

Her father kept his mouth small but did not seem displeased. "They got it wrong," he noted. "My flock last year won the prize at the village fair, not the county."

Chrys smiled brightly. "You see, they always exaggerate. All the other stuff, too," she added hopefully.

"Not the health plan." Her mother sounded puzzled. "The new health plan for all of Dolomoth. They didn't mention that."

So Arion had remembered. Chrys sighed. "You know, I was thinking of visiting home. With a friend." Friends, about a million of them.

Her mother nodded with satisfaction. "True angels always come home."

Chrys returned to Helicon to train Ilia to test the Elf carriers. "I hope you're pleased with your sales," the gallery director told her. "Both originals and copies are doing well—with a surprising range of buyers. Names we've never seen before."

"And some anonymous," Chrys pointed out. "I wonder who bought *Seven Stars and the Hunter?*"

Ilia gave her a look. "He couldn't very well let anyone else have it, could he?"

The morning light spread the turquoise waves with flecks of titanium. Upon the sea floated the seed of Silicon, a dark pod of plast, not unlike Garnet's ball of "flowers." Just a demo, of course, the ceremonial breaking of ground on a world that had none. Around the pod stretched an immense ring-shaped observation platform, full of sensors, controllers, and protective devices. The brains in the back had been busy.

On the platform, Chrys shaded her eyes with her hand, squinting against the wind that tugged at her hair, which she had pulled back and bound as tight as she could. Her gray talar braced itself intelligently in the wind. Wind and water, azure and alabaster—an inspiration for her next piece, her eyes quickly sketched.

Recollecting herself, Chrys flashed a nervous smile at the members of the Board. The sentients seemed pleased, as far as one could tell, while the Elves looked on, their smiles frozen, as the seed sprouted and grew into an outrageous lava-colored dome of the model, each window a swirling spiral galaxy. Next to the board members stood the Prime Guardian of Elysium and the Protector of Valedon, his talar weighted down with gems, and all the other honored guests, humans, worm-faces, and other sentients of every size and description, that had come out to honor the first new city of Elysium to be built in two thousand years. And by the time it's done, she silently told them, some of you will hate me. For good reason.

"Azetidine." Calling her *nom d'art*, the snake-eggs descended, swirling around her, obscuring her view. "Some say, Azetidine, that you yourself are not the real builder of Silicon. Is it true?"

"Of course I'm not the builder. The seed of Silicon was actually built by—" She winked to download the long list of "brains in the back," sentient engineers, most of whom did not even bother to take sonic names, who had physically created the seed and would nurture its growth for the next few decades.

"Nor are you the real dynatect," the snake-eggs pursued. "You did not really design Silicon; you were just a culture dish for those who did. Is that true?"

Chrys stood taller, the wind from the sea already pulling filaments of lava from her hair. "Silicon was designed by the lights of Eleutheria. The light of Truth, ever true to its nature; of Beauty, the kind of beauty to draw the awe of generations; of Sacrifice . . ."

"Silicon is nothing," flashed Lupin. *"Nothing compared to what we're building next."*

"For once, be modest."

" . . . and above all, the Eighth Light of Mercy. Eleutheria is a way of being, a path of endless life. All those who seek to build in truth and memory shall find our way."